PICK YOUR TEETH WITH MY BONES

BOOK ONE OF THE ETERNAL SPRING, INVISIBLE FOREST SERIES

CARRIE NEWBERRY

EDGE SCIENCE FICTION AND FANTASY PUBLISHING
An Imprint of HADES PUBLICATIONS, INC.
CALGARY

Pick Your Teeth With My Bones
Book One of the Eternal Spring, Invisible Forest series

Copyright © 2017 by Carrie Newberry

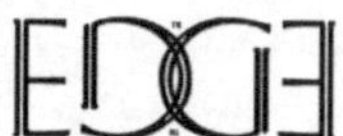

EDGE SCIENCE FICTION AND FANTASY PUBLISHING
An Imprint of HADES PUBLICATIONS, INC.
P.O. Box 1414, Calgary, Alberta, T2P 2L6, Canada

The EDGE Team:
Producer: Brian Hades
Acquisitions Editor: Ella Beaumont
Edited by: Heather Manuel
Cover Design: Brian Hades
Cover Art: Lynn Perkins
Book Design: Mark Steele
Publicist: Janice Shoults
Copywriter: Myles McDonough

ISBN: 978-1-77053-166-6

EDGE Science Fiction and Fantasy Publishing and Hades Publications, Inc. acknowledges the ongoing support of the Alberta Foundation for the Arts and the Canada Council for the Arts for our publishing programme.

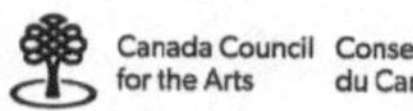

Library and Archives Canada Cataloguing in Publication
CIP Data on file with the National Library of Canada
ISBN: 978-1-77053-166-6
(e-Book ISBN: 978-1-77053-154-3)

FIRST EDITION
(20220829)
Printed in USA
www.edgewebsite.com

Publisher's Note:

Thank you for purchasing this book. It began as an idea, was shaped by the creativity of its talented author, and was subsequently molded into the book you have before you by a team of editors and designers.

Like all EDGE books, this book is the result of the creative talents of a dedicated team of individuals who all believe that books (whether in print or pixels) have the magical ability to take you on an adventure to new and wondrous places powered by the author's imagination.

As EDGE's publisher, I hope that you enjoy this book. It is a part of our ongoing quest to discover talented authors and to make their creative writing available to you.

We also hope that you will share your discovery and enjoyment of this novel on social media through Facebook, Twitter, Goodreads, Pinterest, etc., and by posting your opinions and/or reviews on Amazon and other review sites and blogs. By doing so, others will be able to share your discovery and passion for this book.

Brian Hades, publisher

Acknowledgement

For my parents, who believed in me long before I did. It's really happening! I love you. Thanks to my editor, Heather Manuel, and to the people at EDGE for making my first book a thrilling experience. For my friends at AllWriters, who helped Kellan see the light of day - thanks for believing in us both. And thank you, Kathie Giorgio. When I say I wouldn't be here without you, it's true on so many levels. You reminded me that my backbone was right where I left it, all along. I'm looking forward to lattes and hugs for many years to come.

Chapter 1

Walking a beagle on a leash was the most patience-consuming task known to man. If border collies were born to herd and Siberian huskies were born to howl — I know, supposedly they pull things, but they only do that when they're hooked up to a harness, and they howl all the time — then beagles were born to investigate every single blade of grass that ever dared stick its head out of the dirt. And not just grass. Rocks. Dead worms. Empty pavement.

My going rate as a dog walker was twelve dollars per half hour session. With a lab, I could jog a few miles in that time. With Hanson the beagle, I was lucky to make it all the way around the block without going into overtime.

Don't get me wrong, I love beagles. They're a wealth of information if you know how to ask. But Jesus, could we just take two steps in rapid succession, please?

The nice thing about walking with a beagle was that I could do some sniffing of my own. I'm a shape-shifter; half-human, half-wolf — NOT a werewolf. Werewolves are bitten, shape-shifters are born. So my nose was even stronger than Hanson's. Not that there was much to sniff in this neighborhood.

Just like with every city, each neighborhood in Madison, Wisconsin had its own personality and the reputation that went along with it. The south side neighborhood where I lived, for example, was a past-her-prime exotic dancer — jaded, street smart, and requiring fortitude of character from those who got close to her. This neighborhood, where most of my dog walking clients lived, was the Diane Sawyer of the city. Rich and classy, but not snooty.

Walking around here always made me feel like I had Spaghetti-O's spilled down my shirt.

Hanson and I barely made it down the driveway before I noticed it. A scent that definitely didn't belong. Like all of a sudden Diane Sawyer swore off showers.

Hanson's nose raised to the wind. Usually, when we walked, I never saw his eyes. They were always trained on the ground, where his primary sense held his focus on some scent trail. Now, his eyes met mine.

I sniffed again. More like Diane swore off showers and then rolled around in rotten cabbage.

Actually, it smelled a little like my neighborhood.

I searched the street for the source of the stench. The smell wasn't strong enough to be detected by a human nose. My shape-shifter nose barely picked up on it. I should've realized that sooner, but I only drank two pots of coffee this morning. I was a little slow on the uptake.

My gaze landed on an unfamiliar car. I walked in this neighborhood at the same time every day, so I knew the regular vehicles pretty well. Maybe the car belonged to a visitor. But at ten in the morning, on a street populated by workaholic professional types, visitors were unlikely. Before I could drag Hanson over so I could investigate, a man stepped out from behind the car.

There were a lot of disadvantages to being a shape-shifter. For example, I needed to eat every couple of hours, because if I let myself get too hungry, all kinds of things started to smell like food. Like rodents. And people.

However, the super-sniffer was a definite advantage, and I made good use of it as the man walked toward us. Breathing in deep through my nose, I picked his scent out of the air and examined it. Holy mother of Larry, he stank. Again, not so strong that a normal person could smell it, but I could. Sometimes being in human form was a lot harder than being in wolf form. As a wolf, I could sniff up and down his leg and then pee on him without apology. As a human, I couldn't even make a disgusted face.

Okay, get over it. I took another breath. Musty, like old books. Library? And curry. He ate Indian food recently, or maybe lived near a restaurant. And something citrusy, but not orange juice or lemon oil. Bergamot. He drank Earl Grey.

Yuck. Real men drank coffee, and real women, too, as far as I was concerned.

One more deep breath. Antiseptic? That was weird. The tea and books fit together. But the antiseptic — that was a head-scratcher. Although, germaphobes were a lot more common now than when I was a cub. Frankly, with how fragile the human body was, they should all wear protective padding and disinfect themselves constantly.

Germaphobe or not, he didn't normally wear Eau de Landfill. If that stink was his natural scent, I wouldn't have been able to pick out any of the other stuff. He'd come into close contact with something or someone that reeked, and the scent leeched onto him.

As he got closer, the stink grew stronger, and every one of my muscles clenched. For Pete's sake, I told myself. You clean up doggy doo for a living. You can handle some bad B.O.

But… I didn't like that scent, and it was more than just a gag-reflex thing. It tickled my memory. And it made the wolf in me rise up, shake herself, and prepare to pounce. *Hunt*, a voice inside me hummed.

Clenching my fists to ground myself in my human body, I told myself that maybe he just needed directions. Or maybe he was selling something. That made me feel better. I could walk away from a salesman without a single twinge of conscience.

He spoke, and all hope deflated. "Are you Kelly O'Connell?" Then his eyes widened, as he got the up-close-and-personal view. I knew I made quite a sight. My eyes were amber-colored, and my hair, even pulled in a ponytail, seemed to writhe, a living thing of silver and black waves. But what really made the eyes pop were the tattoos.

Usually, I wore a long-sleeved shirt while I worked, because the Celtic knot-work sleeves down both arms tended to alarm my elderly clientele. But it was already sixty-five degrees outside, and sunny, and I just didn't have the heart for long sleeves that morning.

I heard a growl and looked down at Hanson. I didn't know Hanson could growl. He stood beside me, legs rigid, hackles raised, tail high and straight, glaring at the interloper. The sight disconcerted me even more than the man's scent. It was a little like seeing a woman in a dress with a beard. The mind kept trying to reconcile the picture, and the eye just couldn't do it.

"I'm Kelly." I wasn't Kelly. Well, I was, but I wasn't. The real Kelly O'Connell was born, and died, on May 1, 1977, in Lexington, Kentucky. I borrowed her name a few years ago, because she would've been the right age and because Kellan Faolanni wasn't a name I could use in public. "Can I help you?" When he kept staring, I waved my non-leash hand in front of his face. As much fun as it was to make people's eyes cross, I bored easily. "Yo. Anybody home?"

He finally managed to find his way up to my face. He gave me a crooked smile. "Sorry. I just — you have a lot of tattoos."

"Yeah." I waited. If I was being paid to be courteous, I could manage it for hours at a time. This guy wasn't paying me. When his crooked smile faltered, I sighed, feeling like I just cussed out a third grader. I bit the inside of my cheek and dug deep for more pleasantries. "Don't worry. You're not the first person to do a double take."

The crooked smile was back, stronger than ever. I took a closer look at him.

When meeting people, I rarely noticed visuals until five minutes after the person walked away. I could pick their scent out of a line-up, but their face? Not so much. I needed to make a conscious effort to notice appearance. Tall. Pale skin. No gray hair mixed in with the reddish brown, so probably not old. Clothes — oh, who cares, he was wearing some. He spent a lot of time indoors with people who apparently slept while wrapped in moldy gym socks. What more did I need to know? Oh, yeah. How the hell to make him go away, before that scent made me shape-shift and eat him.

What would a human do? I wracked my brain for my knowledge of "normal" behavior. I stuck out my hand and once again offered him my borrowed name. "Kelly. And you are?"

Oh, that was stupid. Shaking hands meant he entered my personal space, which meant his stink came closer, too. I clenched every muscle in my body to keep from ripping his throat out with my teeth. This meant that when I shook his hand, I used too much force, and he made a pained sound before I managed to release him.

He shook his hand with the sort of furtive movements people use when they hope you won't notice their weakness. "I'm Darcy. Jamison. I'm really sorry to bother you, but it seems I need your help."

Darcy? Seriously? Who names their son Darcy? And I thought my mom was a sadist.

Shaking my head, I focused on the rest of his statement. I could smell he didn't have a dog. But as I was currently wearing my dog-walker hat, I stayed in character. "Oh. I'm sorry." I smiled. "My schedule is full right now, but I can put you on my waiting list."

He looked puzzled.

My smile stiffened. "If you give me your phone number, I can call you if a slot opens up. What kind of dog do you have?"

"Oh." He laughed, a little half-assed sound that set my teeth on edge. "I don't have — that's not what I meant."

I bit the inside of my other cheek, to keep from offering a few suggestions as to what kind of help he should seek. A stronger soap, perhaps. I looked down at Hanson to occupy myself. The beagle was once again sniffing the grass. If this person wasn't going to feed him or pet him, he wasn't worth Hanson's time.

Jamison-like-the-whiskey took my silence as interest, and continued with more confidence. "I have some questions. About, well, this." He slipped off the backpack I failed to notice. All part of the clothes I couldn't be bothered with. I needed to work on my observation skills. The backpack could've been an Uzi, and then where would I be? Full of more holes than a Dunkin Donuts on a Sunday morning.

But, as it turned out, the backpack was the least of my problems. From that unremarkable navy blue pack, he pulled a sheaf of very old papers. Even before I saw the writing on them, in a language that looked like the fugly offspring of Urdu and Welsh, my palms started to sweat and my heartbeat went all wonky.

Those papers — papers that shouldn't exist because we destroyed them all, damn it — reeked like the man holding them. My nose sent up all kinds of distress flares. How did this doofus stumble on these papers, and how did he know to bring them to me? Shit, fuck, damn it all to fucking hell. I started reciting some of my favorite words as I struggled with what to do next.

Kill the fucker, grab the papers, and take them both home with me for a bonfire. Maybe grab some marshmallows and graham crackers on the way.

Except Janus wouldn't let me kill people anymore without clearing it with him first. Damn it.

I considered just stuffing him in the trunk of his car and driving him to Janus. I was sure that, upon meeting the poor bastard, Janus would give me permission to take care of the problem. And if not, at least Jamison would be Janus's problem, not mine.

While I contemplated the various paths to his demise, he continued talking. Not only was he smelly, he was verbose. My lucky day. "...so I tried looking up dead languages on the internet, but I couldn't find this one. And I showed it to a friend of mine, who's a professor at the UW. She speaks eight languages and specializes in Middle Eastern—"

He showed them to a friend? Jesus Christ.

"—but she'd never seen anything like it, either. So, I looked you up." He looked at me, wide-eyed like the prey animal he was. "Can you help me?"

"You looked me up?" I tried to think. Not my strong suit, at the best of times.

"Yeah, online. Your dog-walking website."

My dog-walking website wouldn't have told him where I'd be walking that morning. And it certainly wouldn't tell him that I could read those documents. I felt sweat begin to pool in uncomfortable places.

Should I ask him more questions? I should. "How did you know where to find me?"

"I, um ... she ... I..." She? She who? His breathing grew loud and fast, and even over the rush of the breeze and the sound of his breath, I could hear his heart begin to pound. Then he started to sweat. Not so that anyone without hyperactive olfactory glands would notice, but boy, did I notice. "Cold" sweat had its own scent. It was more sour, it coated the tongue and hung in the back of the throat, and it helped us predators find easy prey.

My second egg sandwich from an hour ago suddenly seemed a distant memory. It wasn't just hunger. It was a desire to hunt, kicked into high gear, building inside me like an orgasm. I could give him a running start. Then I could stalk him, get high off his fear before…

Hanson glanced up at me, his ears twitching back and his nose working. I needed to get us out of there. I couldn't shape-shift out in the open. And I was responsible for Hanson, who, if I went hunting, would probably follow his nose into the middle of the street and end up a pancake. Before I could leave, I needed those fucking papers. But unfortunately, the train had just rocketed past Finesse Station and was barreling toward Massacre Central. We needed a plan B.

Chapter 2

I gave Jamison-like-the-whiskey one last chance. "Give me the papers. I have someone I can show them to. He'll—"

"We can go together," Jamison said. He smiled, apparently pleased at the idea of a field trip.

Last chance burned. Plan B activated. I let my frustration and hunger turn my eyes into glowing gold-and-black orbs. His fear scent kicked up into holy-fucking-shit range. Growling seemed almost superfluous at that point, but I was a big believer in overkill.

I growled, "How 'bout you give me the fucking papers now." Hanson backed away from me, as far as his leash would allow. My mother would've called my technique artless, but she got her ass killed two months after my ninth birthday. What the hell did she know about technique? I chose to call it effective, and hoped I didn't scare the sucker so bad that he went running to the nearest police station.

Jamison blinked at me, his scent flooding the air with the reek of adrenaline. He opened his mouth as if to speak, then apparently thought better of it and closed it again.

To soften the blow, I smiled at him as he handed me the documents. "Thanks. Darcy, was it? Have a nice day now." A tad over the top, perhaps, but I never saw much point in learning the lines to False Courtesy. Okay, fine, you catch more flies with honey. But one thing I'd learned was to play to my strengths and leave the honey to people who didn't mind sticky shit.

As I turned away and took a step toward Hanson, I allowed myself a real smile. I'd talk to Janus, get permission to take care of the loose end, and hand over the documents so he could destroy them. All in a day's work.

"Wait!" His voice prepared me, so when Jamison grabbed my arm, I was ready. Not ready to fight him. Ready to not fight him.

Teeth gritted, hands open and fingers splayed — as far from a clenched fist as I could get — I faced him. "How did you say you got my name again?" I didn't know where the question came from, but I felt grateful it materialized out of the ether. It seemed like a damn good question.

"I — your website." He pulled his lower lip into his mouth. I could smell the blood he drew when he bit down.

I suddenly felt like my tongue was coated in crushed aspirin. He was lying to me, and now that I had the papers, I didn't need to stand and listen anymore. Disgust made my voice cold. "You don't know much about asking for help, do you?"

He didn't speak, just looked at me.

"You did what you came for. You told me your story — and by the way, you might want to consult Webster on the definition of over-sharing — and you gave me the documents. Now you smile, say thank you, and go, so that I don't change my mind about helping you. Understand?"

As fear, anger and despair played three-way tug of war with his scent, he smelled sour and spicy at the same time. My brain translated the scent. He didn't like being talked to that way, but he didn't want to say anything and risk offending me. Finally, he reached into his backpack. I tried not to stiffen, but I watched him closely. He didn't pull out a weapon. He pulled out a piece of paper, tore off a corner, and scribbled on it. Then he handed the scrap to me.

Darcy Jamison – 608-555-4399 it read. I looked back up at him.

Under the parasitic stench, he smelled like lead. Defeat. "So you can contact me. When you get the documents translated. And thank you."

I blinked. I'd never expected him to actually thank me. Because I was shocked, and because some deep-down part of me that rarely got acknowledged really hated the grief in his scent, I said, "You're welcome."

The rest of my dog-walking day seemed to take three years to finish. My brain was consumed with the documents, which were now hidden under the driver's seat of my truck. As soon as I finished my last client, I went through two drive-thrus. The first to get two bacon double cheeseburgers, the second to get two large cappuccinos. Then I parked my truck in a parking garage downtown, and pulled the documents from under my seat. I ate, drank, and read in the privacy of the parking structure's shadows.

The documents weren't in Welsh, Erdu, or any other language known to the world at large. They were in Gaachail. Less than a handful of people alive today could speak the language, much less read it. I happened to be one of the lucky ones who could do both.

I began to read silently.

The Sankhain were created for a single purpose — to protect the secret of the Spring. When a threat is perceived, the Sankhain must deal with it swiftly and without fail. To that end, they will position themselves as needed, around the vastness of the world, to...

I paused, and drained the last of my coffee. A drop fell onto the paper, and my heart seized up as I blotted it with the hem of my tank top. Then I realized I was trying to preserve a document that was supposed to be a pile of ash, long since scattered to the winds. My face heating, I ground my teeth together and kept reading.

The Sankhain, or Watch-Keepers, were founded by a nomad, a young man whose tribe exiled him because they feared his magick. This man stumbled upon a wood, in a strip of land sandwiched between two lakes. Within that wood, he found a natural spring, and when he drank of that spring, he felt the timeless energies of the earth pulse through him with every beat of his heart.

I knew this bedtime story better than I knew my own name. That nomad, Janus, had told it to me himself, countless times. It was one of my earliest memories, my twin sister Mal and I tucked into our bed, and Janus dutifully retelling the tale so we'd shut up and go to sleep. He wasn't my father. Just the thumb under which I was caught. Because I was one of the Sankhain, as my mother was before me and her mother before her. And the document told the truth. We were the booby-trap, set to warn the household of impending doom. And my trip wire just got triggered in a major way.

I shoved the papers under my seat and pulled out of my parking space. As soon as I left the parking garage, I hit speed dial eight on my cell. The phone on the other end went directly to voicemail. He'd turned it off. Finn's voice instructed me to leave a message if I wished a return call. What I wished was that someone would answer the bloody phone. Janus didn't have a phone. I was left with Finn.

I kept my voice cool and deferential. "Finlay, it's Kellan. I have an urgent matter that requires your attention. Please call at your earliest convenience." Then I punched the "end" button, stopped at a red light, and screamed to let off frustration. The woman stopped in an SUV in the next lane stared at me in alarm. I didn't care.

This wasn't the first time I'd called Finn to report a potential problem. My current assignment was to live in Madison, acquaint myself with the dogs that lived there, and glean what I could from their confidences. Dogs are keen observers, Janus told me. He said, *Your sense of smell has taught us how valuable such things can be.*

Sure, I communicated with dogs, mind-melded, kind of like texting, but without the need for a phone. And sure, my sense of smell was valuable to me, because I knew how to interpret it in human terms. The problem came when I tried to interpret dog observations. Dogs noticed things that alarmed them all the time. People in hats. People wearing parkas. And don't get me started on lawn ornaments. Dogs didn't have a way to process these things, so they were alarming. When I first started with this assignment, and I got the message from a dog that so-and-so was a creep, I called Finn right away. Finn sent me a couple Sankhain as back-up, and we did a little investigating. And discovered that so-and-so had a deep abiding love of cowboy hats and boots that made *click-clack* noises when he walked. Creepy? Maybe. Evil? Not so much.

After a few repetitions of that scenario, Finn stopped sending back-up, but my orders were still to report any suspicious activity. Every time a dog gave me some intel, I called to report it. Now Finn would decide this was another wolf-who-cried-boy moment, and take his sweet-ass time calling me back. And I couldn't leave him a message with any specifics because Finn saw an episode of 20/20 about eavesdropping on cell phones, and was now paranoid about how voicemails were worded.

As I drove, I considered my options. I could break the rule about voicemails and leave Finn more information. I didn't like that option much. Breaking rules set by cool, calm Finn was one thing. Paranoid Finn was a whole lot bitchier when I stepped on his toes.

I could sit on the papers and wait for a call back. Just the thought made my butt cheeks sweat.

I could keep calling Finn until his voicemail box was full and he drove all the way here just to strangle me. Hmm. That had potential.

The one option I never considered was going to the Sankhain home base, the forest that housed the Spring. Sankhain were forbidden from entering the forest in daylight. Our entire purpose was to protect the Spring and keep its existence secret. Janus used his sorcerer mojo to make the forest invisible. All his work would be for nothing, if a Sankha walked into the forest, and disappeared from sight with a dozen witnesses. One of the worst incidents happened when one of our younglings, our Sankhain-in-training, stepped out of the forest by accident. A kid walking past saw him suddenly appear and returned that night with all his friends to explore. We were forced to kill them all. We buried them on our grounds, and they're still considered missing persons. Dateline did a story on them last year. Fortunately, this happened forty years ago, before Twitter and Facebook and the constant online documentation of every single aspect of every person's life. If it happened today, we'd have a hell of a time covering it up. This was our golden rule — never enter or exit the forest in daylight.

I chose option C, and redialed Finn's number. As I turned onto my street, Finn's voicemail beeped and I left an almost identical message. I was nearly at my building when I dialed a third time. And then I saw him. Darcy Jamison-like-the-whiskey, sitting on my front fucking stoop. How did he get my address? Directly on the heels of that thought was: Of course he has your address, dumbass. He found you on your dog-walking route. Your address is easy-peasy compared to that.

I hung up the phone without leaving a message, and swore silently. I was too tired and too edgy to deal with the stench and the fear that might still be clinging to him. I wanted to keep driving, but I saw the moment he spotted me. With a growl rumbling through my chest, I turned left into the driveway of my apartment building. The growl grew louder, until I cut it off. I couldn't afford to indulge in wolfish behavior. I inhaled deeply through my nose, trying to ground myself in my human half.

All I wanted was to go upstairs and bury my nose in my dog's fur. Was that so much to ask?

In answer, Darcy Jamison appeared at my window. I squelched the urge to stick my tongue out at him, and opened the truck door. "What are you doing here?" I asked.

"I came to see you."

Ask a stupid question. "I never would've guessed that." I jumped down from the driver's seat. I started to grab the papers, then at the last second decided to leave them in the truck. "What I meant was, why are you here? I told you I'd talk to my friend."

He shuffled his feet and looked everywhere but at me. Then he straightened and looked me in the eye. "Yeah, well, I started thinking and I thought, how do I know I can trust you?"

"You don't. Speaking of trust, how the hell did you know where I live? Or where I work? And don't say my website. That site's the cheapest piece of shit on the web."

Fear ripened, so strong and bright that I started to salivate. His gaze slid from mine again, and this time it stayed focused on his shoes. "I — why won't you let me come with you, to talk to your friend?"

With that, he officially reached pest status. Rage surged to the forefront. Instead of avoiding his fear, I drew it in, let it feed my distaste for this weak human. "Fine. Don't tell me jack shit. Hitch up your skirt, go on home and sit on your ass, knitting potholders and waiting for my fucking phone call, because if you show up on my doorstep again, I'll eat you."

My words landed like a physical blow, and Darcy Jamison twitched. His shoulders slumped. I walked around him rather than shoving him aside, because the thought of hitting him turned my stomach. Halfway to the front door, I remembered that I left the damn papers in the damn truck, and I turned around to go back. And I saw Darcy Jamison square his shoulders, raise his head, and mutter something to himself. I was too far away to make out the words, but from the look on his face and the set of his shoulders, I suspected he was giving himself a pep talk.

Dread made my fingers itch for my Highland dirk, a solid blade with just a hint of ceremony. Because I felt something winding its way through my mind, something like respect for this man, with his polite manners and determination. Better to kill him now, before that nasty feeling spread. But the punishment for killing a human without permission was six months in a solitary cell. Eight if I committed the act in public. Was my apartment parking lot public? Probably. I could lure him upstairs, do it in the apartment.

No, not worth it. Not when I would certainly get permission to kill him, once Janus heard the story. I took a big breath through my mouth, then held the breath as I walked back to the truck, opened the door, and grabbed the papers from under the driver's seat. Without a word, without a glance in Darcy Jamison's direction, I slammed the door and walked away.

Chapter 3

I let myself into my apartment building and took the stairs three at a time. My legs were just barely long enough for this, and I needed a physical challenge to balance the mental hell of the day. Besides, I could heal any injury a tumble down the stairs might incur. Broken bones might take a few hours, but at least they would give me something else to focus on besides my silent cell phone and the papers I clutched in my hand.

I glanced down at the papers as I stood before my apartment door. They didn't look like much. So why did they matter so much to me?

Janus created the language, Gaachail, and began writing down our history long before I was born. He made up his own language rather than using one of the known tongues, because he was a paranoid old bastard, and he thought it would keep the written history safe from prying eyes.

Then, about fifty years ago, a Sankha named Addison McAdams defected. I never knew why. It wasn't like Janus made him fill out an exit interview so we could learn from his disenchantment. The "why" of it didn't matter. The Sankhain had a long and proud history of "my way or the highway" leadership. Once Addison walked away, he was a dead man. Addison knew this, so he decided to try and buy himself some time. He stole twenty pages of the written history, with the idea that he'd send it to a newspaper. He left Janus a note, saying he wouldn't send the translation to the papers if we didn't come after him. Like he could blackmail us into sparing his life. He was wrong.

Janus usually faced the elimination of a Sankha as a solemn event, regrettable but necessary. But I think he enjoyed hearing Mal's and my report of Addison's death. And all because Addison took some papers that nobody outside the Sankhain could read anyway.

As soon as Mal and I returned from hunting down Addison, Janus instructed us to build a bonfire. He and Finn brought the documents — all of them — to the fire pit. Then Janus ordered us to burn the documents.

I asked him why. I mean, that was a lot of hard work, writing hundreds of pages by hand. Not to mention making up a stinking language. I thought somebody should ask, just to make sure he'd thought it through. I didn't want to be the one he tasked with rewriting the damn thing when he changed his mind.

Mal reached out and pinched the thin skin inside my wrist between the nails on her thumb and forefinger, probably to keep me from saying anything else. But before Finn could smooth things over or Mal could distract Janus from my stupidity, Janus surprised us all by answering my question. "They were born of ego. I will not allow the Sankhain to be brought down by ego."

"Oh. Okay." And I started tossing the papers on the fire. Finn and Janus helped us with the tossing, then they left. Mal and I stayed until the fire burned down to embers. We shoveled dirt over it. The next day's rain took care of the ashes.

I saw it with my own eyes. There wasn't so much as a scrap of paper left. Where did these come from? And why did they smell to my nose like the sewage treatment plant on a hot day?

Even before I turned the key in the lock, I heard the clicking of nails on hardwood on the other side of the door. As soon as the door opened a crack, a big square head shoved its way through the gap, revealing a big toothy grin and a waft of hot breath. Galen, my three-year-old Akita, was the best welcoming committee on earth.

I pushed my way inside the apartment, and immediately Galen pressed himself against my left leg like he wanted to crawl inside my skin. Setting the papers and keys on the table by the door, I knelt and rubbed him down.

At the sound of a rattly muffler, I looked outside and saw Darcy Jamison's car pull away. Finally, gone. I slid Galen's harness on him. His name meant "joyful one." He wasn't joyful when I met him, but I saw the potential. Now, as he shook himself and looked up at me, he lived up to his name.

I needed to do something with the papers. I headed for the bedroom, Galen doing his best to trip me up — he didn't understand "just a second." When I stopped before the bedroom closet, he planted himself firmly in my path. I grabbed his harness, hauled him out of the way, and opened the closet door.

Finn insisted that I have a fireproof safe in my apartment. For valuables. I laid the papers inside, closed the door with a *thunk*, and picked up Galen's leash.

Galen and I always sounded like at least twenty people as we thundered down the stairs. It made me smile, hearing our enthusiasm echo throughout the stairwell.

We ran along the Wingra bike path, down to Vilas Zoo. It was a beautiful area, lots of trees. But today I didn't enjoy a bit of it. Memories kept getting in the way. Darcy Jamison, his squared shoulders and downcast eyes. Addison McAdams and how so little of his blood actually splattered on me, because I was behind him when I slit his throat. And more than any other image, I saw Finn's face, his beautiful, straight-angled features, his shining blond hair. Not shiny. Shining, like it had its own light source rather than reflecting something else's light. And I wondered how something so beautiful could be so despicable. I wanted Finn's help. I needed Finn's advice. And he was too busy playing power games, making sure I knew my place in the pecking order, to do his job.

Usually, jogging left me too tired to be angry. Today, jogging failed. By the time I got home, I was even more frustrated than when I left. I gave Galen fresh water, along with a few ice cubes. He liked to crunch them. He thought they were treats.

With Galen taken care of, I pulled my cell phone out of my pocket and hit redial. Once again, it went straight to voicemail. Up to that point, I was respectful, mindful of my place. This time, I tried a different track. "Finn. If you ever want to see me naked again, you will call me back. Immediately. Otherwise, I hope you like yourself, because you're the only one you'll be having sex with from now on. I'll make sure every woman you meet thinks you're a pestilence-ridden premature ejaculator with a penis the size of a macaroni noodle. CALL ME!"

This message was no more likely to get me a response than the previous ones, because Finn knew he was good-looking and charming enough to override any negative reviews I might give him. But the message made me feel better.

I fixed myself some sandwiches and brewed a pot of coffee, trying to fill the gnawing hole in my gut.

I started to pace. Galen sat by the front door, enjoying the draft that leaked in at the bottom of the ill-fitting door, and watched me. Full dark was at least two hours away. I couldn't go to the forest yet. I needed to be patient.

I glanced at my silent phone. Fuck patient. Full dark might be far off, but the sun was already riding the horizon. I could just wait for dusk. That might be dark enough. I mean, it wasn't like I wouldn't be careful. And once Finn saw me, once Janus realized I had the papers and what they meant, they would forgive me for breaking the golden rule. They would. They had to.

In the hall closet I found a canvas messenger bag, and stuffed the papers inside. Then I went into the bedroom, walked to the dresser and opened the second drawer from the bottom. Inside lay an assortment of sheathed blades, and a few loose ones. All of the shorter (eight inches or less) sheathes were modified so I could clip them on the waistband of my pants like a cell phone. Unlike a cell phone, I wore the blades inside my pants, against my skin. Conceal and carry might be legal these days, but I wasn't the type of girl who went around applying for permits.

I grabbed two eight-inchers and slipped one on each hip. I really shouldn't wear eight-inchers that way — they tended to stick out a little when I sat down. But despite my justifications, I felt insecure, and the blades helped. After considering a moment, I also took my belly band out of the drawer. Mal made the belly band for me fifteen years ago, for our two hundredth birthday. She took an extra-wide ace bandage, added some snaps, and sewed sheathes into it. The damn thing was incredibly uncomfortable and made me sweat like a son-of-a-bitch, but it allowed me to carry half a dozen throwing knives under almost every shirt I owned.

At the last minute, I looked down at Galen. I had planned to leave him at home, but now I was rethinking that decision. What if Finn and Janus didn't forgive me completely? What if they decided to be petty or sticklers for the rules, and punished me anyway? If I got held up and Galen suffered for it, I'd never forgive myself. Besides, I liked his company. "All right, big guy. Come on."

Galen strode to the door like his place in the party was a foregone conclusion. Only the slight vibration in his muscles as I snapped on his harness betrayed his excitement at being included. I grabbed the messenger bag and my keys, and we left.

—— ‹›› ——

Even though I was already buzzing with caffeine, I stopped at a gas station for another cup of coffee. The messenger bag went inside with me, and Galen stayed in the truck with the windows down. I could've left the keys in the ignition and no one would try to steal my truck. No dog could do a death stare like an Akita.

Back in the truck, I took a sip of coffee, grimaced at the weak flavor, and pulled my cell phone out of my pocket. No one called. I knew no one called. But I still had to look, because maybe, maybe I'd missed it. I needed to save my rage for the next time I got Finn alone. I smiled and relaxed a little, as my imagination took over. This might call for props. Handcuffs, definitely. Or a riding crop. My pulse jumped, and I felt the skin on my chest grow warm. I loved mixing anger and sex. Finn and I had been sleeping together since my twenty-third birthday. And the only things we had in common were lust and dislike.

My truck practically drove itself to the business park, a couple miles south of my neighborhood. I pulled into our small parking lot, among the dozen cars Finn kept on hand for Sankhain use. It wasn't dusk quite yet, so I took Galen for a short walk around the business park. He peed on a couple dozen trees, tried to chase a squirrel up a telephone pole, and managed to find the one discarded hamburger in a fifty-mile radius. Finally, we made our way toward an empty lot on the outer rim of the business park. I kept my right hand on the messenger bag, and my leash hand hovering near the waistband of my shorts, so I could grab a blade if needed.

We reached the edge of the empty lot. It was marshy, with puddles in random places and vegetation like cattails that wouldn't grow in your average field. A faded sign stuck up out of the weeds, announcing the impending construction of an office building. The building's ETA was completely obscured by the cattails and long grass. I glanced around me, checking for prying eyes. Then I closed my eyes and did a sniff check. We were alone.

Without glancing down, I took a step forward. My foot landed in the center of a rock, smooth to the point of slippery. While anticipation hummed through my blood, I had to drag Galen behind me. My big, strong dog hated getting his feet wet.

I took another step, and found the next rock right where I knew it would be. I should know — I was one of the Sankhain who laid the rockway, as we called it. Big rocks, not easily balanced upon, in a drunkard's path leading into the wetland.

I stepped onto the third rock, much smaller than the others because of sinkage — there wasn't much left aboveground to stand on. I moved hastily onto rock number four, a more comfortable fit.

I placed my left foot on the fifth rock. The anticipation grew, making my palms tingle.

When my right foot landed on the fifth rock, the field disappeared and we were surrounded by trees.

Chapter 4

The invisible forest, a nice little piece of abracadabra, was Janus's brainchild to keep people from wandering onto our land. A marshy field was less appealing to enterprising walkers than a cache of trees. To keep out anyone who might be wearing watertight footgear, Janus cast a second spell over the area. Anyone who came close to our forest would feel an eeriness wash over them, like they were halfway down a dark alley and realized they weren't alone. Most people left in a hurry. Those who didn't were dealt with by our archers, and buried in a field behind the munitions barn. Janus needed to maintain these spells continuously. He could never leave the forest, or the magick would fade.

I hauled Galen tight against my left leg, so his front feet rested on the rock with me. If I could've convinced him to leave the ground behind completely, I would've pulled him all the way up on the rock. But Galen was afraid of heights. It took me three months to coax him up on my bed.

Whoosh. An arrow landed a foot in front of us. Even though I knew it was coming, I almost peed my pants. Galen jumped and tried to pull away from me, but I held him and gave him the command to stay. He did, although I sensed the reluctance in his stiff muscles, his perked ears searching for the threat. She wouldn't hit him, I told myself. But I still started to sweat. *Whoosh.* Another arrow embedded itself in the ground to my right. Galen twitched violently, but held his stay. *Whoosh.* A third arrow, a scant inch from the tip of the rock we perched on. Galen lost it, dragging me off my feet and onto the ground. I kept my grip on his leash, but landed on my hands and knees in muddy leaves. All this, just so she could show off.

"For Christ's sake, Cat," I yelled. I pushed to my feet and dusted off my hands. "You know it's me."

With a rustling of leaves twenty feet away, a girl swung down from a tree and landed with a splat of wet earth. Galen didn't jump this time. He was used to people dropping out of trees. The girl's long, dark blonde hair was full of leaves, and her jeans were splattered with mud. She had a bow slung across her upper body, and a grin stretched wide across her face. "Welcome home, Sankha Kellan."

Kelly O'Connell was my alias. I had a birth certificate stating that Kelly O'Connell was born on May 1, 1977, and a driver's license with my picture on it that stated Kelly O'Connell could drive. Kellan Faolanni, on the other hand, had no birth certificate or other documentation. That was because, even though I looked like I was in my late thirties, I was born Kellan Faolanni about two hundred fifteen years ago, right here in the forest. Only my fellow Sankhain knew me by my real name.

Cat was one of the younglings, a Sankha-in-training. At fifteen years old, Cat would ordinarily be too young for border patrol. She was so gifted in archery, though, that Finn gave her the assignment. As I looked at her, I felt a warmth spread through me, scrubbing away the residue of my anger. Cat was one of my favorite younglings. She had balls.

I was preoccupied with Cat, so Galen heard it before I did — the squishing sound that announced the arrival of another person from deeper in the forest. His ears perked and his head turned in the direction of the newcomer, drawing my attention that way, too. I frowned. Protocol dictated that a member of border patrol must escort any unexpected Sankha through the forest to the camp, where the Sankhain Academy resided. The forest was around a half-mile thick and a couple miles long, and the Spring lay just about in the center. On one side of the trees was the business park, and on the other side was the Academy — a collection of cabins, two dormitories, a few barns and outbuildings, an infirmary and a mess hall. Was Cat's partner going to escort us? But her partner shouldn't have been so far into the trees. Cat's post twenty feet away was the farthest Finn allowed a youngling to position herself from the border. So, if the approaching feet weren't attached to a member of border patrol, then what the hell was going on?

My heart skittered around my chest like a cornered squirrel. I tightened my grip on Galen's leash as I realized what was happening. Janus had seen me coming. He wasn't just our camouflage expert — he was also our security camera. When someone approached the forest, the presence tripped a wire in his head and suddenly he was watching the whole damn thing like CCTV. I had known that he would see me coming. I just didn't for a second think that he might not let me in, once I arrived. But those footsteps squelching across the mucky forest floor told me that I wasn't getting past the gates today.

It must be Finn, I told myself, as Cat turned to greet the newcomer. He would come himself, to chastise me in person. That was the fun part of his job. I could tell him why I was here, and he would let me in. They would yell, stomp their feet, and then forgive me. Or at the very least, take the damn documents off my hands. They might be only ten pages, but they weighted down my shoulder like an unabridged dictionary. Okay, maybe it just seemed that way in my head, but I really didn't want to carry them any longer than necessary.

I braced myself for two reasons. One, Galen hated Finn. Hated him from day one. When Finn appeared from the shadows in a few seconds, Galen would growl and maybe even lunge for him. The second reason was more embarrassing. Every time I saw Finn, I lost the ability to speak. Not because of magick, but because, as I said before, he was just so bloody pretty. Before he appeared and tied my tongue, I brought up a mental picture of him with that "you're so stupid, Kellan" look on his face. It was hard for me to get all wet and gooey with that picture in my head.

As it turned out, my preparations were unnecessary. It wasn't Finn who slowly took shape in the dusk. It was a shape several inches taller, and several muscle layers broader. Skin the color of coffee with too much milk and sugar, close-cropped dark hair, and a voice as melodic as gravel going through a wood chipper. Antony.

Antony was twenty-four years old; a smart-ass youngling who just recently passed the tests, so now he was a smart-ass Sankha. Yeah, yeah, pot, kettle. I was a smart-ass because I needed the aggression outlet. Antony was a smart-ass because he was too dumb to realize how close he came to getting one of my blades through his belly button. Or at least, that was my theory, ever since he joined us at the age of eleven.

Galen only knew Antony in passing, so my dog treated him as he would any man large enough to pull a tractor through the mud. With stiffened muscles and raised hackles, Galen stepped in front of me to protect me from the new threat. Antony stopped when he reached Cat, his gaze locked on Galen. "Hello, Sank— I mean, hello, Kellan."

I smiled, because Antony almost used my title, the address the younglings were required to use. He'd almost forgotten we were equals now. Which suited me just fine, since I didn't consider him to be nearly my equal. In fact, under different circumstances, that little slip would have made my day. But not today. I'd never been more disappointed not to see Finn. I shushed Galen, told him to relax. "I need to see Janus and Finlay."

"No." Antony's Adam's apple bobbed. He was nervous — I could smell his cold sweat.

My temper raised its head and glared at him, but didn't flare. Yet. "No offense, Antony, but compared to you, I'm God here. I say I'm going to see Finn and Janus. You nod and get out of my way."

He cleared his throat. At the sound, Galen stiffened again and leaned into me, trying to push me backwards. Antony stared at Galen for another moment, then looked up at me. "No, ma'a— No. You're not. I am here to deliver instructions of your exile from the forest and the Academy grounds. For the next six months, you are not to—"

"Whoa, whoa, whoa." Galen looked up at me when he heard my tone, but I couldn't reassure him. I was too busy trying to assimilate the information while my heartbeat ricocheted around in my chest. Exile? How did Janus get pissed enough to exile me? He only used that punishment in cases of extreme disobedience. And he hadn't used it in years — he decided that it was more efficient to just kill the disobedient Sankha and assign the task to the next in line. After all, once a dog bites his owner, he really can't be trusted, can he?

Of course, that wasn't true. One bite in a dog's past didn't mean it was a bad dog. Most bites are a case of self-defense. And besides, I didn't bite anybody. All I did was enter the forest. And leave Finn a few messages, the last of which might've been objectionable, but come on. Exile?

And to make matters worse, both Cat and Antony were looking at me with that most hideous of human emotions — pity. I could almost stomach Cat's pity, because I knew she respected me still. But Antony's made me want to hurl something at his head, just to wipe that look off his face.

Cat backed away silently, probably eager to return to her tree and get out of the awkward moment. I wished I could climb a tree myself, but I had Galen. Galen. I needed to focus on Galen. Feel the leash in my hand, hear the sound of his breathing. Stay grounded, as only my dog could make me. I opened my mouth to tell Antony about the papers, but he spoke first.

"Um. The terms of your exile are thus: for six months, you will have no contact with any Sankha. You will not set foot within two hundred yards of the forest. You will not—"

"I know what exile means!" My voice was too loud in the relative silence. Both Antony and Galen jumped. Poor Galen. I needed to stop reacting like a wounded cub and start acting like his alpha. I closed my eyes. "I — please. Just stop talking."

Exile. Fuck. I needed to see Janus, or at least Finn. Talk to them. Pass along the papers. Get permission to kill the outsider. I needed to get the nod to go ahead and do my job.

Antony held his ground. "I'm to escort you to the far end of the forest, where you will exit and not return. For—"

"Six months. Yeah. Got it." I opened my eyes. "Do me a favor, would you? If you're going to be the voice of doom, use your own fucking words instead of being Janus's parrot."

The scent of cold sweat disappeared as the air heated with his anger. Galen tried to push me backwards again, away from Antony, who smelled more and more like a threat. "I'm not a parrot," Antony said. "And don't bitch at me 'cause you were too damn stupid to wait one more hour for full dark."

I didn't like this new world I'd stepped into, where I got exiled and Antony was right about something. I wanted to get away from here before up became down or Galen turned his nose up at a piece of meat because he wanted to watch his waistline. "It's almost dark now. If Janus wants me gone so badly, why don't I just exit here?"

Antony shook his head. "Orders are the far end of the forest. Less risk of discovery."

Exhaustion slammed into me. A day in the sun, a long jog with Galen, and all the stress of the surprise meeting was finally catching up with me. "Fine. Far end of the forest is a long walk. We better get started."

At my capitulation, Antony didn't smirk like I expected. Instead, he said, "All right, let's go," and started walking.

In the forest, the ground was covered by several years' worth of leaves, so we didn't need a rockway. And we never bothered to lay a rockway from the far end of the forest through the marsh, back to civilization, which meant my shoes would be soaked through by the time I reached pavement. Ordinarily, I would be annoyed by the idea of driving home in wet socks. Now, I was too numb to achieve annoyance. I was too numb to do more than put one foot in front of the other.

Galen kept glancing up at me, confusion twisting his scent. He had to be wondering what was going on. When we went to the forest, we walked all the way through to the Academy. And for dogs, life was all about what usually happened. They really didn't contemplate what might happen, so the unusual usually blindsided them. I didn't know how to help him, because I felt totally blindsided myself.

As we walked, I thought about what I was going to do with the papers. I had two options, as far as I could tell. I could give them to Antony, and trust that he would pass along my story to Janus and Finn, hopefully getting my sentence reduced or commuted. Or I could hold onto them, thereby risking the documents falling into the wrong hands, and incurring the wrath of Finn and Janus because I didn't hand the documents over to Antony like I should.

I halted and addressed the world at large. "Does nobody want to know why I did it?"

Antony stopped walking and stared at me. "No." His cold tone brought Galen's hackles up, but the boy didn't seem to notice. "Nobody wants to know why. You broke the rule you never break, Kellan. Shit, you shoulda seen 'em. Finn was pissed, but Janus was so mad the whole camp was practically vibrating. What would you have done, if I just walked into the forest when it was still light out?"

I felt my muscles turn to lead. "I would've knocked you on your ass."

"And I've got the permanent bruises on my ass to prove how much you like to do that. Nothin's worth that, Kellan. Nothin's worth risking somebody seein' you vanish into thin air. They don't care why. It doesn't matter."

"But I waited for dusk." My voice sounded small and useless.

Antony took a step forward and Galen lunged at him, teeth bared. I reined Galen in, but he'd made his point. Watching my dog closely, Antony took two steps back and sighed. "Fine. Then you could've waited another hour for full dark. So why the hell didn't you?"

I didn't want to answer him. He was barely old enough to shave. I had no obligation to answer him. But ... if I told Antony about the documents, Janus would hear. He was watching us right now; I could almost guarantee it. Maybe this was my chance to talk to him, through Antony. I stood up a little straighter. When I spoke in a clear, calm tone, Galen relaxed — finally, I was taking control. "Because an outsider walked up to me this morning and handed me some documents written in Gaachail, in Janus's own handwriting. Because I've been calling Finn ever since and never got a response. And because I'm fucking pissed off at being treated this way, when I know I need help this time!"

Antony was quiet for a long time. Full dark was gathering around us, so I had difficulty seeing his face, but I figured he was thinking about what I said. I scratched the top of Galen's head. "Okay," Antony said finally. "Give the papers to me. I'll deliver them to Janus. I'll talk to him, see if I can convince him to reconsider your sentence. It sure sounds like extenuating circumstances."

"No." The word just popped out, but it felt right. It went along with the pride and rage that made my skin burn. "I'm custodian of these documents. I'll hand them over to Janus and Janus alone. He can summon me back here when he decides he wants them. Until then, they're staying with me, and I guess I'll just have to do my job, and try to get to the bottom of all this on my own. Without help. Since I'm exiled and all."

I could smell the shift in Antony's mood, from reflective to alarmed, as he realized I was serious. "Kellan—"

"And I think, since it's full dark, Galen and I will just exit right here. No sense wasting your valuable time walking me the rest of the way to the far end. So, have a nice day." I turned on my heel and walked purposefully away. Galen pranced by my side, happy that I was acting like I knew what I was doing. At least I managed to fool him.

"I can't let you leave like that." Antony's footfalls were quieter than I expected, for someone his size. "Look, just stay here, and I'll go talk to—"

"Thanks, but no." Blood rocketed through my veins and must've started pooling in my brain, because I felt light-headed and shaky. "You can walk with us, if you feel you must. But we're leaving." I stepped out of the forest, and felt the jarring loss of magickal energy as we left the spells behind.

"Kellan!"

I paused and glanced at him. Unfiltered moonlight gave me a nice view of the panicked *o* of his mouth. "You might want to keep it down. Don't want to call attention to ourselves, do we."

"Your life will be forfeit. Come on. Don't do this."

I broke out in a cold sweat. This could, in a broad interpretation, be construed as extreme disobedience. Janus could say I was deserting. So, I made good and sure my voice was loud enough to be heard inside the forest. "No. My life would be forfeit if I pulled a blade, slit your throat, and gave Janus the finger as I made a run for it. What I'm doing right now? This is following orders. Now stop detaining me."

I turned, stumbled over my own feet, righted myself, and started in the direction of the parking lot. Galen followed, tail lowered.

We were in a field, not unlike the one with the rockway leading to the forest, and the nearest building was half a mile away, so it was fairly dark. But Antony wore a white t-shirt and khaki shorts, so I saw him when he fell into step on my right side. The opposite side that Galen was on. "You're dumber than a box o' rocks with a hole in the bottom," he told me.

"So why not leave me to my stupidity, before you get accused of guilt by association?" I was honestly curious.

His voice was curt. "Because my orders were to escort you to your truck."

I felt a little surprised. That was the smartest thing he could do at this point, really. Short of knocking me over the head with a rock or trying to steal the papers from me, both of which might backfire and land him in the infirmary if he lost the skirmish, all he could do was follow his orders to the letter. It gave him a defense, should Finn question Antony's actions. I never realized Antony had that much going on north of his deltoids.

"So who's this outsider, anyway?" Antony said.

"How the hell should I know? I spent my day trying to get in touch with Finn, not finding out anything useful." This realization, previously lost in the chaos of the last few hours, added fuel to my rage. I'd wasted a day, Darcy Jamison would probably show up at my work again in the morning, and I still didn't have any bloody clue what to do about him.

"Yeah. I got that. I thought maybe you'd want to talk a little, since we gotta walk all the way back to the damn parking lot. But that's fine. Not like I want to listen to your whiny voice anyway."

"My voice is not whiny!" Although it sounded awfully close to whiny, in that moment.

Antony grunted. "Whatever you say."

A breeze blew by, carrying with it the scents of the forest. Janus kept the sights and sounds hidden, but didn't bother with the smells. Since human noses weren't sensitive enough to pick up on anything worth noting, it simply wasn't worth the energy. But my nose was plenty sensitive, and the scent-rich air reminded me of what I was leaving behind. Not just Janus and his inflexibility. Not just Finn and his cold shoulder. But the forest. The decades of memories that only came from one place. Home.

"Kellan?"

I realized that my feet were no longer moving, that my eyes were closed and my face upturned to better capture the scents in the air. With horror, I noted the dampness under my eyelids and the creeping snot that threatened to clog my nostrils. Galen was pressed against my left leg again, but this time, I knew he meant to comfort me, rather than protect me from harm. Slowly, I lowered my face, sniffled, and started walking again. I didn't reopen my eyes until I'd gone a couple steps, until I was sure none of that dampness would leak out onto my cheeks.

"Race you to the parking lot." Antony's voice rattled my raw nerves, so it took me a while to comprehend the words.

It was dark out, we were on wet, pitted ground, and he was wearing hiking boots, not running shoes. He was begging for a sprained ankle, or worse. Plus he had no shot at winning. Antony, like most of the Sankhain, was just a human. I was a shape-shifter, a supernatural being, stronger, faster, superer. This was a pity play. And I was pathetically grateful to him for it. "Okay."

We took off. It should've been no contest. He was more than half a foot taller than me, but he carried an extra eighty-five or so pounds, so his size should've worked against him. But those muscular legs had power, and he kept pace with me. When we were about fifty yards from the parking lot, I started to pull in front of him. Then, over the sound of my breathing and the air rushing past my ears, I heard the sound I'd been waiting for all day — the bleat of my cell phone ringtone. I skidded to a stop, dragging Galen back to me when he tried to keep running. With shaking hands, I dug the phone out of my pocket. Just as it went to voicemail.

The joy of almost winning the race died, as I stared at the "missed call" notification. Finn's cell. A slew of emotions confused my body.

"Who was it?"

I jumped. In my struggle to react, I had missed Antony's approach. "The Easter Bunny." My phone beeped. I had a voicemail.

"Aren't you gonna listen to it?"

I looked down at Galen. He stood in what I called his "ready" pose. Head high, body relaxed, eyes alert, tail curled over his butt. Not wagging, but he could break into a wag at any moment. He wasn't looking for danger, because Galen had every confidence that I would make the right choice. And whatever I chose, he was ready to follow me to the end.

What if Finn told me I had to report back to the forest, that now they wanted to see me? That was what I wanted, right? But Finn's call felt like a snap of his fingers, like he was calling me back to heel after I wandered away. And damn it, I wasn't done being pissed yet. He tossed me out. He could come to me. "Nope," I said, in answer to Antony's question. I stuck my phone back in my pocket and started running again. Beside me, Galen did the happy, bounding run that only dogs and little kids could pull off. More bounce than run. And why shouldn't he? In a dog's mind, the only bad decision was indecision. But a leader who was willing to lead, even if he led you into oncoming traffic, that was a leader a dog could look up to.

I was justifying decisions based on my dog's approval. Gods help us all.

Chapter 5

Antony followed us to the truck and waited while I opened the passenger door for Galen. Galen didn't jump up though, the way he usually did the moment the truck door opened a crack. He stayed standing next to me. Watching Antony.

"All right," I said. "Job well done and all that crap. You can leave now." Please. I wanted him to leave so that I could think in peace, without the threat of inane questions shooting at me.

Antony surprised me again by not asking any questions. Instead, he said, "I know you're pissed. People tend to be stupid when they're pissed. Don't do that."

For some reason, his tone took my anger down a couple notches. "So I'm supposed to be smart and pissed? At the same time? I don't think I'm that talented."

The shadows on his face shifted in a way that I thought might be a smile. "He thinks you are." Antony looked down at Galen. I watched Antony. I couldn't seem to look away. That rattled me.

So, I covered. "Well, he thinks it's a good idea to lick his butthole. Don't put too much money on his picks."

Antony laughed, and I realized that his laugh was a nice sound. A slow, broad chuckle that sidled up next to you and sat down to stay for a while. "Listen to your voicemail." He walked away.

I wanted to stand and watch him disappear, but that might draw attention to us or to Antony, so instead I told Galen to hop up in the truck. Once my dog was safely seated, I slammed the passenger door and walked around to the driver's side. I paused, my hand on the door handle. I should listen to the message. My skin felt tingly and I shivered from a chill that wasn't in the air.

I punched the button for my voicemail as I climbed into the truck.

"Kellan. It's Finn." Duh. "You are to return to the Academy immediately. That is an order. We'll discuss ... everything when you get here. Return now." He hung up.

My stomach roiled at Finn's sudden turnabout. Now that I had something he wanted, he was summoning me to his side. If not for those papers, he never would have called me back. I had never felt so small before, so insignificant. And that pissed me off more than anything else.

"Go fuck yourself, Finn." I looked at Galen, who seemed to confirm my decision with his steady gaze. I nodded and started the truck.

That's when my cell phone rang again.

At the sound, my bowels turned to liquid as I wondered if Finn had heard what I said. The phone bleated again. I had two more bleats before it went to voicemail. I wasn't ready for a confrontation with him yet. But, unable to resist, I picked up the phone and almost fainted with relief when I saw "Mal Cell" on the display. "Hello?"

"What'd you do this time?" My twin sister's words crackled from a lousy signal, but her dry tone came across just fine.

I scowled. "Nothing."

"Really? Because I just got a text saying you're exiled and nobody's supposed to contact you. What'd you do this time? Shape-shift in the middle of Wal-Mart?"

"No. And thank you for the support and confidence in my character."

"Uh-huh."

I slumped in the seat, suddenly missing my only living relative with paralyzing fervor. "I entered the forest."

She was silent for a beat. "And?"

"And, it wasn't totally dark yet."

"And you're still standing? Jesus, Kell, it's not bad enough we had to bury the rest of the pack? You want me to have to bury you, too?"

I was quiet for a while, listening to her harsh breathing and trying not to acknowledge the truth. "Windy tonight."

Mal sighed. "I think the only wind they make here in Kentucky is the flatulent kind. What I wouldn't give for a strong, cool breeze. Why'd you do it, Kell?"

I didn't want to explain. Mostly, I didn't want to hear Mal condemn my actions the way Antony had. "So you haven't heard them lately?"

"No one ever hears them, Kellan. They're dead. It's just an old superstition."

Galen stretched out across the seat and laid his head in my lap. I felt incredibly tired all of a sudden. "I should go. You're going to get in trouble."

She sighed again. "I won't get in trouble. They aren't bugging our cell phones. Yet." She paused. "No, I haven't heard them. And I miss them, like I miss you."

Two hundred years ago, Janus was the one to actually tell us that our mother and sisters were dead. But that's not how we found out. The wind told us first.

— «» —

Not all Sankhain began their lives in the outside world, the way Cat and Antony did. Some of us were born into this life. Janus recruited my great-great-grandmother when he first started the Sankhain. He thought a shape-shifter or two might come in handy. And we did, many times over. Janus lucked out in the sense that we, the Faolanni clan, happened to be a fairly prolific family, up until the current generation, at least. By the time she was my age, my mother had birthed eight children, all daughters. The shape-shifter body didn't seem to tolerate the long-term intrusion of "Y" chromosomes.

My sister, Amalea (Mal), and I turned out to be gross disappointments in the progeny department — we were both childless so far.

By the time Mal and I were born, or whelped — my mother thought it very amusing that she'd finally given birth to a litter of two — we had twelve older sisters. We weren't the only shifters in the Sankhain, either. Janus built a small army of half-animals, some wolves, like us, some birds, some cougars. The type of animal ran in the family. For instance, the Faolannis were all wolves. The Toullenes were all falcons. A falcon never gave birth to a wolf, or vice versa. The fathers were irrelevant, walking, talking sperm donors that never spent the night, much less played a role in their daughters' lives.

Janus called his band of merry women the Hycene — Gaachail for "Special." We were the Sankhain special forces. Janus didn't use the Hycene for border patrol or other grunt work. If the Sankhain were the anvil dropped on the intruder's head, the Hycene were the arrow, loosed to eliminate the enemy. When Mal and I were nine years old, our mother led the entire Hycene into Illinois, leaving us behind because we were too young. I argued with her about that. She left us behind anyway.

In Illinois, they found a nest of nocturnes, right where Janus's intel had told them the monsters would be. Nocturnes were also shape-shifters, but they could shift into the shape of any living thing, including humans. Also telepathic, the creatures could figuratively wriggle inside a person's brain and ferret out the darkest, most desolate secrets. Then they used that knowledge to drive their prey insane, and feed off the negative emotions they created.

Charming.

The nocturnes wanted access to the Spring, the one in our forest. For humans, the Spring acted as a fountain of youth, or rather, vitality. It didn't make them younger. It just cured them of every ailment imaginable and protected them from future malaise. It also froze them at their current age, preventing death by old age. The one thing it didn't protect against was death by mortal wound.

For non-humans, those of us already immortal, the water from the Spring had a different set of perks. It made us ... more. Faster at healing, faster at shape-shifting, stronger in both musculature and sensory perception. My sense of smell increased a hundredfold the night I drank from the Spring. And for as many centuries as we'd been protecting the Spring, the nocturnes had been trying to get a piece of the pie.

So, the Hycene left to stop them before they got any closer. I still remembered the sight. Wolves and cougars, coyotes and badgers. And the sky filled with hawks, eagles, falcons, crows. Every one a shape-shifter. They would spread out once they got away from the forest, to avoid causing a stir. But they left as one. Shock and awe, made flesh.

Two weeks passed without word. Not surprising, given travel time and the lack of speedy communication systems. Then, on the sixteenth day, the wind arrived.

The Hycene had their own traditions, almost like a religion. We had a full-moon ceremony, and we had our own death rites. Janus claimed the Sankhain funeral pyre was his idea, but we knew different. We burned our dead to set them free. The spirits spent eternity riding the wind, and anytime the wind kicked up, it meant our ancestors had something to say. If the wind died completely, that meant we had done something to make the spirits abandon us.

On that early autumn day, the wind tried to tear the roof off one of the barns. Mal looked at me, and we knew.

Janus didn't get official word for another month, after he sent riders to find the warriors who never returned. "Reinforcements," he told Mal and me, because he refused to tell us that he thought our family was dead.

The local humans believed it was a mass animal slaughter, after said animals killed a bunch of people (the nocturnes). Claiming to be from the army, the "reinforcements" dragged all the rotting bodies, Hycene and nocturne alike, onto bonfires and waited until all that remained were bones and teeth. Then they buried the bones on the spot, because the bones weren't important. Our people had already been set free.

By the time the reinforcement riders returned, no one expected them to be accompanied by the Hycene. And yet, Janus made a point of pulling Mal and me into his cabin that afternoon after he talked to Finn, who led the group of riders.

He sat us down in front of the fire. All three of us sat on the floor. Mal was older than me by a few minutes, but she was always smaller. Her coloring was brown where mine was salt-and-pepper. We looked nothing alike. But as we stared at the man in front of us, Mal took my hand, like she always did when shit was headed for the fan.

We laced our fingers together, and waited.

"Amalea. Kellan." Janus always called us by our full names, and always in order of birth. "Your mother is dead."

Mal just sat and looked at him, blank and quiet as always. She wasn't quiet with me, never with me, but she wouldn't show that side to other people, not then.

Of course, she didn't really need to make noise — I made enough for both of us.

"The wind told us that already." My voice rang out, loud and strident, in the confines of the cabin. I deliberately omitted the "sir" I knew he expected.

Mal stirred beside me, but she didn't speak.

Janus twitched. Doubtless he wanted to reprimand me for being disrespectful, but he'd just told me my mother died, after all. A good leader can show mercy. "Kellan—"

"May we go now?" I stood up without waiting for an answer, pulling Mal to her feet with our still-joined hands. Then I dragged her out and slammed the door behind us, hard enough to shake the walls.

"Kellan!" Mal hissed as I walked toward the archery shed. "What are you doing?"

I looked at her, feeling rage swirl in my gut, hot and welcome. "Archery practice. Come on."

The wind once again gained strength, whipping our hair across our faces and tugging at us as though begging us to play. Finn, fresh from the stables and smelling like sweat and horse and blood, arrived to lead our small archery class. Mal and I, along with two other younglings, stood outside the shed with our bows and quivers. Generally, our instructor chose a tree for each of us, and we spent the hour loosing, adjusting, loosing, adjusting, going higher or lower as the teacher bade.

Finn informed us that, because of the wind, practice would be moved to the half-empty cattle barn. I hated archery to begin with, and archery indoors was like watching potatoes grow.

"I want to stay out here," I said.

Finn looked at me. He knew, of course, where I'd been just prior, what I'd just heard. Like Janus, he didn't seem to know if he should reprimand me or leave me be. "We're going indoors, Kellan. Now—"

I never heard what he meant to say next. Probably something meant for the feeble minded, like "Let us go." But I spared us all from the inanity of the moment, because I pulled an arrow from my quiver, raised my bow, and shot Finn in the leg. It was a good shot, right through the thigh. Shattered the bone. Simone healed him easily.

Mal tried to tell Janus that she shot Finn, not me. I told her to be quiet. Not that it mattered what either of us said. There were witnesses. Janus asked me why I shot Finn. I told him that the wind was calling me, and I was tired of having to follow some human around like a cowed hound. And I told him I hated archery.

He said that was a pity, because I certainly seemed to have a knack for it.

I said, "A one-armed blind man could shoot someone from three feet away."

And he said, "Very well," and tried to lead me to a solitary cell. I wrenched out of his grip, dislocating his shoulder, and then I punched him in the groin. I heard yells, voices, one of them Mal's. But it was all just noise, more chaos to fuel the violence inside me.

I dropped to the ground and shape-shifted. The younger a shifter was, the less control she had, and I was never very good at control anyway. I hated them, Janus and Finn, Simone for rushing to Finn's aid, Mal for telling me to stop, my stupid mother and her stupid daughters for not taking us with them, for being stupid enough to die.

Hate was my king, and my teeth were my sword. I would have ripped them all apart, if they hadn't clubbed me on the back of the head hard enough to knock me out.

I earned a month in solitary and a year of kitchen duty for that little scene. And even though she would've ended up in the next cell if she was caught, Mal came to visit me every night I was in that six-by-seven cage, talking and singing to me through the little window. She kept me sane.

— «» —

If Finn knew Mal was talking to me now, he'd send a team to put her in chains and drag her back to a cell of her own. And I wouldn't be there to keep her sane.

I swallowed hard and forced the words out. "You shouldn't be talking to me."

She snorted. "Since when did that stop me? Now tell me what happened."

So I did. I told her about Darcy Jamison, the manuscript, and how I'd fucked it all up by not waiting just a little longer. Galen watched me, his ears twitching every time my voice caught, which happened often enough to shame me.

"He called you?" Her voice rose two octaves with disbelief.

"Yes, but that's not the point. The point is, I don't want to just go running—"

"He just called. He didn't come after you? He didn't show up in person, and tell you he was wrong. He just called his greatest asset and told her to come back. In a voicemail."

His greatest asset? Yeah, right. My temper rekindled. I knew I was only a blunt instrument, and that was fine, but I didn't appreciate my own sister pointing it out. "Don't be a bitch. My day has been lousy enough without you mocking me."

"I'm not — he should've — I don't know why you waste your time with that man. He doesn't value you at all."

Galen raised his head as I stopped petting him, switched the phone to my other ear, and raised my voice. "I know. You've made your opinion of Finn very clear. We're not dissecting my sex life right now. I've got bigger problems."

"I wasn't—" She cut off, and for a long time all I heard was her breath. "Are you going back?"

"No!" Galen sat up and stiffened. I spoke in a more modulated tone. "Not right now. If I saw them right now, I'd probably say something regrettable."

"If you used that as a requisite, you'd never speak to anyone."

My mouth curled in an involuntary smile. She was right, and I loved that she knew me so well. "Thank you, sister dear. Now go away. I have work to do." The wheels in my brain turned laboriously, as I considered how to deal with Darcy Jamison.

Now Mal's voice had an audible smile. "Such dedication."

"Yup, that's why they pay me the big bucks. Later, shrimp." Because she was so much shorter than me.

"Until then, *little* sister." Because I was so much younger.

I hung up, feeling a tiny bit better. Galen, however, was still on high alert. I talked softly to him, stroked his head and ears. By the time he heaved a sigh and laid down, I felt a lot better. As soon as I pulled out of the parking spot, my cell started ringing. This time, I didn't bother looking at the caller ID. I had a pretty good idea who was calling. And I didn't feel like talking to him. What would happen if he got a taste of his own medicine? I didn't know, and even though it made my palms sweat, I decided to find out. I stuck the phone in the glove compartment and turned up the volume on the radio.

On my street, I saw a familiar figure under a streetlight. And I got an idea. I slung the messenger bag over my shoulder, retrieved my phone, and grabbed a plastic bag from the collection on the floor, in case Galen needed to poop. Then I led Galen back to the corner where I had seen Raoul. I smiled as we approached. Raoul's only occupation, as far as I could tell, was standing on the street corner and hitting on every woman that walked past. Maybe he hit on the men, too. He'd paid my legs numerous compliments when I'd jogged with Galen. Probably Raoul was into something illegal, but I wasn't exactly halo material myself.

"Hey there, handsome," I said with a grin. Galen's tail wagged. Galen liked Raoul, probably because I liked him. Galen tended to trust my judgment.

Raoul's teeth were yellowed, but his smile was genuinely charming. "You finally decide to make an old man happy?"

"Aw, Raoul. You're too much man for me. I couldn't handle you." He laughed, and I moved onto business now that we'd addressed the pleasantries. I relaxed my grammar and slid into a more urban dialect. "You see that dude sittin' on my stoop few hours ago?"

He looked at me with mock horror. "Tell me that pale little white man ain't the one you turned me down for, girl." So, he had seen Darcy.

I smiled. "If I was on the market, I'd be all yours, you know that. No, I just was wondering if you saw him around here before today." I thought I saw something flash behind his eyes, but when I tried to read his scent, all I picked up was the usual — cigarette smoke, hot dogs and cherry lip balm.

My phone rang again, causing me to jump. Raoul cocked his head to one side and studied me. "You in some kinda trouble?"

I decided to be honest, since lying would slow me down. "Yeah, maybe. You seen him around? Before today?"

Raoul shook his head. "Not before today. But he showed up a few times today. Always hangin' around for a while. Like he was waitin' for something."

Or someone. "You remember when you first saw him?"

"This morning. Right after the bus picked up the high school kids."

Around eight o'clock. I left the house at quarter to eight that morning. So, Darcy Jamison came here, then found me on my dog-walking route. I felt an overwhelming urge to look over my shoulder to see if someone was watching me. Nobody, not even Finn, knew my dog-walking schedule. How did Darcy find me?

I must've looked like hell, because Raoul's next question sounded tense, almost angry. "You want me to take care of him, he shows up again?"

I blinked and looked at him. Then I looked at Galen and watched his tail go still. Get a grip, Kellan, I thought. You can freak out when you get home. I met Raoul's eyes, smiled and winked. "You're too good to me, Raoul. Naw, I got it. Thanks, though."

"Anytime. You change your mind — 'bout anything — you come let Raoul know."

"I promise." As Galen and I walked away, I put a little sway in my hips. I never did the whole swish-and-sway thing for anyone else, but having Raoul's wolf whistle follow me down the block made me grin. As we walked, I did a mental inventory of my weapons. Ticking off the list of blades relaxed me. Like counting sheep.

When we reached our building, I took a deep breath and found that the dumpster stink still clung to the air. I glanced over my shoulder, and saw that Raoul had followed me home. Not close enough to make me nervous, just close enough to have my back. All the supposed support of my fellow Sankhain, and the guy looking out for me was the neighborhood Casanova. Yeah, Raoul probably dealt drugs from his corner, but who was I to judge? The great thing about the neighborhood was that it existed in the gray areas. If you spent enough time there, you realized that not all criminals were villains. We were all just doing the best we could.

Chapter 6

In the apartment, as Galen trotted into the kitchen to his water dish, I went into the bedroom. I put the papers in the safe and went back to the living room to consider what to do next. I needed to find out more about Darcy Jamison. I needed to come up with a game plan for the next time I saw him, which would probably be in the next half hour, at this rate. And I needed to decide what to do with my cell phone, because Finn seemed determined to employ my own annoy-to-destroy method of calling.

Galen sat down in front of me and looked up at me expectantly. I knew all the things I should do. But I didn't care about those things. I was restless, edgy, angry, and maybe a little scared. I needed some "me time." So, I closed the blinds, stripped naked and crouched down on the floor. Galen knew the routine — he backed off and gave me some space to maneuver. Bowing my head, I focused my attention inward.

My hands changed first. The bones elongated and realigned themselves so they were narrow, flush with the bones of my arms. My ribs popped as my ribcage folded like a piece of paper creased in half, causing me to cry out. My shoulders and hipbones adjusted to the new shape of my torso, while my nose, mouth and cheekbones rearranged to become a muzzle. As fur flowed over my skin like goosebumps and my tail emerged from the small of my back, my cry turned into a howl. If the neighbors noticed the noise, they never said a word to me. This wasn't a Mr. Rogers kind of neighborhood.

I shook myself happily. All the human concerns disappeared, shouldered out of the way by scents, so much richer and more immediate, now that I was closer to the floor. Who cared about phone calls and papers? I needed to reacquaint myself with my little brother.

Some dogs would be freaked out if their owners were half-wolf, but not Galen.

We walked to the bedroom, me a head-length in front of him. I hopped up on the bed first, then Galen followed. We curled around each other, so that when I drifted off to sleep, Galen's tail was draped over my nose.

— «» —

The apartment was still dark when banging jerked me awake. With Galen on my heels, I jumped up and ran to the front door, the source of the noise. I sniffed the bottom of the door, the spot where the draft came in, and my wolf eyebrows drew together in confusion. It seemed the forest lay on the other side of the door. The door banged again. I growled loudly in response.

"Kellan, it's me. Tony," said the forest on the other side of the door.

Tony? I couldn't place the name. In wolf form, I didn't lose my human cognition, but I did sometimes take a little longer to get from A to B. Sensory overload was a common problem for a wolf in the city, especially a wolf rudely awakened. I sniffed the bottom of the door again. Another scent, almost as familiar as the forest, was there, too. Warm, slightly sweet, and thick.

"Kellan? I can hear you moving around."

I growled again in response, then shifted back to human form. As my bones snapped into place, I let out a howl that turned into a scream. It was a painful process. Shifting into wolf form hurt, too, but that was fun. Wolf time was play time. Human time almost always came with burdens, expectations and tedious interactions.

I heard Antony say my name again, more tentatively this time. "Yeah, just a minute. Keep your fucking pants on," I said. A few minutes later, fully dressed, I opened the door and glared at Antony. "What?"

"You didn't answer your doorbell," he said.

"The doorbell doesn't work."

"Why don't you ask your landlord to fix it?"

"Because then people would be ringing it and I'd be expected to answer. What are you doing here, Antony?"

"Can I come in?" He was looking at Galen, who stood, as usual, by my side.

"Are you asking me or him?" I said.

"You."

"That's good. If Galen had his way, he wouldn't allow anyone else in here." I stepped back, pulling Galen with me. "C'mon in."

After I closed the door behind him, I turned on a lamp, because humans had weak vision that required artificial lighting. He seemed even taller and broader in my living room. I watched him look around my apartment. "Why does it smell like old socks in here?" he said.

"Maybe it didn't, until you walked in. Ever think of that?"

He touched the back of my futon, right by the mysterious stain that every re-homed futon seemed to bear. "No."

My patience ran out for the eightieth time that day. "You have five seconds to tell me what you want, before I let Galen go for your balls."

Nothing like a threat to the testicles to focus a man. "Finn sent me. To bring the pages back to the forest."

I imagined I heard the snapping of fingers again. Anger warmed me disjointedly, like someone held a torch to my skin, first to my face, then my belly, my hands, my chest. "No. I told you, I'll hand the pages over to Janus. No one else."

"Then come with me." He said it like it was so easy.

It wasn't. I didn't want to go. I didn't want to hear about how stupid I was, how impulsive, how different from my great warrior mother. "I'm still exiled. As far as I know, that hasn't been lifted." I waited for him to tell me I was wrong. Then I stopped waiting, and felt myself deflate a little. "So, to avoid further unpleasantries, I'm going to follow orders. No returning to the forest. Not until Finn shows up and tells me otherwise. That's the protocol. If an exile is lifted before it runs its course, Finn either shows up himself or sends a proxy with a written pardon. Do you have a written pardon?"

"No." He was wearing a t-shirt that said *Keep talking. I like watching your lips move.*

"Nice shirt."

He cocked his head slightly and studied me, like he thought my compliment was a trap. "Thanks. I'll trade it to you for a cup of coffee."

I glanced at the clock. It was almost five a.m. First light would be coming very soon. "Shouldn't you be getting back to the forest?"

He shrugged one shoulder. "Not without those documents. So, if you're not going to turn them over, and you're not going to carry them yourself, then I guess I'm staying a while. You got cable here?"

"Yes." Annoyed, I wondered how I went from taking a stand to taking on a house guest. "And I really don't think—"

Antony sat down on my futon. "Wow. This is the least comfortable piece of furniture my ass has ever been smacked by."

I instantly felt defensive of a piece of furniture I didn't even like. "Nobody asked you to sit on it."

"So what's next? What's the plan?"

My last bit of patience snap-crackle-popped. I studied him with a critical gaze. "A shot of 'roids with a protein shake chaser, I imagine."

He looked offended. "I don't use steroids." He spread his arms wide, then flexed his biceps. "This is all natural, baby."

"Excuse me, I need to go vomit." I headed for the kitchen. Galen followed, watching me prepare a pot of coffee. He knew that the coffee routine was usually followed by food preparation.

"When you're done with the vomiting, how 'bout that coffee? I've been up all night."

I growled again. "I'm going to make coffee, but not because you asked for some. I'm making it because I want some."

I heard footsteps, then Antony's scent filled the kitchen. His scent wasn't an unpleasant presence, which annoyed me. "Will you share?" he said.

"Maybe. If you shut up for five minutes." I hit the "on" button, and Mr. Coffee gurgled to life.

"I gotta check in with Finn anyway. Where's the john?"

I looked at him. "It's down that hall, but the reception's just fine in here, too."

He seemed to find that very amusing. "I'm not gonna multitask. I'll do one, then the other."

"Whatever. Just try to hit the bowl, would you? I don't like surprise wet spots in my bathroom."

His smile turned suggestive. "No? What kinda wet spots do you like?"

"Just get out of here, would you?" I turned my back on Antony and opened the refrigerator door. Galen inched closer, until his head was almost inside the fridge. As I pushed Galen out of the way with my leg, I heard Antony walk toward the bathroom. His scent lingered in the kitchen.

By the time the toilet flushed, I had assembled a stack of ham and roast beef sandwiches. Antony's low voice preceded him into the kitchen. I listened to his end of the conversation with Finn. Finn answered the phone when Antony called. I would've thought I'd be all angered out, but I still had some rage left to spare. It curled in my gut, a ball of heat that began to radiate, to pulse through my limbs with such power that I thought my fingers should be glowing red.

"No," he said. "No, I wasn't able to make contact in time. She was out when I got here, I only just... No. And now, of course, it's too close to dawn. Yes, I will. Of course, sir." Antony held the phone out to me. "He wants to talk to you."

I couldn't move. The rage was still there, but some other emotion acted as a damper, cooling my arms, making my hands tingle. Not only did he tell Finn a relatively harmless lie about me being out when he arrived, but he withheld some pretty important information about my refusal to either hand over the papers or return to the forest. Why would he do that? Not for my benefit. I was certain I'd never done anything to warrant him being nice to me.

Antony cleared his throat. "Kellan? He wants to talk to you."

"Yeah. Okay." I took the phone. "Hello."

"Are you done sulking?"

At the sound of his voice, I wasn't confused anymore. I'd worry later about why Antony lied. For now, I was going to stick with rage. "No, not quite. So, you answer the phone when Antony calls, hmm?"

"I answer the phone when you call. When I'm available."

"You have never answered the phone when I call."

"Kellan, this is hardly relevant. I have been trying to reach you."

"It's completely relevant, but whatever. I've been unavailable. I might not be as important as you are, but I do have my own concerns to deal with."

"Kellan, please stop this. Now, you will turn over those documents to Antony so he may return them to us."

"No. As I said before, I'm the custodian of the documents. As a member of the Sankhain, I would be remiss if I allowed the documents to leave my hands. You'll just have to come get them."

"That is not an option. I'm very busy, you know. If you insist on accompanying the documents, you may accompany Antony as far as the forest."

The rage shifted, turned cold. So cold, it raised goosebumps on my arms. "So I'm still exiled?"

"Yes, of course."

Of course. The world felt very still. As though not even the cockroaches dared breathe. "Well, Finn, I just don't think that will be possible. I'm very busy, you know. I guess, if you want those documents, you'll just have to find a way to drag your ass over here. Buh-bye." I hung up the phone.

Antony looked reluctant as he took the phone from me. "That sounded unamicable."

"Really? Can't imagine why. You want milk for your coffee? I don't have cream." I pulled two mugs out of the cupboard.

"No. I take it black."

I got the milk out of the fridge anyway and set it on the table. I made my coffee strong enough to strip paint. Even the most die-hard coffee drinkers usually needed a little help choking down my brew. I set the plate of sandwiches on the table, too. "If you want breakfast, I've got toaster waffles and cereal."

"This is fine. Thanks."

We each filled our mugs and sat down at the table. A cheap folding table with metal folding chairs, it was not a comfortable place meant for lingering. I usually ate sitting on the futon. I found myself watching Antony as he took his first sip of coffee. His face contorted as he struggled to swallow. But he managed to swallow, and followed the first sip quickly with a second that he held in his mouth for a while. Like he was getting acclimated to it. He never added any milk or, god forbid, asked for sugar. I couldn't respect a man who added sugar to his coffee. It was just wrong.

He sounded a little hoarse when he spoke. "So. You never told me the plan."

"What plan?"

He chuckled. "The game plan. What're you gonna do?"

"Right now? Drink my coffee."

"Kellan." He didn't say my name the way Finn did, like I was an annoying child. He said it the way Mal did, like there was affection behind it.

"Look. I get that you have a job to do. And I'm sorry that I'm going to make your life difficult, because it's really not your fault Finn's an asshole. But all I care about right now is coffee and sandwiches. The rest of the world can go to hell until I deal with my stomach." To illustrate my point, I shoved half a sandwich in my mouth all at once.

Galen heaved a sigh, as if to remind us that he was there and starving.

"All right," Antony said. He pushed away his coffee mug. "Then do you mind if I try to get some sleep? I'll camp out on your futon."

I considered this. It didn't feel right. "No. You can take the bed. I'm not going to sleep anymore for a while." I rarely slept for more than a few hours at a time anyway, and when I slept in wolf form, the sleep was deeper and lasted me longer. I thought of something, and felt nervous gurgles in my stomach. "Why did you lie to Finn? Before, on the phone?"

"It was easier, I guess."

Easier than what, I thought. I was a horrible liar. I couldn't think of anything harder than pulling off a lie without stammering like an idiot. I felt annoyed that he didn't have a better answer. "Clean sheets are in the bathroom closet. I'm going to get ready for work."

He frowned. "Oh, your dog walking thing."

"Yeah, my dog walking thing."

"You want me to come with you?"

"Why?"

He shrugged. "I dunno. Just thought I'd ask."

I couldn't help myself. "Yes, please. I don't know if I can handle those dogs all by myself. I might need a big, strong man to save me."

"Okay, you know what? Screw you." He got up and left the kitchen, while I laughed.

I heard Antony go into the bathroom, open the closet door. I heard the swish of the sheets being changed. Then I heard the bedroom door close. When all was still, I looked at Galen. "Was I too mean?"

Galen didn't answer, although he looked at me rather reproachfully. But maybe he was just disappointed that I hadn't dropped a sandwich.

I put the leftover sandwiches in a bag, which I set in the fridge for later. Then I realized I needed to go into the bedroom, to get clean socks for my run. Shape-shifters were immune to the common cold, but not to foot fungi. I listened at the bedroom door for a second before knocking. "You decent?"

"Mostly." The sound of Antony's low, rumbly voice on the other side of my bedroom door sent a disturbing shiver down my spine.

I gritted my teeth and opened the door. Antony lay in my bed, the sheet pulled up to his waist. His upper body was bare naked, as was his leg that stuck out from under the sheet. His eyes were closed, so I let myself look over his torso. The well-muscled shoulders weren't a surprise, nor were the chiseled pecs — I figured those out from the way his t-shirts fit. But his abs were a thing of beauty. The man didn't have a six-pack — he had a case of twenty-four. I cleared my throat, trying to force my voice to sound normal. "You better be wearing underwear."

With his eyes still closed, his mouth curled in what I could only describe as a wolfish grin. "And if I'm not?"

My own mouth was drier than a Baptist wedding. "Then I'm burning those sheets." I grabbed the first pair of socks I laid my hands on.

I was almost out of the bedroom when he spoke. "If he knew you weren't answering the door, he might've seen that as further insubordination. Gotta be available and all that shit. He probably would have made me bring you in tonight. The lie gives us some wiggle room."

I couldn't think of anything to say to that, so I just left the room. I put Galen's harness on him, and we went for a run. I wanted to run until Tony's comments made sense. What was in it for him? Why would he need wiggle room? What difference did it make to him if I got taken in to camp, if I got locked up in a solitary cell? It shouldn't. He shouldn't care.

Because I couldn't make Tony's actions make sense, I lost track of time. The run went long. So long that I didn't have time to shower before I left for my dog walking rounds. Not that the dogs cared. The more scent the better, as far as dogs were concerned. But I had one client that day, an elderly woman named Mrs. Bartol, who was homebound and would almost certainly have to smell me.

Domingo was a cocker spaniel who weighed roughly three hundred pounds and was Mrs. Bartol's whole life. I checked my armpits and grimaced. Maybe Mrs. Bartol was old enough that she'd lost her sense of smell.

A little after eleven, I headed home for lunch. My cell phone had stopped ringing after I hung up on Finn, so the truck was quiet. Well, quiet except for the Metallica blaring from the speakers. A perfect morning, mostly. Aside from the exile, the documents, the smelly outsider, and the man that I really didn't want in my apartment. Because I was having such a nice morning, I wasn't at all surprised to see the rusty old hatchback parked in front of my building.

Chapter 7

My hands tightened on the steering wheel as my eyes sought out Darcy Jamison. He was still sitting in his car. I parked my truck behind my building and walked around to meet him. My tone was less cordial than the woman behind the counter at the post office. "Can I help you?"

His face flushed, and he smelled again. He was like a dog that found something dead in the backyard, and kept going back to roll in it so the yummy scent wouldn't fade. "I was just wondering if you found out anything yet. When you went to see your friend."

"No. Not yet. Apparently, dead languages that nobody but God has seen in a couple thousand years take a while to translate. I know. Shocking." A little heavy on the sarcasm, maybe, but those leftover roast beef sandwiches were calling my name.

"Oh. Right. Well, you'll call when you hear something?"

"No, I thought I'd just wait until you showed up again. Yes, I'll call you. Now go away. Don't you have a job or something?"

"Yes. I work at the library."

The question was rhetorical, but oh well. "Bully for you. I work as a dog walker. Which you know, because this is the second time you've interrupted my work day. And I have exactly twenty-three minutes left until I need to be at my next client's house. So, do you mind?"

His flush deepened. "Sorry. Thanks for your time."

There he went again, thanking me. What the hell was wrong with him? "You're welcome. Or whatever. Bye." I left him standing there, entered my building, took the stairs three at a time, and tripped over my own feet as I let myself into the apartment. Both Antony and Galen stared at me from the futon. The TV was on.

"You okay?" Antony said.

Galen, as if remembering that he had a job to do, hopped off the futon and trotted over to say hi. "You didn't feed him, did you? Because he already ate, and he'll overeat, given the chance, and then he could end up with bloat and die. There's no cure for bloat, you know." I was babbling, and I couldn't seem to stop.

Antony looked at me like he thought I might detonate. "I didn't feed him."

"Good." I put Galen's harness on him, to run him outside to pee. "I thought you'd still be sleeping."

"Yeah. The blinds in your bedroom are broken. And I think your neighbors are rehearsing for their STOMP! audition, the way they pound up and down the stairs."

"Are you just going to sit there and watch TV all day? Because that's pretty pathetic." I was being bitchy, and I knew it. But again, I couldn't seem to stop myself.

"Well, I washed all your dishes and vacuumed the dog hair off the living room furniture. And I Windexed your bathroom sink, but you're gonna have to do the toilet, or at least buy me some gloves, 'cause I don't do other people's toilets with my bare hands."

"Oh," was all I could think to say.

"I was thinking I'd go to the grocery store, maybe make some pasta, but I need a key to your apartment."

I felt so confused. "Why would you do that?"

"Because. Sandwiches are nice an' all, but they're not real food."

"Yes, they are."

He looked at me like he pitied me. "No. They're not."

"Fine. Here." I took the spare keys off the nail where they always hung. Where Antony could probably see them but didn't just take them. That annoyed me, and I let the annoyance carry me out the door with Galen.

I let Galen pee on all the bushes in front of the building. Then we went back upstairs and I hit the fridge. "Where are the sandwiches?"

Antony appeared. "I ate 'em."

"I thought they weren't real food."

"Well, I was hungry. And you don't have a lot of food choices."

"So you thought you'd just help yourself to my lunch. That's great. Really nice." I slammed the refrigerator door, but of course refrigerator doors didn't slam in a very satisfactory manner, so I went into the bathroom and slammed that door. When I came back out, the apartment was quiet. I found a note taped to the door frame. "Sorry about the sandwiches. I'll make dinner – Tony."

I looked at Galen. "Well, it's a good thing he signed it, because otherwise I might've thought the note was from you."

I kissed Galen on the top of the head. I lied when I told Darcy I had to get to my next client. My only client that afternoon was Heinrich the dachshund, and I didn't have to be there until five. That meant I had time for a workout.

I took off my shoes and socks, and grabbed my yoga mat from the bedroom. I didn't meditate, didn't consider myself a spiritual person. But yoga did have some value. Something about standing on one leg in a position that looked nothing like a tree didn't just sweep away the clutter in my brain, it blew the clutter away with a giant leaf blower. And that day, I had more clutter than one of those hoarders on TV, the ones that buy sixteen copies of the same book just in case they drop one in the toilet.

Yogi I was not, but the exercise served its purpose. After an hour, I had a brainstorm. I could do an internet search on Darcy Jamison. Day job, address, criminal record, all the relevant things. And, of course, a birth date was always important information. Never take for granted that your quarry was born within a human lifespan.

Maybe the internet didn't seem like much of a revelation, but I was born two hundred years ago. People still sealed their letters with wax when I was a kid. I was a little behind the curve when it came to the information age. After a quick shower, I put a pot of coffee on to brew and set up my laptop on the kitchen table. As it whirred and buzzed, I went back to the coffee pot, all but tapping my foot in anticipation of that first cup. Finally, it gurgled out enough for a mug-full, and I sat down at the table.

Slowly, and with not a little swearing, I finally had some search results for Darcy Jamison of Madison, Wisconsin.

I slanted a glance at Galen, who was watching my struggles with his ears pinned back and his eyes a little too wide. "It's okay, buddy."

Galen didn't look reassured.

I started sifting through the information. Turned out, there were three Darcy Jamisons in Madison. The other two were girls, of course. I wrote down Male Darcy Jamison's address and phone number, as well as the address of the library where he worked as a reference librarian. Next, birth date. Thirty-one years ago. I squeezed my eyes shut, trying to remember whether his physical appearance jived with that number. I was lousy at judging human age. If they were anywhere between seventeen and sixty, they all looked the same to me. Thirty-one probably fit.

Of course, there was always the possibility that his history was manufactured, the way Kelly O'Connell's was. But for the moment, I would go with the facts in evidence. After all, I'd read it on the internet; it had to be true.

I moved on to the rest of the search results, looking for anything interesting. A link to the Madison Times caught my eye. I skimmed the article as I drank my coffee. Darcy ran the local summer literacy program for kids. Last summer, the theme was Pirate's Bounty. Every time a kid read a book, they would get a "doubloon" that they could redeem for a prize at the end of the summer. Not exceptionally original, but probably effective. I didn't learn to read English until I was almost eighty years old. Maybe I would have been more motivated if someone offered me fake gold.

There was even a picture — Darcy Jamison sitting on the floor, reading to a bunch of enthralled children. Jeez. I'd almost hunted the librarian equivalent of Santa Claus. I was a horrible person. Not only that, I was a horrible person who still had no idea why this patron saint of libraries stank like a three-week-old Big Mac. I didn't know what he was so afraid of, or why he kept coming around and getting in my way. I needed more information than the internet had to offer.

I checked the clock and wondered why Antony wasn't back yet. How long did it take to buy pasta? He'd been gone almost an hour and a half.

With a glance at Galen, I got up and went to the fridge. More sandwiches sounded like too much trouble, so I dug a piece of roast beef out of the package and stuffed it in my mouth, then refilled my coffee mug. "Sit," I said to Galen. I tossed him some roast beef and he swallowed it whole. "At least I chewed."

We went into the living room and settled on the futon. I considered my options. I could ignore Darcy and hope he went away. That one was easy to discard. If I had learned anything in the last twenty-four hours, it was that Darcy would keep coming back. Better to deal with him. I wanted to know why Darcy showed up on my radar in the first place.

Antony chose that moment to crash through the door, carrying way too many plastic shopping bags. Which he promptly set down on my living room floor. I caught Galen just before he made a dive for the bags. "Dude! Take those in the kitchen and put 'em away. Before Galen commandeers the food."

Antony looked at me. "You're welcome."

"How do you get from what I said to 'you're welcome'?"

"I just went grocery shopping for you. I bought you milk, cereal, eggs, ground beef, ground turkey—"

"You mean Finn bought me those things. You did use your Sankhain Visa, right?"

"Of course. How else would I pay for all this stuff?" He picked up the bags, three in each hand, and hauled them into the kitchen. "But you might say thank you, since I did you a favor."

"A favor? What the hell am I supposed to do with ground turkey?"

"Cook something with it."

I walked, still holding onto Galen's collar, into the kitchen. "Like what? Do I look like Martha Stewart?"

Antony gave me a long, slow, up-and-down glance. "No. I look more like Martha Stewart than you do."

"Thank you." I peered into one of the bags. "Fake crab meat? Seriously? What possible use could there be for fake crab meat?"

"Just out of curiosity, which is worse, in your mind? Ground turkey or fake crab meat?"

"Really, the worst thing is that I suddenly find myself in a world where such questions are not only possible, but necessary."

"There's more to life than beef, ya know." As if to prove his point, he handed me a phallic-looking green vegetable. "Wash that, will you?"

I didn't move, just stared at it. It smelled like dirt and cabbage. I couldn't imagine wanting to eat this. Galen, on the other hand, was surveying it with interest. He must not have been able to smell it. "What is it?"

"It's a zucchini." He set the fake crab meat in the fridge and glanced at me. "It's not gonna bite you."

"I think I'd trust it more if it did."

Shaking his head, Antony took the zucchini from me and started washing it himself. "What were you doin' when I walked in?"

I had a little trouble switching gears. "Huh? Oh. I was thinking."

"Hard work. What about?"

I watched as he rummaged through the drawers. "About life, love and the pursuit of happiness. What are you doing?"

"Don't you have any good knives?"

"Of course I do." I reached under my shirt and pulled out one of the knives from the belly band. "This is pure—"

"I meant kitchen knives. Like for chopping."

"Can't you just use a steak knife?"

He closed his eyes for a moment. "No. Not if you want your vegetables clean cut instead of looking like a drunken four-year-old sliced 'em."

"What kind of degenerate would get a four-year-old drunk?"

"I give up." Antony turned his back on me and started chopping the zucchini with a steak knife.

"See? It's working fine." I watched for a while. Apparently, Antony wasn't going to leave anytime soon. Maybe I should make use of him. Other than in the kitchen. I was very suspicious of his idea of "food." "So what would you do?"

He shot me a glance. "I'm gonna need a little more information."

"Next. With the outsider. What would you do, if you were me?"

"What have you done so far?"

I told him the story, from the moment Darcy showed up on my dog-walking route to when I saw him a couple hours ago. While I talked, Antony put water on to boil, chopped some red and green peppers, dumped rotini pasta in the water, and assembled a line-up of shredded cheese, alfredo sauce in a jar, and fake crab meat.

"So basically you haven't done squat," Antony said.

"Yes, I have."

"Right. You took the documents from him, you entered the forest before full dark and got yourself exiled, you ignored Finn's phone calls and orders, and you growled at the outsider a few times. Oh, and you Googled him. Well done."

My cheeks grew warm. "The sarcasm is a little excessive."

He laughed. "That's good, coming from you. So, what do you think you need to do?"

"Obviously, I shouldn't be trusted to tie my own shoes, so why don't you tell me what I should do?"

He poured the pasta into a colander. "Don't suppose you have a casserole dish."

With a smug smile, I opened a cabinet and pulled out a long glass dish. "Like this?"

His eyebrows shot up and his scent lightened with surprise. "Yeah. That'll do it. Thanks." He washed my casserole dish, then dumped the ingredients in it and heaped shredded cheese on top. I was still looking doubtfully at the concoction when he slid it in the oven. "It'll be good. I promise," he said, when he saw the look on my face.

"Sure." I reminded myself that I had Pizza Hut on speed dial.

"It's gotta cook for a while. You want to sit down?" Without waiting for an answer, Antony headed into the living room. I hesitated. It bothered me, the way Antony was making himself comfortable here. But I wanted help, right? I followed him into the living room.

He took the armchair. Galen and I settled on the futon again. Antony didn't say anything for a while, and I started to prepare my defense of my actions.

"I'm sorry," he said.

I blinked. That wasn't the opener I was expecting. "Okay."

"I should've been nicer before. You're right. Finn shoulda called you back. The way that outsider keeps getting in your face, it's totally understandable that you acted … impulsive."

I didn't know how to respond to that, so I kept it simple. "Oh."

"I think we should just keep going the direction we're already going. I mean, you found a bunch of information already, right? Where he lives, where he works."

We? Was that like the royal "we?" Or did Antony actually consider himself my ally in this? "What do you mean, 'we'?"

"Finn's gonna assign me to help you."

"Did you talk to him again?" The thought of the two men discussing me without my knowledge made my hands clench. "Who says I need help? I'm doing just fine on my own, thank you."

"No. I didn't talk to him. But I mean, come on. This is the biggest thing to happen around here since, shit, probably before you were born."

"And god forbid that I handle something so big on my own? I've got plenty of experience dealing with big."

Antony leaned back and grinned cockily. "I bet you do."

"Wipe that grin off your face or I'll make you a eunuch."

"You'll make me one? Like outta clay?"

My blood pressure shot so high I felt like my eyes were about to pop out of my head. I had to say something, but my brain wouldn't offer any words, except, "Fake crab isn't real food!" At my tone, Galen lifted his head off his paws and looked at me. I was breathing too fast and too loud. With conscious effort, I took a deep breath and closed my eyes. When I opened them, I focused on my dog. "Well, it's not. It's fake. It's right in the name."

"Of course you can do this on your own." Antony sounded so serious, I had to look at him. "But Finn's gonna need to feel like he's in control. So you have a couple choices. You can answer your phone when he calls, say 'yes, sir' and 'please' and 'thank you,' and listen to his opinion on how you should tie your shoes. Or you could let me do it."

I frowned, totally mystified. "Why would you want to do that?"

Antony hesitated, and I tensed as my mind raced. He probably thought he could advance his career by being the smart one on this operation. Showing Finn how stupid I was and how useful Antony could be. The little turd.

"Last night, you were…" He stopped, and my temper flared.

"What? I was what? I stood up for myself, damn it. I have rights. I shouldn't be treated that way." This time, I didn't bother trying to calm myself. Fight or flight wasn't all bad.

"No. You shouldn't. But Finn's still got a bug up his ass. Every time you two talk, you're just going to make things worse. Both of you. If you let me deal with him, then maybe someday you two can stand to be in the same room again without tearing each other apart."

"Oh."

"And why do you have to assume that I was going to put you down? I was going to say you were, I don't know, inspirational, I guess."

I curled my lip. "Like Billy Graham?"

"No. Like Barack Obama."

Was he serious? He looked serious. But Antony and I weren't nice to each other. He was the cocky kid who thought his size made him superior on the battlefield, and I was the old bitch who took joy in showing him that speed and skill could best brute strength. "What the hell is that supposed to mean?"

He sighed. "Nothing. It meant nothing. Are you done with dog walking for today?"

The topic jump was too jarring. "It wasn't nothing. You don't tell someone they're inspirational for no reason. That's stupid. What did you mean?"

"I meant that you surprised me, and made me want to help you! Jeez. Learn to take a compliment, would you?"

A compliment? "That really wasn't part of the curriculum. My education was more knife throwing and hand-to-hand."

He snorted. "You ever think maybe the reason why nobody gives you compliments is because you'd bite their head off if they tried? Shit."

I felt my cheeks grow hot. "You ever think the reason you spent so much time on your ass in the dirt was because nobody likes a fucking know-it-all?"

He smiled so beatifically, I could practically see the halo over his head. "It's the price I pay for being born wise. Are you done with dog walking, or not?"

Wise, my ass. "No. I have one more client."

"Okay. So you'll do that. I'll hang out here, if that's okay, maybe do another search online for information on this guy."

"I already did an internet search, there's nothing else to find." Considering my crappy computer skills, that was almost definitely untrue, but I wasn't about to admit that.

Antony continued like I hadn't spoken. "Then, after dark, I'll go back to the forest and talk to Finn. Get him to assign me to help you. I'll be back before midnight, probably."

He sounded so damn certain. Like all this was part of the plan. Meanwhile, my mood kept traveling further down the rabbit hole. "Bully for you. I'm sure you'll enjoy sleeping on the futon."

He grinned, which just irritated me more. "Great." He jumped to his feet and returned to the kitchen. As Galen followed him, abandoning me on the futon, I realized my apartment smelled like melted cheese and something else, hot and savory. It smelled not only edible, but tasty. Damn. If it tasted as good as it smelled, I was going to have to acknowledge his efforts. He called from the kitchen, "Soup's on. You hungry?"

"Eternally." I waited a moment, wondering if I could just leave rather than eat his food. I didn't want to be grateful to him. My stomach grumbled, casting its vote for staying. "All right," I muttered, and joined the males in the kitchen.

Chapter 8

Antony and I ate without talking, while Galen drooled on my foot. The food was very good. The fake crab went well with the alfredo sauce, the peppers gave it a little extra zing, and the zucchini — well, hopefully, the zucchini added some kind of nutritional value, because it didn't taste like anything.

The longer the meal droned on, the more uncomfortable I got. Because I was going to have to pay Antony a compliment, and I'd rather gouge out my eyeball with a grapefruit spoon. "It's good. You know. The food."

Antony glanced up at me quickly, then returned his attention to his food. "Thanks. I like doing it. Balanced meals weren't really part of the menu when I was little. I guess I don't want to go backwards."

My irritation faded. I'd never heard Antony talk about his past before. None of the kids that we recruited came from happy homes. Kids from happy homes tended to be missed. Featured on billboards and coupon booklets. That got in the way of our work. We chose runaways. When two Sankhain found Antony, he'd just escaped from the pedophile who bought him from his mother. I knew his history, but as a rule, I didn't ask questions. Emotional healing was someone else's job. Still, I felt compelled to say something. "Um, Antony—"

"Call me Tony." I heard what he wasn't saying — he didn't want to talk about it anymore than I wanted him to.

I started to clear the table, but Antony told me he'd take care of it. I hightailed it out of Emotionally Awkwardville. Once in my truck, I saw it was still too early for Heinrich. I considered my options. I could swing by Darcy's apartment, and if he wasn't there, I could sniff around, literally. But it was broad daylight, and there was really no inconspicuous way to wander around outside a building, sniffing. I would end up looking like a crazy person. Better to do that under cover of darkness. I decided to try his work.

This was a good plan, I told myself. A good use of time, a good opportunity for reconnaissance, and, as a bonus, a good way to get the hell out of my apartment. I kept telling myself how smart I was, as I drove past the library, searching for Darcy's car. It wasn't there, which meant Darcy probably wasn't there, which meant I could talk to his coworkers.

When I stepped through the library doors, I suddenly recognized the flaw in my good plan. Libraries were like grocery stores. Many of them only had windows along one or two walls, windows that never opened, and the only living things allowed inside were humans. Even the plants were fake. And library exits were always interspersed throughout the stacks, meaning if I needed to make a quick exit, I'd have to perform the world's worst slalom.

I took a deep breath, inhaled the air-conditioned stench of old books, dust and perfume, and almost walked back out. But then I noticed a woman sitting behind the reference desk, all alone, perfect prey. Oops. Perfect source of information.

As I crossed the room to the desk, I took in the other patrons. No apparent threats. One less thing to worry about.

When I reached the desk, I turned on my most harmless smile and cleared my throat. Librarian Lady looked up from her computer and returned my smile. She was the source of the perfume I smelled. "Can I help you?" she said.

"Um, yes, I hope so. I was wondering if Darcy Jamison was working this afternoon?"

She cocked her head to one side, considering me. I turned my smile up a few watts and hoped she wasn't one of those people who didn't like tattoos. If she decided I was a bad person, she wouldn't talk. "I'm sorry," she said. "Darcy isn't due in today. Can I help you with something?"

"I don't know. He was helping me the other day ... with..." What did librarians do? "With some information I was looking for."

The woman's face lit up, and I could almost hear her think *Oh! A live one*. She took a step closer, and her perfume hit me like a wall. She must have marinated in it overnight. I fought not to gag. "I'm sorry," she said again. "Darcy's been having to take a lot of personal time lately. With his sister being sick and all."

I nodded, trying not to sneeze. "Right, his sister. He mentioned something, but I forget. What's wrong with her again?"

She whispered, like it was catching, "Cancer." She shook her head, sending another wave of scent my way. "Stage four. They don't think she'll make it much more than a month."

The cartoon light bulb lit up over my head. How lucky for me that White Diamonds Barbie was a blabbermouth. "Well, I'll just come back another time. When will he be back?"

"Tomorrow, I think. If you like, I could help you do another search." She was studying me again, a little too close for comfort.

I sneezed. "No, that's okay." I sneezed again. I had to get out of here. "I'll just come back. Thanks for your help."

I pushed out the doors, breathing deeply the sweet, warm, blessedly perfume-free spring air. And then I smelled it again. That strange scent, faint, but still there. Whatever covered Darcy with that stench visited him here. I wondered if the girl inside had seen him/her/it. I wondered if that information was worth venturing into perfume range again for. Hell, no.

I decided to come back after dark to see if I could track the scent. Frowning, I inhaled deeply, one last time. The scent just wasn't human — almost, but not quite. I shook my head as I drove to Heinrich's house. I knew the scent. It was somewhere in my brain, like a word just out of reach, and the more I tried to place it, the more it eluded me.

Chapter 9

My hour with Heinrich passed without incident, and I decided to stop on the way back to my apartment for a cappuccino. I wondered if I should get one for Antony. Tony. He said to call him Tony. Maybe I could just drink my cappuccino really fast, and not bother bringing one home for him. That sounded perfect.

As I walked to the front door, I noted that the sun was starting to droop. I wondered when Tony would leave.

In the apartment, Galen was waiting for me, as always. That made something inside me relax, that one display of normalcy. Then I heard it — snoring, loud enough to scare Helen Keller's socks off.

I stopped rubbing Galen's butt. "That better be Tony. Or else Mama, Papa and Baby Bear are all sleepin' in our bed."

Galen didn't react. Of course, he'd been listening to the snoring since Tony fell asleep. He was probably used to the noise level by now.

I slipped Galen's harness over his head and we escaped into the evening air, which had cooled off considerably. Dark clouds advanced on us. Rain would wipe out the scent trail at the library. That scent trail was too important to risk losing. Before we left, though, I thought of something else. "Probably we should leave Gigantor a note, right? So he doesn't wake up and think he lost you."

Galen withheld comment. He was the perfect sidekick, warm, strong, and totally nonverbal. We went back upstairs, and I tried to decide what to write. I didn't want to sound like a codependent girly girl. But I also didn't want him to be waiting for Galen and me to come home. Finally, I muttered, "Oh, fuck it," and wrote, "Took Galen out. See you later."

When Galen and I finally got into the truck, the air was heavy with the scent of rain. It hadn't started yet, though.

White Diamonds Barbie said Darcy wasn't working until tomorrow, but I didn't want to take any chances. Running into him would slow me down. Seeing a sign for a bike trail, I pulled onto a side street and parked. Bike trails were handy recon tools in a strange neighborhood. The people who lived there might notice me, but if I was on or near a bike trail, I was just another crazy health nut with a dog. It made my jogging shorts the perfect camouflage.

I opened the truck door and climbed out, then waited for Galen to jump down.

We jogged back to the library, then paused by the building. I leaned over, placing my hands on my knees, as though trying to catch my breath. As Galen searched for something tall to pee on, I inhaled deeply, searching for the scent. There it was. I tried once again to place it in my memory. It was almost like something dead. Zombie? No, not quite. Well, I was getting very good at figuring out what this scent wasn't. Only about a million more possibilities to eliminate and I could figure out what it *was*.

I refocused my nose and started down the sidewalk with the aim of following the trail. Unfortunately, I hit my aim about as well as a three-toed sloth with a slingshot. The trail led me from the front door of the library to a field behind the building. Two steps into the field, the scent trail vanished. It didn't fade, it didn't dissipate — it disappeared. I backtracked and found the trail again. Followed it a few paces. In the same spot, it disappeared again. Now you smell it, now you don't. Except you couldn't fool noses the way you could fool eyes. Even invisible things left behind a scent trail. I searched the field, then the blocks surrounding it. Nothing.

Rain started to fall. Galen glared at me, like the steadily increasing downpour was my doing. With a sigh, I tugged his leash and we began the long, wet walk back to the truck.

As I drove home, I wondered if Tony would still be there. Snoring on the futon? Or maybe in the kitchen, cooking something else? Not that I cared. He was a cocky, irritating son-of-a-bitch. And his cooking skills left a lot to be desired. I mean, anyone who thought zucchini was a viable food source obviously had a lot to learn.

I pointed that out to Galen, in case he was wavering in his opinion of our house guest. Of course, Galen seemed to like Tony. And, well, as much as I hated to admit it, cocky and irritating didn't seem to equal unlikable in my mind, either.

Talking to Tony was kind of like talking to Mal. Except Tony was about a foot and a half taller than Mal, and I knew for a fact that Mal's abs were nowhere near as impressive as Tony's. And Mal's laugh was a kind of high-pitched hee-hee, where every sound Tony made seemed to be low and rumbling. Like it echoed around in that big barrel chest.

I stopped at a red light. The inside of the truck was suddenly uncomfortably warm, like an undersized parka, and I couldn't seem to fix my eyes on any one thing for more than a couple seconds. I rolled down my window and let the rain blow into the truck. Fresh air made everything better, I told myself. To avoid the rain, Galen crawled onto the floor and curled into the tightest ball he could manage. I felt a little guilty, but not guilty enough to close the window. The air from outside felt wondrous, as it wound its way through the truck, pressing against my skin because the humidity weighed it down. My focus returned. I decided that, whether Antony was in the apartment or not, I was going to eat my own food and do my own thing. Like he never existed.

So, when I pulled into my parking lot and saw that the Sankhain sedan was gone, I told myself that I was glad. But I didn't believe me.

Galen and I went upstairs. I saw the note, now taped to my good friend, Mr. Coffee. I noticed some additional chicken scratches under my handwriting. "Thanks for the note. There's still some pasta left in the fridge, if you're hungry – Tony."

"Of course I'm hungry! I'm always hungry!" I crumpled up the note and tossed it in the trash. Then I opened the refrigerator, planning to pull out the roast beef and eat all of it. But I saw the container of leftovers, sitting right there next to the milk. Maybe I should just eat that up, I thought. Who knew how long fake crab stayed good? And all that cream sauce, that would mold in no time. Yeah, probably I should eat the leftovers before they grew green fuzz.

I grabbed the container, took the lid off, and almost moaned at the smell of garlic, cheese, and seafood. Fake seafood, but it still smelled pretty close to the real thing. As much as I loved beef, I had a weakness for shellfish that Mal always thought freakish. My mouth suddenly started watering with such vehemence that I wiped my mouth, checking for drool. Galen supervised every forkful, to make sure nothing escaped. I wondered if Tony was allowed to enter the forest early, since the rain storm basically brought on full dark an hour early. I wondered if he was meeting with Finn yet. I wondered how it was going. I wondered how many "I wonders" it took to get to the center of the Looney Pop.

After setting the container in the sink to soak, I climbed into bed. My brain was still going round and round the mulberry bush, trying to place the scent from the library, trying to figure out how it could just disappear. But the bedroom was dark and cool, and the rain provided a lovely soundtrack, allowing my overtired body to override my brain.

When I woke to the sound of knocking, I was treated to Galen's toenail shoved up my left nostril as he scrambled, cartoon-style, to disentangle himself from the blankets and race to the door. It was with a bloody nose and major bedhead that I followed him.

I opened the door. "Oh my god. What happened to you?" Tony asked.

"Galen kicked me in the head." I turned and walked away, dragging Galen with me.

"And then he turned your hair into a rat's nest?"

I turned to face him, my lip curled in a snarl, which probably looked pretty impressive, considering the drying blood on my face. "What, you don't like my new do?" I wanted to wash my face. A glance at the living room clock told me it was a little after eleven. "Is it still raining?"

"No. Stopped about an hour ago." From the bathroom, I heard Tony close the apartment door and bolt it. Then I heard some rustling noises and boots hitting the floor. I felt a little annoyed that he hadn't offered to tell me about his meeting with Finn. I was maybe also a little annoyed because I could smell Tony's scent in my apartment again, and part of me really liked it being there. Wolves were pack animals, after all. Not that Tony equaled pack, not by a long shot; he was just a measly human, but still. It was kinda nice to have someone else in the apartment.

Tony was pulling out the futon, which was built for someone five foot seven, tops. He was six foot four and at least two hundred pounds of muscle. But I was still considering letting him sleep on it, when he pulled off his t-shirt and started to unbutton his jeans.

"Whoa, there. At least close the blinds first, will ya? Jeez."

"Sorry," he said. His voice was quiet, pulling my gaze to his face. I noticed the bags under his eyes, how blood-shot they were, how he couldn't seem to drag them open more than halfway. "I'm beat."

"How long did you sleep this afternoon?"

"Bout an hour." He yawned so wide, my jaw hurt. He lay down on the futon, still wearing his jeans. The end of the futon hit just below his knees.

That sight annoyed me more than Darcy and the phantom scent put together. "Oh, for Pete's sake. Get up."

"What?" He sounded halfway to sleep already.

"Get up. Go sleep in the bed. I can sleep out here."

"No, it's okay. I—" He interrupted himself with another huge yawn.

"Just go, before I change my mind." I watched him sit up, watched his stomach muscles contract and relax as he got to his feet. I began to salivate again. I wasn't into muscle-bound guys. I'd known too many who thought muscles were the key to domination of the "weaker" sex. But Jesus God on a donkey, the man was something to look at.

"Wanna share?" His voice, lower than usual with extra gravel, made me jump.

"What?"

"The bed." He smiled, slow and warm. I felt the warmth, right down to my... Shit.

"No. Get out of here."

"Are you sure? I could—"

"Antony, I swear to god, if you don't get the hell out of my living room, I'm going to tie you to a folding chair and pour coffee down your throat until you're so fucking awake that you won't sleep for a week."

"I'm going." He paused. "Finn said okay, by the way."

"What?" I said again. Finn? Who was Finn?

"I'm officially your liaison."

"Oh." I slowly found my way back to rational thought. "Great." It helped a lot when Tony left the room, and I wasn't using all my faculties to avoid staring at his pretty, pretty body.

On the bright side, I now had help. Help who could cook. But on the not-so-bright side, I was wide awake and suddenly found myself with about a thousand kilowatt hours of energy to burn. With a sigh, I started lifting weights.

Shortly after midnight, I began to feel tired again. I took Galen outside for one last potty break. The neighborhood was unusually quiet. While Galen lifted his leg on every bush in the front yard, I closed my eyes, raised my face skyward, and took deep breaths of the clean, heady spring air.

His scent appeared out of nowhere, and I almost peed my pants, I was so startled. Galen abandoned his marking ritual to stand in front of me, shielding me. I opened my eyes and took in Jamison-like-the-whiskey's figure as he stepped in range of the porch light. "Darcy Jamison, you are now officially creepy. Do you know what time it is?"

His hand moved, and I twitched for the knife at the small of my back. Then a little green light emanated from his wrist, and I realized he was looking at his watch. "Quarter past twelve."

Everybody's a smart-ass.

I closed my eyes and counted to ten, a technique suggested by Finn. Maybe it worked for Finn, but I didn't find the sequence of numbers calming in the least. Then

Galen brushed up against my leg, and I opened my eyes to find him looking from me to Darcy and back again.

Get a grip, I told myself, before your dog decides to rip somebody's head off. He'd do it if he thought it was what I wanted. But I never let my dog fight my battles if I could help it. Taking a deep breath, I rubbed Galen behind the ear to soothe us both.

"Nice night," Darcy said.

Oh, Christ. If I had to endure small talk, I needed food. And coffee. Lots of coffee. Fuck sleep, I wanted to be high. "Are you hungry?"

"What?"

I smiled, finding it gratifying to hear someone else taken off guard for once. It made me feel better, more like myself. "I'm hungry. If you insist on inflicting yourself upon me, I'd much prefer you did it while I eat. If you're hungry too, we can go somewhere."

"Oh. Okay." He paused. "Maybe you want to shower first?"

I remembered my rat's nest hair, now seasoned with a healthy dash of sweat, and I scowled. "We're not going to La Brioche. We're going to the golden arches for drive-thru." I started walking toward my truck.

I didn't check over my shoulder to make sure Darcy was following us. History had shown that he wouldn't let me shake him so easily. By the time Galen hopped onto the seat of the truck and I was ready to join him, Darcy stood by my side again. I looked at him. "We can't all fit behind the wheel. You're going to have to sit on the passenger side."

"I could just follow you."

"Sure. 'Cause nothing says keeping it simple like a fucking caravan. Just get in the truck."

Darcy peered through the window. "I don't think your dog likes me."

"Yeah, well, he has good taste. Just don't make any sudden moves, and you should be fine." In the interest of good karma, I tried not to enjoy the look on his face too much.

As Darcy climbed in, Galen straightened his spine and puffed out his chest. Since it was just posturing, I let it slide.

Darcy didn't smell so bad tonight. No rotten smell, just his usual Earl Grey and old books. He did smell scared, but it was more the healthy fear that came from sitting next to a large dog who wasn't convinced you deserved to keep your appendages.

At the drive-thru, Darcy insisted on paying. I let him, since he'd single-handedly turned my life upside down over the last forty-eight hours. He went to hand me the money, then looked at Galen, bald suspicion on Darcy's face. I guess I couldn't blame him, since I warned him not to move around too much, so I reached around Galen and plucked the money from Darcy's hand.

Once we had the food, I drove to a park a couple blocks away. Darcy held the coffee tray in his lap, and I held onto the food. At the park, I pulled the truck into a spot next to a picnic table, then hopped out, Galen close on my heels. I wanted to be in a public place where nobody would look too closely at what we were doing or listen to our conversation, and this park was perfect. Nobody minded their own business like drug dealers and their clientele. So, we sat at the picnic table, the dog, the Sankha, and the librarian. Sounded like a Douglas Adams novel.

Darcy carefully laid out his food, then ignored it. "That's a beautiful dog you have." He wasn't looking at my dog, though. He was casting furtive glances into the darkness surrounding us.

"Yeah, he is," I said around a mouthful of fries. Said dog was sitting a few feet away from me, staring at Darcy's burger. Akitas hated to see food go to waste, and to an Akita, food allowed to sit for more than ten seconds was going to waste.

A muffler-impaired car at a nearby apartment complex rumbled to life. Darcy jumped so high, his leg banged the underside of the tabletop. I tried not to roll my eyes. To his credit, he strove valiantly to continue the line of chit-chat. "What's his name?"

I swallowed. "Galen."

When I didn't say anything else, Darcy glanced at me. "Not much for small talk, are you?"

"Did you come here to make small talk?"

"You don't like me much."

"I don't like a lot of things," I said. "For example, the little onions they put on these burgers. There are more onions than meat on this thing, and they're like dried paint. You gotta scrape 'em off with some sort of tool."

"I need to talk to you," Darcy said.

"Ah. So then maybe we can skip the small talk."

He nodded and looked around. I followed his gaze, and saw nothing. For some reason, "nothing" seemed to frighten Darcy even more.

I ate my onion-infested burger and waited for Darcy to start talking, or Galen to leap on the table, whichever came first.

Finn liked to tell me that waiting in silence was a very good interrogation technique. Unfortunately, it required a great deal of patience on the part of the interrogator. I had never quite mastered it. Now, I drank my coffee, counting in my head so I wouldn't get bored. But unless you were two years old and just learning to count on your fingers, counting wasn't a very effective boredom-avoidance technique. I began to think that I would die of old age, waiting here, and considering shape-shifters were immortal, that was saying something.

Darcy opened his mouth and drew in a breath, as if to speak. Then he closed his mouth and looked over his shoulder at the vacant jungle gym.

I swallowed a growl, then chased it with a gulp of coffee. Maybe I wasn't the easiest person to talk to, but Darcy should've prepared himself before showing up on my doorstep. When I found myself hoping Galen would actually put his food-stealing plan into action, I gave up. "Are you going to talk, or am I supposed to divine your topic of choice?"

Darcy's mouth drooped open, and I realized my voice might have sounded a little harsh. And probably I wasn't going to get him to start talking if I kept reminding him I was a bitch.

"Sorry," I said, and tried to sound like I meant it. "I'm having a bad day."

He nodded. "You came to the library today, didn't you? Dolly told me a skinny woman with gray hair was there, asking about me. About my sister. That was you, wasn't it?"

"Yeah." Dear god, the woman's name was Dolly? No wonder she wore so much perfume. Could you say self-fulfilling prophecy?

"Why did you come looking for me?"

"Because I couldn't wait to hear about this year's summer reading program. Why do you think?" More sweat. More fear. But *I* was the one who needed to shower? "I wanted to know if you were for real. You know, make sure you weren't just some stalker or something."

Darcy went silent again. I sipped my coffee and watched Darcy look down at his cup as if he'd just remembered it was there, watched him add sugar and stir. Four sugars. He poured in creamer after creamer until it smelled more like milk than coffee. He saw me watching him. "I don't really like coffee."

"I see that."

He shrugged. "Caffeine is the only thing that gets me through the day sometimes."

Join the club. "What do you want from me, Darcy?" I was surprised at how tired my voice sounded. Better tired than belligerent, I guess.

He seemed to think so, too. "I need you to tell me the truth."

"I have been telling the truth." More or less.

He leaned forward. "You said you couldn't help me. You said you're just a dog walker."

"I am a dog walker."

"But that's not all you are, is it? It can't be. You work, like, three hours a day. Nobody could make a living off so little work."

"Maybe I have a sugar daddy."

He snorted. "No sugar daddy would let you live in this neighborhood."

"Fine, then maybe I deal crack on the side. Everybody needs a hobby. I don't see how this is any of your business."

I was back to belligerent, but I didn't like how much he noticed about me while I wasn't looking.

"How about you stop tossing out maybes? How about you tell me the truth?"

"How about you tell me the truth, Darcy? Tell me what you want so badly, and maybe I'll tell you the story of my life." I pulled my second burger out of the bag and started eating. I looked up to see Darcy watching me, a frown twisting his features. "What?" I said.

He shook his head. "Go ahead and finish your food. Then maybe we can actually talk."

I considered setting my food aside and continuing our little heart-to-heart while my burger got cold. But cold fast food was barely edible, even by my standards. I kept eating.

Darcy took a sip of his coffee, then started shredding his French fries. I'd never actually seen someone do that before. I wondered what level of anxiety made a person rip apart greasy food without realizing what he was doing. It was kind of fascinating, in a lion-disemboweling-a-gazelle kind of way.

When he started shredding the hamburger bun, I spoke up. "You know, I really think that food would do you more good if you actually ate it. No matter the problem, it's much easier to face on a full stomach."

He blinked and looked down at his food. Then he wiped his hands on a napkin, focusing on the action as if he'd never encountered something as exotic as a napkin. "Some problems make food seem trivial," he said to his hands.

I wasn't heartless. Really, I wasn't. I couldn't begin to imagine what would happen if Mal was dying. But this guy was wasting my time. It was really starting to piss me off. "Some food makes problems seem trivial. Which this food obviously isn't, but it's not about enjoying fine cuisine while the world's going to shit around you. It's about having the strength to wade into the shit and do your part. Sustenance helps."

He looked up at me finally. If someone spoke to me like that, while I was enjoying a little self-pity, I would be pissed. Darcy just looked at me, as if trying to glean some kind of answer from my eyes. I let him look until my patience ran out again. "If you're not going to eat that burger, do you mind?" I said.

A slow smile spread over his face, and I realized he was handsome. With that smile, he looked like a little boy who just stuck a frog in his sister's bed. All of a sudden, he looked like someone you'd want to get to know, just to see if you could make him smile again.

Fuck. I liked him better as prey.

I fought to keep my discomfort from showing. I schooled my face into annoyance, my favorite emotion to use as a mask. "What?"

"I don't think I've ever met anyone like you before."

I grunted. "I get that a lot. Does that mean I can have your burger?"

His smile lingered on his lips, reluctant to leave once it finally arrived. "You've inspired me to try eating." He picked up the burger with its mutilated bun and, rapidly gaining momentum, managed to polish it off in about three bites.

"Congratulations. Next time, you might want to try chewing, but you know, one step at a time. So how about answering my question."

He held up his hand and started to drain his coffee cup.

I breathed deep, trying to inhale some tolerance. Instead, I caught a fresh scent in the air. Darcy said something, but I didn't hear him. All I heard was a whooshing sound, like wind rushing in my ear.

Something was coming.

Chapter 10

It looked like Peter Pan's runaway shadow, flying through the air toward us, except this shadow had bright red eyes and long, sharp claws where fingers should be. With my left hand, I pulled the blade from the small of my back, and grabbed Galen's collar with my right. Dragging Galen with me, I ducked under the table and came up on the other side, next to Darcy. "Get down," I yelled. I let go of Galen's collar, hoping he heard "down," took it as a command and stayed under the picnic table. Then I threw myself at Darcy and knocked him to the ground. Hoping that Darcy would stay down, too, I came up in a crouch.

I felt a rush of air over my back. Then nothing. Holding my blade at the ready, I closed my eyes. The easier to hear and smell you with, my dear. I started with a shallow breath, so the sound of air filling my lungs wouldn't distract me. No strange smells, no sound of movement. To my left, Galen's earthy scent told me he was right where I'd left him, under the table. Good dog. Pride lodged in my throat, making it hard to breathe.

"What the hell is going on?" Oh, goody. Darcy found his voice. "Where'd you get that knife? What was that thing? It just shot straight up into the air, like a—"

I opened my eyes and looked at him. I guess I looked scary, because he recoiled. "Sit still, and shut the fuck up." I took a few more deep breaths, but found only a rapidly dissolving scent. It was gone.

Well, I had my answer to the familiar stench. And to the disappearing scent trail at the library. What stunk like rotten flesh and moved through the darkness like a shadow? What could make itself look like anything, but couldn't change its scent? What could be walking along, and suddenly shoot straight up into the air, taking its scent trail with it?

"Nocturnes."

"What? What's going on?"

Ignoring Darcy, I fell back on my butt and tried to stem the flow of adrenaline through my system. I waved my hand through the air in front of me, releasing Galen from his down-stay. He closed the distance between us to press his body against mine, the next best thing to actually crawling under my skin. I couldn't blame him for being shaken. Nocturnes. Bad day, meet worse.

Someone grabbed my right arm. I reacted without thought, without looking. I slashed with my knife; a slash, not a stab, because I couldn't risk my knife getting lodged in flesh, couldn't waste precious seconds tugging it free. I heard Galen snarl and lunge, felt the pressure on my arm disappear, heard a cry, smelled blood. My skin started to tingle as I turned to see what I'd done. Galen stood over Darcy's prone form. I was relieved to see his muzzle was clean — no blood there. Galen hadn't hurt him. That was on me.

"Galen, come." He obeyed. With my dog out of the way, I saw the gash on Darcy's forearm, about six inches long, oozing blood, but not deep. Nothing serious. Judging by the look on his face, Darcy didn't share my assessment.

I offered Darcy a hand up. He stared at my hand for a second, then pushed to his feet on his own. "No," he said, though I hadn't asked him a question.

"Darcy," I said.

"No," he said again. "You know what? I don't need your help. I'm outta here."

Oh, human, you need me more than you ever dreamed. "Darcy, I'm really sorry. I didn't mean to hurt you."

"Wow. I'd hate to see what you do when you mean it." He turned and started to walk away.

I felt panic clench my lungs. There was a nocturne out there. And if my nose was right, it had been stalking Darcy for at least two days. Not that I cared about some puny little human, I told myself. It just galled me to let a nocturne get its way. Hastily, I stuck my blade in the pocket of my shorts, so he couldn't see it. Like maybe then he'd forget how he got that big ole paper cut on his arm. "Darcy, at least let me give you a ride back to your car. I have a first-aid kit at home, I can get you bandaged up."

"That's okay. I'll walk." And he started to run.

I considered running after him. But I needed to find a way to win back his trust, and I was pretty sure chasing him down would only cause further setbacks. I jogged in the opposite direction, to my truck, with Galen close on my heels.

I ran three stop signs on the way back to my apartment. If Darcy raced in a straight line and caught a ride from Spiderman, he could've beat me back to his car. The car was still there, though, and I sighed with relief. Too hopped up to stand still, I started to pace the length of the parking lot. Galen trotted beside me for a few minutes, but when it became clear I wasn't actually going anywhere, he laid down in the grass and watched.

I wondered if I should go looking for Darcy. He might be lost, if he didn't know this area very well. And he was in a nocturne's crosshairs. Wandering the streets alone didn't seem like a good plan for him. But if I left to go looking for him, I risked missing him return to his car.

Pacing no longer felt like enough, so I started jogging backwards across the lot.

No, I couldn't go wandering the streets, looking for him. But I did have the ability to reach out to him, I suddenly remembered. That first morning, he gave me his cell number. Where the hell did I put it?

"Come on, big boy," I said to Galen, and switched gears so I jogged forward toward the front door of the building. I climbed the stairs quietly, opened my apartment door, and slipped inside, Galen following. He trotted to the water dish, and the sound of his slurping almost drowned out the sound of Tony's snoring. Almost. On the living room floor, I found the shorts I wore the first time I met Darcy. I took the paper with his phone number on it, along with my cell phone, a pocketful of Galen's kibble, and Galen himself, back down to the parking lot.

I began another campaign of call bombardment. Like Finn, Darcy didn't answer, which made my hands feel hot and itchy. But unlike Finn, Darcy had a fairly good reason to ignore my phone calls, so I kept the messages as genial as I could. I aimed for concerned and hoped that I at least landed somewhere near apologetic.

Waiting really wasn't my thing. To be honest, performing the same inane task over and over again, yielding zero results, wasn't my thing, either. If I didn't try to distract myself between phone calls, I would soon get pissed off and lose the ability to modulate my voice. The night's events brought several concerns to my attention. One of them, the only one I knew how to fix with ease, was Galen's unreliability with hand signals. While I called Darcy over and over, I drilled Galen on the hand signals for sit, down and stay.

Unfortunately, a pocketful of kibble didn't last very long.

Without the dog training to occupy my brain, I was thinking too much. Maybe Darcy's wound was worse than I thought. Maybe he passed out from blood loss. Maybe he decided his junky old car wasn't worth the risk of running into me again.

Maybe I needed to get a grip and stop playing the "maybe" game.

A nocturne in town was a very bad thing. Like all the worst monsters, nocturnes started out as humans. Usually, they were people who repressed some extreme, dark part of their nature — a pedophile who raped a dozen kids and then stopped, hoarding memories and self-loathing for years, or a mother who fantasized about killing her children while cheering them on at a soccer game. Then, all it took was meeting a nocturne. Just passing one in a crowd. I didn't know if the nocturnes picked specific people to turn, or if it was all accidental, but that incidental contact caused that darkness to ooze out of the person's pores, until it took them over and they literally became a shadow of their former selves. It rotted their soul from the inside out. Hence the stench.

Once turned, they needed to feed on humans, although not like a vampire or zombie. Nocturnes fed on the human aura, absorbing negative energy created by emotions like anger, grief, or fear. The stronger the emotion, the stronger the nocturne grew. Emotional vampirism. Like the poisonous friend that you hated to be around because she sucked the life out of you. Except nocturnes didn't just suck the life out of people. They convinced their prey that there was no escape.

Say a husband and wife had a fight, and then the husband left the house and died in a car accident. The wife would not only feel grief, but also regret about the fight, and guilt that their argument may have distracted the husband and caused the crash.

Enter the nocturne, disguised as a church member, a grief counselor, a funeral home employee, something condolence-related. It could feed on the grief, the regret, the guilt already there, absorbing the psychic energy through its skin. Then it could tease the conflict with carefully chosen comments until the wife's emotions became such a tangled rat's nest that she begged the nocturne to take her life. The nocturne, happy to oblige, would then change forms, back to its natural state, the glowing red eyes, the looming shadowy figure, the long, thick claws, and rip into the woman, usually someplace not instantly fatal. Tearing open the gut was a favorite. The nocturne would continue to feed on the woman's despair and fear until the moment her heart stopped. Those emotions right before death were a nocturne's ambrosia.

I'd never met a nocturne before. Not face to face. But I knew their stench, because one windy autumn day, Finn brought back the necklace my sister Taize always wore. My mother hated that she wore it into battle. Don't make the enemy's job easier, she said. Don't give them something by which to string you up. But the necklace meant too much to my sister.

She told me it was once worn by a boy who tried to follow Taize into the forest because he thought she was so beautiful. Janus made Taize kill the child, because she was the one who allowed herself to be followed, the one who compromised our security. She wanted to make him a youngling. Janus said no, the child would be missed. Better for him to be found dead, mauled by a wild animal. So Taize shape-shifted and ripped open the boy's throat. Then she shifted back to human and walked away with his necklace, refusing to desecrate the body further, though Janus ordered her to do so. Taize was in solitary for a week for her disobedience. When she came out, she was wearing the necklace. She never took it off after that.

Because my family went to battle in their wolf forms, the search party didn't have any clothing items or mementos to bring back for Mal and me. Nothing but that necklace. And the damn thing was saturated, not with Taize's blood, but with nocturne stink. To learn the scent, Mal and I carried it, ate with it, slept with it, for weeks, until the scent all but disappeared. Then we buried the necklace in the forest, next to the Spring.

I knew that smell. It just never occurred to me that the smell on Darcy could be from a nocturne. They were supposed to be nearly extinct. And those remaining were supposed to be so damn scared of the Hycene that they'd never hunt on our territory.

Why would this nocturne reveal itself? Nocturnes usually chose human forms, because humans offered the most versatility. The lore said that human eyes were difficult to emulate, with the pupils that changed size and the colors that shifted with the light, so nocturnes only changed their eyes when absolutely necessary. But when they did change their eyes, it was almost impossible to identify unless you had an ultrasensitive nose. A human like Darcy couldn't smell a nocturne's rottenness. That was why shape-shifters were so valuable to Janus, when defending the Spring. We could ID the riffraff.

This nocturne didn't even try to camouflage itself. Because it knew I would know what it was, no matter what form it took? But still, why reveal itself at all? I would still be standing firmly in Confusedville, if not for the evening's revelation. And why reveal yourself to the one person who could identify you, and not at least try to take that person out? I could understand it leaving Darcy alive. If it killed him now, it missed out on some juicy emotions. But me? I was a threat. Much more sensible for the nocturne to at least try to kill me.

The whole encounter struck me as just plain stupid. And I would've liked to dismiss it as a stupid nocturne, but I didn't really think stupid people turned into nocturnes. It was my experience that only the smart ones repressed their darkness to that degree. The stupid ones just let their dark flag fly.

I wished I could call Finn. I wished someone could give me answers, fill in the blanks. Had nocturnes been around this whole time? If so, why did the Sankhain stop hunting them? Why would it show up when I was there? Did it not know what I was? Did it know now? And what did that mean for me? I felt a deep maw open up inside me, felt rage and, surprisingly, grief rise up out of it.

With my mouth closed to muffle the sound, I allowed myself a short scream of frustration. Galen woke up and trotted over to check on me. Wrapping one arm around his rib cage, I let him comfort me as I pulled out my phone again. This time, instead of hitting redial, I scrolled to Mal's number. It went straight to voicemail, but just hearing her recorded greeting soothed my nerves. I left her a brief message, asking her to call me back.

Now that I was sitting down, I felt the last of the adrenaline evaporate, leaving me exhausted and cranky. Where the hell was Darcy? How long was he going to make me wait? I said I was sorry. Then I heard shuffling footsteps approaching. Darcy! My body wanted to launch to its feet, but I stayed right where I was. I hoped I would seem less threatening if I was sitting while Darcy stood.

I caught a familiar scent in the air. The scent brought to mind an image of fresh-baked bread. Not that he smelled like bread. That was just the image my brain free-associated with his scent. I tried not to sigh with disappointment.

"Her truck's here," Tony muttered to himself. "She can't be taking another run, can she? Poor dog's gonna get shin splints."

"Poor dog is just fine, thank you very much."

Tony jumped, which was very satisfying, then closed the distance between us so he could loom over me, which was very annoying. "I woke up, and you were gone. I was worried something happened. Why are you sitting down here?"

I didn't know how I felt about the idea of Tony worrying about me. "Enjoying a little peace and quiet. Someone's revving a chainsaw in my bedroom."

It took him a minute to put two and two together. He sounded genuinely remorseful. "Sorry. I was snoring?"

"Oh, is that what that was?" I pushed to my feet. My gaze fell on Darcy's car, and I growled. Where was he?

"Whose car is that?" Tony was watching my face.

I didn't like Tony watching me so closely. "Could we maybe continue this conversation later? Like after I change my pants?"

He raised his eyebrows. "You really have been down here a long time, if you need a change of pants."

"The ground's wet, okay? It rained. Jeez." Maybe my tone was a little harsh, but I was allowed. After all, my panties were moist for no good reason.

"Kellan, whose car were you staring at?"

I didn't appreciate his tone, since it was very similar to the tone Finn liked to use when he was about to tell me I'd done something stupid. "I said I wanted to wait to talk. Is it so much to ask to have dry underwear? This is America, right?"

"I musta missed the part in the Constitution about the right to dry underwear."

"Oh, fuck off." Giving up on Tony altogether, I turned to Galen instead. "I'm tired," I said to my dog. "And my butt cheeks are cold."

"Come on." Tony's voice was quiet. At the sound, I felt my temper cool slightly. "You can take the bed for the rest of the night. All right?"

"I can't sleep, I have to keep watch."

"For what?" The story was too long and I felt irrationally annoyed that he didn't know it already. Like he should've been awake and in the park with Darcy and me. There must've been something in my expression, because Tony's lips twitched up. "Never mind. How 'bout you and I go upstairs. We'll open all the windows. You'll be able to hear anyone approaching. You can have something to eat while you tell me what's going on. Then you can go to sleep, or maybe shower, and I'll take over the watch." His voice was still low and quiet, like I was rabid or something.

Because I was feeling prickly, I searched for holes in his plan. I came up empty, but rather than admitting his idea was valid, I just started walking toward the front door. We walked upstairs in silence, which I appreciated because I was straining my ears. While I opened the living room windows, Tony went into the kitchen. It was three a.m. It didn't seem possible that only three hours had passed since I took Galen out to pee and we found a Darcy on our front stoop. Too much happened for it to be so short a time. I stood up and felt my shoulders sag under a weight that I couldn't name.

When Tony reemerged, he was carrying a glass of milk and a slice of bread thick with peanut butter. "Thank you," I said. The words felt awkward, like my lips and tongue couldn't quite coordinate.

Tony chuckled. "That sounded painful. Why don't you eat before Galen decides to help himself?"

"He wouldn't steal from me." Then I eyed Galen, eyeing my bread, and I felt a little less sure than I sounded. "He wouldn't."

"He must really love you, then."

I glared at Tony, sure he must be mocking me. But his face appeared serious. I shook my head to clear it, and changed topics. "The car belongs to the outsider."

"The one with the Gaachail documents?"

"No, the one I took the Gaachail documents from."

His mouth twisted, like he just bit into a wormy apple. This also reminded me of Finn, and I waited for him to say my name disdainfully. Instead, he said, "So he came back to see you? Again?"

"Yeah, he's been hovering around. I can't shake the guy. And now that I finally want him to show up, so I can keep him from being nocturne kibble, he's Mr. Elusive. Shit." I polished off the bread and drained the milk.

Tony closed his eyes for a second, and again, I waited for him to tell me to speak in complete thoughts, one of Finn's favorite requests. But again, Tony surprised me. He opened one eye, squinting at me. "Okay. Nocturnes are those shape-shifters, the ones that feed off emotions? And there's one on this outsider's trail?"

"Yes. Didn't I just say that?"

"So how did you lose the outsider?"

"I didn't lose him. I could've caught him. I let him go."

"Okay. But why? You see what I'm trying to get at here?"

I did, but I felt so off-balance. He wasn't acting the way I expected. He was being so … nice. "Um, yeah. I think."

He cocked his head to one side, looking at me. "All right. I don't need to know everything now. You've got a few hours before you have to start dog walking, right?"

Dog walking? Oh, shit, I still had a day job. "Yeah. I start at nine. Ish."

"Good. Get some sleep, and I'll go down and watch the car."

"But Darcy doesn't know you. What will you say to him?"

He smiled, like he had a secret. It made me want to move in closer; it was such an inviting smile. I felt myself start to lean in.

Shit. I was more tired than I thought. "Yeah. That sounds great. You keep watch, I'll sleep."

Tony went back down to the parking lot, and I went to the bedroom. I would've taken a shower, except my BO wasn't going to matter very soon. I stripped off my clothes and knelt down on all fours. Then I shape-shifted. As a wolf, I slept deeper. A little sleep would go a long way, and I had a feeling a little sleep was as much as I could hope for.

Once I finished the change, I noticed something I'd been too preoccupied to notice before. My sheets smelled funny. Like a tall, well-muscled man had been sleeping on them. Okay, maybe I couldn't tell from the smell that he was well-muscled. But my brain recognized the scent, and my memory filled in the rest. Scent recognition was the ultimate free-association exercise. No way to control what the scent brought to mind.

I saw Galen sniffing the sheets, too. I was never going to be able to sleep with this foreign scent in my den, so I did what any self-respecting wolf would do. I rolled around on the bed, rubbing my scent over his, until the bedroom once again smelled more like me than him. Then I let my muscles relax and I started to slide toward sleep.

Chapter 11

When ambient sunlight began to seep through the windows, I gradually came awake. First, I became aware of smells. Galen's familiar musk was beside me. Tony's scent still lingered, and in my post-sleep state, I didn't dislike it. So much so that it made me very uncomfortable. Desperate, I sought out other scents. Exhaust fumes from outside helped me relax. Other senses started to put in their two cents. The sound of muffler-impaired vehicles driving past. The taste of sleep on my tongue. Finally, I opened my eyes and let the world all the way inside.

The first thing I saw was Galen staring at me. I knew that stare. He needed to go outside. I got up, stretching my front end, then my back legs, before I shifted back to human form. After dressing, I hustled Galen outside.

Right in the middle of Galen doing his civic duty, Tony walked around the corner of the building. As soon as I caught his scent, I felt warm in some very surprising places. The memory of waking up and breathing in his scent, and how … right it felt, made the rims of my ears burn and my girlie parts throb. I couldn't look him in the eye, which was okay, because he was staring at the pile Galen left on the lawn. "Wow, that's a lot of shit."

"He's a lot of dog. What the hell did you expect?" I started walking toward the parking lot, because I had plastic bags in my truck, and because I didn't want to stand there smelling him anymore.

"Kellan?" He followed me. Of course, he followed me. Because it would just be too much to ask for him to drop dead of an aneurysm or something. "Did you not sleep or something?"

"I slept fine." I opened the back of the truck and dug out my bag full of bags. When I turned, Tony was studying me in a way that made me all hot and throbby again. "What?"

He blinked, and I realized that my tone was a little on the harsh side. "Nothing," he said. "You're being perfectly normal. I think I'll just go stand over by the big pile of shit. That'll be more fun than standing here."

I sucked in a breath and blew it out. "I'm sorry."

He frowned at me as if looking for the trick. Was it so unbelievable that I could sincerely apologize? Yeah, I guess it was.

My pocket began to ring. I checked the caller ID and swore under my breath. It was Mal. I didn't want Tony to know I was in contact with her. If word got back to Janus, she would get in trouble, too. My conscience couldn't handle another burden. "Hello, O'Connell Dog Walking Service, please hold." I put my thumb over the mouthpiece and looked at Tony. "I'm hungry."

He stared at me. "What?"

"I'm hungry, and I want Drive-thru." I dug a couple of twenties out of my pocket. "Here. Go get some breakfast. I'll have two sausage and egg biscuits. No, make that three. And an order of pancakes. With sausage. And get yourself something."

"Three?" He looked shell-shocked.

I raised my eyebrows. "You need me to write it down?"

He shook his head. "I got it. I'll be back."

I gave him the keys to my truck and he drove away. Then I put the phone back up to my ear. "Sorry. You still there?"

"What the hell was that?" Mal wasn't much of a morning person.

As I filled her in on the night's events, I wandered around the edge of the parking lot, letting Galen sniff-and-lift. Mal was silent for a long time.

"Well," she said finally. "If I was talking to someone with an imagination, I might think you were making this up to make your life sound exciting. But since I'm talking to you..."

I growled, "If you don't have anything useful to say—"

"Keep your fucking mouth shut," she finished for me. "Yeah, I know. Sorry. Hell, Kell, you sure attract the nutters."

"Again, not helpful."

"Yeah." After a pause, she said, "Nocturnes? Shit. And which one's Tony?"

"Looks like the Incredible Hulk, except not green."

"Oh, right. He actually survived long enough to pass the tests, huh? I thought for sure you'd end up snapping his neck in one of your sparring sessions. So he's your 'help?' They really don't like you."

"Why do I even bother talking to you?"

"Because no one else will listen." Oh, yeah. That's right. "You need to tell Janus about the nocturne. If you don't, he'll get pissy that you kept something so big from him."

"And how am I supposed to do that? I'm exiled. No contact allowed."

I heard her let out a sigh. "That's why you have a liaison, right? Let him liaise. This is actually pretty nice for you. You don't even have to be the one to deliver the bad news."

She was right. I tasted on my tongue an uncomplimentary combination of annoyance with, and longing for, my sister. "Does it ever get old, being so damn smart?"

"It's exhausting."

I heard footsteps, and caught the scent of Earl Grey. "Mal, I gotta go."

"Everything okay?"

"Yeah. Thanks for the help. I'll call you." And I hung up, slid the phone back in my pocket, and tried very hard to look nonthreatening.

Darcy didn't see me right away. From the slump of his shoulders, I judged that he was exhausted. Not wanting to spook him, I scuffed my boots on the ground to announce my presence. He turned and instantly tensed. I tightened my grip on the leash, not wanting Galen to get involved in the conversation. "I'm not going to hurt you." I walked toward Darcy, stopping a few feet away. "But we need to talk."

"So now you want to talk." I heard an edge in his voice that sounded more like anger than fear. Interesting. I breathed in more of his scent. His anger smelled hot and spicy, like ginger tea.

I held up my hands and kept my words vague. "I'm sorry about before. With the knife."

"You cut me." Compared to some of the other angry scents I'd smelled in my life, ginger tea didn't have a whole lot of threatening feel to it. It was nice to know Darcy was capable of anger, though. It made me respect him a little more. "With a knife. What kind of an — an ass-butt does that?"

Ass-butt? Some people just shouldn't try to curse. I lowered my head, chin to chest, and closed my eyes as I swallowed a laugh. "I'm sorry. I didn't realize it was you."

"Who did you think it was? Santa Claus?"

Oh, goody, he was going to be sarcastic. I felt a snarl coming on. "Maybe I'm a little jumpy. I've had this creepy guy following me around. Maybe I have the right to flip out a little. And I said I was sorry." Galen tried to take a step toward Darcy. I pulled him back and told him to sit. He hesitantly obeyed, but he kept a close eye on Darcy and his anger.

Darcy was quiet for a while, and the scent of anger slowly faded. "Sorry. I guess I didn't think about how it might make you feel."

Apologies always surprised me. I shook it off. "Why did you come looking for me, Darcy?"

His voice fell to a whisper. "My sister is sick. She's dying."

I knew this, of course. Dolly the Super-scented Librarian had told me about Darcy's sister. But to hear him say it, to breathe in his scent as it went from full of life to the dried-up nothingness of grief, brought his reality home to me like a punch in the va-jay-jay. I didn't have to fake the hushed shock in my voice. "I'm sorry, Darcy. That's horrible. But I still don't know what you think I can do. I'm not a doctor."

"No, you're a Sankha."

He pronounced it with a Midwestern twang, not the pseudo-British precision Janus affected.

How did he know that word? My stomach was performing a Cirque du Soleil routine, but I snorted in what I hoped sounded like disbelief. "A what? You should lay off the crack, dude. It's messing with your head."

Darcy took a step toward me. His pupils looked too big, and his cheeks were flushed. His voice was hushed and hurried. "I know, okay? I'm not going to tell. But I need your help. I need you to take me to the forest. To the Spring."

Well, on the up side, at least I knew how much he knew. On the down side, I was having a really hard time maintaining my poker face. I stared at him, trying to get my brain in gear to come up with a plan.

Okay, I thought, as I looked into those puppy-dog-on-speed eyes. It was one thing to think maybe he'd stumbled on some old documents while digging through somebody's dumpster. Less plausible than world peace, but I supposed it could happen. It was another thing entirely for him to know those words. Sankha. Forest. Spring. I couldn't let him run around town now, especially not with a nocturne looking to turn him into an Unhappy Meal.

I could follow him. Except in order to follow, I had to get him to leave first. And since Darcy left his mild-mannered librarian life behind to morph into the Amazing Persistence Man, he was getting more and more difficult to push away without the use of weaponry. I could stop trying to push him away and take him up to my apartment. Then all I'd have on my plate would be the papers, the nocturne, and the Man Who Knew Too Much. Piece of cake.

God, I wished Mal were here. She was always complaining about how nothing interesting ever happened, and here I was, up to my elbows in interesting, and all I wanted was to go home to my forest and pull the covers over my head. Except the forest wasn't mine, wasn't an option, and even if it was, I didn't know if I wanted to be that close to Finn and Janus right now.

Letting Darcy into my apartment wasn't just a bad idea, it was an extra-large bad idea pizza, piled high with poor choices and sticky situations. As bad as it was, though, I was faced with two blinking neon signs. One said: Avoiding Darcy doesn't seem to be working. The other said: You have a bucket of nocturne bait standing right in front of you. Might as well dive into the bad idea pizza.

I took a deep breath and dove in. "Oh. Why didn't you say that was what you wanted? Well, if you know that much, then you know that it's not as simple as buying a ticket and going to the show. Before I can take you to the forest, I'll need to get permission." Not that I planned to take him anywhere near the Spring, but he didn't need to know that.

Desperation made humans so gullible. If he'd been a supernatural being, he could've sniffed out the lie. But he wanted to believe me, so he didn't look at the tension in my shoulders or the fact that my eyes didn't match the rest of my expression. Instead, he was nodding like one of those felt-covered dogs people put on their dashboards.

I heard the approaching rumble of another muffler-impaired vehicle, and seconds later, Tony drove into the lot. I felt torn. I could smell the food through the open windows of the truck, which made me happy. But I also knew that now I had to figure out how to get Tony to go along with my bad idea pizza, which annoyed the piss out of me.

First, though, I had to secure the Darcy part of the problem. I turned my back on Tony and the smell of breakfast, and focused on Darcy. "Look, it might take a while for the request to go through channels." Look at me, talking all bureaucratic. "Maybe you should stay here, with me, in the meantime. That way, when I get the okay, we can just head right over there. I won't have to waste any time tracking you down."

More incessant nodding. I pictured a Darcy bobble-head sitting on a dashboard. Then I pictured popping off the bobbling head and tossing it out the window. I imagined watching that head bounce down the side of the highway, and then I imagined the blissful quiet that would follow. If only. I decided I'd have to tell Mal about that image. She'd enjoy it.

The truck engine cut off, then I heard the door creak open and slam shut. "Hey, sweetie. Who's this?" Then, because apparently his words weren't weird enough, Tony came up behind me and kissed my temple.

My poker face had already taken too many hits that morning, but I think I managed to smile convincingly. "This is Darcy Jamison. I mentioned him to you, didn't I?" I wracked my brain for a pet name that I could say without gagging. "Sunshine?"

"Oh, yeah. Right. Hi, nice to meet you." Tony held out his hand like this was all normal, like we were just normal people meeting on a normal day in a normal world, instead of the Twilight Zone. "I'm Tony. Just don't call me 'sunshine.' She's the only one who gets to do that."

"Hi," Darcy said, looking from Tony to me and back again. He looked doubtful, like he wasn't buying the whole sweetie/sunshine routine.

As much as I didn't want to get any deeper into this charade, I decided I needed to be an active part of the conversation, since I was Darcy's "contact." I wracked my brain for words to fill Tony in without revealing my discomfort. I wanted Darcy Jamison to have confidence in me.

"Darcy's going to come up to the apartment and stay for a while. He needs to go to the Spring. I haven't called it in yet to get permission."

If Tony was surprised, he didn't show it. No widening of the eyes, no tightening of the mouth, not even a shocked jerk of the shoulders. He just nodded and then gave me a playful cuff on the back of the head. "You should've called me. I would've picked up some breakfast for him, too. Oh, well. Lucky for you, Darcy, I got a few extra sandwiches. I never know how hungry she's going to be."

I was going to have to kill Tony. It was that simple. As my face grew hot, I pictured a Tony bobble-head bouncing down the highway alongside Darcy's. This made me feel better, and I was able to smile quite convincingly.

"I don't think I got enough coffee for three, though." Tony frowned at the tray in his hand.

"That's all right," I said, and pinched Tony on the ass. Not because I wanted to, of course, just to finally get a rise out of him.

It was even better than I hoped. He squealed like a mouse that fell into a toilet. But then he leaned down and breathed in my ear, "Don't start something you can't finish. Sweetie." And I shivered, because the combination of that deep voice and the tickle of his breath sent an electric charge down my spine.

Galen began to stir at my side. He was gazing lovingly at the bag in Tony's hand. "All right," I said. "Let's take this party upstairs before Galen gets hungry enough to do something stupid." At the look on Darcy's face, I shook my head. "I didn't mean that he was going to take a bite out of you. But he's not above grabbing that bag of food and making a run for it."

Tony raised the bag over his head. "Not on my watch."

Thank god he didn't call me "sweetie" again. While we trooped up to the apartment, I tried to think of a way to get Tony alone so I could ask him what the hell possessed him to start this absurd pretense. He and I were lovers like peanut butter and mustard. Of course, there was that moment this morning, when I woke up smelling his scent and my body reacted so ... vividly. And that other moment, when he came around the corner of the building and I smelled his scent again... And he made me dinner. And listened when I talked. And didn't mock me after listening to what I had to say.

I shook my head. Didn't matter. The whole "sweetie" thing was still way left of center. And now we were stuck pretending to be lovey-dovey for the foreseeable future. Ick.

By the time I entered the apartment, I could hear Tony closing a cupboard in the kitchen. He stepped into the living room, holding three plates. The clatter of plate-on-plate made my stomach rumble. "How many places should I set?" he asked me.

I just stared at him. Was the Sankha educational system so poor that Tony, a recent graduate, couldn't count to three?

"I know you have to leave for work soon," he said. "It's almost nine."

I looked at the clock and swore. I'd completely forgotten about dog walking, what with the bad idea pizza and all. "You're right. I'll take mine to go. I just need to feed Galen and then I'll take off. Thanks." Then I smelled a worry-bordering-on-fear scent. I turned and saw Darcy watching me with those sad-puppy-on-speed eyes. What was I going to do about Darcy while I took care of my clients? "Tony?"

"Yeah, babe?"

Upon hearing this latest nickname, I felt my blood pressure shoot up about six hundred points, but I kept my voice even. "Are you free to stay here with Darcy while we wait for the good word from the forest? It might take a while. You know how slow-moving these things can be."

He popped out into the living room again. "Yeah, of course. I've got the day off." Tony dipped his head down and placed a soft, almost careful kiss on my lips. I was momentarily distracted by the warmth of his mouth. "Why don't you feed Galen, then I'll walk you downstairs."

"Okay. Sure." I felt a little dazed. I hoped I didn't sound dazed. That would be embarrassing. Galen and I went through the ritual of food delivery, and then I turned to Darcy. "I'll call my supervisors while I'm walking my first dog. Then I'll let you and Tony know as soon as I hear anything back. Okay?"

He still smelled a little anxious, but he nodded. I closed Galen up in the bathroom so he wouldn't try to steal the food that now sat on the table. I took two of the four egg sandwiches and three of the four coffees. "If you need more coffee, you can make more. You know where I keep my coffee, right?" I said to Tony.

"Yes." For some reason that made him smile, which annoyed me. "Come on. Dogs are waiting with their legs crossed."

"Right."

Tony told Darcy he'd be right back, then the two of us walked in silence down the stairs and out the front door. And I turned around and punched Tony in the gut. Not a real heavy punch, since he was a human and humans were breakable, but heavy enough that it couldn't be mistaken for a love tap. "What the hell are you thinking?" I hissed, because the apartment windows were open and I didn't want anyone to hear. "Sweetie? I've killed people for lesser offenses."

"I'm sorry." He sounded a little winded, but not particularly sorry. "I couldn't remember your outside name, all right? I drew a total blank. 'Sweetie' was the best plan I could come up with. And it's a good fucking plan. It explains why I'm here. Maybe you wanna explain why you thought it'd be a good idea to tell the outsider about the forest and the Spring? And told him you'd take him there? And then brought him home to stay in your apartment? Shit. I leave for fifteen minutes and you fall apart."

"I did not fall apart!" My voice cracked with the effort to keep the volume low. "And I didn't tell him about the Spring or the forest. He knew, okay? And the dumbass has a nocturne on his tail. I couldn't just leave him to stumble around with a head full of knowledge for a nocturne to poke around in, now could I?"

"He knew?"

"Yes."

"How?"

"Well, gee, Sherlock, I'm sure glad you showed up, because it never occurred to me to ask how!"

"So you asked?"

I twisted my mouth into an s-shape. "No."

"Why not?"

"Because we didn't get that far, okay? I was just trying to figure out a way to keep him close so the nocturne doesn't find him. Then you showed up and fucking kissed me and all of a sudden, I'm having to pretend I like your sorry ass!"

"You didn't think my ass was so sorry a few minutes ago, when you groped it."

"I pinched it. That's totally different from groping. And I was trying to hurt you."

"Oh, it hurt, all right. But it's one of those sweet kinda aches."

"Jesus Christ." I closed my eyes and counted to ten. "I have to go. Not because of my dog walking clients, but because I need you to babysit the nocturne bait today and if I snap you in half, you won't be able to do that. Go up there and talk to him, and see if you can find out a thing or two. Or maybe you could come up with a disgusting nickname for him. Pumpkin or something."

"Sure, sweetie. Have a nice day."

"And my name's Kelly!" I spat. Then I stomped toward my truck. I reached the driver's door before I realized I didn't have my keys. "Tony! I need my fucking keys."

When I turned to look for him, he was standing right behind me. "Come on. We're partners here. Ask me nicely."

I gave him my dead-fish-eye look. "That was me asking nicely. It's about to get not nice. How about you give me my keys before things get out of hand?"

"Here." He handed me the keys, then held onto my hand for a moment. "Don't forget to call your supervisors and schedule that tour of the forest."

"Bite me." I felt sick to my stomach at the thought looming in my head. "Hey, Tony?" He paused and looked at me. "Do you think I should call Finn? I mean, there's the nocturne. He'll probably want to know about that."

Tony thought about it for a second. "Yeah, he will. But why don't you let me call him, okay? Darcy looked like he was about ready to pass out from exhaustion. I can call after he falls asleep. Don't want Finn getting pissy because you violated your exile."

"Right. Thanks, I guess."

Tony laughed. "God, that sounded painful. Don't worry. 'Thank yous' are like sit-ups. They get easier the more often you do 'em." Then his mouth tightened and flattened like a rubber band pulled too tight. "This is some deep shit we're in, huh? Don't suppose it could all be one big coincidence. The papers, the outsider with the inside track, the nocturne. All that happening at once."

"No. I don't suppose it is a coincidence." My skin broke out in goosebumps, despite the bright morning sun. "I'm not that lucky."

"If you're not cool with the pretending-to-be-a-couple thing, we can stage a break-up when you get home."

I considered it and discarded it in the course of a second. "No. You're right. It explains why you're here, nice and simple. Sorry I yelled at you."

He reached out and ran his thumb down my jawline, making me jump with surprise. Before I could think of a response, like another fist to the gut, he turned and walked away, and I was left alone with my cooling coffee and an all-consuming mental picture of his abs lying in my bed. "Fuck," I said to the world at large, and I got in my truck and drove away.

Chapter 12

The dog-walking job wasn't about income. Janus covered my living expenses, as he did for all the Sankhain. When a Sankha like myself brought in a paycheck, it went into a communal account. Fortunately, most of the Sankhain made more money than I did. We had lawyers, a couple doctors, and a lot of small business owners. Auto shops and chain restaurants mostly, though we did have three hair stylists and one Sankha who owned a tattoo parlor. All that income got pooled together, and Janus made sure we always had at least two accountants on the team to manage the intricacies of the budget.

Since my income, or lack thereof, didn't matter much, I didn't schedule myself too heavily. My first Tuesday-Thursday clients happened to be two of my favorites. Simba and Nala were typical Scottish terriers. They barked at everything, growled and snarled at dogs ten times their size, and loved to scare the crap out of people. In addition to dog walking, I worked on training the two dogs. I got to charge more for that.

Training Scottish terriers was a little like reasoning with a two-year-old, mid-tantrum. Scotties had selective hearing, they "forgot" things as it suited them, and they always, always tested the humans.

Unfortunately, that morning, I was too tired and distracted to pick up where we left off in training. Instead, we went for a two-hour long walk, so the owners still got their money's worth out of me. While we walked, I rolled the events of the last twenty-four hours through my mind. I batted them around like a cat with a ball of yarn: nocturnes, sweetie, outsiders, dying sisters. It didn't help. By the time the walk was done, I felt more entangled in a mess than ever.

I finished my clients by one o'clock. I should go back to the apartment, I told myself. Instead, I sat in my truck and stared out the window at a giant red maple. I loved red maples. They put on the most spectacular show in autumn. Being spring, this tree looked just like every other maple, but I knew what it would look like in five months or so. I leaned my head back and imagined. The next thing I knew, I was jolting awake to the jangle of my cell phone.

I saw the caller ID and wanted to pretend I was still asleep, even though he couldn't see me, and it would be stupid to play possum over the phone.

"Hi, Finn. How's it hanging?"

He didn't acknowledge my warm greeting. Not that I expected him to. "What in the name of all things wretched have you been doing?"

Rage blinded me, stole my vision and my breath for a long minute. "I've been fumbling around in the dark with my thumb up my ass, just like you wanted me to. Go fuck yourself. If you need any suggestions on how to achieve that, I've got a few for you."

"Kellan—"

"No. You know what? You don't get to judge my performance. You don't get to treat me like I'm stupid. You want me to do my job a certain way? Then don't cut me off without any support. Try answering your phone once in a while. And, I don't know, maybe you could pull your head out of your ass long enough to see what considerable assets you have at your disposal, and actually try appreciating us once in a while."

All was quiet for several Mississippis. Then, "Are you finished?"

I considered. "For now. But I reserve the right to start up again."

I heard the deep, weary sigh that was the musical accompaniment to so many of our interactions. "When will you be returning to your apartment?"

"Um." A paranoid voice in my head wondered if he wanted to corner me so he could arrest me. Take me back to camp. Throw me in solitary until I went mad and ripped out my own throat. I told that voice to shut the fuck up. "I'm done now. I'll be home in less than twenty."

"Very well. We will be joining you after dark. Have the outsider out of the way so we may meet in private."

Out of the way? "You mean kill him?" My intestines roiled at the thought.

"No. Unless you feel you have gained all the information he can offer you. It sounds as though, from what Antony said, there is still quite a bit we need to learn from him."

"Why don't you take him with you? You could interrogate him. You're so good at that." Flattery wasn't my strong suit, but I thought it couldn't hurt to try.

"No. Under no circumstances will that outsider be brought near the Spring. We cannot risk that the nocturne will follow his trail from a distance."

"What if the nocturne is watching my apartment, and he follows you back to the Spring?"

A beat of silence. "Have you not been taking precautions?"

"What do you mean, precautions? It's a nocturne, for Christ's sake. Am I supposed to have some sort of surveillance of the skies?"

"Well, have you at least been checking the perimeter of your building for foreign scents?"

Rage turned icy, settled over my skin like a wet blanket. "Oh my god. I never would've thought of that. Finn, what would I do without your supreme brilliance? Please, hurry over here so I can kiss your feet."

"If you intend to be belligerent, I am ending this conversation."

"If you don't want me to be belligerent, don't be such an ass!" I hung up, ending the conversation for him. Then, with my mouth clamped shut, I screamed.

That man was such a — a — damn it, now I couldn't even think of an insult bad enough to suit him. The way he treated me, like I was a youngling. Like I was some stupid human who only used sight to observe her surroundings. I was Hycene! I was the one who identified the damn nocturne. But did I get a thank you? A "Job well done, Kellan?" No. I got interrogated like a kid with a pocketful of weed.

Shoving the key in the ignition, I turned the truck for home. After I failed to see a stop sign and almost t-boned a Buick, I decided I needed to cool down before driving further. Fortunately, the golden arches were straight ahead, and I was starving. Two double cheeseburgers and a large coffee later, I felt calm and in control.

At home, I walked through the door and Galen raced to greet me. I'd never felt as happy to see him, as grateful for his boundless enthusiasm, as in that moment. To my horror, I felt tears lodge in the back of my throat as I knelt down and buried my face in the thick fur of his neck. I reached up and started scratching behind his left ear. That was one of Galen's sweet spots, and he melted, leaning into me. Gradually, the lump in my throat dissolved.

When I finally looked up at the rest of the room, I saw Tony watching us. Well, watching me. I doubted the look of worry on his face was for Galen. I didn't want to deal with it. "Where's Darcy?"

Tony stood and walked over to us. "The bedroom. I hope you don't mind, I told him he could sleep in the bed. He could barely stand up by the time I came back upstairs this morning."

"Sure. Whatever." I was going to have to move. My bedroom already smelled like Tony. Now it would be saturated with Darcy's scent, too. Gods only knew what I'd wake up picturing tomorrow morning.

Tony knelt down and scratched Galen's hindquarters, making my dog's tail start to wag. "What happened?" he said, his eyes focused on Galen. I didn't think Galen's tail was fascinating enough to hold Tony's gaze, so I figured he was giving me time to collect myself.

I started to say something smart-ass, to stop the moment in its tracks. But I was tired and raw, and I didn't want to be in this alone. "Finn called."

"Oh." He didn't say anything else, just seemed to be waiting.

"He seems to think this is all my fault. Like I invited Darcy and the nocturne over for tea and crumpets. Like I should've donned my psychic cap and prevented the whole damn thing from happening."

"It's not." His reply came so fast, I knew Finn called him, too. And Tony spent the time in between preparing what he was going to say when I got home.

The idea that he put thought into this moment made all kinds of voices start to clamor in my head. I blinked forcefully, trying to clear the Etch-a-Sketch. "What?"

"It's not your fault. You know that, right?" His eyes zeroed in on my face, held me in place like a tractor beam. That gaze further unnerved me.

And I didn't know. I mean, obviously the nocturne wasn't my doing. But bringing Darcy home still sounded like one of my stupidest stupid ideas. Part of me agreed with Finn there. But with Tony looking at me like that, I couldn't admit it out loud. "Yeah. I guess. I mean, yeah. I know it's not my fault. But he doesn't."

"He does. He just — I don't know. There's something wrong at Home." I heard the capital letter in his voice. "The tension levels are through the roof, and none of us peons know why. He's been blowing up at younglings for stupid shit. And nobody's seen Janus for weeks."

"Really?" How did I not know this? "Why didn't you tell me before?"

He shrugged. "You got enough on your plate. I was hoping I could absorb Finn's venom for you."

I stared at him, my mouth hanging open a couple inches. "Why?"

He narrowed his eyes, then abruptly stood up. "Are you hungry? I can make you a sandwich. And there's coffee."

I considered letting it go. After all, the double cheeseburgers were almost half an hour ago, I was always hungry, and I never wanted to get involved in an emotionally-charged conversation. But if Tony was my ally, possibly my only ally, then I needed to know his motivations. "Why, Tony? Why do you want to help me?"

He walked into the kitchen. I followed and leaned against the fridge, waiting for him to answer. Instead, he stared at my one piece of art in the apartment, the one "thing" in this place that I cared about. A lovely Pollyanna Pickering print of two wolves curled up together. "You miss it?" he asked suddenly.

"What?"

"Having them around. Other wolves." He didn't meet my eyes, seemingly entranced by the painting.

I took a deep breath, scent memory flooding over me. The musky, dark smell of my pack. Even though I was pretty young when most of my family died, I still remembered that scent.

Yes, I thought. I missed them all the time. Sometimes people said "all the time" and they meant "occasionally." I meant the words. I never really felt whole or secure without my pack around me. Lone wolves were a romanticized notion. The reality was, lone wolves died. The pack survived. I blinked, coming back to the present.

Tony watched me, his face carefully casual. "My mom was a heroin addict. She traded me to her dealer for a lifetime supply of drugs."

I nodded. I knew his story. All the younglings had similar tales, some more violent or violated than others. But generally, kids from happy homes didn't run away to become warriors. It was the broken ones who came to us to weld themselves back together.

"I hated her," he continued, like he was reading the nutritional content on a box of cereal. "And you know what? Sometimes I wake up, thinking I hear her voice, and I miss her so much, I think I'm gonna puke."

I focused on pouring two mugs of perfectly equal amounts of coffee. "By human standards, my mom was probably a sociopath. She didn't like kids, but she had fourteen daughters to perpetuate her bloodline. She wanted nothing to do with us until we were old enough and good enough to fight by her side. She never liked me. I was too soft." I paused, pulling the cream out of the fridge. "And I still do things the way she taught me. Like maybe someday, I'll do it well enough for her approval."

Tony took a deep breath like he was about to say something, then held the breath too long. On one big burst of air, he said, "Because you don't do pity."

I frowned, a little lost. What the hell did that have to do with my mother? "Oh. Okay." This was possibly the least comfortable conversation I'd ever had, and a girl could cram a lot of uncomfortable into two hundred years.

I saw his fists clench, and I automatically made note of Galen's position. If Tony started throwing punches, Galen would go for his throat. I didn't want that to happen. Whatever Tony was fighting right now, I could tell it had nothing to do with me.

"You asked ... why ... I wanted to help you," he said. Like he had to drag the words up from the bottom of a tar pit with a fishing pole. "You don't do pity. You never pity any of the younglings. You just expect them to stand up for themselves. To fight. To win. And you never pulled punches."

"If I pulled punches, they'd never learn."

"I know." He smiled down at his shoes. "Some of the Sankhain assume the younglings are weak. Because they were victims. Abused. You ... respect them. Us. You respect us." He raised his head like it weighed two tons. "We respect you back. And they should respect you more. That's why."

I felt like my lungs shrunk two sizes. I couldn't take a deep breath. And without a deep breath, my brain was too oxygen deprived to come up with a response. I changed the subject. "Finn wants Darcy out of here before he arrives tonight." My voice only sounded a little breathy. Yay, me.

"Yeah." Of course, Tony knew that already. He was the liaison.

"I don't want to let him leave." The words slipped out without my knowledge, but as soon as I heard them, I knew they were my truth.

Tony nodded. "The nocturne might find him."

Knowing that Tony agreed with my truth gave me a little strength of conviction. "And what if he goes blabbing about us or the Spring to somebody? The guy has major verbal diarrhea."

"He does like to talk."

"So we can't let him leave. What do we tell Finn when he gets here and the outsider's cozied up in my armchair, watching must-see TV?"

"Shit, I don't know," Tony said. I glared at him. He grinned. "Gimme some time to think about it. We've got a few hours before it even starts getting dark."

"Yeah. I guess." I cast my gaze around the room, searching for a task to keep me occupied for that time, so I didn't have to stand here and have any more heart-to-hearts with Tony. As it usually did, my gaze landed on Galen. "I'm going to take him for a run. You okay to stay here?"

He got a funny look on his face, like he had a stomach ache. "Sure. I can stay here," he said without emotion.

I realized he was probably stuck in the apartment all day. We Sankhain weren't used to being caged for so many consecutive hours. We tended to be a restless bunch. "You want to come along? We could leave Darcy a note or something."

Tony's face lit up. "That would be great."

"Um, okay." For some reason, the sweet twist of his scent that came from happiness made me feel very uncomfortable. Like I just walked into a Billy Graham tent, wearing a "Ride 'Em Hard" t-shirt. I needed to take him down a notch. "You better keep up, though."

For some obnoxious reason, this just made him laugh. "Hey, I'm not the one who's got two centuries under her belt. If you need to go get your cane, I'll wait here."

I scowled, because that was a good zinger. "No. But you need to write a damn note for Darcy if you're coming."

"Okay." He went directly to the drawer in the kitchen where I kept a steno pad. I barely had time to wonder how he knew which drawer it was, before he asked me, "Should I tell him we're on some kind of Sankha business?"

How the hell should I know? "Uh. No. Then he'll expect to hear about it when we get back. I think we can stick with the truth for once."

"All right. I guess it's not unusual, the two of us walking the dog together, seeing as how we're involved."

I almost said, "Involved with what?" but stopped before I embarrassed myself. He meant *involved*. Ick. "Sure. Great. I gotta pee."

He didn't look up from his writing, so he must not have picked up on the desperation in my voice. I couldn't see my cheeks to be certain they were red, but I didn't think my face could feel this hot without some visible evidence. I ran to the bathroom and shut myself inside. Once there, I realized I did need to go. Five coffees and counting.

After flushing and washing my hands, I stared at myself in the mirror. Considering how little time I'd put into my appearance the last forty-eight hours, I didn't look too bad. My minimal sleep was enough to erase any shadows under my eyes. My hair wasn't greasy but did look like I'd been on the wrong end of a wind storm. Bright side, I didn't have blood or dirt caked on me anywhere.

I raised my arm and sniffed. Making a face, I tried to remember the last time I showered, and couldn't. Bad sign. But I wasn't about to shower before a run. If Tony couldn't take it, he'd just have to jog upwind.

When I opened the bathroom door, Galen was sitting on the other side, giving me his best poor-puppy-all-hope-is-lost look. I sighed. "I'm sorry I locked you out," I told him.

Tony came around the corner, notepad in hand. His eyes looked darker in the shadowy hallway. More like emeralds than jade. Blech. What the hell was wrong with me? "What was that?" he said.

"Nothing. I was talking to Galen." I felt my cheeks warm again. Because I was caught talking to my dog. Not because I was comparing his eyes to gemstones like some dumbass harlequin romance damsel.

Tony looked from Galen, seated just outside the bathroom, to me, just inside the bathroom. "You usually take him in the bathroom with you?"

Suddenly feeling very grumpy, I curled my lip in a snarl. "No. Usually, there's nobody else in the damn apartment, so I just leave the damn door open and he can come and go as he pleases. He's probably fucking traumatized at being shut out of his own home."

Tony's scent soured with what I assumed was worry, and I felt like an ass. "Oh. Sorry."

I rolled my eyes, although whether my exasperation was with him or with me, I didn't know. "I'm sure Galen will survive. Did you finish the note or not?"

He held up the pad. "You wanna read it?"

"No. Just put it somewhere he'll find it and let's go." I didn't want to say it, but I knew that if I had to spend one more minute standing in that condensed space with him, I was going to go crazy. He smelled so good. So warm. So male. Not like cologne. Just like testosterone and a little sweat, and that musk that males had that females just didn't.

Tony set the notepad in front of the bedroom door, a pretty ingenious place to put it. I would've done something stupid like tape it to the outside of the door, where Darcy most likely would've never seen it. This knowledge just made me grumpier.

I grabbed a plastic bag out of my stash in the closet, and was already strapping Galen into his harness when Tony made it into the living room. I looked at his footwear doubtfully. "You're going jogging in biker boots?"

"I don't have running shoes with me."

"How many blocks are we going to make it before you wimp out and start whining like a little girl about how much your tootsies hurt?"

"Tootsies?" He closed the distance between us. I straightened up, instinctively unwilling to be that close to a body that large without making full use of what height I had. "Sweetheart, feet this big ain't ever called tootsies."

He was so close. Too close. I either had to crane my neck back to stare up at him like he was the moon, or stare straight ahead at the middle of his t-shirt. I could've taken a step back, but I refused to give ground. So instead, I took a step toward him, eating up what little breathing space there was so that I was almost pressed against his chest. "What are they called?" I asked in a deliberately soft voice, head cocked to the side as I looked up at his face.

He lowered his head so his mouth was next to my ear. I didn't feel his lips, but his breath tickled. "Boats. Big fuckin' boats." Then he started to laugh, and he stepped back.

I looked down at my dog so that Tony wouldn't see how unnerved I was from the sensation of his breath in my ear. It didn't help any that his voice was so deep and gravelly, the sound was palpable, like bass drums vibrating through my chest. Damn. I needed to get laid. Maybe Finn could stick around for a quickie after he ripped me a new asshole tonight.

The thought stopped me, and made my stomach flip-flop to the point that I feared my double cheeseburgers might make an encore appearance. Was I really so pathetic that I still wanted physical contact with Finn, even though he obviously thought I was less than worthless? No. Because the thought of touching him, or looking into his eyes as I guided him inside me, made me want to hurl. I wasn't pathetic. I wasn't worthless. I was a strong, fierce woman who could damn well take care of her own needs when she got in the shower in about an hour and a half. With a deep breath that carried entirely too much of Tony's scent, I picked up Galen's leash and grabbed my house keys from the table. "Let's go."

I took off at a run, not a warm-up walk or slow jog, but a flat-out, run for your life, wind howling past your ears kind of run. To my surprise, after only a few strides, Tony appeared on my right side, the side not occupied by Galen. After a couple blocks of blatant racing, which nobody won, we called a truce and settled into a more comfortable pace.

When I decided it was time to turn around, I slowed to a jog, then a walk. Tony ran ahead a little, then turned and jogged in place, looking at me. "You tired?" he said. After how far we ran, those few syllables were probably all he could string together at one time.

"No. But Galen will be. I don't want him to hurt himself."

Tony nodded once and jogged back to us. I noticed Tony was sniffling a lot. "You okay?" I asked.

"Yeah." Then he sneezed. He glanced at my face. My expression must've been asking a question, because he said, "Allergies. It's not a big deal."

"They make pills for that, you know."

"I don't need drugs!" The force of his words, like a physical lash, made me tighten my grip on Galen's leash.

"Okey-dokey then. No pills for you." I tugged Galen away from the tree he was about to christen, and started walking faster.

His voice cracked as he said, "Kellan. I'm sorry."

Shit. As soon as I heard that ragged edge to his voice, I knew why he didn't want an antihistamine. I opened my mouth to say that he didn't need to explain, but I wasn't fast enough.

"My mom was an addict. I kinda got a thing about pills." He'd already told me about his mother, but I didn't think he was saying it again to inform me. More like he said it the way an alcoholic introduced himself at AA. Admitting he had a problem.

I could go two ways. I could go with pity, but he said earlier that my lack of pity was one of my more attractive qualities. I didn't think I possessed enough attractive qualities to start knocking them off, so I decided to go with callous smart-ass. "I'm talking Benadryl, not OxyContin." I glanced at him out of the corner of my eye. The rims of his nostrils looked red. So did the rims of his ears, although I didn't think that was allergen-related.

"Yeah. I just don't like to take 'em if I can suck it up and go without. You know?"

I wanted to say, "Not really," but I thought he might take that as being rude, so I just stayed silent. The fact of the matter was, I truly didn't know. I'd never been sick. Anytime I got injured, I either healed fast enough that I didn't need chemical help or my body burned through the painkillers too fast for them to be worthwhile. I didn't know what it was like to have the option.

Tony sneezed again, then blew his nose on a tissue that he pulled from his pocket. He started to stuff the tissue back in his pocket.

"Ew. Don't do that. Give it here." I held open the plastic bag that I had yet to need for Galen.

He looked at the bag. "I might need it again."

I looked at the tissue. A blind man could see that Tony had already used up all the good in that poor thing. "Then use your t-shirt. That'd be less disgusting than reusing that thing."

He pressed his lips together. I had a feeling he was battling something deeply ingrained, like the pill hatred.

"Tony. Let it go." I didn't really know what "it" was, but I didn't think I was talking about the tissue.

"I... Um. Okay." But he still hesitated for a long second before carefully dropping the tissue into the plastic bag.

I felt like he deserved a round of applause. I settled for a sigh of relief. Looking down at Galen, I said, "You had enough leg-lifts for a while?" Without waiting for an answer, I started to jog. We took it slower on the way home, because Tony was having a harder time breathing through his nose. But I still felt like we made good time. As we climbed up the front steps toward the door of my building, I looked at him with approval. "You do good running in those butch boots of yours."

He barked out a laugh. "Gee, thanks. You do pretty good on those skinny-ass legs of yours."

"Skinny means less baggage to carry around. So, what're you going to make me for dinner, sunshine?"

"Anything you want." He sniffed. "Long as you take a shower while I do it. Damn, girl. If I can smell you right now, you know you gotta be ripe."

This surprised me into laughing. "Yeah. I guess so. Considering the rate at which you're producing mucus."

"Damn skippy."

My shower was delayed yet again, however, when we got upstairs. Darcy was sitting on the futon, looking bleary-eyed and a little lost, but definitely more awake than asleep. I looked at Tony. He leaned over and murmured in my ear, "Rock paper scissors?"

I snorted and stepped past him. "Hi, Darcy. Sorry we weren't here when you woke up. Can I get you anything?"

"Hmm?" He blinked at me.

Having used up all my perky with the previous breath, I turned my attention to Galen and pretended the rest of the room didn't exist.

"You smell," the nonexistent entity on my futon said.

Tony's deep chuckle turned into a cough. I ignored them both. Once he was free from his harness, Galen shook himself and trotted into the kitchen for a loud slurp of water. I followed him, intending to do the same.

"Do you think he's okay?" Tony asked me.

"Go blow your nose, dude. You're making me sniffle."

"I'm serious. He seems … off."

I glared at him for a second, then went back into the living room. I knelt in front of Darcy and looked him in the eyes. His pupils looked normal. "Darcy, are you on something?"

"You really smell."

"Thank you. Noted. Darcy, did you take any pills? Or drink something? Like absinthe?"

"No. No pills. What day is it?"

"Thursday."

"Still? Or a different one?"

A teeny fluttering of worry in my chest. "You think you slept for a week?"

"No," Darcy said, but he didn't sound very sure. Then he seemed to think about it and gain certainty. "No. No, I don't. I just — I don't sleep much. My sister, she's sick. I've been staying at the hospice most nights. I guess … I guess I was really out." He started patting down his pockets. "I should call her. I haven't — she must be wondering where I am."

I stood up and turned to Tony. "I think he's okay. Try giving him coffee. Strong coffee. Make a big batch, will you? I'd do it, but apparently, I need to shower."

"Yeah, 'cause you smell," Darcy said.

I closed my eyes, counted to ten, then opened them. "Come on, Galen. You're with me."

"Kell?"

In the bathroom doorway, I turned and looked at Tony, who stood a few feet away. "Yeah?"

He spoke softly, presumably so Darcy wouldn't hear. "It's almost five. Dark is getting closer."

"Okay."

"What are we going to do with him?"

"Fuck, I don't know. I thought you were going to think about it. Come up with a plan."

"Maybe we could just tell him the truth."

I stared at Tony, not sure how to take that. "Tell him our colleagues are arriving to discuss how best to extract information from him?"

"Tell him we're discussing what to do about the request to enter the forest. Tell him it's an insider-type meeting. He can't attend, but we still want him here so when the meeting is over, we can talk to him right away about the outcome. Something like that."

I thought about that. "And just stick him back in the bedroom?" Tony nodded. "Huh." It could work. Except... "What do we tell Finn?"

"Who cares? He's gonna be pissed, no matter what."

I felt a smile blossom across my face. Suddenly, I was very glad that Tony was on my side. "All right. The truth. It's radical, but I'm game."

"Okay. Any dinner requests?" He sneezed.

My stomach twisted uncomfortably, as I noticed how puffy his eyes looked. But I wasn't supposed to pity him. "Yes. No snot in the soup, please."

He grunted and turned to go.

"Tony."

He looked back at me.

"Do you need anything?" I didn't specifically mention the allergies again, because I figured he'd be more likely to ask for help if we kept things vague.

He sneezed again, then swore softly. "You got any Kleenex?"

"Yes!" I felt inordinately happy that I could do this for him. "I'll get you a box." I grabbed a fresh box from the bathroom closet and handed it to him.

"Thanks." He didn't meet my eyes, but he ripped open the box, set it on the floor, pulled out a tissue and mightily blew his nose.

Then I watched as Tony stuck the tissue in his pocket. "Dude. The trash can is two feet away. You can just walk over and throw it away."

He went still as the dead. "Oh. Yeah." But he didn't pull the tissue back out of his pocket, or walk in the direction of the kitchen trash.

"Tony? I have six more boxes of Kleenex. We're not going to run out anytime soon. Please, lose the used one."

His breathing was shallow and uneven. I could hear his heart pounding and smell the adrenaline flooding his system. "I — yeah. I will."

I wanted to shower. I felt like I had hangover mouth, all over my body. But I instinctively knew that he wasn't going to throw away that tissue. He was going to try to reuse it, and I couldn't accept that. "Tony, what's the deal?"

He wouldn't look at me. "Whad'you mean?"

"That tissue is done for. Its structural integrity is severely compromised. Why do you want to hang onto it?"

"I — I might need it." His hands were now clenched.

I took a deep breath and tread carefully. "No. You won't. I promise."

"But—" He shuddered, and I couldn't breathe for a second as I watched him. When he spoke again, his voice was so low and soft, I had to strain to hear. "These things don't grow on trees. You can't waste shit like that." Then I thought I heard him say, "Beat it into you."

"Tony. Look at me." He hesitated. I hated to push him, but I needed to pull him out of his waking nightmare. I forced my voice to be firm. "Antony. Look in my eyes, please."

He blinked several times, then raised his gaze. He looked at my nose, which was close enough.

"Antony, this is the new rule. You have to throw away tissues. After one use. If you don't, I'll be forced to…" I couldn't threaten to hurt him. I dug around in my brain for a threat that I could stomach. "I'll chain you to a really uncomfortable chair and make you watch the golf channel. For at least three days. Straight."

This surprised him enough that he met my eyes. "What?"

"I'm serious. I'll make you watch a marathon of white guys in ugly pants, hitting a tiny, tiny ball over and over again. With the mind-numbing NPR style commentary. I'll force feed you coffee so you can't even fall asleep to get away from it."

He stared at me for a few more seconds, then his gaze flitted away. "Well, that would be awful." His voice sounded a little better. A little more solid.

"I'll say. By the time it's done, you'll have an inexplicable desire to wear pink polo shirts. So you better start saying adios to those tissues."

"I guess I better." A smile haunted his face for a moment. He turned to leave again.

"Tony. The tissue's still in your pocket."

"I'll throw it away in the kitchen."

"Am I going to have to frisk you when I get out of the shower?"

He paused. "Mmm. Sounds like fun." His voice lacked the usual electrical charge, but at least he was trying.

"Oh, shut up." Then I turned and went into the bathroom, closing the door behind me so he wouldn't see the relief on my face. Galen snuck into the bathroom before I could close the door. I looked down at him. "Whew."

He wagged his tail, as if in agreement.

As I stripped and got into the shower, Tony's tortured face hovered in my mind. I washed my hair twice and still felt like my scalp was crawling with fleas. I tried not to think too much about the lives of the younglings before. Before us. Before they were rescued, brought to a place where no one would touch them in unwelcome ways, unless it was in a sparring session. Before they discovered what it was like to have enough to eat, anytime they felt hungry. Before they saw a future for themselves that didn't involve drugs, or booze, or selling any part of themselves. Every once in a while, though, I was forced to see that, for them, the lines weren't as clearly defined. It wasn't *before* and *after*, for Tony. It was just his life, and it was all jumbled up in a trunk full of memories, and he somehow still managed to think and speak and walk and be a far more decent human being than I would ever be.

I adjusted the water temperature, but it didn't do any good. I could boil myself and still feel cold.

Chapter 13

When I got out of the shower, I couldn't make myself put on my sweat-encrusted clothes for even the short walk to the bedroom. I wrapped a towel around my body and opened the bathroom door a crack to listen and check for male scents. I heard the television and male voices from the direction of the living room. Feeling safe, I hurried down the hall to the bedroom. Then I heard the laugh. From the living room. A laugh much too high and breathy to be Tony or Darcy.

I froze. Breathed deep through my nose, this time searching for estrogen-rich scents. I was too far away to pull anything identifiable. I tried to be rational. If there was an intruder, I would hear the sounds of battle, not laughter. But all I knew was, there was a strange female in my den, and I needed to defend my territory.

I clothed myself without looking at colors or fabrics. Then I grabbed my short sword, and crept toward the living room.

I heard a second female voice as I entered the kitchen. The voice sounded vaguely familiar, but in my adrenaline-charged state, I couldn't place it. I recognized the scents just as I, with sword raised, entered the living room.

"Seriously, what is it? Human growth hormone?" Leanna released Tony from an embrace, and looked over at me. "Wow. Nice sword. Are you the welcome wagon?"

Trini shushed her partner. "Stop it, Lee. It's her home. I'm sure Finn didn't even bother to tell her we were coming."

"That would be like ol' Finlay. Such a master communicator." Leanna looked at my face rather than my blade. "Sorry if we startled you. We were on our way to camp. Just got done in California. Finn called and rerouted us here. Hey, Galen."

I looked down at my dog. He was wagging his tail. It had been a long time since he last saw Leanna and Trini, but in general, he trusted women more easily than men. With jerky motions, I lowered the sword and noticed my clothes. I wore a bright orange t-shirt that I usually reserved for night jogging, along with a pair of olive-green cargo shorts with frayed pockets. I looked like I was all ready to go out panhandling on State Street.

I glanced at Darcy, who was watching the interaction with rabid fascination on his face. "It's a little crowded in here," I said, trying to be cryptic.

"Oh, don't worry about Darcy," Tony said. "I introduced him to Trini and Leanna. Since he knows all about the Spring, I figured we didn't need to keep him in the dark."

"Sure. Of course." Inside, I was screaming at him for making such a bold decision without talking it through with me first. But it was too late now. I struggled for a normal tone of voice. "So, Tony. I thought you were going to make dinner."

Leanna snorted. "He cooks, too?"

"Damn straight," Tony said. "Helluva lot better than you."

"Hey, as I recall, you enjoyed my goulash," Leanna said.

That's right, I thought. Trini and Leanna were the ones who found Tony on the street. They brought him into the Sankhain fold.

Tony scowled. "It was Hamburger Helper, and it was two years out of date. I got the runs from that shit." But as he walked around her to get to the kitchen, he gave her shoulder a squeeze.

I watched him go, a suspicion growing in my mind. I almost said something, but changed my mind at the last minute, not wanting to embarrass him. I followed him into the kitchen. "Hey. Do me a favor and turn out your pockets."

He froze. "What?"

"You heard me. You don't want me to say it any louder."

His scent heated with shame. I found myself imagining what might have happened when he was a kid, just a kid with a runny nose, nothing he could help or change. What might've happened in a place where nothing was sacred and nothing was safe? Then I made myself stop before I did something stupid, like burst into tears.

A muscle in Tony's jaw twitched. "I told you I would—"

"Great. Then there's no reason you can't turn out your pockets so I can see that you followed through."

He still didn't move.

"Golf channel, Tony. Pastels that don't see the light of day in any other context, and quiet clapping, like the sound of a babbling brook. It's enough to drive a person mad." Still nothing. Getting pissed, I said, "Tony, if we're in this together, if we're a team, then I need to be able to trust you. And if I can't trust you over something as stupid as a tissue, then we're in trouble."

He swallowed and, in painfully slow motion, turned out his pockets. Inside the left front pocket was the blasted tissue. "I didn't use it again," he said, sullen.

"And the world is a more beautiful place for your restraint. Now throw the damn thing away. And wash your hands before you touch any food. Do you want help?"

"I think I can manage."

I realized he thought I was offering to help him throw away the tissue. Given that he was supposed to dispose of it ages ago, I could've questioned his assertion, but that wasn't what I was offering to help with, so I didn't. "I meant with dinner."

"Oh." He finally tossed the tissue in the trash can under the sink. Then he turned on the hot water and started washing his hands. "No. I got it."

It occurred to me that if I wasn't helping with dinner, then I would be expected to entertain our guests. "Are you sure?"

Tony pulled a mug out of the cupboard and filled it with coffee that smelled dark and thick. "Here. They won't bite. Now suck it up and go into the living room."

"I can't believe I'm being told to suck it up by a guy who needed assistance from the National Guard to throw away a Kleenex."

"Yeah, well." Much more relaxed, Tony opened the fridge and started rummaging around. "We've all got our battles to fight, I guess."

I was good at fighting battles. It was what I was born to do. But my sword wasn't going to help me make small talk with three people who, through no fault of my own, seemed to have taken up residence in my living room.

Tony pulled his head out of the fridge long enough to look at me and say, "Do I need to threaten you with the golf channel?"

I stuck my tongue out at him and stalked away.

Leanna and Trini were both sitting in my armchair. Well, Leanna sat in it and Trini perched on the arm. They were telling Darcy a story about some pier they'd gone to in San Francisco. I stood and watched for a while, sipping my coffee. I liked Trini and Leanna. They'd been lovers for centuries, and their scents now intermingled to the point that I couldn't tell where one ended and the other began. I sat down on the floor and let Galen cram his torso onto my lap.

I was probably closer to sharing a scent with Galen than with the man I'd been fucking for the last century and a half. That made me a little bit sad.

I turned my attention back to the conversation. Where was San Francisco? Was that southern California? I never really bothered to learn geography. I already outlived a few versions of the world. Why bother memorizing a bunch of crap that was only going to change again in fifty years or so? "Is San Francisco southern California?"

"No, northern," Trini said, not batting an eye. She knew me well enough to understand my irritation with geographic nuances. I wasn't the only Sankha who felt that way, either.

Darcy, however, was staring at me like I just crawled out from under a rock and requested a cup of tea. "You don't know where San Francisco is?"

I shrugged. "I do now."

"Where did you go to school?"

I hesitated. Sure, he knew about the Sankhain and the Spring, but that didn't mean he knew how a Sankha's life began. "I was, um, homeschooled."

"By whom?"

The way he said it irritated me. Like I'd said, "Really? The world is round?" I wasn't a moron. I just thought geography was a waste of time. Hell, you could get maps on your phone, along with turn-by-turn directions read to you by a mechanical woman. Plus, he used the word "whom," and in my experience only dickwads used the word "whom." "By Snow White and the seven dwarves. I may not know geography, but I can whistle with the best of 'em."

"Sorry," Darcy said, and I thought he meant it. "I've just seen people who were homeschooled that have very … odd understandings of the truth. I guess I'm a little biased."

"Yeah, well." I looked at Trini, not sure what to say. "I guess that makes sense. I mean, the first time I saw a full-sized man, I was scared shitless. After all that time with Dopey and Doc."

Trini smiled at me, and Darcy surprised me by laughing. "That's funny," he said. Like he hadn't thought me capable of humor. Just because a girl carried a few knives and wasn't afraid to use them.

I wondered how much longer Tony would be in the kitchen. I wondered what he was making. It smelled like spaghetti. I wondered if it would be odd if I just got up and left the apartment without offering an explanation. I was reasonably sure there wasn't enough oxygen in here to sustain this many life forms.

An eternity later (or maybe only fifteen minutes), Tony stuck his head in the room. "Kell? You got any more chairs?"

"No." I felt my face get hot. Almost as if I was embarrassed to be caught with my hostess pants down.

"Oh. Spaghetti isn't really a plate-in-your-lap kinda food. Maybe we should eat in shifts."

"That's okay," Trini said. "We ate after the flight. We're not hungry right now. Right, Lee?"

Leanna nodded. "If there's leftovers, though, we might take something later."

I heard Tony banging plates and silverware around. Leanna started channel surfing, while Trini perused my bookshelves. Darcy was staring at me with a familiar look on his face. A question was coming. Sure enough, three seconds later: "So Tony doesn't live here?"

He caught me by surprise and I responded without thinking. "What? No. Of course not."

"Oh." Darcy cocked his head to the side and stared at the bare wall. "Huh. I guess I just thought he did. You two seem so … close."

Realizing my mistake, I tried to recover. "Well, we are, but, you know, I — he — he doesn't live here." Then, desperate for a distraction, I walked over to Trini. My reading tastes were eclectic, but I leaned strongly toward literary fiction. I lived a fantasy novel. I didn't want to spend my time reading about it. "Go ahead and borrow whatever you like," I offered to her.

"What's good?"

"All of it. I give the crap ones to Goodwill or the library."

"And the library thanks you," Darcy said.

I couldn't tell if he was yanking my chain or not. "Well, I figure you can sell them at one of your fundraiser things."

"Yes. We do. We appreciate the donations." He paused. "Although, once in a while, if you wanted to throw a non-crap book into the mix, that might be nice."

Now I was sure he was yanking my chain. I debated the merits of duct-taping his mouth shut.

Then he grinned. "I'm teasing," he said. It was such a rare sight, Darcy full-on grinning, that I felt like a deer and her doe just ran across my path. It made me feel warm and fuzzy on the inside. Which weighted down my limbs with icy dread.

"Tony, how's that food coming?" I almost ran into the kitchen, which was infinitely smaller and still felt like wide open spaces compared to the overcrowded living room. Galen followed and planted himself directly in front of the stove, where a pot of red sauce and what looked like meatballs sat steaming. "How'd you make meatballs so fast?"

"Frozen. I took 'em out of the freezer this morning."

"Oh." I didn't realize meatballs came ready-made. Maybe I should try going to the supermarket. I usually did my shopping at Casa de Sankha, where there were always buckets of leftovers and dry goods to spare. "Smells good."

He flashed me a smile. "By the time you and Darcy get to the table, I'll be ready to dish up."

"Okay." With a deep, fortifying breath, I reentered the living room. "Darcy? Soup's on."

He hesitated. "My appetite's been kind of funky lately. Stress, I guess. I'm not really all that hungry."

I was weary of this conversation. "I don't care. Tony made food. You're going to eat it." I turned and walked away, picking out a seat at the table.

"Galen, you're going to get boiling water poured on your scalp," Tony said to my dog. Galen didn't budge. I knew Tony wouldn't really let any boiling water hit Galen, so I didn't intervene. Tony shook his head, hefted the pot of pasta and held it over the sink, where a strainer waited. Sure enough, Galen was unscathed, although a little water did splash on Tony's bare leg.

"Ouch," I said. I was up and kneeling beside him before I realized I moved. "Are you okay?" I examined the patch of skin, which was already growing red.

"Yeah, I'm fine," he said. I continued to peer at the red spot. Unable to resist, I poked the skin. Tony yowled. "Jesus! What the hell are you doing?"

"Um." I really didn't know what I was trying to accomplish by poking it. "Checking to see if you're cooked all the way through?"

The crowd of people that used to be in my living room decided to cram themselves into my teeny tiny kitchen. "Everything okay in here?" Leanna asked.

"We're fine. Go away." I was too abrupt, but I couldn't help it. I already felt myself suffocating on too much steam and not enough air.

Leanna raised her eyebrows and looked at me. "Tony?"

"I'm fine. Boiling water. Bare skin. Doesn't hurt too bad. Unless you stick your finger in it."

"I said I was sorry," I said.

"Actually, no, you didn't," Tony said.

I stood up and walked back to my chair, hoping that if I put a little distance between me and the humans, I might be able to breathe. "Well, I thought it. That's gotta count for something, doesn't it?"

I smelled him before I saw him; his usual scent, comfortable as home-baked bread, now coated with the smells of garlic, tomatoes, and beef. Pressing up against my back, Tony reached around me and grabbed my plate off the table. "It counts," he said in my ear. "I'll dish up the plates. Too hot to load up the table. Unless you have trivets?"

I was flustered at his proximity. "What the fuck's a trivet?"

Darcy finally joined me at the table. "It's something you set hot dishes on, so they don't burn your table."

Everybody else knew what a trivet was. And where San Francisco was. "I really am a moron, aren't I?"

"No, you're not." Tony slammed my plate on the table with enough force that one of the meatballs rolled off and splatted on the floor. Galen hoovered it up before the steam had a chance to rise. "How do you expect someone like Finn to respect you if you don't respect yourself?"

It was really starting to creep me out, the way Tony kept defending me. At least, "creeped out" was what I chose to call this tightness in my gut, this feeling that felt so similar to fear, but with more warmth in my extremities. After a far-too-long silence, I gave up on finding words and just started eating.

My arms and legs felt weightless, I was so hungry. I watched as Darcy, despite his protests, dug into his food with the devotion of a lifelong glutton. When he paused in his aggressive consumption to take a breath, Darcy asked, "Who's this Finn that you keep mentioning? Is he one of you?"

I ignored the question, because I just didn't feel like explaining anything. Tony didn't answer, either, just looked at me. Darcy, contrary to what I knew of his character, let it go. By the time Tony, Darcy and I finished eating, Trini and Leanna said the wonderful smells from the kitchen were making them hungry, and they took their turn at the table.

The apartment grew darker. Finn would be here soon.

Dread halted the digestion process. Spaghetti sat in my stomach like a flour-and-tomato brick. I must've looked ill, because Tony suggested that I take Galen for a walk around the block. Then he invited himself along. Maybe Tony and I had some moments of enjoying one another's company over the past few days, but I still wasn't comfortable with having him around. Tony wasn't just a cocky smart-ass kid anymore. He was something more complicated. And I was full up on complicated.

But, since there wasn't a reason to say no, I let Tony come along on the walk. He waited until we were half a block from the apartment building before he started yakking. "You worried about Finn?"

"What?"

"That look on your face back there, in the kitchen. You looked like you were gonna hurl."

"Words every woman wants to hear." I took a deep breath, relieved to smell only the usual rottenness. Ripe garbage cans, the occasional piece of dropped food lying in the grass. Sweaty bodies that didn't wash often enough. Nothing to cause alarm.

"He can't hurt you unless you let him."

I stopped and glared at Tony, suddenly sick to death of this child acting as my life guru. "What the hell is that supposed to mean? Shit. You sound like a cross between a fortune cookie and a domestic abuse hotline."

"I just meant—"

"He can hurt me all he wants. He has all the power. Or did you miss that company memo?"

"All the power, huh?" Tony glared right back at me. "He had the power to stop you from walking out of the forest and not turning over those papers? He had the power to make you obedient, respectful? Why do you think I want to be a liaison for you? Because you don't let anyone stop you from saying what you think, and one of these days, it's probably going to get you killed, and I'd really prefer if that day didn't come for a long, long time!"

I didn't know what to say, so I just walked away. Unfortunately, Tony followed.

"The kind of power Finn holds is in the mind, Kellan. I mean, yeah, he could have you killed. But he probably won't unless he absolutely has to, because he knows you won't go down without a fight and you'll take some of his best warriors down with you. I think Finn has power because you let him. Because you don't trust yourself to make the wise decisions, so you leave it to someone else. But you can stop that anytime you want. I think you already have. Don't go backwards. Don't give him back the power you took for yourself."

This, from the kid who got his ass kicked by a snot-filled tissue? If being a victim of mind games made him an expert on them, then maybe he should focus on learning to escape his own mental choke hold, instead of lecturing me on how to live my life. I opened my mouth to tear into him, then snapped it shut again. He was trying to be kind, I told myself. He was trying to help. I managed to keep my mouth shut, though I felt my nostrils flare from the effort.

"You're stronger than he is," Tony was saying now. "You're—"

I found myself looking over my shoulder. Searching for hidden ears that would pass along Tony's borderline treasonous words. "Shut up."

"No, Kellan. You need to—"

"I get it. Thanks for the pep talk. Now shut the fuck up. Those aren't words you want anyone else to hear."

He didn't look happy, but he did fall silent.

We got home just as the sun sank below the building line. As we walked up the stairs, I said, "Did you tell Darcy he's going to be sitting out the meeting?"

"No, not yet." Tony pulled a tissue out of his pocket just in time to sneeze into it. He saw me watching him. "I'll throw it away when we get inside." He sounded a little testy, which brightened my mood.

"Okay. I'll give you fifty bucks if you get Darcy to stay in the bedroom with a minimum of fuss."

"I offered to liaise for you with Finn. Darcy's your problem." His refusal of my request should've pissed me off, or at least annoyed me. But instead, my mood brightened further. In my world, nice equaled weak. Nice got you dead quicker. Bitchiness kept you alive. Some part of me that I didn't care to acknowledge really wanted Tony to stay alive.

When I opened the door and stepped into the living room, I saw Leanna slipping something in her pocket. "Finn just called," she said. "He wanted to make sure you were prepared. He plans to be here around nine, maybe nine-thirty."

"Okay. Great." That was more than two hours away. What the hell was I supposed to do with my band of merry men in the meantime? And Finn didn't care if I was prepared. He was just calling to make sure I stayed on edge, that I didn't relax and enjoy the company of my guests. If bitchiness was going to keep me alive, I currently had enough fuel in my furnace to keep me going until the sun exploded. "What did you tell him?"

Leanna shrugged. "Who am I to judge your preparedness? I told him I'd pass along the message, and if he wanted more specific information, he should contact you."

I loved Leanna in that moment. Nodding, I took off Galen's harness, gave him food and water, and then, back in the living room, I looked down at Darcy on the futon. "Walk with me, please."

He blinked at me. "Why?"

"Because the Lollipop Guild just told me it was time to follow the yellow brick road. You coming or what?"

Tony cleared his throat, giving me a disapproving glare. I scowled unrepentantly. My problem, remember? I led the way out of the living room, toward the bedroom.

"Thank you again for doing this," Darcy said as I closed the bedroom door behind us. That pissed me off. Nice equaled weak.

"Thank me one more time and I'm backing out." As soon as I said it, I saw the shock on his face, and felt my stomach twist. "Look, just ... don't go around thanking people for shit that you already thanked them for, okay? Move on. I've got a couple things I need to go over with you before my supervisor gets here."

"Is that Finn? Your supervisor?"

Stomach twisting led to stomach ache, and I wasn't in the mood for Q&A. "Do you want to hear about what's going to happen tonight? Or not?"

He now sounded subdued. "Yes, please." Like Oliver, asking for more gruel.

I took a deep breath and blew it out through pursed lips. I couldn't take too many more niceties. I needed to get laid.

Whoa. Where did that come from? Swallowing hard, I clamped down on that vein of thought. Couldn't be thinking about sex when Finn arrived. Backbone and libido never coexisted well within my body. And I needed backbone more than I needed a mindless fuck that I'd just regret.

All of a sudden, Tony's sleeping form sprawled across my bed popped into my mind. Possibly, my brain wanted to give me an alternate option.

"Okay," I said, trying to focus. On something other than Tony's abs. "So, yeah, Finn's kinda my boss. And he's coming here to talk about your request. But he's kinda touchy about having outsiders in official meetings. It's a breach in protocol. We depend on secrecy. You understand."

Darcy nodded. A speck of spittle in the corner of his mouth made him look rabid.

"But we want you to still be in the apartment with us, so that we can consult with you as soon as our meeting's done. To finalize the arrangements and all. I thought you could stay in the bedroom here, while we meet with Finn. How does that sound?"

He hesitated, giving me several brief, sidelong glances before speaking. "Well, I'd rather be in the meeting, I guess. But I totally understand about the secrecy thing. It makes perfect sense. So yes, I'll just stay back here while you all talk."

That was easy. I was happy enough with the outcome of our conversation that I offered Darcy a smile.

Then he slapped me with, "Are you sure I can't just, you know, sit in the kitchen and listen? I won't say a word. You won't know I'm there, I promise."

The man couldn't keep his mouth shut for three minutes. He really expected me to believe he could sit in silence during a meeting of a secret society he believed had the power to save his sister? It would've been hilarious, if it wasn't so irritating. I growled and said, "I'm sure."

As we walked back to the living room, I heard the opening strains of Breaking Benjamin's *Saturate* album. With raised eyebrows, I looked at Trini, who stood next to the CD player. Trini wasn't really the type to help herself to someone else's music. She smiled and said, "With a name like Breaking Benjamin, and a song called 'Polyamorous,' how could we resist?"

"So very true."

I walked over to the CD player and hit the "seek" button, skipping ahead to track 3. Then I turned around, bumped into Trini, who backed up into Tony, who stepped on Galen's foot. Galen yowled and bared his teeth at the offending boot, while my claustrophobia flared. "All right. Either everybody finds a chair for their ass, or you can wait outside until Finn comes."

Darcy claimed the armchair, probably because after about thirteen minutes, the futon started to get really fucking uncomfortable. Trini walked over to the corner behind the door, where two duffel bags were propped against the wall. She dug around in one of the bags and pulled out a deck of cards. "Anybody in the mood for Texas Hold 'Em?"

While Darcy curled up in the armchair with one of my books — A. Manette Ansay's *Midnight Champagne*, an excellent choice — the four Sankhain sat at my kitchen table, drinking coffee and playing poker. Trini proceeded to whup all our butts. When we accused her of cheating, she informed us that we all had obvious tells. "Tony drops his left hand into his lap when he bluffs," she said. "Kellan, you always scratch Galen behind the ear, and Leanna, you're the most obvious. You lean back in your seat and exhale through your nose."

We stared at her. Tony spoke first. "No way. I don't have a tell. You're making that up."

When Darcy spoke up, I jumped, having mostly forgotten he was there. "No, she's not. Your tell might not be the most obvious, but you are the most consistent with it." Then, apparently realizing all eyes were on him, he turned a deep shade of port.

Trini sent him a brilliant smile, then gathered up her winnings. We played for Tootsie Rolls. I snagged a piece of candy from Trini's pile, moving out of reach before she could snatch it back.

"Don't make me shoot you, Faolanni," she said. "You might not die, but you'd bleed all over your beautiful hardwood floor."

I grinned and popped the chewy chocolate goodness into my mouth. "Might be worth it."

Something started to ring, and we all checked our phones. When I saw that it wasn't mine, I stood up and walked over to Darcy. I didn't have to listen to the conversation. I knew who was calling. It was dark outside. Fun time was done. Finn time was about to begin.

"Come on." I almost took Darcy's hand to lead him back to the bedroom, like I was going to tuck him in. A sudden sadness gripped my throat. Was Finn going to tell me to kill this man? Of course he was. I knew that I should be more suspicious of Darcy. How did he know what he knew? But what I knew of Darcy was how sad he sounded when he talked of his sister, and how desperate his hope smelled, and how guileless his eyes looked, even after I accidentally cut him last night. All my senses told me Darcy was an innocent.

But our job wasn't protecting the innocents. That was someone else's job. Our job was the Spring. Period. I started to close Darcy in the bedroom. At the last moment, I paused. "Were you able to talk to her?"

"Who?" he said.

"Your sister. You were going to call her earlier."

"Oh." In the light from the streetlamps, I could see his Adam's apple bob. "Yes. She, um, she's not really all that with it these days. I don't — that's why I like to, you know, be there. I don't know if she remembers the phone conversations. I'd rather just be there, where she can see me."

His words were like a round kick to the solar plexus. I wasn't prepared, and my breath developed a hitch to match the one I heard in Darcy's. Mal's face popped into my head, and I wondered if this unpleasantness in my chest was what empathy felt like. "Why don't you go, then?"

"What?"

I opened the door and stepped aside. "Go see your sister. Instead of sitting in this room with your thumb up your ass for the next hour. Go to the hospice. Let her see you. But don't linger outside, okay?" How could I explain why I didn't want him standing around outside, where the nocturne could find him? "Maximize your time with her, but when we call you, hurry back here so we don't lose a single moment. Okay?"

"Yes! Yes, of course." Relief flooded his scent. "Thank you."

His gratitude irked me. I might not know exactly what Finn was going to say when he got here, but I knew it wasn't, "Gee, let's help the poor sod save his sister's life." Darcy's gratitude was gratingly misplaced.

Blaming him for my discomfort, I scowled. "Hurry up about it. I'll walk you downstairs." As we passed the kitchen, I told the room that Darcy was going to visit his sister, and would return when our meeting was done.

"Finn's down there, waiting to be let in," Tony said.

Why hadn't one of them gone to get him?

As if reading my mind, Trini said, "We wanted to give you time to get Darcy settled."

"Oh. Okay. Thanks. I'll take Darcy downstairs and bring Finn up. Perfect timing." Perfect like sneezing when you have a full bladder.

"I'll come with you." Tony stood up from the table.

The thought of Tony, Finn and me in the stairwell together sent my adrenal system into overload. That was a lot of personality crammed into a small space. But Tony was the liaison, and I couldn't think of a good reason to deny him. On the way downstairs, Darcy kept up a running commentary about how excited and grateful he was for all we were doing for him. I curled my hands into fists to avoid smacking him. At the bottom step, I paused and took a deep, cleansing breath. This was my territory. I made Finn come to me. This was a victory. At least, that's what I told myself. I might've believed it if my stomach wasn't eating its own lining.

"Kelly?" Darcy said, sounding a little less excited.

I didn't respond, but I did manage to take that one last step so I stood before the door. Chin up, shoulders back. For once in my life, I wished I had some cleavage to distract the man on the other side of the door. Oh, well. Mal got the cleavage, I got the balls; that's what we always used to say. The memory made me smile, and gave me the courage to open the door. "Hello, Finny. What a pleasure."

Finn's scent reminded me of earth. Rich, loamy dirt, the kind that can grow anything. Except when he was angry. Like now. Right now, he smelled like the middle of the Sahara. "What took so long?" he said in greeting.

"Well, you know, it's been kinda busy around here." I closed my eyes and inhaled through my nose. Filtered out Finn's scent, searched for others. Nothing nocturne-ish. Satisfied, I opened my eyes and turned to Darcy. I wondered if I should introduce him to Finn. I decided to see if I could get away with skipping the intros. "So, we'll call you when we're ready. Enjoy your time with your sister."

Darcy gave me a funny look, glanced around me at Finn, then looked at me again. But he didn't say anything, and I was allowed one moment of hope that we wouldn't go into the awkward introductions. Then Finn's voice rose up from behind me like a sea monster. "Who is this?"

Darcy spoke before I could. "Darcy Jamison. It's nice to meet you." And he stuck his hand out to Finn.

Finn stared at Darcy's hand. "We're on a schedule, Mr. Jamison. If you will excuse us?"

"Yeah, he was just on his way out." I took a step forward across the threshold, forcing Finn to step back. That gave Darcy enough room to walk out the door. I shoved the corners of my mouth into a smile as Darcy passed me. "I'll call you soon, okay?"

"Okay. Thanks." Darcy glanced at Finn one more time, before he jogged down the sidewalk toward the parking lot.

When I turned back toward the door, I saw Finn was still standing on the front stoop, because Tony filled the doorway. Tony's expression was calm, blank, but his scent was heavy with testosterone. "Shall we?" he said to me.

"Yeah. Sure." I didn't know what was going on, why he was blocking Finn's entry, but I wasn't about to argue with him. He was my ally.

"Was that the outsider?" Finn said.

I wanted to say "Duh." Instead, I said, "Yup."

"I thought I told you to make sure he was out of the apartment before I arrived."

"Yeah, well, didn't work out that way. You want to go upstairs or not?"

Finn's voice was precise, one of the few giveaways that his temper was rising. "What do you mean, it didn't work out that way?"

I felt a rush of hot blood between my ears. I was getting to him. It made me want to see how far I could push him. "My apartment got awfully crowded all of a sudden. I guess he just got lost in the shuffle." I walked past Finn, trusting that Tony would move out of the way and let me lead the way upstairs. He did.

"Kellan!"

I smiled. Finn, speaking in exclamation points? This might just be fun. Then I straightened my face and tossed over my shoulder, "Around here, it's Kelly."

Tony and I reached the second-floor landing first. He leaned in and murmured, "Well played. Kelly."

He smelled good. Warm, and male, and yummy. That rush of blood that made me want to push Finn suddenly made me want other things. I tilted my head back to look up at Tony, and his face was so close, our lips almost brushed. Then Finn rounded the corner, and I jumped a mile in the air, shoving Tony away with enough force that he stumbled backwards. Instead of diminishing, Tony's scent grew stronger, filling the stairwell. I could barely smell Finn, meaning Tony was agitated. Agitated was supposed to be my job. "Liaise," I said to him, to remind him of his job.

Tony blinked, looked at me, took a deep, cleansing breath of his own. Then he smiled and winked, while his scent returned to a normal volume. "So, Finlay, sir, I made spaghetti and meatballs for dinner. There's still a little left. I could heat you up a plate."

Finn's scent softened a little. Whether it was the offer of food or the use of the word "sir," he seemed to relax. "Ah, no. Thank you."

Well put, Monosyllabic Man. "I'll take some more," I said. I didn't really want any — my stomach still felt like a cinder block in quicksand — but I felt like I needed to support Tony's efforts.

"You got it." Tony's hand came to rest on the small of my back. Finn's eyes followed its progress, and his scent dried up once again. I wanted to elbow Tony in the gut. He called this liaising?

I opened the apartment door. Galen sat just far enough from the door that I was able to take one step inside. Trini and Leanna were standing across the room, staring at the door with enough intensity that I wondered if they had weapons handy, just in case. Watching and waiting for what might come next. I grabbed Galen's collar and ignored the women. "Come on in."

As Finn gazed around and focused on the futon, his mouth twisted into a very uncomfortable-looking shape. I tried to remember when I'd acquired my latest piece of shabby chic furniture. Then I tried to remember the last time Finn had been in my apartment. It was at least six months ago. He really didn't like leaving the forest; he hated the sounds of the city, the exhaust fumes and the people who tended to stare at this god walking among them. He only came to me when he was really horny. Which, come to think of it, wasn't nearly as often as it used to be. So I guessed that this was the first time he had seen the futon.

That look on his face, like he just unintentionally swallowed something slimy, was getting to me. I felt an apology bubble up, so I killed it by finding my mug, pouring a fresh, hot cup, and gulping a few mouthfuls, searing my vocal chords and eliminating the threat of submissive posturing.

Once Galen saw that I was only getting coffee, not food, he meandered back into the living room. When I followed, Finn saw the mug in my hand and gave me a pointed glare. God forbid he actually ask for something. I should offer him a cup. I clamped my lips together and stared right back at him.

"Kellan? Did you still want more spaghetti?" Tony asked, reminding me that there were other people in the room.

My stomach was telling me the coffee was risky enough. I didn't want to add tomato sauce to the mix. Puking up Tony's food might diminish my attempt at support. "Ah, no. I guess I'm more full than I thought. Maybe later." To my left, I felt Galen's eyes on me. I knew from his scent that my dog was relaxed. Maybe even a little impressed by my sudden display of authority.

Finn didn't smell impressed. He was waiting for me to do the proper thing, to offer him refreshments and make clear my role as the loyal subject to his highness. I gritted my teeth. I had all night, and no inclination to offer a damn thing.

Once again, Tony came to the rescue. "Would you like some coffee, sir?"

"Yes. Thank you. Cream, if you have it."

"I don't," I said, to remind the men that the apartment was actually mine, the food in it was mine, and therefore should've been mine to offer.

"There's milk, though, isn't there, Kellan?" Tony sounded tense.

"Yeah. If it's not sour."

Tony exhaled loudly through his nostrils. "I just bought some. I think it'll be okay." Tony walked around me to the kitchen, giving my shoulder a little shove as he passed. When Tony returned, he handed Finn a mug. "Should we sit?"

Boy, once he decided to liaise again, he really jumped head first into the empty pool. I should make it easier for him. But I just didn't want to. "Yeah. Sure." I sat down in the armchair. Left the futon for Finn.

He chose to stand. Trini and Leanna took the futon instead. Their mutual scent wafted toward me. Finn and I had been together twice as long as Leanna and Trini, and I never smelled my scent on him, not even right after sex.

My relationship with Finn wasn't exactly two peas in a pod material. The sex was dynamite. But it never occurred to us to embrace in greeting, or for any other reason. We didn't hold hands, or stand so close to each other that it was almost teasing, waiting to see which one of us would move those last few inches and give us what we both wanted. Finn walked into a room and, though I enjoyed the view, I often felt more alone than before he arrived.

My lungs were too small, and my skin too tight. I couldn't stay in this room with the proof of my romantic ineptitude. When I started to fidget, Galen moved to stand by the door. "Galen needs to go out," I said, my voice sounding giddy even to my ears. Of course, he just got back from a walk. But Finn didn't know that.

Finn's mouth once again twisted into a shape heretofore unseen outside of a Dr. Seuss illustration. "Be quick. We are on a schedule." This time, he actually pronounced "schedule" the British way: *shed-jewel*.

A number of catchy retorts came to mind — Of course, Jeeves, do bring the tea and biscuits into the parlor for us — but I decided that silence was the better part of valor in this case. Instead, I strapped Galen into his harness and slipped out the door. I took Galen around to the back of the building, dropped his leash and told him to take his time. The instruction wasn't necessary — give a male dog the opportunity, and he'll mark every blade of grass from here to Hades.

I sat on the ground, feeling the cool blacktop through the fabric of my shorts. The events of the last twenty-four hours swirled around in my head. Surprisingly, the nocturne wasn't the featured item. The memories that persistently plagued me were of Tony's eyes as he threw away the tissue, and Darcy's voice as he explained about his sister's state of mind. I didn't want to replay those scenes. Not ever. I deliberately watched my dog, studied the movement of muscle under fur, the way the yellowed streetlight turned his coat into one of a thousand colors, instead of just four.

"Kellan!" Tony looked down at me from the balcony. I was impressed that the rusty metal held his weight. "Hey. Finn's getting impatient."

"Tell him to go suck a—" I started to say, then reconsidered. After all, this was what I wanted all along, help from the master plotter. I pushed to my feet and called Galen's name, so he knew to zip it up. "We'll be right there."

Tony nodded and disappeared back into the apartment. I sighed and raised my face to the moon one last time. "Next time I complain about being lonely," I told Galen, "bite me on the ass, okay?"

He wagged his tail at me, another happy resident of doggy oblivion. "Come on, Tonto, let's go." With my trusty sidekick at my, well, side, I went back upstairs.

"Where did you take him, Chicago?" Finn asked as I closed the door. He sat in the armchair now, so, after unharnessing Galen, I walked over to the futon to stand next to Tony.

"Nah. Chicago traffic's a pain in the ass. So, what's the plan, Stan?" I didn't bother to hope he would ask for my input. This wasn't a consultation. This was a delivery.

"My plan is simple." Uh-oh. Finn's simple rarely translated into a normal person's simple. And he looked entirely too pleased with himself for my comfort. "You told him you would take him to the forest, so that's what you are going to do."

Yup. Definitely not simple. "Huh?" I said.

"Well, that's what you will tell him, anyway." He couldn't have just said that first? "Instead, you will take him to Diesel's farm. Lead him through one of the pastures, keep him occupied long enough for the nocturne to find you. Take care of the nocturne and the outsider with one rock."

My shoulders felt heavy. "I think you mean stone. Two birds with one stone, that's the saying."

Finn shrugged. Of course, cliché accuracy probably wasn't foremost on his mind.

Diesel was a Sankha who used to run a small dairy farm, about twenty-five minutes from my apartment, right outside a little three-bars-and-a-church town called Mount Vernon. About ten years ago, Diesel got reassigned to Nova Scotia, but the Sankhain still owned the farm land. "Darcy's not blind, you know. He'll probably notice we're in the middle of a field, not a forest."

Finlay didn't look happy that I was showing off my critical thinking skills. "You will explain to him that the forest is a short hike away from the road."

Despite the scent of scorched earth filling the air, I kept pressing. "A short hike with no trees in sight?"

Finn clipped off the ends of his words like his tongue was a pair of pruning shears. "As I recall, there is a copse of trees in the southwest corner of the property. You will take him there."

"Big difference between a copse and a forest."

Tony cut in on our little dance. "So by take care of, you mean what, exactly?"

Everyone just stared at him. He couldn't be asking because he didn't know. Even the dumbest youngling didn't graduate without knowing what "take care of him" entailed. Sankhain didn't leave loose ends. Our existence depended on secrecy. The moment he approached me, Darcy's life expectancy shrunk by about sixty years.

As the silence dragged on, Tony's jaw tightened. This was an ugly part of the job, and some Sankhain never got used to it. Usually I didn't have a problem with "take care of it," but then, usually I didn't spend time with the target before I killed him.

Without thinking, I said, "Maybe we could let him go. He's a smart guy. If we explain to him—"

"Kellan." All Finn said was my name, and I knew it wouldn't do any good to argue any more.

Tony and I looked at each other, then looked away. I didn't like Darcy. I didn't. He was a bane, a boil on the bottom of my foot. My world would be a happier place once he was dead. That should've been the truth. But a voice deep inside me screamed, "LIAR."

I sat on the floor and pulled Galen to me. "Are you sure the nocturne will be able to find us, all the way out at Diesel's?"

Now that I was asking reasonable, submissive questions, Finn's mood cooled down. "Yes. It tracked you from here to that park last night." He turned to Trini and Leanna. "You two will go ahead, scout out the property. Act as sentries. You have scopes for your rifles?"

"Of course," Leanna said, obviously insulted. Trini elbowed her, and Leanna said, "Sir."

Finn checked his watch. "I should be getting back," he said. On his way to the door, he stopped and stood over me. "Be careful," he said.

Maybe he'd cooled down, but I was still pretty cranky. So I mangled his name to bring him down to my level. "Oh, now, Findred, don't be pretending you give a shit. It'll ruin this whole indifferent-god thing you've got going on."

The corners of Finn's mouth turned down. "I'll expect a report when it's done."

I glared up at him. "Assuming the good guys win, how exactly am I supposed to give it to you? By phone? And what, I should leave a voicemail when you don't answer? Or maybe you want me to do it in person? Kinda tough, since I'm exiled and all. Oh, tell Janus I said hi, by the way."

Apparently done with me, Finn turned to Tony. "Time to go."

"What?" I said. "No. No way. I need him."

Finn frowned. "He was assigned as liaison. This entire episode will be over in a matter of hours. There is no need for him to continue in this post."

Frantic and not wanting to know why, I scrambled to out-logic Finn. "You're wrong. He's good at thinking on his feet. Better at bullshit than me. He's proved how valuable he can be, many times over." Tony's head swiveled to look at me. I couldn't blame him for the shock on his face. I felt the same way. "And, besides, we're dealing with a nocturne. I need back-up."

"If we have too many bodies in the field, the nocturne may choose not to strike," Finn said.

"And if we don't have enough, it might just kill us all!" I shot to my feet and stuck my nose in Finlay's face. Both of us huffed and puffed. Who would win? The big, bad wolf? Or the little pig? My voice dropped to a threatening growl. "Do you really want to be responsible for another nocturne massacre? What are you going to tell Janus when you lose another Hycene, one of only two remaining? And let the nocturne go free?" I let him think about that, then drew back and straightened my spine. "Tony stays."

I didn't wait for his response. Instead, I turned on my heel and walked into the kitchen, and started a fresh pot of coffee. My hands shook so bad I spilled grounds all over the floor. I gave up and just closed my eyes, leaning my head against the side of the fridge. I heard the apartment door open and close, hard. I couldn't be certain, but it sounded like one set of footfalls, not two. Was Tony still in the living room? I didn't move to look.

"We should probably hit the road then, huh, T?" Leanna said. Her voice was casual, but their shared scent grew stronger. Adrenaline ran high for all of us, right then.

"Yeah. Get set up, find our vantage points. See you soon, Tony." My heartbeat raced. The door opened and closed again.

I finally returned to the living room. Sure enough, Tony still stood there. "So," I said, "do you want to call Darcy, or should I?"

"You can have the honors." His voice sounded funny, thicker than it should. His scent was strangely empty. Bone-deep sadness was the only thing that stole a scent so completely. He turned and left the room without further comment.

The thought occurred to me that maybe he didn't want to stay. Maybe I should've let him leave with Finn. I didn't like that thought very much. It tasted like bad fish. I looked at Galen, who was watching me. "Guess I should make that call, huh?"

Galen didn't offer to do it for me, so I pulled my phone from my pocket. Darcy's phone rang and rang. By the fourth ring, I was on my feet and starting to pace. He finally answered after five rings. "Hello."

"Took you long enough. Were you at the urinal or something?"

"What? No. I — the — my sister was having some pain. I was getting the nurse to help her. She's on a morphine drip, you know, pretty powerful dose, but the pain still gets through sometimes." His voice drifted off.

I tried to imagine what it would be like, to know that Mal was in pain, and the best the medical community could do was shove a needle in her arm. I cleared my throat. "We're ready, if you want to head back this way. Remember, no dawdling. I don't need to tell you, we don't want to waste a single moment." I wanted to tell him to call me when he made it safely to his car, but I didn't want to scare him.

Tony reentered the living room. His eyes and nose looked red. Allergies? Maybe. But his scent was still subdued. Picking up Finn's discarded coffee, he carried it into the kitchen. I followed and watched him rinse the mug. As he wet a paper towel and started mopping up the grounds I spilled, the bad-fish thought popped up again. Maybe, given the fact that he apparently didn't want to kill Darcy, Tony would've preferred to go back to the forest. Maybe I should ask him.

But, the thought of being alone in this made my sphincter clench in a very unpleasant way. So I pretended not to notice the red-rimmed eyes. I'd rather play shallow and stupid than risk losing the closest thing I had to a friend.

"Darcy's going to die, for something that isn't his fault," Tony said.

I shrugged. "Lots of people do."

Tony turned on me. His anger smelled like jalapeno foccacia. "I'm not talkin' about lots of people. This isn't some freak bus accident we're talking about here. We're gonna take his life."

The fact that his words so perfectly mirrored my previous apprehension just pissed me off. "What did you think the job was going to be? Picking daisies? You wear that gun for shooting squirrels? And he's not completely innocent, you know. I gave him plenty of chances to walk away."

Tony's face shut down, lost its animation. And I felt a tightness in my chest that made it hard to breathe. "Look. We have to do our jobs. But, you know, if our captive were to escape before we got the job done... Even just long enough to say one last good-bye to his sister... Well, even the best Sankhain make mistakes."

Tony stared at me, his mouth dropping open slightly. Why did I say that? I wasn't the disobedient type, but I agreed with him. Darcy didn't deserve to die. He was just a stupid human who stumbled on something he didn't understand. Tony closed his mouth and squared his shoulders. "You'd get in trouble."

I shrugged, thinking of my earlier conversation with Mal. "I'm already in trouble. What are they going to do? The only punishment worse than exile is death, and I don't think Janus would kill me over this."

"You don't think so?" His voice implied that perhaps I should have something more concrete to say.

I didn't have jack. "Besides, who would he send to kill me? No one's good enough, or suicidal enough."

"Somebody's got healthy self-esteem."

"Hey, if it's true."

"Your sister's good enough."

I didn't even have to think about it. "She'd fight him on it. It's not a kill-worthy offense."

I could hear the frown in his voice, even if it was getting too dark to see it. "So she wouldn't wanna do it because it's not kill-worthy, not because she's your sister?"

"If I did something stupid enough that warranted my death, she'd take care of the problem. But this doesn't fall into that category. I think."

His scent grew stronger as he moved closer. "And you'd take that risk, all for him?"

I'd never just listened to his voice before. Now, in the dark, with only his scent and his sounds to judge by, I listened. It was a low, rumbly sound, like a dog who'd just been awakened from a dream. I swallowed hard. His voice must sound like that because of all the steroids. "It's not that big a risk." I remembered the sound of Darcy's voice, as he explained why it took him so long to answer the phone. "And it's not that small a thing."

"Hmm. The tin man has a heart."

One corner of my mouth tugged up. "Now if only the scarecrow could find a brain."

That low rumble took on an indignant tone. "If you're implying—"

"Not implying."

"Sweetheart, nobody's ever mistaken me for a scarecrow."

He'd taken another step closer. He was close, too close. The apartment was too damn small. I cleared my throat. "We should go."

"Yeah. Trini and Leanna will wonder what we're up to." His tone told me exactly what kinds of things he thought they'd be speculating about.

"Tony, there aren't enough hallucinogenic drugs in the world to make their imaginations go there. I gotta get dressed."

"Want some help?"

"I'd rather wear these clothes until they rotted off my body," I shot back over my shoulder. His low chuckle followed me to the bedroom. I didn't need clothes, exactly. I needed to arm myself, and adjust my outfit accordingly. I surveyed my closet and grabbed the sixteen-inch mini sword in a sheath that I wore between my shoulder blades with straps like a backpack. Then I needed a long-sleeve button-down shirt to hide the sword. My long hair hid the top of the hilt, where it peeked out from under the collar of the shirt. I strapped on my forearm sheathes and dug a pair of clean socks out of my dresser.

"I was thinking. We should blindfold Darcy," Tony said, when I returned to the living room.

"Why? You got a piñata in your pocket?"

"No. But I do think it'll help sell the whole illusion. Why would we let him see where the forest is? We blindfold him for the ride, and take it off when we get there."

"Oh." The idea was actually pretty smart. But I already sang his praises to Finn. I didn't want to feed his ego anymore than I already had. "Sure. What should we use for a blindfold?" I looked around, as if the perfect blindfold would jump up in my hand.

"I was thinking dishtowel. Do you think it'll draw attention to us? Riding around with a guy wearing a blindfold?"

"Not in this neighborhood. 'Don't ask, don't tell' has a whole different meaning here."

— «» —

Not wanting Galen to become a broken egg for this omelet, I left him at home. Just as we exited the building,

Darcy's car turned onto my driveway. He didn't look so good. His eyes were very bright, his pupils very large, and his face had an unnatural sheen to it. Like if I touched him, I might be able to dip my finger into his skin and scoop something out. I wondered which was harder, sitting by his sister's deathbed, or walking away from it.

Tony explained the necessity of the blindfold. "You understand, right? We need to maintain the safety of our secret." It was a little awesome, the way Tony could make anything sound legitimate. Like he did this all the time. Just another day at the office.

"Yes, of course." Darcy's voice, like his eyes, was about six shades too bright. Maybe we wouldn't have to kill him. Maybe he'd just drop from an overdose of adrenaline.

Once Darcy was blindfolded, loaded and buckled in, I handed Tony the truck keys and slid in next to Darcy.

Tony climbed in. Immediately, I understood my mistake. I was trapped, sandwiched between two strong scents. It was one thing to deal with a single person's scent in a cramped space, or multiple scents in a larger space. But to be bombarded with more than one foreign scent in such a small space, with no easy exit? No matter how my mind tried to be logical, my body told me I'd been cornered, and I better defend myself before I got hurt.

Tony put the truck in reverse, then slammed on the brakes as he looked at me. His voice was approaching-a-rabid-raccoon cautious. "You okay?"

With my jaw clenched, I could only breathe through my nostrils. Not a good plan. I was too afraid to switch to mouth breathing, though. If I moved any muscles, I might lose control completely.

"Kellan." Tony's voice was more insistent now.

"Kellan? Your name's Kellan? Is Kelly a nickname?"

Darcy's voice grated on my nerves. The urge to shift forms rose up in me, hard and fast like a sudden sneeze. If I didn't get out of that cab soon... I turned to Tony. "Move."

Tony followed my order instantly. I pushed past him and stumbled several feet away, until I couldn't smell either of them anymore. I breathed in the stench of the nearby trashcans like it was the sweetest potpourri.

I heard the scuff of boots on cement a split second before I caught his scent. "Kellan," Tony said. I didn't turn. I didn't want him to see the fear on me. "Look, I think I can get Darcy to talk. About how he found out about us, where those documents came from. But I'll need to spend some alone time with him. Would you be willing to ride in the bed of the truck?"

Christ, I forgot about the reason we were in this bloody mess. Darcy and where the fuck he'd found those papers. How did Tony figure out that I couldn't ride in between them? For now, I was just weak-kneed with gratitude for the out he offered. I tried to sound annoyed instead of pathetically relieved. "I guess I could."

"All right. Thanks."

Head held high, I walked past him, and even managed not to trip over my own feet as I went. Time to go hunting.

Chapter 14

It was a damn rough ride in the back of the truck. Apparently, those seat cushions made all the difference. I didn't mind, though. The cab could have been filled with Tootsie Rolls and rib-eye steaks, and I still would have been grateful for the scent of grass clippings and French fries that filled the covered bed.

When we arrived at the farm, I waited for Tony to let me out. Through the partition, I watched him remove Darcy's blindfold and tell him to sit tight. A quick check of my weapons made me feel prepared and brought the anticipation rushing back. I was already sniffing the air, even before Tony popped open the gate.

"Well, Lassie?" he asked. "How's it smellin'?"

I growled deep in my chest. "Fine, except Tony's about to get his ass tossed down a well."

"I think you mean Timmy."

"Nope. I said what I meant." As my eyes adjusted to the dark, I looked around the field. Why couldn't the moon ever be full when you needed it to be? We were two days past new moon, and while I could see fairly well, I knew Tony would be at a disadvantage. So would our lookouts, although I was willing to bet Trini had a night vision scope on her rifle.

I handed Tony the giant flashlight I kept in the truck. If we were really going to the forest, we'd never risk drawing attention to ourselves with flashlights. But we were trying to draw attention to ourselves. A giant beam of light worked even better than a bull's eye, considering our quarry would probably approach from above.

I angled my head toward the cab of the truck. "Did he tell you anything?"

Tony shook his head, sending a wave of scent my way. Odd, how someone who smelled like trash made me want to hunt, and someone who smelled like food didn't. I suddenly realized Tony was talking, and I had to ask him to repeat himself.

He rubbed his hand over the top of his shaved head. "I said, we didn't really have time. But I think he'll talk eventually. He seems to like me."

"Hmm, well maybe I should just let you two take your moonlit walk and have some privacy."

He patted me on the shoulder. "No need to be jealous, just because he likes me better than you."

"Yes, well, he hasn't known you very long. Give it an hour." I reached between my shoulder blades and loosened the sword in its sheath. "Just go get him so we can get on with this."

Tony placed a hand on the small of my back and pulled me against him. Before I could react, he kissed me. Pulling back slightly without loosening his grip, he murmured, "I took the blindfold off before I got out of the truck. Darcy's watching. Just wanted to be convincing."

Convincing, huh? I planted my hand on the back of his neck and pulled his mouth back down to mine. He tasted like coffee. His mouth was firm, and if he was a little bulkier than I usually like my men, I couldn't deny that all that muscle and potential strength felt good under my hands. I didn't exactly hate the kiss, and that realization was what made me let go.

I really needed to work on impulse control.

Tony's scent mirrored my icy shock and not-so-icy musk of … something I did not want to think about. Just to have something to do, I knelt to retrieve the flashlight. "Go get Darcy. Let's get this over with."

As Darcy came around the truck to stand a few feet away, he looked around. "Where are we?"

Yes, there is such thing as a stupid question. "At the forest, dumbass."

Tony stomped on my foot. I returned the favor by kicking him in the shin with my steel-toed hiking boot. He grunted, but didn't try to strike back. "What she means is, we brought you to the forest."

"That's what I said."

"Minus the dumbass."

"Well, I'd love to be minus the dumbass, but I seem to be stuck with two of them."

"Okay, enough." Darcy rubbed his temples. "Jeez. Aren't you two supposed to be the protectors of the universe or something?"

My face heated as his chastising hit home. "Or something."

"You act like a couple of third graders. Now are we going into the forest?"

I opened my mouth to say something scathing and witty, but Tony cut me off. "Yes," he said. I kicked him again. "Ow, stop doing that."

Darcy threw his hands up in the air. "For crying out loud. They couldn't have sent me to someone competent? They had to send me to Moe and Curly."

My ears pricked up. I wanted to pin him down and make him tell me who "they" were, but history had proven that approach ineffective. Instead, I tried continuing along the path of annoyance. Maybe if I kept pushing him, he'd slip up. "Hey, we brought you here, didn't we? Stop whining."

Tony stepped forward, hand outstretched, but he didn't have time to reprimand me.

"Whining?" Darcy said. "We're in a field in the middle of nowhere, and you're trying to convince me that we're at a forest."

"Think it through, genius," I said. "If the forest was there for everyone to see, every tree-hugger in the state would want to wander its paths. Not very conducive to secrecy, is it? The forest is invisible."

Darcy snorted, and it made me like him a little better. "Invisible? You really expect me to believe that?"

"You're just pissed because your benefactors didn't let you in on that little part of the story."

"Well, obviously, they didn't know, or they would have—" Darcy cut himself off, apparently realizing how much he'd said.

"They would have what?" I asked. Next to me, Tony was silent. Either he'd figured out that my bitchiness had a purpose, or he just didn't want to get kicked in the shin again.

Unfortunately, Darcy was silent now too.

"Okay, you know what?" I said. "I'm not going anywhere until you tell us what we want to know. You can talk and move forward, or you can stop right here. Do not pass go, do not collect two hundred dollars. It's up to you."

Fear scent rolled off him, but I didn't care anymore. Time and patience were luxuries of the non-predatory. After reaching into my pocket for a piece of gum to stem my urge to hunt, I leaned back against the truck, chewing loudly, and waited for Darcy to make his choice.

After several lifetimes of silence (or maybe it was five minutes), I began to doubt my strategy. Maybe he wouldn't talk. My gum was losing flavor, and I was craving something with a little more meat. "You promised you'd help me," Darcy said.

"Tough shit."

Tony jumped in. "But if you were to tell us what we need to know, that would make our job that much easier."

I caught the scent of fresh adrenaline, heard Darcy's heart beating faster. "I'll tell you," he said. Darcy's biorhythms told me there was a "but" in our future. "Right after you take me to the Spring."

I had to give the guy credit. We held almost all the cards, but Darcy was going to hang onto his one and only until he got what he wanted. Unfortunately for Darcy, I spent a couple centuries perfecting my stubbornness. He didn't have a prayer of winning this one. I turned to Tony. "All right. Let's go. Obviously, he doesn't want this all that bad." I started to climb back into the bed of the truck.

"Wait!" Darcy's voice cracked. I stopped, trying to feel satisfaction but feeling sick instead. "Do you have any siblings?"

Aw, jeez, not empathy, not again. I could have lied, but I didn't. "One. I have one sister left."

The smell of Darcy's hope was so much worse than his fear. "Then you understand. If it was your sister—"

"If it was my sister, and all I had to do to save her was answer a few questions, I'd sit up and bark like a fucking sea lion." I stared him down, trying to ignore my churning stomach, my tense shoulders. We weren't going to save Darcy's sister. I didn't even know if we could save Darcy.

I turned on the flashlight and shone it at Darcy. The beam made a fun-house clown out of his face. I saw the moment he gave in. His shoulders slumped slightly, and his head bowed. Then he raised his head and met my eyes. "Ask your questions."

If I hadn't been born with mostly silver hair, I would have blamed every gray hair from here to eternity on this blasted human. I opened my mouth to speak, then realized that I didn't know which question to ask first. Looking over at Tony, I spread my hands in front of me. The show's all yours, the gesture said.

"How did you find out about us?" Tony asked. "About the forest?"

Oh, good one.

Darcy hesitated again. He reeked of fear, and I could hear him taking shallow breaths through his mouth. "I — I can't."

"Darcy," I said, as gently as I could manage. I wanted to get this over with before the nocturne arrived and cut our interview short. I swallowed my impatience and forced my eyes to meet his, nice and steady. "I understand about secrets. But some secrets — it's better to tell." When he didn't respond, I kept trying. "Whoever gave you this information, they might have claimed to be helping you. But tell me the truth: who do you think you can trust? Them? Or us?"

Beside me, Tony made an approving sound. Darcy seemed to appreciate my tone as well — his eyes were slightly less wide, his breathing a little deeper. "I don't know who they were," he whispered, as though afraid they would hear him.

"Okay. That's fine." I waited some more.

Slowly, he gave us his story.

A few nights before he met me, Darcy was visiting his sister at the hospital. She was having a bad night, and the doctors encouraged him to consider moving her to a hospice. Darcy's voice cracked again. "So she could die comfortably."

I forced myself to take a deep breath, so I could more easily swallow the emotions rising up in my throat.

At about one in the morning, Darcy went to get a cup of coffee. He was sitting in the waiting room, drinking burnt coffee and trying to get a grip on himself, when they approached him. A man and a woman. Medium height, medium build. The only remotely interesting thing about them was that the man wore sunglasses. Indoors, at night. Darcy thought maybe he was blind, but then the man looked right at him. "He saw me. I know he did."

I nodded, keeping my expression blank. Lazy-ass nocturne didn't bother to change his eyes. You'd never see me shape-shifting half way.

Darcy told us that the couple started to make conversation. Who was he visiting, so sorry about your sister, how sad. Darcy thought about how he needed to talk to someone who wasn't going to bombard him with facts and terminology. What good luck that these two happened to come in at that moment.

I tilted my head back and looked at the sky. Luck. If it sounded too good to be true, it was probably going to kill you.

In his gratitude at finding a couple of confidants, Darcy never asked who they were or why they were at the hospital. When his coffee was done, they got up and wished him the best, and walked away. Darcy went back to his sister's room, and would have forgotten all about them if not for the following night's events.

He worked at the library until close. Shortly after eight-thirty, when the library was nearly empty, the door chime signaled someone entering. Darcy turned to let the newcomer know that the library closed in less than half an hour, when he saw it was the same couple from the hospital the night before. The man even wore the same sunglasses. At first, Darcy was suspicious at the coincidence, but he told himself he was being silly. Everybody went to the library at some point in their lives.

I couldn't keep my mouth shut any longer. "Darcy. Don't take this the wrong way, but — don't be one of those people who proves Darwin right, okay? If you have an instinct about something, *listen to it.*"

He was quiet for a long time, so long that I began to worry he wouldn't start talking again. I heard Tony's intake of breath, as he prepared to say something, when Darcy spoke. "You're right." He kept his eyes fixed on the dirt at his feet. "I knew it was weird, but then they started talking. About how they knew someone who could help my sister." He finally looked up at me. "They told me about you. They gave me those documents, said that the papers would lead me to a miracle cure. It was stupid. But I wanted so badly for it to be true."

I wanted to hate Darcy for being such an easy mark. I wanted to say he was better off dead, because clearly, he was too stupid to live. But Mal's face wasn't the only one crowding my mind. Taize, Sache, Regina, Vivi, all my sisters. I hated them for dying. But I hated myself, for failing to save them. Sure, it wasn't my fault, as I wasn't even allowed to follow them into battle. But since when did logic hold much sway in the realm of grief? Mal and I could've slipped into the ranks. We could've hidden among the cougars until we were too far from the forest for our mother to send us back. We might've been the difference in the outcome of the battle.

Neither the time nor the place. Even though I was sure Darcy was telling the truth, I didn't know what to make of his story. The man with the sunglasses was a nocturne, I was reasonably sure of that. What other reason would he have to wear sunglasses indoors two nights in a row? But where would a nocturne get Sankhain documents? And who was the woman? While nocturnes often lived in packs, they usually hunted alone. They didn't share food well. So why the change in hunting patterns? "Did they say anything else? Was that when they told you about the Sankhain?"

Darcy shook his head. "That happened later. The only other thing they said that night was not to tell you where I got the information. They said you—"

We all heard the noise, a rustling like something large moving through the dry grass. I closed my eyes and sniffed the air. Beside me, I heard the sound of Tony pulling his gun.

I didn't know where he kept his holster, and I didn't care. The smell of gun oil comforted me.

"Nocturne?" Tony asked me softly.

The wind was blowing the wrong direction. "I don't smell anything."

Tony did a bird call, our signal to Trini and Leanna. Then we waited.

Silence.

Not only were they not the ones rustling around in the brush, but they didn't respond at all.

Fuck.

"Maybe they're, ya know, gettin' busy." Tony's voice wanted to be hopeful, but failed.

I kept my voice soft, but still managed disdain. "Getting busy? Okay, nineteen ninety-three. Maybe you'd be the type to 'get busy' while you're on sentry duty, but they're professionals."

"What is it?" Darcy whispered behind us.

Well, Darcy, this is the part where you play worm-on-the-hook. Make it Oscar-worthy. "I don't know," I said instead. "Might just be a rabbit."

"Big fuckin' rabbit." Tony's voice sounded harsh. True, the noise was too loud to be anything smaller than a coyote. I didn't really think it was a nocturne, either. Unless it had taken human form, the nocturne would have made less noise than Thumper on tiptoes. Why would the nocturne expend the energy to shape-shift into a human and then hide in the bushes? Maybe it had seen me and Tony, and got scared off when it realized Darcy wasn't alone.

Too much thinking. Time to act. I wanted to know where Trini and Leanna were. I tossed the flashlight to Tony. "You go right, I'll go left. Meet you in the middle. Call if you find … anything." I ordered Darcy to get in the truck. "Lock the doors, and don't open them for anyone. Not even me or Tony. Okay?"

I couldn't see his expression in the glow of the flashlight, but I saw his head bob unnaturally fast as he backed toward the passenger side door. I waited until Darcy was safely locked in the cab of the truck before I took off. If the nocturne was waiting for us to leave, it might decide that the easiest way to get Darcy out of the truck would be by disguising itself as Tony or me. Hence my instructions. It was the most I could do to keep him safe.

I could barely hear Tony off to my right, and only hoped that I was making as little noise as he was. Then I let go of that thought and gave myself over to the scents around me. Filtering out the expected fauna and flora, I searched for things that didn't belong.

As I drew even with the spot the rustling originated from, I found what I was looking for — a scent that stood out like a green mohawk at a Republican convention. Fresh blood, of the human variety. Human blood smelled a little sweeter, less tart, than animal blood. I followed my nose to the source, then dropped to my knees. Leanna lay in the grass. I could hear her heartbeat, but blood flowed from her scalp into the ground. I could smell the mingling of the two, earth and iron, a heady, succulent scent. My stomach growled.

Pulling off my long-sleeved shirt, I pressed it to the wound and trilled my tongue in a call to Tony and Trini. The breeze on my sweat-soaked arms chilled me.

As I waited, I searched the ground around me. I found a jagged rock with Leanna's blood on it, just as the beam of the flashlight announced Tony's arrival. He shone the light in my direction.

"Bright." I dropped the rock and raised my hand to shade my eyes.

Instantly, he lowered the beam. "Sorry." I heard the sharp intake of breath that meant he'd seen Leanna. His scent changed to an anxious sourdough smell, but his voice was steady. "How bad?"

"It looks like somebody hit her over the head, and cut her scalp in the process," I told him. "Shallow, but it bled a lot. We should get her to Simone." I asked if he'd found Trini. He hadn't. I sniffed the air. Useless. Between Tony and Leanna's scents, and all the blood, I didn't have a prayer of finding Trini. I tied the shirt around Leanna's head. "You still have the truck keys?" I asked. When he nodded, I said,

"Good. You take her to the truck, and check on Darcy. I'll find Trini and meet you back there."

He nodded and carefully picked Leanna up. As he walked away, I sought out the rock I'd dropped. Raising it to my nose, I took a deep sniff. And started sneezing. Under the blood, the scent of strong perfume clung to the rock. As I wiped my nose on the hem of my tank top, I felt understanding dance cold over my skin. Unless Leanna's attacker had colossally bad taste in toiletries, I suspected that they knew who and what I was, and tried to mask their scent accordingly. And that made no sense. The nocturne already revealed itself to me. Why try to hide its identity now?

Wait a second. The librarian, Ditzy or whatever her name was. She wore enough perfume to make a bomb-sniffing dog cry. Was she the woman, the other half of the nocturne pair? But no, Darcy knew Ditzy. He said he'd never seen either one of mysterious visitors before. Besides, I couldn't see Ditzy hitting anyone over the head with a rock, much less an experienced warrior like Leanna.

But what could get the drop on Leanna?

I shook my head, stuck the rock in my cargo pocket, and started moving again on the same track. More questions, more thinking. Just give me something to fight, already. Was that really so much to ask for?

And where the hell was Trini? I knew she and Leanna would have split up — no sense in having two sentries in the same spot — but it didn't make sense for her to be too far out, either.

After going about thirty more feet, I was ready to start back and hope I found her somewhere along the path Tony took. Then I caught it, that same scent of blood and earth. I broke into a run. There was a stand of trees up ahead. When I was still a few feet from the trees, I stopped for another sneezing fit. Perfume-face spent quite a bit of time here. Lying in wait, perhaps?

When my nasal passages cleared a little, I caught another scent that gave me pause. Gun powder. And blood that wasn't human. Had Trini gotten a piece of her attacker?

I hadn't smelled any non-human blood by Leanna, which either meant that the perfume-wearer attacked Leanna before Trini, or that it healed very fast.

When I finally reached Trini's prone form, I knew that it was the latter. Trini was attacked first. First, and more thoroughly. The ground around her body was squishy with blood, and I counted three stab wounds. I held my breath as I knelt beside her. I couldn't hear a heartbeat. I placed a finger to her carotid artery.

She had a pulse! Barely, but it was there. I was afraid of the damage I might do if I moved her. Nothing to be done about it, though — if I didn't move her, she'd die where she lay.

As I picked Trini up in my arms, I held my breath, waiting for her to moan in pain. Of course, she didn't. She was far from conscious.

When we got close to the truck, I saw the bob of the flashlight, as Tony paced just behind the tailgate. He looked up at the sound of my footsteps, and when he saw what I carried, ran to meet me. "Don't," I panted as he moved to take her from me. "She's worse than Leanna. Stab wounds. She needs Simone. Fast."

He halted. I laid Trini beside Leanna, on the blankets Tony must've spread across the bed of the truck. Then I doubled over, planting my hands on my knees. I struggled to catch my breath. I really needed to start carrying weight on my back when I jogged.

A ridiculous train of thought, but I grabbed onto anything to forget I was covered in the blood of two good friends.

Tony's feet came into view. "Come on, get in the truck. We gotta get to camp."

I shook my head. I'd thought about it as I carried Trini back. "Darcy can't go to camp. He'll slow down the process. You go. I'll call ahead, let Simone know you're coming. After you get them to Simone, you can come back for Darcy and me."

Tony tensed. I straightened up and looked him in the eyes. "Tony. They need you. Get your ass in the fucking truck and go."

His scent ebbed back to normal. Give a guy a job and he won't be afraid. "Darcy won't let me in the cab."

"You have the keys."

Tony shrugged. I marched over to the passenger side of the truck cab. I knocked on the window. Darcy jumped. Good. I hoped he peed his pants. Just a little, not enough to soil my upholstery. "Darcy," I said loudly. Then I saw the gun. I looked at Tony. "Who gave him a gun?"

His head ducked as he studied his boots. "I put one in the glove box. While we were driving here, I told him that if anything happened, he should get the gun to defend himself."

I stared at him. "He's a librarian, Tony, not Rambo." I motioned for Tony to go around to the driver's side. "Stand by the window and try not to do anything stupid, okay?" Then I turned back to Darcy and made sure I spoke nice and clear. "I know I told you not to open the door. You did a great job. But Tony has the keys. See?" I pointed to the driver's side, where Tony obediently held up the keys. "And he needs to drive my friends to the doctor. You and I are going to stay here. We still have to go to the forest. Open the door and get out here."

Darcy hesitated just long enough that my temper flared. I reached back over my shoulder to draw the sword and give him something real to think about. Before I even loosened it from the sheath, he popped the lock on the door and opened it. He didn't get out yet. "We're still going?"

I closed my eyes, took a deep breath. "Yes, Darcy. I'll take you to the North fucking Pole to see Santa and his reindeer if you just get out of the truck."

He slid down off the seat. Before Darcy's feet even hit the ground, Tony opened up the driver's side door and vaulted in. I relieved Darcy of his misbegotten weapon and, after checking that the safety was on, shoved the little peashooter into my pocket. I slammed the passenger door as Tony put the truck in drive.

As I watched the taillights melt into the night, I pulled out my cell phone and hit speed dial six, for the infirmary. Simone answered. I told her what had happened, and that

Tony was on his way. She thanked me and hung up the phone. No time for chit chat when you're the one who keeps all the Sankhain alive.

Sticking the phone back in my pocket, I sat down on the ground. While I kept a close nose on my surroundings, I took advantage of the quiet to rest a little. I imagined Trini and Leanna bouncing around in the bed of the truck. I pictured Tony's lips pressed together in a thin line as he drove as fast as he could, while knowing that with every bump he was probably hurting his saviors even worse. Simone would have younglings with stretchers waiting at the edge of the forest. And maybe Trini and Leanna would survive. Lots of people believed in far less plausible things.

Darcy sat down next to me and picked up the flashlight. "Are you going to tell me what's going on?" he said.

Maybe when we finished talking, he could give me a root canal. Then we'd really have a party. "Can you be more specific?"

Darcy made a strangled sound. "What happened to your friends? Why did you make me lock myself in the truck? Why did you tell me not to open the door, even for you?"

"I was afraid that was what you meant." I swatted a mosquito and put off answering. Even though the technique never worked, I still clung to the hope that if I ignored something long enough, it would go away.

Once again, that logic proved faulty. "So?" Darcy said. "Are you going to tell me?"

"If I say no, will you stop asking?"

I could feel the weight of his glare. When he answered, he sounded a little angry. "No."

Still, I didn't answer. I didn't know what to say, how much to say.

He bolted to his feet. "Why can't you just talk to me? What else could you possibly have to hide?"

Seriously? He'd die of old age before I could finish the prologue to the answer to that question. You might think, she's been doing this for two hundred years, one would expect she'd be better at this by now. But most of my life I spent at camp, doing odd jobs and handling the younglings that the rest of the instructors gave up on. Even after Janus decided he wanted me out in the field, I didn't have to deal with explaining myself. Nobody knew about us, so nobody asked me questions. Until now. Just because I'd been alive for two centuries didn't mean I couldn't land in new brain-paralyzing situations.

Maybe I could just explain that to Darcy. I'm sorry, sir, but that isn't my department. Let me forward you to the Department of Human Lies and Misdirection. One moment please.

If only.

I chose my answer and turned to face my inquisitor. "Why don't you start by telling me what you do know? I'm not really in the mood for telling stories you've already heard."

"I asked you first." He smelled afraid. I began to wonder if I'd misjudged his natural scent, and he just reeked like fear all the time.

I stared him down, feeling anger, frustration, and inadequacy burn in my chest. "What are you, five years old? Those women could die, because they were waiting out here for us. For you. Suck it up and tell me your story already."

In the light of the flashlight, I saw him blink at me, then avert his eyes to the grass. "I'm sorry about your friends."

I sighed. I preferred his anger to his sympathy. If he was angry, I got to respond in kind. I felt my vocal chords grind together, like their gears lacked lubrication. "Thanks." I tried to remember where Darcy left off in the telling. "So, the night the noc—" I stopped. I hadn't told Darcy about nocturnes yet. Keep it simple until you absolutely, positively can't. "Um, when the couple came to the library. You said they told you not to tell me about them?"

Darcy kept his eyes on the ground, loudly breathing in and out through his nostrils. "Right. Well. What they said was, you would want to know, and if I kept it from you, I could make you help me. Blackmail you with it, I guess."

After Darcy confronted me the first time, he said, they showed up at the library again. They asked how his meeting with me went, and when they heard how I took the documents away from him, they sat him down. "That's when they told me about the Sankhain. They explained how important secrecy was to you, and that I needed to mention the forest and the Sankhain, but not to say where I got the information. If you needed information from me, you would give in and take me to the forest." He smiled bitterly and angled his head so he could meet my eyes. "But you haven't done that, have you?"

The burning in my chest spread to my face. This should be Tony, I thought. He should be talking to Darcy, and I should be driving the wounded back to camp. He was better at talking, and I was better at driving like a crazy person. Except Tony wasn't exiled, so he could enter the forest without tripping over red tape. "What makes you say that?"

"If you're taking me to the forest, why are we still sitting here?"

The best lies have a grain of truth to them, right? "I need to make sure it's safe, before we go anywhere."

"Safe? From what? From whoever hurt your friends? You think they're still here? Then why didn't we go with Tony? What are we doing just sitting here? Why—"

"For god's sake, shut up." The venom in my voice surprised even me. "I don't know. But if you just give me a minute to think, maybe I can figure out this super-sized bucket of shit. Okay?"

He wanted to pursue it. I could smell his secondary line of attack poised and ready. Then he seemed to pull back. Maybe he heard the desperation in my voice, or maybe he finally realized it was a bad idea to piss off the chick with the sword. I was grateful for the peace.

Gratitude made me magnanimous. "You're safe with me. These blades aren't for show. I'll protect you."

He looked at me doubtfully, which annoyed me.

"What?" I said. "You gotta have testicles to protect someone? Welcome to the twenty-first century."

"Sorry."

I waved my hand and pulled some long weeds from the ground. Without realizing what I was doing, I started to make an effigy.

"What's that?" Darcy said.

I looked down at my hands. When Mom of the Year was off waging war and Mal and I felt scared, Janus taught us to make effigies, little grass dolls. Put your intentions into them as you weave them, Janus told us. Sacrifice them to fire, and in return, fire will offer an answer. Some people might say fire can't talk, but they'd probably say women can't turn into wolves either. Some people don't know as much as they think they do. As we got older, we taught ourselves different ways to weave the body-grass together, making it look more like a solid thing and giving us more time to concentrate on our intentions. I didn't want to explain all that to Darcy. Turned out, I didn't need to.

"It looks like an effigy," he said.

I didn't bother trying to hide my surprise. "That's because it is an effigy."

"May I?" He held out his hand, and I placed the half-finished doll in his palm.

"Be careful," I said. Silently, I finished, *my intentions are in there*.

He nodded, studying my handiwork. The weaving was a little ragged — it had been years since I bothered with the old stuff, effigies and purifying with herbs, protective stones. Nostalgia pulsed through me for a moment before I turned my attention back to the problem that held my magick in his hand.

"I've seen pictures of these," he said. "Nothing this intricate, though. Where'd you learn how to weave one like this?" He teased at the weaving, as if he would unravel it.

I plucked it out of his hand and spoke before my brain could stop me. "I've been making effigies since before your grandfather's grandfather was in short pants. And don't unravel someone else's effigy. It's rude."

When I realized what I admitted, I held my breath. All the possibilities for his next question crowded my head. But I never imagined that he would say, "It's the Spring, isn't it? It's some kind of fountain of youth?"

I stared at him. He didn't know what the Spring was? Mental head slap. Had I gotten us into this mess over some guy who'd been fed a bunch of keywords, who didn't actually know anything? "What exactly did those people tell you about us?"

His eyes went wide. For someone with enough information stored in his brain to recognize a half-finished effigy at twilight, he didn't have a whole lot of sense, and he seemed to realize it now. As he answered, his fear scent increased tenfold. Somebody wasn't accustomed to deception. "They, um, they told me everything."

"Darcy, Helen Keller could hear the lie in your voice." I was getting hungry, and all my emergency energy bars were in the glove box of my truck. Then I remembered the Tootsie Rolls in Trini's duffel. "Come on," I said. "We need to find something."

As we walked, Darcy didn't ask any questions. I found his silence oddly disturbing. I began to hum Metallica's "Enter Sandman" to fill the void.

I found Trini's duffel stuffed in the tree she must've been hiding in. It was nestled in the V formed by the thick branch and the trunk. I climbed up and grabbed it, then jumped back to the ground. My ankles groaned as they absorbed the shock of the ten-foot jump. I shook my legs out and I was fine.

Darcy was staring at me. I started humming again and ignored him as I unzipped the duffel bag. I dug out a handful of candy and offered some to Darcy. He started to shake his head, then changed his mind and grabbed a few pieces. "Keep up my strength, right?" he said with that charming smile.

I sighed. Just when I forgot that he possessed any likable qualities, he pulled out that smile. Reminding myself of how he'd manipulated me, I waited until he swallowed his mouthful of chewy goodness before I repeated my question. "How much do you really know? The truth this time, or so help me…" My voice trailed off, but it carried the promise of a threat, even without the specifics.

"Look," he said. "I didn't mean to give you the wrong impression."

I raised my eyebrows.

"Okay, maybe I did." He sounded nervous, but as he spoke, his fear lessened. "But I didn't want to do it. They just made it very clear that you weren't going to do this for me out of the kindness of your heart. You had to think I knew everything. You had to think I was a threat."

Who woulda thunk it? The pale-ass little librarian managed to fool the big bad wolf. Yeah, it occurred to me once or twice during our encounters that he was lying. But I never would've guessed that he didn't know what he was talking about.

"You're wasted on the public library," I said. "You should have joined the CIA."

He looked a little surprised. His fear scent dropped to a level consistent with someone who just witnessed two mangled women being carried out of the darkness. "I really didn't want to do it," he repeated.

"Good. Don't do it again."

Darcy told me the exact words the nocturnes fed him. Just tell her you know about the Sankhain, and the forest, and the Spring. Tell her you need her to take you to the Spring. And when he asked for clarification— "They got really quiet," he said. "The one with the sunglasses lost all expression. No smile, no frown, no raised eyebrows. Nothing." He paused. "It scared the crap out of me. I said, you know what, I don't need to know any more. Then they smiled and were all friendly again."

Again, I shook my head. "Why did you throw your lot in with the Creepy Twins? Honestly, Darcy. You said they scared the crap out of you."

"My sister."

I sighed and rubbed my eyes. Without considering the consequences, I said, "Darcy, I can't help your sister. None of this is going to help your sister. All it's going to do is get you killed."

He frowned. It took him a long time to work through that information and form a reaction. "But you said—"

"I lied," I told him. "People do that. Especially people who wear sunglasses at night so you can't see their eyes."

He pointed his finger at me. "We aren't talking about him. We're talking about you. You lied to me."

"Yeah, and you lied to me. Wow, look at that. Everybody lied. How disillusioning."

He stood up. "No. You don't get to make jokes about this. This isn't funny. You led me on, about my sister's life."

He was right. And what he did to me wasn't even in the same tax bracket as what I'd done to him. The thick, sweat-riddled nausea of guilt settled over me.

It didn't matter now. I rose to my feet and faced him, wishing I was about eight inches taller. That would make intimidation so much easier. Ah, well, guess that was what knives were for. I reached back and scratched my neck, causing the hilt of the sword to shift into a more visible position. Then, when his eyes were focused on the hilt, I responded to his accusation. "You're right. This isn't funny. But I'm not the one who gave you false hope, Darcy. They did that." He opened his mouth to disagree, but I couldn't let him do that — I needed to bring him over to my side, even if it meant manipulating the truth. "I never told you I could help your sister. I said I would take you to the forest. If you chose to believe something beyond that, it's not my fault. I'm a bitch and a liar. But without my help, you will be dead too, very soon."

His mouth hung open for a moment, then snapped shut. In the air around me, I could smell his anger, the spicy scent of ginger tea. Not the scent of fear. For once, I would have liked Darcy to be afraid. If he wasn't afraid, it meant he didn't take me seriously.

"Why should I believe you're here to help me?" he asked finally. "You already lied to me. Why should I trust you at all?"

Hmm. Tough question. If he survived the nocturne, and that was a big if, I'd be the one to kill him. But he might survive, and I could maybe postpone his execution. Telling him all this, however, seemed an unwise course of action. "We're out in the middle of nowhere, with no transportation and a homicidal something-or-other out there in the dark. You should trust me because I'm all you've got."

He was quiet again, his muscles slowly relaxing as he down-shifted from anger to resignation. "What do we do now?" he asked.

Boy, he was just full of difficult questions tonight. I shoved the effigy in my pocket, unwilling to toss it away. It held some of my energy, after all. Just as I struggled to come up with my next move, I heard the best sound in the world — the distant rumble of my truck. "He's back," I said, relief thinning my voice.

I took off at a jog, glancing over my shoulder every few strides to make sure Darcy still followed. We covered the distance in a fraction of the time it took me to carry Trini. When Tony pulled up, he put the truck in park, but left it running. He hopped out and strode over to me. He pulled me to the other side of the truck, where we could see Darcy, but he couldn't hear us.

I opened my mouth to ask what was going on, when I smelled more blood. It didn't belong to Trini and Leanna. After a quick search of his body, I noticed the cut on his forehead. Automatically, I reached up to touch it. "What happened?"

He waved my hand away. "It's nothing."

"It's not nothing, you're bleeding. What happened?"

"I—" His jaw was tense. "I disagreed with Janus about my orders."

Sudden anger made me go still. "He hit you?"

"Never mind. I shouldn't'a — I coulda been more diplomatic. Anyway. Orders are to take you immediately to camp. To incapacitate you if I have to."

I blinked at him, surprised. Incapacitate me? I hadn't done anything insubordinate. This time. "Did you tell him about the plan to..." I lowered my voice. "Let Darcy go?"

Tony's scent warmed with annoyance. "Of course not." His next words sounded like they belonged to someone else. "Janus is very displeased with this operation, and wishes to discover the reason for its colossal failure."

"What failure?" I hissed. "It's not my fault the nocturne attacked Trini and Leanna instead of Darcy. It was their stupid plan."

Tony's eyebrows fused into a single line. "It was our job to execute the plan. And please don't call it stupid to his face, ah 'ight?"

The slip in grammar meant he was worried. Tony worried was as disconcerting as Darcy silent.

Tony said he was taking *me* to camp. He never mentioned Darcy. I doubted we were going to just drop him off at home and thank him for the lovely evening. No, Darcy wasn't leaving Diesel's farm. Mal's face flashed in my mind. A person should be able to say goodbye to his sick sister.

I'd done everything by the book so far, and all it got me was a couple of badly wounded friends and an attachment to a stray librarian. The book wasn't working. Besides, killing Darcy now made no sense. We had a nocturne to catch, and Darcy was still our best bait. Janus would see that when we brought him the nocturne's head. Maybe I didn't need the effigy after all. "We have to swing by my apartment to pick up Galen," I told Tony.

Tony stared at me. "I think your ponytail's too tight. Cuttin' off the circulation to your brain. We gotta go to camp."

"But Galen's all alone. He needs me. Of course, if we made any stops… Things happen. Prisoners escape. If we make a stop."

Tony's eyebrows relaxed. "We'd get in trouble. But then, we already are."

"And if something were to happen, I am an awfully good tracker, after all. I could find him again." I might still have to kill him, but he'd get to say goodbye.

Tony leaned in close. His mouth stopped a mere breath from mine. "I like the way you think, wolf." A shiver rode my body at the way he uttered "wolf." In Tony's deep growling tone, it came out a cross between a compliment and a come-on. "We better go get Galen. Wouldn't want to make him wait."

Do what you're told, be a good soldier, and get your jollies by annoying as many people as possible. Those were the commandments I lived by. Allowing Darcy to go free broke all my rules, even the last one, since I had a feeling jollies weren't in the cards tonight. I waited for the trepidation, the resistance about going against my leader's wishes. But all I felt was certainty. "Okay. Let's go."

Chapter 15

As I rode in the bed of the truck and tried not to breathe the scent of blood, I wondered why the Thing in the Bushes didn't come after me and Darcy. It ambushed Trini and Leanna. Did I really look so badass that I scared it away? Doubtful. Leanna looked a lot more badass than I did. And Darcy looked about as badass as Big Bird, so it wasn't like my back-up scared it off.

When we pulled into my parking lot, I was already waiting by the tailgate. As soon as Tony opened the gate, I sprung out. "Good, I'm starving," I said.

"You're so weird." The awe in Tony's voice made me smile.

I glanced back at Darcy, who was still sitting in the cab of the truck. "I was thinking we should let Darcy beat us up."

Tony looked at me skeptically. "You make Hitler sound like the voice of reason. What the hell are you talkin' about?"

"If we show up at camp all bloody and bruised, we can say that he knocked us out and got away."

His skepticism lingered. "And they're gonna believe this librarian got the jump on two trained warriors?"

Hmm. Hadn't really thought about that part. "Well, there's no one to contradict us."

"Kellan, if I was Janus and two of my Sankhain came in with that story, I'd kill them. If they're lying, they're hiding something from me that could be a threat to the Spring. If they're telling the truth, they're completely incompetent."

He really was better at this than I was. "Well, what do you suggest?"

He shrugged. "There's always the be-honest-and-face-the-music route."

"Yeah, I don't really like that one. You got anything better?"

He didn't even bother thinking about it. "Sorry. I think that's the best one."

"Damn." I was going to get locked in solitary for a month. Then Darcy turned and looked at us through the back window. I saw the hope on his face. Some part of him still believed we could help him. "All right. Let's get this over with."

I walked around to the passenger door and yanked it open. "Go away," I said. No need to sugar coat anything.

Darcy looked confused. "What do you mean?"

"I mean, get in your car and drive. Go back to the hospice and sit with your sister. Go to your apartment and sleep. Go to Disney World and dance with Cinderella. I don't care, just get out of here."

"But—"

"Oh, yeah, almost forgot." I reached into the glove box and rummaged until I found a pen and a piece of paper. Jotting down my cell number, I handed it to Darcy. "If you see that couple from the hospital, call me. Then run far, far away."

Darcy's frown deepened. "But—"

I pulled him out of the truck and slammed him into the hood of his car. Pain usually got the point across. I made sure I looked him in the eyes, and tried to ignore the hurt look they carried. "Go. Away."

"Tell me what's going on."

Darcy had that stubborn look on his face that meant he would keep coming back. Like herpes. I glanced at Tony. He shrugged. "This is your show, babe."

I took a deep breath that accomplished two tasks. One, it allowed me to belatedly scan the area for scents that didn't belong. And two, it calmed me so I didn't punch Tony in the nose for calling me "babe." Not that he didn't deserve it, but he'd been bloodied enough for one night.

Before me, Darcy looked immovable. Next to me, Tony cleared his throat. His scent washed over me as he leaned in close to my ear. His stubble abraded my cheek. "Okay, I'll take this one. But you owe me."

I opened my mouth to reply, but Tony started talking. Probably just as well — I had absolutely no idea what my reply would have been.

"You know how, in horror movies, there's always that guy who believes in ghosts long before everyone else, and when everybody else starts believing, he gets to say I told you so?"

Darcy frowned at Tony, and I joined him.

"Well, me and Kellan are that guy, and you're everybody else. Guess what. All those things you see in horror movies? They exist, and then some. It's the 'and then some' that's hunting you."

Darcy thought for a long time. I couldn't blame him — I knew what Tony was talking about, and it took me almost as long to unravel that knotted, twisted statement.

Darcy's eventual question proved he managed to unravel it. "What do you mean, hunting me?"

"Those people at the hospital," I said. "They didn't just happen upon you and offer the information out of the goodness of their hearts."

Tony and I took turns telling Darcy about nocturnes — what they were, what they did. Why they were after him.

Darcy's eyes got wider and wider, and he finally held up a hand to stop us. "This is insane."

Invisible forests and magick cures, documents that looked like they were written under the influence of hallucinogenic drugs, and he only now reached his crazy threshold? This guy was either really impressive or just as crazy as we were. "You're not the first to think that," I said. "Unfortunately, truth is usually crazier than fiction."

Darcy thought for a while longer. "If this is true," he said, then stopped. After a deep breath, he tried again. "If this is true, then I assume it was a what? Nocturne? A nocturne that was out in that field with us."

"I'm not sure about that." The words shocked me, but they felt true. The nocturne wouldn't have bothered with perfume to hide its scent from me. Something else was in that field, and tracked down and tried to kill my friends.

Tony made a surprised sound. We never got to discuss the perfume, with all the bleeding going on. But I didn't want to explain my supernatural sniffer to Darcy. I laid my hand on Tony's arm to keep him from interrupting with inconvenient questions.

Darcy was forming another thought. "Were we out there to catch those things? Were you ... using me as bait?"

Goddamn, this guy was good. Too bad he was under a death sentence; he could come in handy. "Well." I drew the word out into several syllables to delay having to continue the sentence.

"Oh my god, you were." The scent of lemon-ginger tea told me he was angry. "You used me."

"Oh, for Pete's sake, it's not like I fucked you and never called."

Darcy took a step toward me, his face a savage mask. "You all manipulated me. You're all monsters."

Because it was true, I almost quailed, almost took a step back. "I'm not the one who handed you the false hope to begin with. They sent you on a wild goose chase, so that when the time came to kill you, you'd taste like veal rather than stew meat."

"You opportunistic..." He searched for the right word. Five letters, started with "b" and rhymed with "witch." But of course, not everyone was as willing as me to use the right word. "You're an opportunist who twisted the situation to serve her own ends."

Anger heated my skin. I backed away, toward my apartment building, shouldering Tony out of my path. "You know what? I give up. You're right. Like I really wanted to spend my entire evening in the company of a naïve little human, to risk my life to save someone who obviously doesn't want to be saved. Go, fly, be free. Just try not to get killed in my parking lot. I don't want to have to explain the bloodstains."

With both men staring at me, I turned and walked away. Just before I rounded the corner of the building, I looked back at Tony. "You coming or what?" When he looked at Darcy, I made a disgusted sound. "Leave him. I'd hate to inflict our opportunistic opportunist selves on him any longer."

With a scent like jalapeno foccacia bread, that promised loud questions as soon as we got inside, Tony followed me to the front door and up the stairs. Then, when the apartment door closed behind us, he turned to face me, the sharp bite of his frustration growing stronger in the air. "What the fuck was that? You didn't have to be so awful to him. His sister's dying."

I knelt to greet Galen, who was wagging his tail until he passed Tony. Now Galen positioned himself between Tony and my body. I could smell him going into high alert mode, so I stood up. Hard to be authoritative on your knees.

I made a gentle shushing sound. "It's all right, big dog, you done good. He'll behave now." I looked up at Tony. "Right?"

Drawing in an audibly deep breath, Tony slowly lowered himself into a crouch. Rather than looking into Galen's eyes, a direct challenge to a dog, Tony glanced up at me. His voice a quiet rumble, he said, "I'll behave."

Galen's scent relaxed. I, however, felt a suspicious tightness in my throat. Tony did everything exactly as he should, right down to making himself submissive to me. Maybe he did it to keep Galen from ripping his throat out, but I didn't think so. No, call me crazy, but I was pretty sure he did it just to make Galen feel better.

I looked away from Tony, who still crouched before us, watching my face. Wandering over to the window, I looked out to see Darcy's little beater turn left out of my driveway. "Good," I murmured. Turning away from the window, I walked past Tony to enter the kitchen. I was still hungry.

With Galen's head right beside mine, I rummaged around in the fridge, searching for sandwich fixings. I piled bread, cheese and ham on the cutting board, nudging Galen out of the way. "You want a sandwich?" I called to Tony.

His scent mingled with that of the food as he wandered into the room. "We should get back to camp."

"You'd rather get drive-thru on the way?"

"Ugh. No. Want some help?"

I started slicing the cheddar. "It's complicated stuff, but I think I can manage."

Tony made an indecipherable sound and started to leave the kitchen.

I felt bad, like I just kicked him out of his domain. The kitchen was more Tony's area than mine now, even though he'd only been here a couple days. "Actually, you want to put on a pot of coffee while I do this?"

"You really think we should take the time for coffee?"

I laughed humorlessly. "I think the outsider is still alive and we're late for Judgment Day. Coffee may be essential to surviving the ass-kicking."

"Right. Extra-strong coffee, it is."

I smiled down at my bread.

"What was with the schizo mood swing down there?" he said, starting the coffee. "One minute, you were all helpful info-desk girl, the next you were, well…"

My smile widened. "Come on, Tony, you can say it. I was a bitch."

"Oh, so you do realize that."

I handed him a sandwich. "Of course I do. You think I go around under the delusion that I'm Miss Congeniality?"

I downed a sandwich in two swallows, then immediately reached for a second. I used my hip to push him away from the coffeemaker, then poured two cups. The smell hit me long before I had the mug to my lips.

"Wow." I got high on the fumes. "Good coffee." It was almost too strong to swallow without choking. "Mmm. I love coffee."

"Honey, Juan Valdez and his donkey don't love coffee as much as you do."

Breathing deep, I took another slower sip. Tony watched, like he saw something way more entertaining than my face. The warmth of the coffee inside me extended farther south than it should've.

With the bipeds so distracted, Galen took advantage of the situation. Rearing up on his hind legs, his front paws never even touching the counter, Galen swiped the remaining two sandwiches off the cutting board. He seemed to swallow without chewing, so by the time I set down my mug and pried open his jaws, the food was already down his throat.

Tony topped off my coffee mug. "He eats even faster than you."

Surprised out of my self-annoyance, I laughed. "You hear that, Galen? He just paid you a compliment."

Tony watched us with a lingering grin before turning serious again. "You never answered my question. Why were you so mean to Darcy?"

I drained my coffee. "You about done? We should get going. We can talk about this in the car."

He nodded. We left, with Galen prancing along between us. This time I drove, and Galen claimed the passenger window seat. After I explained that he'd be less likely to puke up the sandwiches if he could stick his head out the window, Tony gladly let the dog have the window and he sat in the middle. Then he looked at me expectantly.

I picked up the conversation where we'd left off. "We needed to get rid of him, remember? And he wouldn't leave. We wasted all that time telling him about nocturnes, and then he started getting all worked up because we used him as bait."

Tony grunted. "Sort of understandable."

"He was going to be hunted by the nocturnes regardless. We just tried to set up a ... hunting season."

Tony grunted again. "So anyway."

"So anyway. Based on past experience, I knew Darcy could go on forever if he got something stuck in his head. So, I ended the conversation."

"But—"

"He has my cell number," I pointed out.

"Which he may not use, because you were a bitch." I glared at him. He raised his hands. "Hey, your word, not mine."

"Okay. But I didn't see you diffusing the situation."

Tony shrugged and fell silent.

"Oh, I forgot the documents. They're in the safe, in the apartment." I turned the truck around and headed back home.

"The—? You still have them?"

"Yeah."

"I thought you destroyed them already." His voice rose.

Galen looked over at him. "You might want to take it down a notch," I said. "Galen likes you, so I think he'd really hate to have to rip off one of your appendages."

"Sorry." He sounded genuinely contrite. "I just assumed that, since you weren't talking about the documents, you already took care of them. I shouldn't've assumed." As I pulled into the parking lot, he spoke again. "Where do you think the documents came from?"

I shrugged. "If I knew that, my life would be a lot easier."

"You said the documents smelled like the nocturne. Maybe the nocturnes created them to give to Darcy."

I shook my head. "No nocturne could speak Gaachail, much less write it. There aren't that many Sankhain that know the language anymore. Mal never even bothered to learn it. Besides, the documents smelled old, not like something recently manufactured."

"Could something have survived the fire?"

"No, no way," I said immediately. "Nothing was missed."

He didn't say it. He didn't have to. Obviously, I was wrong. Something got missed. But how?

Because I never used the safe, I never bothered to learn the combination. I picked through the clothes hanging in the closet, found a threadbare plaid flannel shirt that had once belonged to Mal, and from the left breast pocket, I pulled a slip of paper with the combination on it.

I took the documents from the safe and grabbed my messenger bag off the floor. With the bag slung over my shoulder, I ran back down to the truck.

While I started the engine, Tony dug into my bag and pulled out one of the papers. He raised it to his face and sniffed. I smiled a little. He'd never be able to smell what I smelled, but I appreciated the need to try. "Why didn't you destroy them yet?" he said.

"Because nobody told me to."

He apparently didn't have anything to say to that, because he changed tracks. "What'd you mean, when you said you didn't think the nocturne attacked Trini and Leanna?"

I explained to him about the perfume on the rock.

"You don't think the nocturne would've worn perfume? To hide from you or something?"

I shrugged. "It's possible, but it doesn't make much sense. I already know the nocturne's in town. Wearing perfume only makes it more likely a human would notice them coming. My bet, the perfume wearer was someone else."

"And you think whoever it was didn't want you to identify his scent?"

"It's a guess." The coffee hummed through my veins, making me edgy. I wished I could slip my skin, race through the woods as a wolf.

Tony waved the papers. "Why give these to Darcy?"

I was tired of questions. "What?"

"Well, if the nocturne wants to hunt Darcy, approaching him in the hospital makes sense, I guess. Kinda tenderizing the meat before you cook it. But the rest of it? I mean, getting you involved, telling Darcy about the Sankhain and the Spring? It just increases the odds that the nocturne's gonna get hunted right back. Seems kinda stupid, if you ask me."

I swallowed a growl. "Maybe the nocturne thought we'd take Darcy to the Spring. Maybe it thought it could follow us there. It could sneak in, drink from the Spring. Its powers would increase exponentially, and it'd probably be impossible to kill. Pretty high motivation."

"So the nocturne knows enough about us to know the Spring exists, knows that this is a Sankha document, knows who you are and where to find you, but he doesn't know that you're never in a million years gonna take an outsider to the Spring?" Tony turned in his seat to face me. Galen looked at me, too, like he agreed with Tony.

"I don't fucking know." The steering wheel jerked as I turned my head to look at them. With clenched jaws, I looked forward again, my hands at ten and two on the wheel.

"And if he knows who you are, why not just follow you to the forest? Why involve Darcy at all? Plenty of time for hunting once he drinks from the Spring. If he lost Darcy, he could find another vic. Why multi-task?"

I let the growl loose. It filled the car and made Galen lower his head and look at me through his eyelashes. I felt a little bad, but not bad enough to soften my voice. "You plan on helping me answer any of those questions, or are you waiting for God to send down some tablets? How many fuckin' times do I gotta say I don't know?"

Tony was quiet for a long time. "Sorry."

Now I felt like shit, hearing that tiny voice come from his throat. "Just … enough with the inquisition, okay? My head hurts."

"Yeah. Sure."

I listened to the silence for half a block, until I couldn't take it anymore. I told Tony how much Darcy didn't know. Tony actually seemed pleased, although I had no idea why. When we reached the parking lot, I pulled into a space and cut the engine. Neither Tony nor I moved. Then Tony's cell phone rang. He pulled it out and glanced at it. "It's Finn."

"Turn the ringer off."

Tony answered, and explained that we were just outside the forest. I got out and walked around to the passenger door, opening it for Galen. Galen started picking his way across the wet field, lifting whichever front paw wasn't supporting his weight like a yuppie drinking tea with his pinkie in the air. We walked a few feet into the invisible trees. When I stopped, Galen sat beside me, and Tony came to a halt on the other side. I closed my eyes and flared my nostrils, scenting the night air.

Tony's scent had that sourdough flavor to it — he was nervous. Galen's musky scent calmed my own nerves. Various night creatures played predator-and-prey. And moving through the trees toward us were two humans. I recognized Cat's scent, but the other was unfamiliar.

No theatrical displays of archery tonight. In fact, those of us without super-sized olfactory glands had very little warning of their approach. When a snapping twig announced someone's presence, Tony's muscles tensed almost audibly, and his scent doubled in strength.

"Who goes there?" came Cat's strong voice.

"Antony and Kellan," Tony said.

Cat and her partner, a young man whose narrow features looked vaguely familiar, stepped from the shadows. What was his name? Deke? Derek? "Your presence is expected," Cat said. "Dirk will escort you to Master Janus."

Dirk! That was it. How could I forget a name like that? He held his head so high, it looked painful, and his shoulders were thrown back to puff out his chest. I could hear his heartbeat quicken, but his butterscotch scent wasn't anxious or afraid — it was simply strong. Dirk wanted to escort the two wayward Sankhain to their doom.

Tony and I thanked Cat. She held my gaze a moment, like she was trying to tell me something telepathically. Then she slipped off through the trees again. I looked at Dirk with raised eyebrows. He took a step toward me, his hand extended, and Galen stood. I guess he didn't like Dirk's deportment, either.

When the youngling noticed the big dog's eyes on him, he faltered. "I'm supposed to take your weapons," he said. His voice cracked, and he cleared his throat. "If you would hand them over, please."

I briefly considered trying to keep at least the blades in the belly band. He couldn't see them, and he didn't seem willing to frisk me. But Finn might frisk me, and Janus would hear the deception in my thoughts. And then we'd be in even bigger trouble.

Next to me, Tony wasn't exactly rushing to hand over his personal armory, either. Dirk glared and held himself straighter. Like he was growing a backbone right before our eyes. "Your weapons," he said in a deeper voice.

With a glance at Tony, and a shared shrug, we began to disarm. Tony didn't take long — he only had his handgun and a Swiss Army knife. With all my little throwing knives, though, I took considerably longer. I'd be damned if I was handing over the belly band. My tank top kept getting in the way, so I slipped it over my head and handed it to Tony. Out of the corner of my eye, I saw Dirk look away, but Tony went right ahead and stared.

"Nice," he said. "How many sit-ups can you do?"

I didn't look up from my task. "I usually go for at least five hundred."

"Not bad." He tried to sound casual, but I could hear that he was impressed.

Dirk cleared his throat loudly. The boy's attitude was really getting on my nerves. I pulled the last of the throwing knives out of my waistband and tossed it at his feet. When he bent to pick it up, I said, "Careful. They're sharp."

Tony coughed again, and I resisted the urge to look over at him. Instead, I looked down at Galen, who was watching Dirk a little too closely. I clucked my tongue to bring his attention to my face. I praised him softly and told him to leave it. To Galen, "leave it" meant don't touch it. Usually, the command applied to not picking up chicken bones off the sidewalk, but it would work in the case of Dirk, as well. With a scratch behind the ear and a final "good boy," I felt confident Galen would leave Dirk alone, as long as the youngling didn't do anything stupid.

Dirk straightened and looked at me. "Is that all?"

Because a short sword and a dozen throwing knives weren't enough? My mouth twisted as I pretended to think it over. "Yup. I think that about does it."

"What about him? Does he have any?" Dirk was studying Galen.

Like what? A pen knife in his collar? "Yeah. A whole mouthful. You want a demonstration?"

Finally, a little fear from the boy. But he recovered his ego quickly. "Please put your shirt back on."

Without taking my eyes off Dirk's face, I held my hand out to Tony. He placed my tank top in my hand and I slowly lowered it back over my head, sliding my hands down my sides to smooth it into place. From Tony, I caught the musky scent of arousal. From Dirk, nothing.

Hmm. Now, I may not have been the prettiest chickie in the pen, but for a boy Dirk's age, boobs were boobs. Unless boobs weren't his thing. The poor kid was in the closet. Terrible place to be, no room to move. Even among the younglings, who lived on the fringes, it was difficult to be different. As I motioned to him to lead the way, I considered who in the Sankhain was gay. Maybe I could get someone to talk to him, mentor him a little.

Dirk's duffel clinked like wind chimes, and I felt a wave of nakedness. My shirt was back on, but the accessories that mattered were in Dirk's duffel bag. As we walked toward camp, Galen trotted along at my side, sneaking glances at me every now and then. I murmured a couple reassurances to him, to which he responded with the skepticism they deserved. "Sorry, buddy. We seem to be in a mess."

"What?" Tony said, glancing at me.

"Nothing. Talking to the dog."

"It's going to be fine," Tony said. "Tell him it's going to work out just fine."

Sweet of him to say, but I never lied to my dog if I could help it.

Chapter 16

The Academy never bedded down for the night, not completely. Younglings slept in shifts, assuring that someone always kept watch. Janus also thought it was important to teach them the same combat skills in the dark as we did in the light.

By the time we got through the forest, it was almost midnight. The Sankhain Academy wasn't terribly big. The mess hall and the two youngling dormitories stood in the center of a ring of small cabins. Most of the cabins were occupied by Sankhain-in-residence. Off to the left, a slightly larger cabin held the infirmary, and off to the right stood Janus and Finn's cabins. Along the outskirts of the property were barns for storage and paddocks where we held classes — archery, hand-to-hand combat, sharpshooting. All the basics.

I saw lights burning in the infirmary, and a flutter of concern ran through me. Trini and Leanna. Sneaking a glance at Tony, I saw his eyes locked on the infirmary windows. His anxious scent strengthened until I wanted to reach out and touch his arm.

I scuffed my feet and leaned close to him. "I'll let you cop a feel if you tell them it was your fault he got away."

He jerked. "What?"

I repeated myself.

He laughed softly. "Sorry, sweetheart, but I saw what you're offering, and frankly, it's not worth it."

I stopped and glared at him, hands on hips. Not that I'd really expected him to accept the offer. In fact, it was heartening that he was still able to joke, despite his worry. But I couldn't just let that go.

At my side, Galen sat and watched with interest. I made my voice a silky growl. "Maybe my muscles are bigger than my cup size, but you'd be amazed at what a strong woman can do."

As I heard Galen's tail swish in the grass, I saw Tony's Adam's apple bob. What he would have said in reply, I'll never know, because Dirk turned and saw we'd stopped. "Do the foreplay on your own time," he said. Both Tony and I turned our attention to the younger man. I couldn't see Tony's expression, but mine was one of warning. Dirk flinched a little, but then he straightened his shoulders and raised his chin even higher. "My orders are to escort you to Janus. No delays or pit stops. Ma'am. Sir. If you don't mind?"

Maybe his tone was a little too acidic for my tastes, but at least he got the words right. I moved to follow him again, and Galen followed my lead. Tony didn't move. I glanced up at his face, and understood Dirk's flinch. I grabbed Tony's wrist and pulled the mountain along behind me. "Come on, Gigantor. He's obnoxious, but he's right."

Tony followed. "You can be right without being obnoxious."

"Really?" I smiled at him. "I've never figured out how."

"Doesn't mean I'm wrong." But he closed the distance to walk at my side again.

In all my years, I didn't think I'd ever felt less prepared to walk through Janus's door. I disobeyed orders, let an outsider go. I had no excuse for that, or at least, no excuse Janus would accept. But what really concerned me was that the night's mission had gone badly, and that they blamed me for it. I always took responsibility for my screw-ups. But this one wasn't my fault, and that made me more nervous than the things I'd actually done wrong tonight.

A few feet from Janus's cabin, I remembered that Janus hit Tony earlier. I tried to picture it. I couldn't. I could easily see Janus muttering a few words and sealing Tony's mouth shut for a few hours. But throwing punches? That was beneath him. His words, not mine. Then I remembered what Tony said yesterday. Or maybe it was the day before.

That no one had actually seen Janus outside of his cabin for weeks. My skin started to crawl.

Janus's cabin was made up of two rooms, plus a small bathroom. The first room, the outer office, looked like the waiting room of a dentist's office, right down to the magazine spread on the small end table. Of course, most dental receptionists didn't pack the kind of hardware the youngling behind the desk did, but presumably dental receptionists didn't have a need for broadswords. Janus liked to wait for the youngling in the front room to announce any visitors. He said it reinforced his authority.

Tevin, this week's gatekeeper, waved us through without going through the motions of announcing us to the court. That lack of pageantry did nothing to calm me, nor did the scene that greeted us in Janus's inner sanctum. Well, the scene itself didn't look out of the ordinary. Finn stood at the head of Janus's long table, head bowed, though he looked up at us as we entered.

At the far end of the room, near the bed, Janus stood with his back to us, staring at the fireplace with its overbearing fire. He was a small, slight man, not quite as tall as I was. But his figure drew my eyes. His short hair looked mussed, and he had a stain on his khaki slacks. Not his normal, fastidious appearance, but what made my shoulders tighten, made my steps falter, made Galen tense up next to me, was the smell. The room stank of an unfamiliar scent, sour and acidic like vinegar. It was so strong, I shallowed my breathing, so I didn't take too much in at once.

Tony, of course, didn't smell it, and when I tripped over my own feet, he looked at me questioningly. I shook my head and straightened, wrapping one hand around Galen's collar, setting loose his scent into the air to mingle with the foreign smell. Instead of making it better, though, the intermingling just seemed to corrupt Galen's scent. Unable to stomach the perversion of my favorite smell, I slid the satchel off my shoulder and set it on the table.

Finn glanced at Dirk. "Thank you. You're dismissed." The youngling bowed, set the duffel bag full of weapons on the floor, and left in such a hurry, I felt a draft. Finn walked over to us, picked up my messenger bag and looked inside at the documents. Some of that golden glow paled, until his skin looked almost like an average man's. Then he set it back on the table and returned to ignoring us.

Tony fell into a parade rest position — feet hip width apart, arms hanging loose, hands clasped — and I followed, although I kept one hand on Galen's collar. Then we waited. A long time.

Coming into the over-heated office from the relative cool of the outdoors, both Tony and I started sweating within seconds. The physical discomfort gave me something to focus on besides the heavy silence. And interestingly, the scent of Tony's sweat blotted out some of the nasty vinegar smell. I began to relax a little.

"It was a simple job." The disapproval in Finn's voice raised my hackles. Galen's hackles as well. "One I would expect a *Hycene* more than capable of completing."

Was I supposed to speak? Usually, when I thought it was my turn to speak, it wasn't. I decided to keep my mouth shut for now.

"Well?" Finn looked at me. "Explain."

"I'm sorry, *sir*." Even on the best of days, I had trouble calling Finn "sir" with a straight face. I knew too much about him, like how he loved to drizzle honey on his cock, then hum random notes while I sucked it off. Visuals like these made respect rather difficult. "But I'm unclear about what exactly I'm supposed to explain."

The vinegar scent filled the room until I could almost see it, a smog only I could sense. It made the need to shape-shift rise up inside me again. Something needed hunting. I swallowed hard and tightened my grip on Galen's collar, tethering myself to that one solid thing.

Oblivious to my internal struggle, Finn answered my question. I didn't hear him, and was forced to ask him to repeat himself. This did not make him happy. "My apologies, are we boring you?"

"No, sir." Nerves brought the respect to my lips more easily this time. "I was just … thinking. How are Trini and Leanna doing?"

Not even close to my actual thoughts, but the women seemed a good excuse for being distracted. The lines around Finn's mouth softened slightly. "Leanna is going to be fine. Her injuries were fairly minor. But Trini— Simone says we'll have to wait and see."

I nodded. "Thank you. Sir."

Janus shifted his weight, a slight rustling of fabric that sent a fresh wave of smells my way. Oh, god, the scent was coming from Janus. I thought I knew all his scents. Tonight, I expected his angry scent, the one that smelled like sparks and melted plastic. But he was so upset, he needed to go and create a new scent for the occasion? That knowledge rocked me back on my heels.

"If I may," Tony said carefully. Finn abandoned my gaze and turned his attention to Tony. "The situation tonight got out of hand. We should have anticipated that the nocturne might find our sentries. The assumption was, it would attack Dar— the outsider, despite the presence of Kellan and myself. But it was a step ahead of us, and we should have accounted for that beforehand."

Impressive. It sounded like he said it was our fault, but really, he laid the blame at Finn's and Janus's feet. They were the ones who sketched out the assignment to begin with. Tony reminded them, sans yelling and cursing, that they were part of the "we."

Finn, being several centuries more accomplished at manipulating a room than Tony, knew exactly what Tony was saying. Probably Janus knew, too, but he still faced the fire, so I couldn't be sure. "Well, at least the problem of the outsider is taken care of," Finn said. "Now we focus on tracking down the nocturne."

"Um, about that," I said. Tony stiffened. Probably he wanted to do the talking, find some diplomatic way of breaking the news. He was more likely to find a unicorn up his ass. Better to let me handle the undiplomatic stuff. "A few things you should know. First of all, the nocturne isn't alone."

Finn narrowed his eyes. "I thought you only saw one in the park."

"Well, yes, that night one nocturne came at us. But from what the outsider told me, he was approached by two beings, one in male form, the other female. They were the ones who supplied him with information about us." I watched Finn work to fit this piece into the mammoth jigsaw of his mind. I kept talking, not wanting to give him too much time to think. "Also, I smelled a strange scent on Trini and Leanna, a very strong perfume. Like someone was trying to cover up their personal scent. I don't think it was a nocturne — it had no reason to hide its scent from me. I don't think Leanna and Trini were attacked by a nocturne. I think the nocturne's working with someone who wants to hide herself from me." Oh, how I wished I had a blade to comfort me as I broke the remainder of the news. "And, about the outsider. He's actually not as taken care of as you might think."

I was so focused on Finn's reaction, I never saw Janus cross the room. Stupid, stupid, stupid. Suddenly, Janus was in front of me, and I was choking on his scent. "What," he whispered, "does that mean, precisely?"

I held myself very still. "It means he's still alive. Precisely."

One second, I was standing there, waiting for a verbal sand-blasting, the next, I was on the floor, the left side of my face a mass of pain. When I fell, I let go of Galen's collar. He leapt at Janus, but fortunately, Galen had to jump over my legs first, and I was able to grab him.

I had to do the same with Tony, who moved forward to stand between Janus and me. His scent had shot from hot and sweaty to jalapeno angry. I grabbed the hem of his shorts and yanked him back. When he looked down at me, I held out my hand. "Help me up," I said. I didn't want the help, but my knees felt like overcooked ravioli, and I needed to distract Tony before the situation got any worse.

Tony took my hand and pulled me to my feet. By that time, Finn had come around the table and laid a hand on Janus's arm. He turned to look at me. "Go. Wait outside."

I felt light-headed. Shock, probably. I should've been angry. Tony and Galen were angry. Why wasn't I? My entire head throbbed, making me wonder just how hard Janus hit me. Janus? Hit me? What the fuck was happening?

When neither Tony nor I moved, Finn repeated himself, slower and with greater venom. I bit the inside of my cheek to keep from laughing out loud. This whole thing was so absurd, so wrong. It couldn't possibly be real. Before I descended into hysteria, I forced my feet into motion, pulling Tony and Galen along behind me.

When we walked into the waiting room, Tevin suddenly became very busy, shuffling papers around on the desk. I ignored him and kept moving. Outside, I leaned my back against the side of the cabin and slid down to sit on the ground. My head was throbbing harder and in a more consistent rhythm. My skin felt moist, and I shivered. I crossed my legs and pulled my far-too-big-to-fit dog into my lap. Galen curled up the best he could and laid his head on my knee. "Well, that didn't go how I expected."

Tony was pacing. He stopped and stared down at me. "That's good. Because if that's what you had in mind, you really need to up your meds." I started laughing, then clamped my mouth shut. I could hear a padded room, just on the other side of that laughter. With a loud exhale, Tony sat down beside me. "You okay? He hit you pretty hard."

"I'm okay." I shuddered again. "All good."

When Tony reached a hand toward me, Galen raised his head to track Tony's movements. "You're already bruising." He touched my cheek. I knew his hands would be calloused and strong. But the gentleness surprised me. That whispering touch set sensors in motion that had nothing to do with pain.

I met Tony's eyes, and he pulled his hand away. By silent agreement, we leaned back against the building and looked at anything but each other. When the door opened and Finn stepped out, I was almost relieved.

Finn came to stand before us, looking down at us. The imposing stance made Galen's muscles tense under my fingers. I flashed back to Mal and myself as little kids, maybe five years old. Mom caught us playing with her knife collection. She was furious, not because we were playing with knives — she'd taught us to handle knives as soon as we had the dexterity to hold them — but because we'd gotten one of her daggers all muddy and then shoved it back into the sheath. She stood over us, just like Finn did now.

I didn't think it boded well for our sex life if I started making associations between Finn and my mother.

Just so I could feel like a grown-up again, I pushed Galen off my lap and stood up. The ground tilted and the trees shuddered for a second, but then I got my bearings. Finn was watching me. His only reaction was a tightening at the mouth, which for Finn could mean any one of a dozen things. "Your assignment remains the same. Track down the outsider and eliminate him. This time, you'll bring the body here for disposal." He paused, then tilted his head to the side. "Exactly how did you fail to eliminate the outsider?"

Enough with the euphemisms. I blurted out the truth without thinking. "I failed to *kill* Darcy Jamison because I let him go."

I heard Tony rise to his feet and make a sound as if to interrupt, but I held up a hand. I couldn't unsay it. Better to just let Finn react without trying to make excuses.

After staring at me for a moment, Finn closed his eyes and pinched the bridge of his nose. "You let him go."

"Yes."

He squeezed his eyes even more tightly shut. "Why?"

Again, Tony took a breath to speak, but I beat him to it. "Because it was the right thing to do."

Now Finn's eyes whipped open and he skewered me with his gaze. "The right thing?" He took a step closer to me, until our noses almost touched. His damp earth smell shifted to the scent of brushfire. "The right thing, Kellan, would have been to follow orders. From the beginning of this bloody mess, that would have been the right thing to do."

"Not when the orders make no sense." I felt the heat in my face leaking into my voice. "We have a nocturne out there, and Darcy's our best chance at luring it into the open. And you'd have me kill him, because he might tell someone about invisible forests and secret societies? The poor bastard doesn't even know anything. The nocturnes just fed him a few words to say, they didn't give him details. If he did tell anyone, they'd have him pumped full of Thorazine so fast, he wouldn't have time to notice the straitjacket."

Finn stared at me. I had a sneaking suspicion he was trying to figure out what Thorazine was. Not that he would ever ask. "Your assignment is to eliminate the outsider. No detours, no alterations. Do it right this time, Kellan."

As shock wore off and rage took its place, I wanted to say, "Or what?" Would he smack me around too? But part of me was afraid of the answer. An hour ago, I would've said Finn would never lay a hand on me, but then, I would have said the same for Janus. As if sensing my uncertainty, Galen moved to stand between me and Finn. Not surprising. When Tony put his hand on my shoulder, though, that surprised me. I didn't pull away. For once, I let the boys do their macho thing.

Finn looked from my face to Tony's. Whatever he saw there made his eyes go cold and dead. "You may stay here," he said to Tony.

"That's okay, I'd rather go with Kellan," Tony replied casually, but his hand on my shoulder tightened.

Oh, brother. Enough macho. I handed Galen's leash to Tony. "Galen needs to pee. Take him over to the trees." Judging by his narrowed eyes, Tony wasn't at all fooled by my ruse, but he nodded. I smiled at him, even though it hurt like a son of a bitch. After they left, I turned to Finn. "Look. I know I'm supposed to follow orders, okay? But come on. If we don't use Darcy to get the nocturne, it's going to move on to another victim, and we may not find it again."

Finn's scent slowly cooled. "He won't listen to reason." I didn't need to ask who he was referring to. He raised a hand, as if to touch my face, but he never made it there. His hand dropped stiffly to his side and I let out a breath I hadn't realized I was holding. "He needs this mess finished. You need to take care of it. Before you get—"

Before I got hurt? Too late. I forced the lid back on my incredulity. "Trini and Leanna are lying in the infirmary because of that nocturne and its friend. *That's* not right. Let me show the monsters that the Sankhain still protect their own, Finn. And if I'm using Darcy as bait, he'll never leave my sight. No chance of exposing us."

I wanted to keep talking, press the issue, but I knew I needed to let him think. If I gave him enough time to think, he'd see I was right. He stared at the ground for so long, I started to bounce up and down on the balls of my feet as an outlet for the nervous energy. Finally, he blinked. "You will *never* let him out of your sight. If he urinates, you will hand him the toilet paper. Understood?"

I nodded, unwilling to speak for fear of breaking the spell.

"I have three conditions." Finn ticked them off on his fingers. "One. Before you kill the nocturne, discover the identity of its friend. Two, find out why it sent its prey looking for you. That troubles me."

I planned on doing all that anyway. "Okay."

"And third. When he's no longer needed as bait, you eliminate the outsider. Immediately and efficiently. Understood?"

Pride reared its over-coiffed head. Once upon a time, Hycene were given a certain amount of autonomy. We were revered warriors, not dogs requiring a heavy leash. My mother never would have stood for Finn's tone or his conditions, even if they did make sense.

I wasn't my mother. She truly was a revered warrior, while I — well, I was the person Janus just beat on. My head pounded, my stomach rolled, and anger shouldered pride out of the way. Maybe I wasn't as strong or as smart as my dam, but I deserved better than to be treated like a puppy that just piddled on the carpet. I would kill Darcy when I was damn well good and ready. I crossed my fingers behind my back. "Sure. But I want Tony to come with me."

"Since when are you and Antony such good pals?"

He was jealous. I decided to poke the dragon with a stick, see if I could get it to breathe fire. "Since you tossed him to me like table scraps."

His jaw was so tight, I was amazed he could open his mouth. "He's good in difficult situations. His ability to improvise is prodigious."

I inhaled his scent, which reminded me of moldy leaves on a forest floor. I fought a smile. "Mmm, that's a good word for it. Yes, he's very ... prodigious."

He narrowed his eyes. "You have no need for him anymore. You're more than capable of handling this yourself."

"Really? And here I thought I just won Fuck-up of the Year."

"If you want help, I can find someone—"

"I want Tony. He's familiar with the situation and Darcy knows him. Tony comes with me, or I go back in Janus's office and tell him he's lost his mind, and if he wants to find it again maybe he should check his asshole 'cause it might've gotten shoved up there when he stuck that big pole—"

"Very well!" Finn rubbed the back of his neck, glaring at me. "Just get the task done this time."

I blinked at him with wide doe eyes. He didn't specify which task, so I could play stupid later if necessary. "Yessir."

I wandered over to where Tony stood. I was sure he'd watched the entire exchange between me and Finn. I took the leash from him, and Galen happily came to me and leaned against my leg. "We're going hunting."

His shoulders slumped. "Darcy."

"Eventually. But we've got bigger fish to shoot first."

"Finn's gonna get Janus to agree to put off Darcy's death?"

"Next best thing. I got Finn to agree to put it off."

Tony shook his head, but he had a smile spreading across his face. "Janus is gonna kill us."

"Definite possibility," I said. "But at least we get to hunt a nocturne first. That's a hell of a lot more fun than hunting a librarian."

Tony led the way into the forest. "Depends on the librarian."

"True," I said.

"If Angelina Jolie played a librarian in a movie, she'd probably be an ass-kicking kind of librarian."

I struggled not to laugh. "Darcy's not Angelina Jolie."

Tony sighed. "Too bad."

I gave up and laughed. Then I smacked him upside the head. "Get your blood back above the neck, Gigantor. We've got work to do."

Chapter 17

When we got back to the truck, I slid behind the wheel, then jumped when a hard object connected with my tailbone. Digging behind me on the seat, I pulled out my cell phone. It must have slipped out of my pocket. I flipped it open and saw that I had a voicemail. I turned the key in the ignition while I waited for the message to play. It was Darcy. He sounded garbled, like he had a mouthful of water. "She died. My sister died. So — thanks for nothing."

I swore, dropped the phone on the floor, and slammed the truck into gear, tearing out of the parking space. Galen dropped, hugging the seat to keep from sliding.

Tony stared at me. "What the hell's wrong with you?"

"Darcy called."

"What happened?"

I squealed around a corner. "Hang on," I said belatedly as Tony wrapped an arm around Galen. I could smell Galen's fear, and Tony's mash-up of alarm and frustration. Once I was back on a straight-away, I relayed Darcy's message.

"So you thought you'd kill us while the dying's good?" Tony said.

I slammed on the brakes as the light I was barreling toward turned red before I could make it to the intersection. I reached over to give Galen a reassuring pat. "The nocturne will be all over him now. We have to find Darcy before it finishes him off."

Tony sighed. "Yeah. Where're we goin'?"

"Darcy's neighborhood is this way."

I parked on Darcy's street, pointing to the building. Even as I turned off the truck, Tony jumped out and started around back to the parking lot. I told Galen to stay and headed for the front door. I was leaning on the doorbell for the second time when Tony jogged back around the corner of the building. "His car's not here," he said.

"Yeah, he's not answering his bell, either." I closed my eyes and inhaled. No trace of rotten eggs — no nocturne — but no trace of Bergamot, either — no Darcy. "He hasn't been here for a while," I said, opening my eyes to look at Tony. We jogged back to the truck.

Tony snapped his seatbelt in place. "Hospice?" he asked.

I shook my head. "Don't know where it is." Overloaded with adrenaline, I tapped my feet on the floorboards and drummed my fingers on the steering wheel.

Tony reached across the seat. "Give me your phone."

"Why?" Even as I asked, I dug around on the floor to find my cell.

"Because I need his number." He took the phone from me and started pressing buttons. Then he pulled out his phone and dialed a number. With a smug smile, he raised the phone to his ear. He straightened his spine and threw his shoulders back, and suddenly, his voice sounded like that of a stuffy white man. "Darcy? Hi. You don't know me. I'm Dolly's … friend. Anyway, Dolly gave me your number, 'cause she's really sick and she can't go in today."

Realizing our next destination, I threw the truck in drive and started for the Beltline. Tony continued with his White Yuppie impression. "Oh, I'm sorry. That's horrible. Well, I guess she'll have to go in — oh, no, hon, in the bucket." He held the phone away from his head and made some retching sounds. Galen stared at him, fascinated, as Tony finished retching and returned to the phone. "What? Oh, no, you shouldn't have to do that, not when you just—" Pause. "Really? Oh, I know she'd appreciate it. I mean, I'll tell her when she's done with—" More retching sounds. "Well, I'll tell her. Thanks. And sorry about your sister." He hung up the phone.

I stared at him.

He snapped his fingers a few inches from my face. "Watch the road. You're a bad enough driver when you're actually lookin' where you're going."

Any compliments I intended to pay him for his Emmy-winning performance evaporated. "Bite me."

"Much fun as that sounds, we have to go to the library."

I rolled my eyes. "And what do you intend to tell him when he gets to the library and finds out it was you on the phone?"

He shrugged. "Who cares? We know where he's gonna be and when. Maybe he'll be relieved that Dolly isn't puking her guts out."

"Yeah, I'm sure he'll be thrilled." I was avoiding the real question — what we'd do with him once we had him. "Why'd you use your phone to call him?"

"I didn't want to risk him recognizing your number on the caller ID."

Hmm. That was actually pretty smart. "Not bad." His only answer was another smug smile. Grateful I didn't have to hear whatever thoughts went along with that smile, I checked the clock on the dash. "Good, we have time for breakfast."

"How can you be hungry after the ride-so-psycho-even-Six-Flags-won't-touch-it?" I just looked at him. He shook his head. "Right. Stupid question," he said.

A few blocks before the library, we stopped at a drive-thru. I ordered three egg sandwiches and four coffees. Tony got a yogurt, with another coffee for himself. I looked at him with raised eyebrows. "Yogurt? Really?"

"We don't all have shape-shifter metabolisms."

I grinned as I pulled into a parking space in front of the library. "Oh, honey, I don't care what those mean sales ladies told you, those shorts do not make you look fat."

He scowled at me.

Picking up on my amusement, Galen sat up straighter, not wanting to miss any of the fun. Beside him, Tony dunked a napkin in his coffee and wadded it up before placing it in his spoon and launching it at my head. It hit me in the temple. I yelped, caught the napkin before it landed in my lap, and threw it back at him. Laughing, he swatted it away before reaching into the bag and grabbing one of my sandwiches.

"Hey!" I said.

Unwrapping the sandwich with admirable speed and dexterity, he shoved it into his mouth all at once and gave me an egg-filled smile.

A laugh slipped out before I could stop it. "That's disgusting. Why don't you get out here so you can walk to preschool, with all the other three-year-olds."

After some difficult chewing, Tony managed to swallow his food. My food. I nabbed what was left of Tony's yogurt and held it in front of my dog. Galen cleaned out the plastic cup before Tony had time to utter, "That's mine!"

"Well, after that sandwich, I figured you didn't really need the calories."

He looked like he was going to catapult another wet napkin my way, when his expression changed. "Showtime," he murmured.

I followed his gaze. Darcy was early for work. Jeez. The library didn't even open for another half hour. Then again, his sister just died. Probably he didn't have any place more pleasant to be.

We got out of the truck, taking Galen with us this time. Darcy saw us coming and his shoulders slumped. "I told you, I don't need your help anymore."

I stopped a few feet away. "I got your message," I said. "I'm sorry about your sister."

Darcy was edging toward the library door. "I have to go to work."

"Actually," I said softly, "you don't. Dolly's just fine."

He frowned at me. "How did you — oh." Realization dawned. He looked up at Tony. "It was you?"

Tony's arm brushed against my back as he shrugged. "Sorry," he said, without any audible remorse. "But I didn't think you'd agree to see us."

Darcy scowled. "Well, you were right. You guys are nuts, and I don't want anything more to do with you, or your crazy world."

"Glad to hear it." I took a step toward him. "Unfortunately, it's a little late for that. It'll be coming for you soon."

His heavy-lidded glare conveyed his irritation. "Who? The shadow person? I don't care. Let them come."

I took another step toward him. While Galen followed me, Tony stayed where he was. I kept my voice soft, soothing. "That's what everyone says, you know. 'Let them come. I'm not afraid.' That's what they say right up until the time comes to die. Then they wish they'd accepted help when it was offered."

Darcy paled a little. "In your case, I think the cure is worse than the disease."

With one more step, I closed the remaining distance between us. "You were willing to do anything to save your sister. Don't you think she'd want you to do the same for yourself?"

"You don't know anything about my sister," he said.

"You're right. But I know a little about you. You care about people. You cared enough about your co-worker to come in to cover her shift, on the day your sister died. You cared enough about your sister to risk trusting the crazy knife lady." This earned me a snort from Darcy and a choked laugh from Tony. I reached behind me with my leash hand and flipped Tony off. "Now I need you to trust me just a little bit longer. I have no reason to lie to you. Okay?" That was a lie, but oh well.

Darcy hesitated, then nodded.

"Okay. I understand that you're grieving, and that maybe you don't want to live so much right now. I get it. I'm not asking you to be all *mourn not but rejoice* or some crap. All I'm asking is that you listen. See, this thing, this nocturne? It'll kill you. And maybe you're okay with that," I paused for dramatic effect, "but it won't stop with you, Darcy. After it's squeezed every last bit of worth from you, it'll move on to the next person. And the next and the next. Maybe I'll catch it somewhere down the road. It's possible; I'm pretty good at my job. But how many people are going to die before that happens?"

Darcy's sweat glands revealed his discomfort. He was wavering.

"I don't know where to look for it, Darcy. I need your help to protect all those people who aren't as ready to die as you are. I need you."

He wanted to refuse. It made the wolf in me look down on him. You didn't lie down and die just because a pack member was lost, not when the rest of the pack needed protecting. I almost ran out of patience with Darcy. But, thanks to Galen choosing to lean against my leg, my patience held, and Darcy's conscience finally won out. "All right," he said. "But you have to be honest with me. If you're going to use me as bait, tell me."

All righty then. "Darcy, I'm going to use you as bait." I put a hand on his shoulder and started to lead him toward the truck.

He looked down at me. "Seriously? Just like that?"

I shrugged. "You asked me to tell you."

Rather than going to the truck, though, I found myself pulled to the left instead. Galen was dragging me toward a patch of grass on the edge of the parking lot. Tossing Tony the keys, I told him to get in the truck, then we walked to the grass.

My only excuse was that I was distracted. As Galen started to poop and I realized I didn't have anything to clean it up with, I swore softly. Turning to call to Tony, I caught the scent — full dumpster on a hot day. No sooner had I smelled it than I heard Tony cry out, Darcy yell my name, and I caught a fresh scent — blood.

I dropped Galen's leash and ran for the truck. When I rounded the hood, I stopped and stared. Tony lay on the ground, his chest and abdomen slashed with long, deep gashes. He wasn't moving. Darcy crouched next to him, staring up at the man before him. Tall, thin, sunglasses, trench coat. It looked like your average Columbo wannabe, or perhaps your friendly neighborhood flasher, except for its hands. They weren't hands, but long-taloned claws.

Galen came up beside me, and I gave him the hand signals for down and stay. He obeyed for now. Better kill the fucker and be done with it. I reached for my throwing knives, then stopped cold. My throwing knives, along with my other blades, were right where I left them, on Janus's mother-fucking table.

I had a Bowie knife in my truck, under the passenger seat, but no way to get to it. I glanced at Tony and felt a nice ball of rage where my stomach used to be. Who needed weapons?

I positioned myself between the nocturne and the men. Judging from the smell, Tony was still leaking fresh blood. He was alive for now.

"Mmm, it cares for the human," came the nocturne's soft, high-pitched voice. "Delicious. What would it do if I killed it, I wonder?"

"It would rip your sorry head from your shoulders with its bare hands," I answered. "Although, come to think of it, I'm going to do that anyway."

"And yet, it doesn't fight." The nocturne studied me as if I were a bug and it was trying to decide which wing to pull off first. "Why is that? Maybe … it can't. Poor little Hycene, with none of its little knives to play with."

I sensed movement behind me and inhaled deep and fast, anticipating another nocturne's stink. What I smelled instead was gun powder. Tony, I thought. Somehow, he was okay.

When I heard a bullet move into the chamber, I got the hell out of the way.

It wasn't Tony that emptied six rounds into the nocturne, though. It was Darcy who held the gun. He fired the shots like an experienced marksman, absorbing the recoil without flinching. What kind of librarian knew how to shoot?

After a split second to stare in amazement, I trotted over to Darcy. I told him to give me the gun, and he obeyed. Then I returned to the nocturne. Bullets wouldn't kill it, not even six bullets, but they weakened the nocturne to the point that I could overpower it.

I straddled its body, getting all covered in stinky nocturne blood, and I told Darcy where to find the blade in my truck. I would need the knife to finish off the nocturne. While Darcy searched, I held the gun to its temple.

"Silly girl. Your little toys won't kill me."

"Nope, but they'll hurt like a son of a bitch. Here's the deal. You'll tell me what you're really after, why you broke pattern and sent Darcy to me. Then you'll tell me where you got those documents. Then, as your reward, I'll cut off your head and kill you nice and fast. If you don't, I'll make you scream a hundred times for every scratch you inflicted on my friend."

Before I could react, it brought up its claws. The four long, blade-like nails gouged deep grooves in my chest and the blow cracked my ribs. The strike rocked me back, but somehow I managed to hang onto the gun and keep my seat on the nocturne's chest.

My first thought was, well, that'll be a bitch to heal. My second thought was that the interrogation was done. My wounds were too severe for me to stay awake for long. Fifteen, maybe twenty minutes. I'd need that time to get Tony to Simone. No time for answers. Finn wasn't going to be happy. Staring into the nocturne's eyes, I squeezed the trigger, emptying the rest of the clip into its skull.

I fought to draw enough oxygen to stay conscious. I was pretty sure I had a punctured lung. As I dropped the gun, I caught the scents of musky dog and Bergamot oil. Reaching one hand out to Galen to tell him I was okay, I held the other hand out to Darcy. He placed the hilt of my blade in my hand. I thanked him, then got to work.

I grabbed the nocturne by its hair. I pictured Tony bleeding out on the pavement, but I had more pressing concerns — the nocturne wasn't dead yet. I sawed its head off with a blade that was meant for stabbing and slashing. Then I cut its chest open, cracked open the rib cage and ripped out its heart. A nocturne's regenerative powers were even greater than mine. The only way to kill it was to remove the head and the heart.

Distantly, I smelled vomit and heard retching, but I couldn't care about that. I prayed that Darcy was the only one puking, not an entire audience of library employees and patrons.

I coughed up blood, and spat into the accumulating pool on the pavement. My chest was busy mending itself, and I could feel myself weakening with the effort.

The smell of vomit grew stronger. "You're — you're hurt," Darcy said.

"I'll be fine." But my voice was thin, and even I didn't believe me. "I need your help."

I got Darcy to help me load the pieces of nocturne into the back of the truck. He gagged the whole time, but he did it. Then he helped me lift Tony into the cab. We laid him on his back on the seat, with his legs bent awkwardly. I glanced at the massive blood puddle Tony and the nocturne left behind. Probably someone would call the police. I just hoped nobody saw anything, to bring cops to my doorstep.

I squeezed onto the passenger seat, with Galen curled at my feet and Tony's head and shoulders cradled in my lap. I wondered if I should apply pressure to his wounds. Then I looked at the mess that was his chest. Nope. Instead, I lightly rubbed my fingers across his forehead. His skin felt cool and moist, and he moaned. The sound made it even harder to draw air into my lungs.

After giving Darcy directions on where to drive, I pulled out my cell and called Simone. When she answered, she didn't sound happy. "Kellan, I'm busy. I don't have time to go searching for Finn or delivering messages, so—"

"Would you just shut up for a second?" My voice was harsh, and cracked on the last word. I coughed, tasting more blood. I rolled down the window and spat. Tony's face spasmed as my body shifted under him, but he didn't open his eyes.

"What's wrong?" Simone's voice instantly took on that air of concerned authority.

"We—" I shivered violently. "We were attacked. Tony's hurt bad, he's unconscious. I think he's in shock, and he's all cut up. His chest. Nocturne claws." I licked my lips with a dry tongue. "I — I'll be okay, but we're on our way now, and I need someone to meet me at the edge of the forest. I can't carry him myself."

"How badly are you hurt?"

"I'm fine. It's just Tony. Oh, and—" Now my teeth were starting to chatter, as all burnable calories went to healing my wound instead of heating my body.

Darcy turned a corner and Tony almost slipped off my lap. I grabbed his shoulder and he cried out, but he didn't fall on the floor.

Darcy. Shit, what was I going to do with Darcy when we got to the forest? "Um, I've got an outsider with me. He's driving. He helped me with... And he had the gun. I had to bring him along, he's driving." I was babbling, but I couldn't remember what I already said, what I needed to say.

Simone interrupted me. "Where are you now?"

I looked around, started describing everything I saw because I couldn't remember the name of the road or how long it took to get to the forest from our position. "Tree. Fast food. Tall building. Light post."

"Okay," Simone said, her voice strong and calm. I could float on the surface of her voice for a thousand years. "I'm sending someone to meet you. Park on the grass, as close to the edge of the forest as you can get. Bring the outsider to camp with you. We'll deal with all that later."

We entered the business park as I hung up, which was a good thing because the edges of my vision were starting to go black. I raised my arm to point out where we should park, and the contracting muscles screamed. I heard panting and looked down at Galen. He wasn't panting. It was me.

Two younglings with a stretcher emerged from the fog-laden field. Their arrival was hidden from the surrounding buildings by the truck. I tried to open the door, but it was too heavy. Darcy had to reach across my lap and shove it open.

To the younglings' credit, they took in the scene with only a slight scent of fear, before they worked together to get Tony off my lap and on the stretcher. His shirt stuck to my shorts, our blood mingling into a half-dried, tacky glue. So much blood. I could recoup the loss. Could he?

I looked down at the ground, marveling at how far away it was. Galen hopped out of the truck and looked up at me, worried. He had blood on him. Was he hurt? I started to climb out of the truck, but ended up falling. Superman — no, too freckly, must be Darcy — swooped out of the sky and caught me. Then I was close enough to Galen to be able to tell that the blood wasn't his, it was Tony's. And mine. "Oh, good," I murmured, and passed out.

Chapter 18

Blood and disinfectant. The blood, I didn't mind, but the disinfectant made me sneeze. That was how I woke, sneezing hard enough to give myself a headache. Sitting up, I forgot all about the headache when my chest exploded with pain. Eyes watering, I turned my body on the cot so that I could lean back against the wall and dangle my legs over the side. I closed my eyes and tried to remember how to breathe.

The smell of disinfectant was shoved aside by the smell of blood and roses. Simone's personal scent. I didn't know where the roses came from, but the blood was pretty self-explanatory. She laid a warm hand on my forehead. "What are you doing, girl? Sitting up that fast. I've got ten-year-old younglings here with more sense than you."

I shivered, keeping my eyes closed. "Sorry." Then I smiled a little as another scent rushed toward me. Without opening my eyes, I reached out a hand to meet Galen halfway. Simone let a dog into the infirmary. I must have been in worse shape than I thought.

Her hand moved from my forehead to my chest, and I jumped, my eyes bolting open. That was when I noticed I was naked except for a pair of panties and a huge bandage that covered most of my chest. Fortunately, we were alone in one of the small private rooms in the infirmary, so nobody else could see me. The infirmary also had a big room with eight beds in it, for overflow. I was very grateful today was a slow day on the job.

Alone. We shouldn't be alone. Where was Tony? Oh, god, Tony. Horror settled like an icy brick in my gut as the image of him lying in a pool of his own blood took up residence behind my eyes. I closed my eyes tight, like that would make the mental image go away. Nothing would.

Just what I needed. Another image for the nightmare bank. If not for Darcy — wait, where was Darcy? Was he dead already? Fuck. I needed out of this bed. I started to pull away from the wall, and let out an undignified squeak at the sudden pain.

Simone's voice was cool and authoritative. "Sit still."

I started to ask about Darcy, but she pulled the bandage away and fresh pain made me cry out.

"Sorry," she murmured. "You had a lot of dried blood there, made it stick. Good news is, the wounds have completely closed."

Digging my hands into Galen's fur to fortify myself, I forced my eyes open and looked down at my chest. "Bad news is, I look like I lost a fight with Edward Scissorhands."

She frowned at me. "Who?"

"Never mind." I pushed myself into a more upright position and drew the sheet up to cover my chest. "Lots of pretty new scars."

"Hmm. Well, since you're still alive, and the nocturne isn't, I'd say you won the fight."

I wondered if anyone cleaned out the back of my truck, or if I had rotting nocturne waiting for me there. Oh, well. I had a more important question, but I was so afraid of the answer, I could only get out one word. "Tony?"

Simone's sigh sent a fresh wave of her scent my way. "He lost a lot of blood."

Fear, strong enough that I was glad I couldn't smell my own scent. "Is he going to be okay?"

She hesitated. "I think so."

"Honest?"

She looked at me critically. "Yes. I'm still keeping a close watch over him, but I think he'll be all right." Relief made me weak enough to pass out again. I must have looked it, because Simone's hand returned to my forehead. "You should lie back down. Rest some more."

Another scent approached, of damp earth and leaves. "I don't think that's going to happen," I said, inclining my head toward Finn in the doorway.

Simone turned and looked at him. "She needs to rest."

Finn gave her a gently charming smile. Never trust a charming man. "I only need a minute," he said. "Please?"

Simone's raised eyebrow told me she wasn't fooled by his smile, but she stepped back. "A minute. I'm timing you."

Galen wasn't so easily put off. His chain of command started and stopped with me, so when I didn't stop him, he positioned himself in front of my legs. Finn side-stepped him, then leaned in close.

"You scared me," he said, then nibbled my earlobe. I felt myself melt a little. Then I heard what he whispered next. "Janus thinks you were ambushed while hunting the outsider. And that you couldn't kill him because, after you and Antony were injured, you needed someone to help you drive here. I assured him you will finish the job as soon as you are capable. He's upset, but I believe I have him sufficiently calmed down. It's in your best interest to keep it that way."

My brain was a little foggy. "Why was he upset?"

Finn pulled back and looked at me. He studied my face like he'd never seen it before. "Are you joking?"

"No." Anger flared behind my breastbone. "All I did was survive, and get Tony back here before he bled out."

"You not only allowed the outsider to live, you brought him to the forest with you."

"So that I could get Tony to Simone."

"You brought an outsider—"

"Yeah, yeah." I refrained from telling him to shut up. All Finn had to say to Janus was, she killed the nocturne, didn't she? And maybe I showed poor judgment, letting Darcy drive us to the forest, but I was gravely injured. Finn could've stood up for me. Should've stood up for me. But he didn't, and now Janus was pissed at me. Again.

"If I lose my standing with him," Finn said, "then you'll be lost. With me there to mediate, I can talk him down from whatever punishment he might consider."

I would have laughed, if I wasn't so angry at myself. To think I actually believed he would stand beside me. Finn was too busy with his big picture to trouble himself with little things like a person's trust, and what it meant to lose it.

Finn reached up and ran his hand down my cheek. I swatted it away, causing new pain to flare across my chest. My sharp intake of breath was more than my dog could stand for. Without so much as a growl of warning, Galen snapped at Finn, his big jaws clamping shut just shy of the man's arm. Like a little girl with a bumblebee caught in her pigtail, Finn let out a shriek and jumped back, rubbing his arm. Point made, Galen sat at my side once again.

I didn't bother to hide the laughter that bubbled up. "Maybe you should go," I said. So I could praise the hell out of my beautiful dog.

He met my gaze, his scent holding some cross between the sourness of fear and the uncomfortable spice of anger. "Think about what I said." And then he was gone.

Simone came back as soon as he left.

"He didn't look happy," she said.

I felt dizzy, disconnected from my body. Dimly registering the chills that wracked my body, I murmured, "I didn't eat."

She helped me lie down before I fell over. Once she had me safely horizontal, she called to one of the younglings who helped carry Tony's stretcher. "Go get some food. And coffee. Lots of hot coffee."

Before I could speak, the blackness closed in again.

— «» —

This time, when I woke up, Simone had a tray of sandwiches waiting on the counter, across the room. I saw a coffeemaker beside the tray. When I sat up and reached for a sandwich, I barely felt a twinge from my chest. My ribs felt normal, too. Healing nicely, though I still felt dizzy and cold.

As soon as I ate a couple of sandwiches, the dizziness went away. It would take a while for the chill to leave, but the coffee helped, warming me artificially. When Simone stuck her head in to check on me, I thanked her.

She smiled self-deprecatingly. "It's been a while since I had a shape-shifter in here. I forgot about the food."

I shrugged. "So did I, and I'm a shape-shifter all the time."

Her smile softened. "Your color looks better." Snagging the carafe, she topped off my mug. "I need to go check on a few things. You okay here?"

I nodded, then said, "Wait." Galen, who was curled up next to me on the cot, raised his head at my urgent tone.

She turned and looked at me.

I wrapped my hands around the warmth of the mug, grateful for Galen's weight next to me. "How's Tony?"

"So far, so good." What the hell did that mean? But I guess it was better than some alternatives. Before I could ask about Darcy, she headed for the door. "I'll have Smack bring you some clothes," she said over her shoulder.

Absently fingering Galen's ears, I drank my coffee and waited for Smack. I hadn't seen Smack in a while. The fourteen-year-old refused to tell anyone her real name, or even where the nickname came from. None of the connotations for "smack" made it seem like a name I'd choose, but to each her own. Sometimes the best way to keep people from degrading you is to make the degrading terms your own. That made me think of the way I felt when Tony called me "wolf." In my stomach, coffee churned like a whirlpool, bubbly and too hot to be comfortable.

I looked up when the scent in the room shifted. Smack stood in the doorway, a thin pile of neatly folded clothes balanced on one hand. Too young to have come into her own scent yet, she just smelled like sweat and dirt. She was probably in the practice yard before her infirmary shift. Belatedly, I smiled at her. "Hi, Smack. Thanks for the clothes."

Like Tony, Smack's race was indeterminate. She had dark skin, but her black hair was too fine and straight to claim solely African-American lineage. Smack's personality, though, was even harder to peg. Her voice was soft, implying submission, but if you managed to catch her words, they were quite the opposite. She had a biting wit and a vocabulary to put a sailor to shame. She said what she thought, even if nobody could hear her. And yet, just as she was quick to deliver a verbal right hook, she was also quick to smile, and had a warmth about her that made you like her, even as she ripped you to shreds. Frankly, I couldn't wait to see what she smelled like when she grew up.

For now, though, she inclined her head and entered the room. Without a word, she set the clothes on the cot next to me, then stood, staring at the floor, but sneaking glances up at me. She was biting her lip in a familiar attempt to stay silent.

My smile turned wry. "What is it? Come on, just say it."

Her head stayed down, but her eyes locked onto mine. Something told me that Smack kept her sanity by belittling her abusers in her subsonic voice, while playing the meek little sheep. "If you like," she said quietly, "when you're dressed, I could help you out to the archery yard." At my raised eyebrows, she clarified, "You could stand in for one of the targets."

My chin shot up. "I beg your pardon?"

"No disrespect, Sankha Kellan." A sure sign that something very disrespectful was coming. "But from what I heard, you went after a nocturne without a weapon. Seems to me, someone who'd do that is either stupid or suicidal, and either way, that person's not good for much but target practice."

At first, her words stung, because I'd thought the same thing when I found myself weaponless in that parking lot. But then I remembered that I armed myself before I left home. I wasn't totally useless. "Watch yourself, youngling. You don't know as much as you think you do."

"You told me to say it." Her voice was so soft, I didn't think anyone but a wolf could have heard it. But her dark eyes were hard and accusing. "And you know if one of us did it, you'd rip us a new one."

Leave it to Smack to hit the nail on the head, then pound it in so hard, it came out the other side. But she didn't know the whole story, and I was getting tired of people telling me I did something stupid. "If one of you did it, you'd be dead."

"Yeah," she said. "Unless we were lucky enough to have a pasty-ass outsider along for the ride."

Darcy. "Smack. I won't tell Janus how you just spoke to me—" her eyes grew wide "—if you answer a question for me."

"Yes, ma'am."

"Where is the pasty— I mean, where's the outsider?"

She grinned at the floor before raising a serious face to me. "He's in the solitary cells, Sankha Kellan. I, um, I heard Sankha Finlay set Ryder to guard his cell, saying that—"

She cut off, looking up at me. I could smell her fear, and I sighed. I did not want to hear the end of that sentence. "It's okay, Smack. What did he say?"

"He said that you would be comin' soon to handle things."

Jaw clenched, I thanked Smack and dismissed her. Before she left, she held her hand out to Galen. He sniffed it, then shoved his head under her hand for a pat. Smack walked out with a smile wide enough to make her look like what she should've been — a kid.

While I dressed, I ate the last sandwich and polished off the coffee. The t-shirt was three sizes too big, enough to hide the fact that I didn't have a bra. The shorts looked like scrub pants that had been cut off at the knees, comfortable, but also big enough that, even tied as tight as it would go, the drawstring waist threatened to slip over my hips. I shifted my shoulders experimentally. The new scars still looked red and angry, but as long as I didn't go around beating my chest like Tarzan, I'd be okay.

Galen looked up at the sandwich in my hand, and I wondered if anyone fed him while I was out. I pulled the remaining roast beef out of the sandwich and tossed it to him. I shoved the bread into my mouth as Galen's jaws clacked shut around the meat. "Come on, bud," I said thickly, then swallowed. "We've gotta go see a blond-haired ass about a horse."

I found my socks and boots. The socks were stiff with dried blood, but I put them on anyway. I couldn't wear hiking boots without socks, and I wasn't about to confront Finn in my bare feet. Simone came bustling out of one of the other rooms. "Oh," she said, skidding to a stop. "You're leaving?"

"Apparently, I have some business to attend to." I saw that Simone's shirt, clean the last time I saw her, was now bloody. Her blood-and-roses scent was tinged with the smell of feces. I swallowed hard. That was a death smell. I met Simone's eyes. "Tony?"

She hesitated. "No. Not Tony."

I took a noisy breath that was too shallow and too fast. Shoving a hand through my hair, I sat down hard enough to bruise my tailbone. Galen stuffed his head under my arm to crawl half in my lap. He knew that smell too. "Who?" It was the ultimate in questions that you didn't want the answer to, yet had no choice but to ask.

Simone hesitated again. Feeling a scream building in the back of my throat, I sniffed the air, searching for the scent that would give me my answer. One scent reminded me who else lay in the infirmary. I wanted to say their names, but I couldn't seem to summon enough spit to open my mouth.

Finally, Simone answered. "Trini." She wore every one of her nine hundred years on her face. "It was Trini."

I started to shake as memories rolled over me. Trini's face, eyes laughing as she told us how transparent we were, sweeping the Tootsie Rolls off my table. Her scent, mingled inextricably with Leanna's. Her blood under my hands, as I failed to save her.

I could still feel her blood between my fingers. I had to wash it off. I stood up and stumbled to the sink, turned on the water and tried to scrub away the memory.

A weight, barely noticed, against my leg. When I didn't respond, Galen pulled away, then rammed into the back of my knee, causing my leg to buckle. Gripping the edge of the sink to keep from falling, I turned my head to yell at him. Then I stopped when I saw his eyes. He couldn't protect me from a foe inside my own head, those eyes said, but he at least had to try.

I took a deep breath, then let go of the sink. Turned off the water. Dried my hands on the oversized t-shirt. Plenty of time for self-flagellation later. Right now, I had another hunt before me. I didn't know if I was looking for a nocturne or some other type of creepy crawly, but whatever it was, it killed Trini. "I'm going to cut out the fucker's heart while it's still alive." My voice shook with rage, not sadness or guilt. Galen looked alert, his scent sharp with anticipation. Mama was back, and mad as hell.

I called good-bye to Simone and left the infirmary. I should have checked in on Tony, but the thought made my throat close up. I'd never really learned how to look human frailty in the face. If I had to see Tony, more-lively-than-a-six-month-old-terrier Tony, lying in a bed, all pale and bandaged, I might forget how to breathe and never regain the knowledge. I took the low road and left.

The setting sun was so near, compared to the fluorescent light of the infirmary, that I closed my eyes for a moment. With the brightness shut out, I let myself enjoy the warmth, while also soaking up the sounds of the Sankha camp. Younglings shouting. A whistle blowing. A teacher barking orders. And laughter. With a longing so strong it stole my breath, I wished I could just stay here, on this spot, and never leave.

But that wasn't happening. Raising my face to sniff the air, I followed my nose to the practice yards. Finn leaned on a fence there, watching the younglings. I knew he was evaluating not only the younglings, but also the instructor. Although I was sure he noticed me coming toward him, he never took his eyes off the field. When I reached him, I stood with my hands on my hips, glaring. Finally, he glanced at me. "Yes?"

His eyes flicked to Galen, who stood beside me. I didn't need to look to know that Galen was in full-on protective mode. He'd never forgive Finn for making me hurt. That bothered me surprisingly little. "I need to take the outsider back to the city."

Finn blinked at me, his eyes cold enough to burn. "No, you don't."

"I need to continue with the original plan of using him as bait." At my raised voice, a couple of the younglings paused in their practice, earning them a sharp reprimand from their instructor.

Grabbing my arm, Finn pulled me away from the fence. "Lower your voice." An order, through clenched teeth.

"You have about three seconds to let go of my arm before Galen makes good on his threat. If I don't bite you first."

His jaw tightened, but he let me go. "He is your mess. Janus wants you to take care of it, now."

After watching Tony bleed all over me and getting the news about Trini, I was all dried up inside. Prime conditions for the forest fire of rage that blazed through me. I felt the pressure inside my head that meant my eyes were glowing. Even my voice crackled when I spoke. "No."

Finn's scent flashed to angry, causing Galen to tense beside me. I wrapped a hand around Galen's collar, knowing that if he bit Finn, this conversation would be over and I'd lose. I tapped the fingers of my free hand against my thigh, and waited for Finn's response.

"He's an outsider. With intimate knowledge of our world. There is only one response to that."

"Darcy saved my life! He saved Tony's life. Do you even care about that?" *Or do I mean that little to you?* Forget that he and I were lovers for the last hundred and eighty years. I was damn good at my job. Didn't I matter to him at all? I had a feeling I already knew the answer, and I hated how much the knowledge hurt. But I'd let a nocturne fuck me up the ass before I let him see that I was hurting.

"Of course I care." But his voice was distant, making me question whether he cared about me, or just about losing a well-trained Sankha. Good help is hard to find.

I made my eyes and voice go cold, a skill I picked up from Finn. What good was it to spend time in the bed of the coldest man on earth, if I didn't learn a thing or two from him? "We had an agreement, you and I. I use the outsider to hunt the nocturnes, and then I kill the outsider. I'll do my job, Finn. But I'm going to get the whole job done."

He opened his mouth to interrupt, but I steam-rolled him. "I have one more creature to hunt. I have to obtain answers. I'm going to use the outsider to draw them to me. I'll be your whipping girl. But let me do my job first, or you better believe I'll be telling Janus all about our little arrangement. And I won't leave out the part where you said something was wrong with him and he wouldn't listen to reason. He may not believe me, but he won't trust you the same way, either."

As the anger in his scent slipped away, I knew he would give in. Finn liked his job. He didn't want to be out shoveling shit with the rest of us.

"Very well," he said. "I will make an excuse. Ryder is guarding the cell; he'll follow your orders to step aside. But

Cat is heading border patrol tonight, and she'll expect an explanation. I will send word to her."

"Thanks so much, dear." At my tone, the corners of his mouth turned down, like he just bit down on a mouthful of aspirin. A howl from the infirmary made us both jump. Galen whined. "Leanna's awake," I said softly.

"Why do you—" I saw Finn's mind work like a deck of cards being shuffled. Then it went still, and his face fell at the card he drew. "Trini."

I nodded. He closed his eyes, then laid a hand on my shoulder. He left it there for a moment before raising his head and walking toward the infirmary. I watched him go, the thickening colors of the sunset providing a perfect backdrop for his lithe form. "Damn him." Just when I decided I could officially hate him, he did something, well, noble. There wasn't enough prime rib in the world to convince me to walk into that building, stand before Leanna, and witness her pain. And with barely any hesitation, Finn just did it. "Damn him," I repeated, then headed for the solitary cells, which lay beyond the mess hall, farthest from the forest.

It was easy to figure out which of the outhouse-sized buildings held Darcy. For one thing, a tall youngling named Ryder stood at the door, armed with a quarterstaff. For another, the surrounding air stank of Darcy's scent. The cells weren't ventilated well, with only a couple of small windows up near the roof, and the temperature had to be at least eighty degrees. Galen trotted alongside me, stepping in front of me when I stopped before Ryder.

Ryder bowed his head slightly. "Sankha Kellan."

"Ryder. I hear there's a package in there, waiting for me."

"Yes, ma'am." He stepped aside.

I opened the reinforced steel door cautiously. When I got the door all the way open, I saw him crouched in the far corner, squinting.

I stepped into the doorway to cast a shadow, allowing him to see me. "Come on, Jamison. Time to go."

Darcy didn't move. Behind me, Ryder shifted nervously. "Sankha Kellan? Ma'am. I thought you were going to ... take care of it here."

I turned and fixed Ryder with a stare. "Well, I guess you don't know everything. Your duties here are done, youngling. Dismissed."

I was being a jerk and I felt bad about that. I actually liked Ryder. He wasn't the brightest berry on the branch, but he had a lot of heart. And I was making him feel an inch and a half tall. I gritted my teeth and held my ground. Ryder only hesitated a moment before bowing and hustling away. I turned back to Darcy. "Well?" I said. "You coming or what?"

"Why should I?" His voice was rough, cracking around the edges. I guessed that nobody brought him sandwiches and coffee. I didn't even see a water jug in the cell. Rage, always accessible, rekindled as I imagined being locked in this brick oven for hours with no water.

A snuffling noise stole my attention for a moment. Galen was taking the opportunity to sniff around the inside of the cell. Personally, I wasn't too fond of the smell of fermented urine, but if it had to be there, somebody should enjoy it. I walked over to Darcy and held out a hand to help him up, noticing finally that he still wore blood, Tony's and mine, on his clothes and skin. My heart did an unpleasant little jig in my ribcage. "Come on. We'll get you some water once we're out of here."

Darcy stared at my hand, but wouldn't take it. "Where are you taking me?"

"Shoe shopping. What do you care? You're sprung."

Darcy just looked at me.

I blew my breath out with an exasperated grunt. The dizzy feeling was returning. I needed to eat again. "We're going to find the other nocturne. If it is a nocturne."

He glanced at the open door, then at his hands. He picked at the dried blood on his right forearm. "I have to call the funeral home. My sister — I have to make sure she's taken care of."

Emotions swirled in my gut, thick, slow-moving, and very heavy. "Okay. No problem." He finally stood up, and the words popped out with no prompting from my brain. "Thank you, Darcy. I'm sorry for the way you were treated, but thank you for getting us here. You — you saved Tony's life." Then

I looked away, because I didn't want to see whatever crossed his face as he thought about the fact that he'd saved a life for me, but I hadn't saved any for him.

Tail held high, Galen trotted outside and stopped by the door to wait. I stepped behind Darcy. "I'm sorry about this." I held him as though he were my prisoner, with my left hand on his shoulder and my right wrapped around his right wrist, twisting his hand behind his back and up toward his shoulder blades. Moving my lips as little as possible, I spoke softly. "Hold your head up, but don't look around. Keep your eyes straight ahead. Walk slowly, and when I push you, I want you to trip. Got it?" I gently pushed him out the door of the cell. He obligingly tripped over his own feet, grunting in pain. When his steps faltered, I pulled him up by the back of his shirt. "Very good."

"Like I have a choice," he muttered.

"Quiet," I said, loud enough for others to hear.

We continued that way until I got him into the forest and we were no longer visible to inquiring eyes. I released Darcy's arm. "All right," I said. "Now follow me, don't deviate from the path, and don't make any noise. We don't want to attract attention."

Darcy swung his arm in a circle to loosen up his shoulder. I'd been the victim of that particular hold more than once, and I knew it hurt. But he smelled angry, more so than a jammed shoulder warranted. "Why not?" he said.

I told Galen to heel and started moving at an almost-run. "The forest doesn't take kindly to strangers."

Although cold sweat added fear to his scent of anger, outwardly he held it together pretty well. At least until something crashed through the brush a few yards to our right, and he jumped two feet in the air. "Come on, keep up. Trust me, you don't want to be caught alone."

His fear scent grew stronger, so I slowed down slightly, which cut down on the adrenaline. As we neared the border of the forest, I caught the scent of the border patrol. It was dark, but just to be safe, I pulled Darcy's hand behind his back again, once again positioning us as captive and captor. We went about ten yards further, and suddenly Cat swung down out of a tree right in front of us. Because I smelled her there, I wasn't too shocked, but Darcy didn't have that advantage. He jumped, which caused me to unintentionally yank his arm.

Cat ignored his yelp, focusing her attention on me. "Sankha Kellan. I wasn't aware that you were removing the outsider from camp."

Finn must've forgotten to send a message to Cat, what with Trini dying and all. As senior member of her border patrol team, Cat had a reasonable expectation of being informed of those things. I couldn't brush her off as easily as I did Ryder. But I could try. "Last minute change of plans." Oh, please, don't ask why.

"Why?" She gave Darcy a narrow-eyed glare. "Everything you need is here."

Since the day I met her, I appreciated Cat's intelligence. She reminded me of Mal. At that moment, I would have given anything for her to be dumber than a monkey with a nail-gun. Since I couldn't outsmart her, I had no choice but to pull rank.

"Stand at attention, youngling." She did as I ordered. I felt time weighing on me like guilt, and I needed to move before it smothered me. "Finn was going to send word, but he got distracted, because Sankha Trini died and Sankha Leanna is crazy with grief. Now, I'm taking the outsider. That's all you need to know. Stand aside."

"Yes, ma'am." Cat said it through clenched teeth, but she said it. And I shoved Darcy into motion, walking past her without further incident.

Even so, as I glanced around the parking lot, I half-expected someone to come running after us. But no one did. The business park looked quiet. When we got to the truck, Darcy dug in his pocket with his free hand and pulled out my keys. I noticed, happily, that someone had disposed of the nocturne carcass. Dead body, hot day, and enclosed space added up to *ick*. Since I knew the border patrol was still watching, I made Darcy get into the back, promising softly that I'd let him out as soon as we were out of sight. Then Galen and I got in the front, and we headed off.

Chapter 19

True to my word, I pulled over at the edge of the business park and let Darcy get in the cab, Galen on the seat between us. I pulled a bottle of water from under the seat and handed it to Darcy. He shifted in his seat to glare at me. "Are you going to tell me where we're going now?"

I frowned. His anger scent was growing stronger. "My place. I need to raid the armory."

It was a mark of the bizarreness of the last few days that Darcy didn't question further, only sank into a sullen silence as we drove.

Nothing annoyed me like sullen silence. It made me feel like I needed to apologize for something. "Look," I said as I pulled into my parking lot. I shut off the truck. "If this is about getting locked in that solitary cell, I'm sorry. But a solitary cell's a whole lot better than a pine box. And I got you out, didn't I?"

Perhaps not the most empathetic of apologies. And though his anger scent grew stronger, he didn't have a chance to answer because Galen interrupted. He clambered onto my lap and started whining. "Hungry, big dog?" He wagged his tail and whined again.

We went up to the apartment. While Galen inhaled some kibble, I asked Darcy if he was hungry. He said no, but I made him a sandwich anyway, since I was making two for myself. He stared at the sandwich, then at his hands, which were crusty with blood. "Look, we don't have time for you to shower, but in the bathroom there's washcloths, wet wipes, soap. Help yourself to whatever."

Darcy disappeared into the bathroom and closed the door. I went into the bedroom and strapped as many knives on my person as I could manage. I was disappointed that I didn't have my short sword on me. Maybe I should get a spare, I thought, positioning the forearm sheathes at the optimal spot. As I dug around in the closet, I discovered my machete shoved in the back. Not exactly a subtle weapon, but it would be awfully helpful in the beheading process. I grabbed it. Even in this neighborhood, I couldn't walk around with a machete hanging on my waist. I searched fruitlessly for my duffel bag.

After slipping on a fresh long-sleeve shirt to cover the forearm sheathes, I went back out into the living room. Darcy was standing at the front window, every line in his body tense. A few feet away from him, Galen stood sentry. I studied the scene, wondering if Galen was guarding Darcy or guarding against him.

"Did you call the funeral home?" I said. My voice was loud.

He sounded robotic. "Visitation is on Saturday. Short graveside ceremony for family to follow."

I found myself wondering if he had any other family. I caught a whiff of gun powder and, upon looking around, saw a duffel bag in the corner. Not mine, but Trini's. Tony must have brought it up earlier. It smelled strongly of Trini, and faintly of Tony. Feeling a slight twinge in the chest area, I shoved my machete in the bag and slung it over my shoulder. "Ready?"

Darcy turned to look at me, the shift in the air sending more of his anger my way. "He attacked us during the day."

I frowned, struggling to catch up to his train of thought. "The nocturne?"

"Yeah. I thought they only came out at night. You know. Nocturnal?"

I rubbed my eyes. For someone who'd been unconscious all day, I felt surprisingly tired. "Can we do Theory of Monsters on the way?"

The anger wavered, though only slightly. "You in trouble?"

"I will be." I jingled my keys.

Darcy didn't move. "How much?"

"More than usual. Let's go."

Even though I shouldn't have, I decided to take Galen with us. I didn't want to put him at risk, but I felt like I needed back-up, and Darcy didn't count. Never make your bait your back-up. We made it as far as the door before Darcy stopped to glare at me again. "Are you going to kill me?"

I blinked. "I — why do you ask?"

"I heard them talking outside that outhouse they locked me in. It sounded like they were expecting you to kill me."

I hated dealing with smart people. "They were. They are."

For once, he didn't smell angry. He didn't smell scared, either. He just smelled empty. "Why?" he said.

I took a deep breath, looked down at my dog, then looked back up at Darcy. "Because you were in possession of documents and information that you shouldn't have been."

"You kill people over that?"

I shrugged. "Gotta put food on the table."

Apparently, that answer didn't tickle his funny bone — he smelled enraged again, more so than ever. "What's the big deal about those papers? They're not the Dead Sea Scrolls."

My temper finally slipped its inadequate leash. "How the fuck would you know? You probably don't know the Dead Sea Scrolls from a roll of toilet paper." Biting off the end of each word, I told Darcy briefly what the papers meant. "Can you imagine what would happen if someone managed to translate them? If they leaked the information to the media? Even if the only place to print the story was some rag like Weekly World News, people actually read that shit. We don't need those people running around Madison, with the papers as a treasure map, hunting down the invisible forest and its fountain of youth. We destroyed the documents."

"Apparently not."

I tried to tell myself that he was grieving and I should cut him some slack. "Yeah. Thanks for reminding me." I paused, unease settling in my lower intestine. "I don't know how that happened. There weren't many of us at the burning. Me. Mal. Finn, Janus." Darcy didn't know who Mal and Janus were, and I didn't bother filling him in. I was too busy trying to remember who else had been there. I came up blank.

Mal would remember. As I led the way down the stairs, I pulled out my cell phone and hit speed dial two. At the bottom of the stairs, Darcy asked who I was calling. It wasn't until after I said, "My sister," and his face fell from barely interested to devastated to stone-cold in a millisecond, that I realized my faux pas. I hung up the phone and stared at him. "Aw, man, I'm sorry." The two most inadequate words in the English language, but they were all I had, so I repeated them. "I'm sorry."

I watched him flip through a half-dozen emotions, his eyes fixed on a second-story window. Sadness, anger, despair, anger, fear, anger, icy stillness. And silence. I tried to think of something else to say, but even "I'm sorry" stuck in my throat now. I pushed out the front door, hitting speed dial two again.

When Mal picked up, she sounded bothered. I asked her if she was okay. "Yeah," she said. "Just a little busy. Was it you who called just now? How's life in the toilet?"

I loved my sister. She was so supportive. "The water's fine, you should jump in." I listened to her low chuckle, enjoying the sound. "Who was there that night? When we burned the documents?"

Silence. "Me. You. Janus. Finn. I think that was it. Why? You still dealing with all that?"

I sighed. "Yeah. It's been more trouble than I expected."

Another pause. "I'm surprised Janus is letting it drag on."

"Well." I told her about the meeting in Janus's cabin, when he hit me. "And then things got even worse. We—"

"He actually hit you?"

Her tone made me a little afraid for Janus's safety. "Well, yeah, but I did disobey him."

"He doesn't get physical. His hands are too delicate. What's going on there?"

I snorted. "You mean aside from the documents that shouldn't exist, the nocturnes that are changing their hunting patterns, and the outsider caught up in it all? Nothing. Just your average day at the office."

"Because I don't have better things to do than listen to your sarcasm? All I'm saying is, I hope you slugged him back."

"No, but Tony almost did." The memory made me warm.

Beside me, Darcy cleared his throat. "Maybe the girl talk could wait?" His tone irritated me.

Mal must've heard him. "Who's that?"

"The outsider."

"What — why — you know what? I don't want to know." Mal paused, then said, "Be careful. Don't get dead."

"Aw, I didn't know you cared." But the sudden warmth in my chest made the mocking tone difficult to pull off.

"I don't. It's just with all the shit you pull, you make me look really good."

Yup, my sister was supportive. Like a training bra trying to harness a couple of D-cups. "I guess I better stay alive, since I'm your only hope of looking good." I hung up.

We no sooner got the truck started than Darcy repeated his earlier inquiry. "Nocturnes."

I felt the iron vise around my throat loosen. At least he was talking. That thought stopped me. Since meeting Darcy, all I had wanted was for him to shut up and go away. Now I was grateful he was talking again? But the lightness in my belly could only be described as relief. "Yes, they are nocturnal. But they're not vampires. They can come out during the day, they just don't like to."

"Why not?"

Was this how it felt to talk to a three-year-old? "I don't know, maybe they have sensitive eyes."

With an impatient noise, Darcy's anger scent flared again.

Maybe it wasn't about being locked in solitary all day. But then why was he so mad?

"Are you going to answer?" he said.

What would he do if I said no? Probably better not to find out. I had enough battles to fight today. "Best guess? In daylight, nocturnes have to hold a shape longer, which drains energy. At night, they can slip in and out of shadows, but during the day, shadows are more scarce. Makes it more difficult to blend in. But I've never bothered to ask, so I can't say for sure."

Darcy nodded, then stopped mid-nod as he looked around. "This is my neighborhood."

Give the boy a cookie. "Yeah, I know." I ignored his repeated questions about why we were here. When we were still several houses down from his building, I parked the truck and opened the door.

"If you don't tell me what's going on, I'm going to get out of this truck and leave and you'll lose your bait. So you better—"

"Jesus Christ, do you ever shut up?" Galen's ears stiffened and flattened back against his head.

Darcy shut up with an audible click of teeth.

"Thank you." I took a deep breath. "Okay. We're here because, as my bait, your home is the most logical place for the nocturne to be waiting for you."

Darcy glared at me. His anger choked me. Literally. I coughed around the scent lodged in my throat. Galen's muscles tensed against my side, and I knew we needed to get out of the truck before Bad Things happened — i.e. Darcy losing appendages. I jumped down from the cab, dragging Galen behind me.

Darcy got out and walked around the front of the truck. He looked deep in thought. Uh-oh. "The nocturnes. They feed off bad emotions?"

I nodded.

"They were waiting for her to die, so they could feed on me." No question mark, but still a question.

My breathing developed a hitch, like a hiccup. "Yes."

He turned to face me, and the look in his eyes sent a thrill of excitement through me that I chose not to examine too closely. "Do you have a spare gun?"

I studied him. Never give a grieving man a weapon. Basic survival rule. Another survival rule: don't trust an angry person unless you know what they're angry about. When I saw Galen sniff the air, I followed suit. The spice of anger had dissipated, as the cold, calm scent of frozen tea filled my nostrils.

Survival rules were for sissies.

Opening the tailgate, I dug around in the duffel while keeping my eyes on the street around us. Deciding against a rifle — too conspicuous — I pulled out a handgun and slipped it to Darcy. Using his body to shield the gun from street view, he slid the cartridge out and checked that it was loaded, then slammed it back into place. I watched him, my mouth drooping open slightly. "Jesus. What kind of librarian are you?"

His only answer was a startlingly hard and humorless grin, and that thrill of excitement traveled down my spine again to pool in my stomach, making my pupils dilate and my hands itch for a blade. I bared my teeth in a return grin. Galen's tail swished once against my leg, and he practically vibrated as he sensed the imminent hunt. "All right," I murmured. "Let's play."

Chapter 20

I wiggled the blades on my forearms, loosening them in their sheaths so I could pull them faster. I caught a whiff of Darcy's scent as he turned his head to look at me. "Inside?" he asked.

"Not yet." I sniffed the air. As I recalled, the trash cans were at the far side of the parking lot. Too far away to be leaking their smell all the way out here. Which meant the stench coating my tongue came from something else. I pulled the blades from the forearm sheathes with a soft *snick* sound.

The scent was definitely stronger to the left. I decided to go the long way around. Motioning to Darcy to follow, I led the way to the right corner of the building, then around to the back. If the confrontation had to happen here, in this populated place, I wanted to get away from the street.

When we reached the back of the building, I knew I was right. The scent was strong enough to trigger my gag reflex. The parking lot was darker than a Stephen King novel. Stepping onto the pavement, I felt a crunch under my boot, then caught the dusty scent of crushed glass. Someone broke the bulbs in the security lights. Swearing silently, I held up a hand in front of Darcy's face to stop him. Then I turned to Galen. Darcy and I could walk on broken glass, but Galen didn't have the benefit of shoes. Rubbing my fingers together in a near-silent swishing sound, I got Galen's attention. Then I gave him the hand signals for down and stay. My beautiful dog only hesitated a moment before he obeyed.

The nocturne could be anywhere, and the sound of broken glass under my feet announced our arrival. I didn't move again, choosing instead to wait for the nocturne to come to us. For all my lack of patience, I had experience waiting out my prey. More experience than Darcy did, anyway. He stood very still for about ninety seconds, then he started to fidget. At first, it was just a twitching of the hands. Before long, his feet started to move. More glass crunched.

Its scent grew stronger, and I thought I saw movement to our left. It was hard to tell. The nocturne must be in its natural form, I thought. It could find us by scent just as well as I could find it. And if it kept those glowing red eyes closed, I wouldn't be able to pinpoint its position until it attacked.

When it spoke, its voice oozed from the shadows, making it all too clear why humans feared the dark. "He's mine, wolf. Give him to me."

"Mmm," I said, pretending to mull it over. "Nah. If you want him, you'll have to take him from me."

The only warning we got was that tell-tale swooshing sound, and a rush of hot rancid air. I pushed Darcy aside, raising my blades in an X shape to slash at the creature as it passed overhead.

It easily dodged me, and, with a flash of red as it opened its eyes, it swung back around to swipe at me with its claws, latching onto my right shoulder.

I grunted in pain. Brought up my left hand to slice its arm. I felt the blade slide through flesh. It tore its claws from my shoulder, taking a chunk of my shirt and my muscle with it.

I swallowed a scream. Anger slammed my already-charged system with even more adrenaline. I growled. "Darcy. You gonna fire that thing, or what?"

The nocturne came back for another pass. This time, it tried to push past me to Darcy. I leapt into the air to ram it with my uninjured shoulder.

Darcy's voice. "Where the hell is it?"

My feet hit the ground. I dropped into a crouch, and sniffing deeply, I said, "Left!"

Darcy fired and missed. I could smell the nocturne coming back toward us. "Wait for it," I hissed. "Wait for it." In a louder tone, "Come on, you stinking pile of monkey shit! I'm right here."

Not even nocturnes liked being called names. I finally saw the red eyes open and stay open. They were fixed on me.

It was going to pass only a few inches from Darcy as it dove. "Now!" I said.

I raised my blades just in case, but Darcy came through. He waited until the nocturne was close enough to kiss, then pulled the trigger. The nocturne dropped to the ground, and I straddled it. Déjà vu hit me as I used my legs to pin its legs down.

"Stand on its hands," I said to Darcy.

"What?"

The revulsion in his voice made me take my eyes off the nocturne to look at Darcy. "You shot the damn thing, but it offends your moral compass to crush a couple fingers?"

I smelled anger, hot and spicy, fill the air, almost overwhelming the nocturne's stink. Then the creature under me screeched in pain as Darcy stomped first one booted foot, then the other, on its claws.

"Your shoulder." Darcy sounded ill.

My right arm was slick with blood, but as the flow had almost stopped, I didn't think it was the blood that made him want to hurl. No, it was probably the fact that my shoulder was beginning to knit my deltoid back together, like some horrific fast-forward film. I could actually hear it, an awful squelching sound.

The healing meant that I would need to cut my interrogation short. A second major injury in twenty-four hours meant I could lose consciousness again before long. First things first, though.

"I'm fine," I lied, and then turned my attention to the nocturne. "Are there more of you?"

It raised its shoulders off the ground, bared its teeth, tried to lunge at my face. I slammed my left blade into its shoulder. It started to scream again, but this time I used a well-placed fist to its throat to cut off the sound. "That's enough of that," I said. "Now, I can keep crushing your throat, or you can answer my questions. Blink those nice red eyes once if you want more knuckles, twice if you want to cooperate."

It blinked twice.

"Good boy." I eased up on its throat, keeping just enough pressure in place so I could cut off any more screams. "Now. Tell me. Are there more of you here in town?"

Its voice was barely audible. "Yes."

"Very good. How many?"

"Don't know."

I twisted the blade in its shoulder, using my other hand to keep its scream to a sickly gurgle. "Try again. How many?"

It gasped as I let up on its throat. "Don't know. That one does not tell me such things."

I narrowed my eyes, dimly registering the sound of sirens approaching. "What one?"

"Kelly?" Darcy said. I shushed him.

The nocturne's blood smelled like boiled cabbage. "No name. Does not tell me such things."

Well, this was getting old. "Fine. One last question. Where did you get those documents?"

"Documents?"

I twisted the blade again. "Yes. Documents. The ones you gave to this human." Without moving my hands, I tapped Darcy's leg with my elbow. "Where did they come from?"

"That one does not—"

"Tell me such things," I finished. Out of patience and out of time, I picked up my other knife from the ground and slashed its throat.

The sirens were closer than I thought. A couple blocks away now. No time for beheading or behearting. As I heaved the somewhere-between-dead-and-not nocturne onto my shoulders, I told Darcy to go grab the duffel bag from the front of the building and meet me at the truck. I grunted as the nocturne's weight hit my injured shoulder and pain dazzled my vision, almost making me pass out right there. I shoved both blades into my left cargo pocket. The hilts stuck out, but since I was carrying a body on my back, I wasn't too worried about the hardware. I called to Galen. When he trotted up and sat before me, I praised him like he just achieved world peace.

"Okay, bud," I said, hitching the nocturne into a sturdier position. "Let's run."

Galen could've left me in the dust, but he stayed with me. We made it to the truck about three minutes before two police cars wailed up the street. Darcy was waiting with the tailgate down. I eased the body from my shoulders and crawled into the truck bed. After taking the duffel bag from Darcy and giving him directions to Diesel's farm, I settled in. Galen stayed in the back with me, apparently deciding that this was his chance to protect me. As I was feeling steadily weaker, I was happy for the company.

Looking down at the nocturne, I felt a spark of uncertainty. I needed to find out more about the nocturnes and their plan. Should I keep the thing alive until we got to the farm, try to squeeze more information out of it? Problem was, it didn't seem to know much of anything.

While I debated, we went over a bump and I lost my balance, jamming my shoulder against the side of the truck. My vision went black for a moment. When it cleared, I saw that I wasn't the only one jarred by the bumpy ride. The nocturne was sitting up and looking at me.

I saw in the glow of the streetlights that it looked stunned, probably the only reason I wasn't already dead. That was my last piece of good luck. The nocturne moved, back-handing me and sending me flying into the tailgate. My head banged against the metal and my vision went black for the second time in as many minutes. I didn't lose consciousness, though, and as I blinked furiously, I used my other senses to find the nocturne. The scent of boiled cabbage filled my nostrils.

When my vision cleared, I saw Galen standing over it. What looked like half the nocturne's throat was dangling from his mouth. That couldn't taste good. Swallowing bile, I told Galen to drop it. He obeyed. The flesh hit the truck bed with a *squelch*.

No more interrogation. I dug my machete out of the duffel and brought the blade swinging down on what was left of the nocturne's neck. The truck took a sudden turn, and I looked around. We were in a convenience store parking lot. Good, maybe I could get coffee. And food. I felt weak and cold.

I waited until Darcy stopped the truck before starting to relieve the nocturne of its degenerate heart. That was how Darcy found me when he opened the tailgate: kneeling over a headless body, prying open its ribs with my bare hands. Darcy threw up again.

After I cut the heart out, I sat back and took a deep breath. I regretted it instantly; the smells of death and vomit mingled with the scent of nocturne to create a perfume even Dolly the hyper-scented librarian wouldn't wear. That tickled something in the back of my mind, but the thought was too slippery — I couldn't grab on. I picked up a rag and wiped off my blades, then put them one by one into the duffel bag.

The sound of retching stopped. I waited a moment to be sure he was done. "You okay?" I said.

He started laughing. Uh-oh. Inappropriate laughter, definite danger sign. I turned and sat on the edge of the tailgate, letting my legs dangle. Galen sat on one side of me and I pulled Darcy down to sit on the other side. I looked around, checking for witnesses. Nobody. We were surrounded by fields, and the only vehicles in the parking lot were my truck and an old Saturn sedan with no side mirrors. I still had enough adrenaline pumping through me that I thought I would stay conscious for a little longer.

"No," he said. "No, I am not okay. My sister's dead, my life's a train wreck, and I'm sitting on Jack the Ripper's tailgate. No. I'm not okay."

"Don't forget you're covered in vomit."

"And you're covered in blood."

God, I wished Tony was here. He would've really enjoyed this conversation.

I looked around. We needed to move. If we had to pick a place to be sitting around, covered in blood and vomit, we couldn't do much better than a deserted convenience store, but still. No sense tempting Fate; she could be a right skanky bitch when she wanted to be.

Okay. Prioritize. As soon as possible, I needed to dispose of the body. I also needed to formulate a new plan, since I doubted the "take the bait to Mohammed" scheme would work a second time. But before I could do any of that… "I'm hungry."

Darcy slanted a glare at me. I shrugged and slid off the tailgate. Galen hopped off after me. Darcy stayed seated. I took off my torn shirt and examined my shoulder. I had a new mass of scars, but no more gaping wound. Using the remains of the button-down shirt, I wiped off the nocturne's blood, then tossed my brand new blood-rag into the back of the truck. "Can I get you anything? Water, coffee? Valium?"

"You think they have valium?"

"No."

"How about a wet wipe?" He looked down at his vomit-spattered shoes.

"That I can do." I walked to the passenger door of the truck and, after some rummaging, pulled a package of baby wipes out of the glove box. I pulled out three, and wiped down my arms and legs. Then I handed the rest to Darcy. "Have yourself a party. I'll be right back."

I went inside, got each of us a mammoth coffee and a donut, added two oily hot dogs for myself, and topped it all off with some matches and lighter fluid. The cashier, who looked fourteen and bored out of his skull, made eye contact only with the magazine he thought he was hiding behind the counter. Darcy, Galen and I climbed back in the truck and started for Mt. Vernon, and Diesel's farm. No better place to burn a body than a field in the middle of nowhere.

With the help of the coffee and the protein in the hot dogs, I felt closer to normal. Good enough that I took over behind the wheel. Darcy wasn't doing so good. He kept shaking his head and muttering under his breath. The thought occurred to me that maybe he'd finally cracked, but I let him be. I needed to think about what the nocturne told me.

More nocturnes in the area. Maybe that explained them hunting in pairs. Not enough food to go around? No, that didn't make much sense. Madison housed plenty of humans with negative energy to feed on. And I still didn't know where they'd gotten the documents from, or why they sent Darcy to me. And why were there nocturnes here at all, when they avoided wandering into our backyard for the last couple centuries? I sighed and turned on the radio. If I thought much more, I'd be joining Darcy in the Padded Wall Society.

I let the sounds of Disturbed and Seether seep into me, loosening my muscles and soothing my tired brain. The music seemed to have a sedating effect on Darcy, too. He stopped his muttering, sat back in his seat, and gazed out the window. The only member of our party who didn't appreciate the music was Galen, who curled up with a resigned set to his ears and ignored us both.

When I stopped the truck and turned off the ignition, Darcy glanced around. "What are we doing here?" He didn't sound terribly interested in the answer.

Hmm. Maybe he wasn't soothed, maybe he was just depressed. Then a breeze through the open window brought me a whiff of his scent, and my eyes widened. Nope, not depressed. Depression didn't have a smell — it tended to suppress a person's scent just like it did everything else. Darcy definitely had a scent to him, and it was hotter than ginger tea spiked with Tabasco. Galen caught it, too, and he stood up on the seat, shielding my body with his.

My tone careful, so neither male took the situation any further than it needed to go, I told Darcy that we needed to burn the body. He didn't bother to respond, just followed my lead as I got out of the truck. I considered asking him what was wrong, but the fact was, I didn't really want him to answer. Emotional honesty fell outside my purview. Just let me burn the body and get on with my day.

So, in blessed, but sullen silence, Darcy helped me gather wood for the fire. It took a pretty big fire to burn up a body, so we needed a lot of fuel. When the pile looked right, I carried over the nocturne's bits and pieces and laid them on top. Then I emptied the bottle of lighter fluid on top of it, lit the entire book of matches, and tossed it from a few feet away.

I put Galen in a down-stay at my side. We watched the flames and breathed in the scent. Charred nocturne smelled absolutely nothing like chicken. More like burnt rubber.

With that scent filling my head, I couldn't help but go back to the interrogation, if you could call it that. Nocturnes in Madison, not just two, but multiple. With a leader, no less, known only as "that one." I felt sick, and I didn't think it had anything to do with the smell.

I was pulled out of my head by an agitated scent. Some kind of cross between anger and fear. I turned.

Darcy was looking at me. Well, not looking so much as burning holes in my skull with his eyes. "You," he said. "This is all your fault."

Okay. This wasn't unfamiliar territory for me, but usually I knew what I did to get me there. "Huh?" I said eloquently. I heard Galen shift his weight slightly, but he didn't break his stay.

"It's your fault. Your fault I'm here. Your fault I feel so insane." Darcy closed the distance between us.

The fire must've masked the growing agitation in Darcy's scent. I only hoped that I could keep the situation from devolving any further. Galen rose, quivering at my side. I held a hand in front of his face to tell him to stay, although I wasn't sure he would continue to obey. Without taking my eyes off Darcy's face, I reached for the machete strapped to my waist.

Darcy continued his rant. "It's your fault she's dead. It's your fault. You could have saved her. They were telling the truth. You could have saved her, it's your fault."

I felt the situation slipping from my control. "Darcy—"

"You brought me here. You didn't think I'd recognize this place, that I wouldn't remember how you manipulated me? If you didn't waste so much time, if you just helped me like you promised, she'd still be alive."

My hand rested on the handle of the machete, but I didn't pull it. The wolf in me rose up and howled, but I pushed her away. I couldn't convince myself to fight him, when he had every right to his grudge.

When Darcy punctuated his last remark with a shove to my newly healed shoulder, Galen sprung. Without a sound, he pushed himself between me and Darcy. Before I could stop him, he knocked Darcy to the ground and stood on top of his chest. I came to my senses before Galen wrapped his jaws around Darcy's throat. "Hey!" I barked. "Galen. Here."

Galen trotted over to me. My hands shaking, I put him in another down-stay. Then I turned my attention back to Darcy, who smelled faintly of urine. He sat up slowly, like he wore a lead-lined toupee.

I needed to pay more attention. To Galen, and to my surroundings. "Sorry about that," I said. "Sometimes, if I don't defend myself, he steps in. Gets a little overzealous about it. Now listen closely, Darcy Jamison. You might be right. Maybe there was some remote, walking-on-Mars chance that I could've helped your sister. But I didn't, and that's over and done." I paused, swallowing hard before setting my jaw in stone. I would not apologize. The world was what it was. I didn't create it, I just walked its paths. "So you have to choose what battle you want to fight. You want to fight me? Or you wanna help me hunt down those nocturnes who were waiting to capitalize on your pain?"

He shook his head over and over, hands buried in his hair, making it look like he was pulling his head from one side to the other. "There's no point. No point. She was the point, and—" The sentence cracked in two, the second half falling away into silence. He swung his head to look at me, the scent of salt matching the wet sheen of his eyes. I longed for the scent of his anger. "It's a dream. Tell me it's a dream. Tell me I'm going to wake up."

I remained silent.

"Tell me!"

Humans these days were never prepared for layers of pain. They expected the world to stop at one. They said, "Okay, you took my parents, just leave me my sister. All right, you took my sister, but at least let me keep my sense of reality." But it never worked that way. Humans used to understand this, in the days when women birthed a dozen kids in the hope that a few would survive to adulthood. But now, when the mirage of a merciful world got shattered, humans invariably shattered along with it.

I tried for rational, talking-him-off-the-ledge language. "I'm sorry, Darcy. It's real. But that doesn't mean there's no point." Point to life? Point to fighting? Didn't know, didn't care.

He shook his head again, so violently I wondered if adults could give themselves shaken baby syndrome. "No. It doesn't matter what I do. Nothing matters. Nothing."

"Look. You've gotta keep going. There are still nocturnes out there. Help me, before they hurt someone else."

I could smell the moment he crashed. The last of his anger slipped away, leaving the nothing-smell of depression. "I can't," he whispered. "I can't. It's not worth it anymore."

Fuck talking him off the ledge. I wanted to slap him. I settled for leaning down, grabbing his shoulders and giving him a good shake. "Survival," I growled into his ear, "is always worth it, Darcy Jamison. Now listen to me. If you want to drive down the Straitjacket Expressway, fine. Be my guest. I'll even give you gas money. But first, you're going to help me get those nocturnes. Okay?"

He blinked at me.

I straightened up and held my hand out to him. "How 'bout you get up off the ground before a snake bites your ass?"

A snake biting his ass around here was about as likely as Minnie Pearl jumping out of the bushes and leading us in a square dance. But Darcy jumped to his feet.

We had to wait until the body was done before we left. Darcy didn't talk much at all. It was lovely, just me, my dog, a crazy, but silent human, and a nice bonfire. If not for the roasting dead body stinking up the place, it could've been a fucking postcard.

The only thing bothering me was my sudden reluctance to follow orders. The other day, I refused to give Finn and Janus the documents. And now, I wouldn't kill the outsider that threatened everything we stood for. This was Sankha 101: protect the Spring, even against poor hapless humans who just stumbled into the wrong place at the right time. It wasn't like this was the first time I killed someone as part of my job. Killing was the pinnacle of my skill set. And following orders made the world make sense. If that was gone, how could I know what was right?

The enormity of the questions threatened to crush my ribcage, so I shook my head and moved on to more pressing matters. I didn't really think Darcy was all that useful for bait anymore. Two nocturnes killed ought to make Darcy about as desirable to them as Tofurkey — containing the possibility of sustenance, but not really worth the risk. I still didn't want to kill him. The boy was handy with a gun and, now that he passed through the anger stage of grief, he seemed pretty compliant. I could do it by myself, I didn't really need back-up. But I was a wolf, part of a pack. It wasn't as much fun to hunt alone.

I was starting to feel like the Dread Pirate Roberts, from *The Princess Bride*: Good work, Darcy, sleep well, I'll most likely kill you in the morning.

Sooner or later, I'd run out of excuses.

Chapter 21

By the time the body burned down to bones and the fire was low enough that I could put it out, the sun was starting to rise. At the sight of the color-streaked clouds, a line from a Dar Williams song flitted through my head. I started to sing softly as I shoveled dirt on the embers, burying both ash and bones. Sudden and sharp, I felt a pang of loneliness. Mal and I had started harmonizing together before we learned to form actual words. Galen was my spirit brother, and he was wonderful, but I missed having other wolves who spoke and thought in the same language I did. Clenching my jaw, I cut off mid-verse and bent my head over my task.

"Please don't stop."

My head jerked up so I could look at Darcy. "What?"

His voice was so soft. "The singing. You have a nice voice. It sounds… Please don't stop."

I cleared my throat. Must have been the smoke, making my throat close up like that. I looked away. But I started singing again. It was a sad-sounding song, until you listened to the words. It was about finding yourself, and choosing to live.

When it was done, I let my voice fade away. Darcy came over and took the shovel from me, finishing the task. His eyes focused on the dirt, he said quietly, "Thank you."

Aw, shit. Gratitude again. He actually meant it, too. I could hear it in the simplicity of his voice. What was it about this guy? He brought down my defenses in a way that I couldn't fight.

Feeling hot, impotent rage bubble up in me, I grabbed the shovel from him. "We better go."

I tossed the shovel into the truck bed with more force and noise than necessary, then slammed the tailgate shut. Usually, slamming things made me feel better. Not this time. I opened the driver's side door, let Galen jump up on the seat, and followed, slamming the door behind me. That wasn't enough, either. Leaving Galen inside, I got back out of the truck, slammed the door, and then started banging on the side of the truck. I kicked and punched and yelled obscenities until I was hoarse and my knuckles were scratched and bloody. Leaning my head against the truck, I inhaled the combined metallic scents of blood and steel. I saw Darcy watching me. Looking at me like I was the crazy one.

I didn't make a sarcastic comment or an inappropriate joke. I couldn't think of one. Instead, I looked into those irritatingly human brown eyes and said, "I don't want to kill you."

He blinked. "Okay."

I shook my head, backed away. "No, not okay. I'm supposed to kill you. That's my job. My orders. I follow orders. But—" I looked in his eyes again. "I don't want to."

His eyebrows drew closer together. "Then why do you keep saving my life? Wouldn't it be easier to just let me die?"

I blew my breath out in a frustrated noise. "Apparently not." I squinted at him. "Fuck. You say thank you. For things like singing a stupid song. Who does that anymore, past the age of, like, five?"

His eyebrows separated and raised an inch. "Plenty of people."

"Not in my experience."

"Maybe that's because you're not a very nice person most of the time."

His honesty surprised me enough that I laughed. "Yeah." The sound of Galen's frantic whining finally reached my ears, and I moved to open the door of the truck. He hopped out and sniffed around me, seeking the reason for my agitation. Not finding it, he sat in front of me and stared up at me, waiting for a hint about what was going to happen next. I looked up at Darcy once again. "If I don't do it, someone else will."

He met my gaze. "If someone has to do it, I want it to be you."

My mother's philosophy slapped me in the face. *If you have to do a shit job, hold your head up high and own it. Don't cringe and pretend it's someone else's fault.* I nodded once at Darcy. "We better go," I said again. *But I'm going to do my damnedest to keep you alive.* He was a person who said thank you. I didn't care what he said. That was rare. And rare things should be saved.

Chapter 22

In the close proximity of the cab, I was jarringly reminded that Darcy had vomited on his shoes. "Christ, you smell like you've been sleeping behind a dumpster."

He gave me an up-and-down glare. "Yeah, well, you look worse than I smell."

I laughed out loud. At the comfortingly normal sound, Galen thumped his tail on the seat. "My apartment, then," I said, scratching Galen behind the ear. "We can clean up there."

As I drove, Darcy fidgeted — leg jiggling, fingers drumming, shoulders twitching. The more he fidgeted, the more annoyed I got. Fortunately, just as steam was about to explode from my ears, I saw salvation in the form of golden arches. "I need coffee," I growled, and pulled into the lot.

I ordered my usual three sandwiches and as many coffees, then looked at Darcy. He shook his head. "I'm not hungry."

By my count, the only thing he'd eaten in the last eighteen hours was half a donut. And people said I had freakish eating habits. I turned back to the drive-thru and ordered an egg sandwich and some hash browns. After scanning the menu, I saw they had hot tea, so I got him one of those, too.

As I parked, Darcy opened his mouth, probably to protest, but I didn't want to listen. I snagged the hash brown patty and shoved it in his mouth. After choking a little, he chewed and swallowed. Then he ate like a good little piggy, even if he did glare at me the entire time. I didn't care. I had coffee. Nothing else mattered.

Except the nocturnes. And the outsider that I was supposed to kill. And the documents that still never should've existed. With a sigh, I pounded more coffee, and started once again for my apartment.

"Are you and your sister close?"

I was so busy enjoying my caffeine buzz that Darcy's question smacked me upside the head. A little smile touched my lips before I could stop it. But Darcy's tone was so careful, it made me hesitant to speak. Finally, I just said, "Yeah."

"She live around here?"

"She used to. Ten years ago or so, she moved away."

When I glanced at him, his face seemed shadowed, although the sun shone bright through the windshield. He didn't ask if she was one of the Sankhain, the question I expected. "But you see her a lot?"

"Yeah, she was just here last—" I broke off. Now that I thought about it, Mal hadn't been to visit for over a year. How did a year go by without seeing her? "Well, she's here a lot."

Emotion leaked into Darcy's voice, and I once again smelled salt sprinkled over his scent. "You should spend more time with her. Make it a priority. You never know—"

I held my breath for a minute, to avoid the scent of grief. Galen curled up on the seat and laid his head in my lap. Not daring to exhale, I nodded and made an affirmative sound. With a quiet sniffle, Darcy turned to face the window. Sipping my final cup of coffee, I turned onto my street.

Home sweet home. I wondered if I had time for a shower. Might as well, I thought. If Darcy was still alive at sundown, the only thing waiting for me was the inside of a solitary cell. Better get my showers while I could.

I was about to hop out of the truck when Darcy's voice stopped me. "I'm sorry."

I turned back to him. He, in turn, stared at the glove box like it was an oracle.

"About before. It — it's not your fault. I just—"

Suddenly, the cab was much too hot, and I was regretting that third coffee as my stomach rolled. "Come on, vomit boy. I think I've got some clothes upstairs that'll fit you. If you're nice to me, I might even let you use my shower." He was going to bathe if I needed to hold him under the shower head and lather him up myself. Saying he smelled like he'd been sleeping behind a dumpster was an insult to dumpsters everywhere.

When we got up to the apartment, I pushed him into the bathroom with a clean towel and a promise of clean clothes. While Galen snarfed down his breakfast, I went into the bedroom to find some clothes that would fit Darcy. I found a pair of men's running shorts — I never bought women's shorts, as I never cared to have my butt cheeks on display — and a t-shirt that was baggy enough to fit Tony.

I thought of Tony suddenly, remembering the feel of his breath on my neck as he whispered in my ear. Something tight and heavy wrapped around my chest, until I could only breathe in short gasps. I didn't want to put a name to that emotional vise, so I ignored it and focused on the clothes in my hands. I carried them to the bathroom door, behind which the shower still ran.

I opened the door without knocking and set the clothes on the counter. I started to slip the door shut again, when I heard a sharp, wet intake of air. I froze. More gasping, then a horrible strangled keening sound. I glanced behind me at Galen. My dog's head was cocked to one side, as he listened to the noises Darcy made. Probably, I should leave Darcy be. If I were him, I'd want to be left alone in the shower until I was done crying. But god, it sounded awful.

"Darcy?" The noises cut off with a cough and a thump. "You okay in there?"

"Fine," he said thickly. "Almost done."

That tightness in my throat must have been from thirst. I decided I needed more coffee, even though my stomach was still churning like a milkmaid at Oktoberfest. I told Darcy the clean clothes were waiting for him. "Take your time," I said, and closed the door softly.

Hightailing it to the kitchen, I made a pot of coffee and polished off a cup by the time I heard the bathroom door open. I was working with Galen, trying to teach him to roll over. It wasn't going well. Galen nuzzled the hand holding the roast beef, and I decided to cut my losses. I put Galen in a down-stay and made him hold it until Darcy walked into the room. Then I tossed Galen the meat, which he caught in his mouth. Allowing myself a brief smile, I watched Galen trot over and sniff Darcy up one side and down the other. Then, as Darcy turned to face me and his scent drifted my way, I realized why Galen found him so fascinating. With my clothes on him, my scent mingled with his in a very intimate way.

I didn't see that coming. Nor did I anticipate how my body would react to those intermingled scents. *Pack*, my body said. *Mine*. I felt an almost overwhelming urge to stand next to him, breathe in that scent, maybe rub up against him, place my face against his skin and—

I shook myself. "Okay, so I'm going to shower, help yourself to anything, and um, yeah, whatever." And I scooted past him as fast as I could, locking myself in the bathroom before I did something embarrassingly wolfish.

Even though the water was lukewarm, that shower was quite possibly the most sublime experience of my life. I left my bloody clothes on the floor next to Darcy's. Maybe I could wash them together, and give Darcy his clothes back later. Or maybe he'd be dead by sundown. I sighed and rinsed the last of the soap off my legs. No. That wasn't going to happen, not on my watch. I needed to keep Darcy Jamison alive. My brain had labeled him as pack, and that superseded orders. Orders be damned.

At least I was getting better at thinking it. I didn't feel the need to punch or maim anything, this time.

I wrapped myself in a towel and went into the bedroom to dress. When I came out, I found Darcy in the living room. He sat on the futon, Galen standing before him. He was scratching Galen's back end. As Darcy's scent hit me again, I wondered if I could ask him to take the clothes back off. My head spun, not uncomfortably, as I rode another wave of desire. Not sexual. Just a craving for contact, skin to skin. It had been so long since I touched someone who smelled like me. *Pack. Mine.* I wanted to shape-shift, to get him to shape-shift, to be true pack mates.

Except Darcy wasn't a wolf, I reminded myself. Darcy couldn't shift.

Jeez. Humans were lucky. They might have ridiculously short life spans, but at least they didn't have a sense of smell making them want things they couldn't want, not really. I was so wrapped up, I almost missed what Darcy said.

"You said I could help you."

My mind went in a direction that was probably very different from Darcy's intention. "Huh?"

"With the nocturnes," he clarified. "What could I do? You don't seem to need much help."

I grinned. "Lots of people would disagree with you there, but since you're not talking psychological help…"

Darcy snorted.

I pulled out the Glock .45 that Darcy left in the bathroom with his clothes. "For starters, you can take this."

He took it and once again checked the ammunition, looking like the action was automatic.

I narrowed my eyes. "Seriously. Where'd you learn to handle a gun?"

He smiled, soft this time. "My dad was a cop. My mom insisted that if his gun was going to be in the house, even under lock and key, he needed to teach me and Gwen how to handle a gun so we didn't shoot each other. At least not accidentally."

I wasn't sure if that last sentence was joking or serious. "You keep up with it?"

"Once a week, I go to the range. And before you ask, I'm a decent shot. Gwen—" His smile drooped a little. "Gwen was a lot better than I am. She won a few competitions when we were kids. But I do okay."

"Hey, as long as you shoot the nocturne instead of me, I don't care if you can't hit the broad side of a brontosaurus."

He grinned, and even if it was a little sour, it was still better than tears. "I'll do my best."

"Great." I stared out the window at the now-bright morning. "Now if only I knew what the fuck happens next."

I hadn't meant to say that last bit out loud. I was supposed to be the hero here. Heroes never wondered what to do next, and they certainly never said fuck. Boy, was I not hero material. But I was the best we had.

Galen materialized at my side and leaned against my leg. Breathing in his scent, I felt a little steadier. Then Darcy's his-and-hers scent grew stronger, and my heart thumped like a Labrador's tail. He was right beside me. When he spoke, I jumped. "Talk it out."

I glanced at him. "What?"

"Talk. About what happens next. You need to find the nocturnes, right?"

"Yeah, but I have no idea how. I don't have any bait anymore, since the nocturnes probably gave up on you, and I have absolutely no usable intel."

Darcy exhaled. "Well, then, maybe you go in a different direction. What else do you need?"

I lowered my head, rubbing the back of my neck with my right hand. "I guess I need to find out how the nocturnes got the documents in the first place, but I don't have any leads there, either. Maybe if I still had the documents, but I handed them over."

"That's not exactly true." When I stared at him, Darcy shrugged. "I kept a couple pages."

"You ... what?" My voice was dangerously quiet. Galen stiffened and watched me for a cue.

Darcy repeated himself. "I kept a couple of pages. I hid them in my apartment."

Rage, with him, with myself, burned slow and all-consuming. "Why? How?"

Darcy looked like he was realizing just how hot the water was. "Well, I ... well, I was curious. I thought maybe if you didn't come through for me, maybe I could ... well."

"You..." My voice drifted off. I couldn't make my tongue obey.

"Listen. You said there were four of you that burned all the historical documents, right? And so, doesn't it stand to reason that only those four people could've stolen the documents?" Darcy's voice was patient, with a tinge of desperation.

I thought about it. "Yeah. Just the four of us. I stood guard over the record room before the burning. No one else went in or out, until everything was destroyed."

"Okay." He moved to stand in front of me, sending another distracting breeze of scent toward me. "Well. It wasn't you, so that's one down. Who else did you say was there?"

I closed my eyes, took a deep breath. This thinking thing moved so damn slow. "My sister. Mal." I heard Darcy's intake of breath and cut him off. "Before you ask, no. No way in hell. She had less reason to steal the documents than I did. She can't read the language."

Darcy's feet shuffled as he began to pace, his scent moving hypnotically from left to right. "Okay. So. Then there was ... your leader? Janus, right?"

I opened my eyes and frowned at him. "How'd you remember that?" I couldn't even remember his sister's name, and he just said it five seconds ago.

"I'm a reference librarian." When I continued to stare blankly at him, he clarified. "It's my job to know weird and arcane facts, or at least know how to access them. Janus was a god, in some ancient culture. It stuck in my head."

Shaking my head, I closed my eyes again. I seemed to think more clearly when I wasn't forced to process sights. I confirmed that Janus was another member of our torching party, and that Finn, his head lackey, was our fourth.

"Finn," he said slowly. "The guy with the blond ponytail?"

"And the golden poker up his ass."

Darcy made a noise that might've been a snort of amusement, or it might've been a hiccup. "Can you eliminate either of them?"

Asking my brain to analyze the situation was like asking mud pies to taste like tiramisu. I squeezed my eyes even more tightly shut, but all that did was make my face hurt. "I don't know," I exploded finally. When I opened my eyes, it took them a moment to focus. "I'm no good at this."

Darcy stopped pacing. "You've managed to keep me alive so far. I'd say you're doing all right."

Whoa. What was going on? I was receiving a positive critique from the guy who, not long ago, blamed me for everything that was going wrong in his life? "Yeah, great, I kept you alive. I'm supposed to be killing you, remember? I can't even get that right."

"What is it with you?" he asked. "You can't just choose for yourself? Sankha don't have a right to free will?" He still pronounced it "sanka," like the instant coffee.

"No. We don't." My voice was so matter-of-fact, even I pitied me.

Darcy pitied me, too. "Of course you do. Everyone does," he said.

I flopped down on the futon. Galen shoved his head in my lap and I absently stroked him. "You're just saying that because you don't want to die."

"A couple of hours ago, I practically begged you to let the nocturnes have me. You talked me out of it. If I want to live, it's all your fault."

I started laughing, which brought Galen's head up and set his tail to wagging. "You're right." My laughter faded, and I felt empty. "I wouldn't know what to do with free will if somebody made it into a dagger and pointed me at a target. But that's not the point."

Darcy sat down beside me. "No. It's not. You need to find a mole. All right. What would set this person apart? Why would someone want to steal these documents, then decades later turn them over to nocturnes?"

Well, if I knew the answer to that, I'd be done with this bloody job by now and enjoying a little peace and quiet. I didn't say that out loud, though, because Darcy actually seemed good at this analysis thing, and I needed the help. We talked until almost noon, going round and round the mulberry bush, until I hit my wall.

Darcy was saying, "I just think, from what you're saying, that both Finn and Janus are good possibilities. Finn's a jerk, although you say that's pretty normal for him. But Janus's behavior has changed recently, right? So—"

I stood up. "Let's go," I said. I was halfway to the door before Darcy even rose.

"Where are we going?"

"Your apartment. We're going to get those papers. Maybe if I smell — see them again, I might be able to recognize — something."

A horrible thought occurred to me, and my hands shook as I clipped Galen's leash on his harness. Why didn't I catch a familiar scent on those papers? If they really were pocketed by one of us, I would have recognized the scent of the Sankha who took them. At first, I thought maybe the paper-napper handed over the documents to the nocturnes so many years ago that their scent had long faded. But what if I didn't recognize a scent because the Sankha's scent had changed? And I knew of at least one person whose scent recently changed in a big way. "Janus," I said.

Galen shoved his cold nose against my cheek, pulling me back from the edge. I nuzzled him gratefully, then rose from my crouch and walked out the door. Darcy followed us downstairs. "So, Janus, huh? You think it's him?"

I wanted him to shut up. I wanted him to take off the clothes I gave him so he didn't smell like a pack member when he said those things. I wanted to wake up from this insufferably long nightmare. "I don't know. I'll have a better idea when I can examine the documents."

Darcy was quiet until I yanked open the front door. "You've known him a long time?"

"My whole life. Pretty long."

"It must be hard," he said carefully. "Having to look at your friends this way."

Not as hard as it was going to be when I found out for certain it was Janus. Not as hard as it would be to kill him.

My jaw tightened again, and I fell silent as I drove.

Darcy led the way upstairs to his apartment. I shortened up Galen's leash, keeping him close by my side. The building had a sterile, hairless smell that screamed a "no pets policy." Just as Darcy was pulling the key from his lock, the door behind us opened. I spun, reaching for the blade on my right forearm, hidden once again by a long-sleeve shirt. Fortunately, I didn't pull it, because the young woman standing there with a baby on her hip probably wasn't much of a threat.

"Darcy," she said. "Oh, thank God. We were so worried about you."

I stiffened, but Darcy stepped out from behind me. "Hi, Sarah. What's wrong?"

"You didn't hear? Oh, God." Voice hushed with attempted horror and vibrating with morbid fascination, Sarah told us all about the gunshots that went off the night before, right behind this very building. I looked at the baby that she shifted from one hip to the other. He — she? — smelled like shampoo and baby wipes. Apparently a well-cared-for child. But I still had an urge to steal it away and give it to a guardian who didn't think gunshots were quite so much fun. Not that I had a lot of stone-throwing room, living in my glass house.

Darcy made some soothing noises while I pushed his apartment door open. Grabbing the back of his shirt, I pulled him with me as I backed through the doorway. The mother gave me an odd look, but before she could say anything else, I shut the door in her face.

Darcy turned and frowned at me. "That was rude."

I shrugged. "So go tell the teacher on me, hall monitor."

"She's my neighbor. I have to live next to her."

"Yes," I said, annoyed. "And you're a terrible liar. How long do you think it would take for that woman to figure out you were hiding something?" As I spoke, I dropped Galen's leash so he could wander. For a moment, he stayed by my side, but then curiosity got the better of him and he started the slow, methodical sniffing that would give him the History of Darcy's Apartment.

Darcy's scent wasn't angry necessarily, but it wasn't calm, either. Not ginger tea, more like bad chai. Better move things along. I made a sweeping motion with my hand. "How 'bout those documents, Sparky?"

"I'm not that bad a liar. I hid the fact that I took those papers from you, didn't I?" But he moved deeper into the apartment. "Come on. I stuck them in my dictionary."

I followed to the bedroom. His bedroom was the size of my bathroom, and it only had one window. I had a little trouble breathing as my claustrophobia made me think the walls were actually closing in on us. The trash-compactor effect was enhanced by the bookcases. Every inch of wall space was hidden by bookcases, taller than I was, jam-packed and looking like they'd fall over if you sneezed on them. The dusty smell of old paper turned my attention to the nearest case. Eyes wide, I ran my gaze over the collection of what looked like antique books and first editions.

"Wow."

Darcy, who'd been flipping the pages of a dictionary that looked like it weighed more than Galen, looked up. "What?"

"That's some collection." My hand reached, of its own accord, toward a copy of *Pride and Prejudice*. At the alarmed noise Darcy made, I managed to stop myself short of actually touching it. "Where'd you get all these?"

His tone was soft, fond. "A lot of them were my mom's. She loved them, the older and more delicate the better." He chuckled. "She was always easy to buy Christmas presents for. Find her some old book that was falling apart and she'd cry like you gave her a bag full of diamonds." With a shrug, he returned to his mammoth dictionary. "After she died, Gwen took a couple and I got the rest. Every once in a while, I see one that Mom would've liked and I add it to the collection."

My lungs shrunk three sizes. I was grieving the magnitude of his loss, and I'd never even met his family.

Mumbling that I needed to make a call, I stumbled toward the living room. I stood before the front window, resisting the urge to press my nose against the screen to get some fresh air. He came from a family — *the* family. The sort of obnoxiously happy family that all us dysfunctional types dreamed about. No wonder the nocturnes wanted him enough to risk a fight with a Hycene. The loss of that last tie to happiness would create a gluttony of emotion.

Pulling out my phone, I dialed Mal's number. I counted the rings — six — before it went to voicemail. Not bothering to leave a message, I took a couple more deep breaths before heading back toward the bedroom. Galen raised his head as I passed. I stopped. He trotted over to me and let me pet him before he got distracted by some long-past spill in front of the refrigerator.

I was just about to turn left into the hallway leading to the bedroom, when Darcy rounded the corner and bumped into me. "Oh! Sorry," he said. He stooped to gather the papers he'd dropped.

Once again I grew distracted by the combined scent he sported. I inhaled deeply, my eyes sliding shut. Who knew the musk of wolf and the tang of tea would mix so well together?

"Um, Kelly?" My eyelids reluctantly relinquished their grip. Darcy was looking at me a little funny. "You okay?"

Yeah, sure. I'd be even better if you let me lean a little closer, press my nose to your skin. Would that be okay? I cleared my throat. "Yeah, just a little tired."

Taking the papers from him, I carried them into the living room and sat down. Galen trotted in, sniffed the papers, and growled, a low, dark sound that made the hair on my arms stand up. Then he looked up at me, waiting for me to take action against this paper that smelled like our enemy. I met his gaze for a moment, then shrugged. I didn't like the smell either, but I needed the information these pages could provide me.

I tried to think of a way to sniff the papers without being obvious about it, but I failed. I raised the top paper to my nose and inhaled. On the second page, I thought I smelled something under the nocturne stench. I closed my eyes, shutting out all the other stimuli around me, and held the dusty paper as close to my face as I could. I inhaled until I felt like I was drowning in oxygen. Holding the breath in my lungs, I blanked all thought from my head. An image, a face, tried to form in my mind. But it stayed just out of reach.

I avoided looking at Darcy until I set the last page on the pile. As soon as my eyes met his, he burst like a cotton-wood pod. "What on earth are you doing?"

I raised a tired hand. Inhaling so much rotten air drained me. And I felt genuinely shaken. I must have recognized a familiar scent on that page, but it was like my brain was preventing me from connecting that last dot. I felt a howl build in the back of my throat, but whether it was a howl of frustration or despair, I didn't know.

Darcy repeated his question, then tacked on an addition. "What are you doing? Did you find anything?"

I sighed and explained, in a way that revealed as little as possible, that I was smelling the papers to see if anything jumped out at me. "You know, a perfume or something."

"Does this have anything to do with how you were able to heal like that?"

I hesitated. He already knew a lot more about my world than I wanted. "A little, yeah."

He measured me through narrow eyes. He was quiet for a long time. Then, suddenly, his head bobbed in a single nod. "Probably comes in handy."

I let out a held breath. "Yeah. It does." I waved my hand at the documents. "Unfortunately, not handy enough. I thought I almost recognized something, but..." I shook my head. "Just wishful thinking, I guess."

Darcy padded over to me. He was still barefoot, I noticed. Still wearing my clothes, too. When he knelt in front of me, I froze. What the hell was he doing? "Close your eyes," he said.

I wanted to shake my head and say, no way, Jose. He smelled too good; I was afraid if I closed my eyes again, my instincts would win out. I'd end up wrapped around him like a bloody boa, and I'd have to kill him just to end the embarrassment. But he cocked his head to one side, his mouth set in a stubborn curl that told me this wasn't a yes-or-no question. With a sigh, I gave in and closed my eyes.

I felt a shift in the air, and the scent of nocturne magnified. Darcy must've picked up the sheaf of paper and raised it to my face. He held it there a moment, then asked softly, "Don't think, just answer. What do you smell?"

I frowned and opened my eyes, grabbing the papers from him. "You need to change clothes."

Poor guy. Even I was having a hard time following my train of thought, and I was supposed to be behind the wheel. But with him there, smelling like that, I couldn't register anything more than the surface stuff. Any time I tried to scent deeper, I got a nostril full of Darcy, which made the rest of the world cease. I didn't know if I wanted to fuck him or just curl up in his lap. Until he took off the clothes that gave him that scent, I wasn't going to be worth spit.

And the thought occurred to me that even if he did take off the clothes, I'd still be fixed on his scent. Once a pack member, always a pack member. "Please," I said. "Just — change. Please."

He opened his mouth as if to question me further, but finally just nodded. When he rose from his crouch, I had to bite back a whimper. Part of me really wanted him to smell that way, forever. Mal had been my only pack for so long, even a 2-D substitute like this seemed worth clinging to. To avoid looking at him, I once again held up the papers to my face. Mmm, nothing like some good, rotten nocturne scent to put a damper on a mood. I kept them there until Darcy disappeared into the back of the apartment.

When he returned, he was wearing his own clothes, the clothes I loaned him neatly folded in his hand. I almost told him to just burn them, then realized that might seem rude. Instead, I forced a smile as I took them. "So," he said, obviously trying not to ask what the hell was wrong with me. "Did you pick up any smells?"

I hesitated. Was there any way to answer that question without sounding crazy? Not that I could see. I cleared my throat. "No. Your, uh, your scent was too — strong."

"But I showered."

I laughed humorlessly. Yes, he showered — in my soap — and dressed — in my clothes. "I didn't say it was a bad smell. Everybody has a scent. It doesn't mean they need to be taken out back and hosed off."

"Oh." He took a moment, then looked at me with big, earnest eyes. "Will you explain it to me sometime?"

My throat shrank to match my lungs. "Yeah. Sure."

"You want to try again? To smell the papers?"

"Yes." But first, I needed to get away from him and put those clothes someplace where they wouldn't interfere. A biohazard container, perhaps? Or the back of the truck. "Do me a favor. Stay here. I need to check—" I thought for a moment. "I just want to make sure there aren't any more nocturnes around. Before we leave. Okay? I'll be right back."

Without waiting for a response, I held the clothes and the documents to my chest with one hand, grabbed Galen's leash with the other and scooted out the door. I resisted the urge to lean against the door and breathe. I felt like I'd just narrowly escaped something.

"Wait!" Darcy's voice followed me down the stairs, but I didn't even slow down.

I tried to make my voice upbeat. "Be right back," I repeated over my shoulder. Once outside, I took in several gulping breaths of hot, humid air. Then I scowled. This Darcy-as-pack thing was really messing with my head. Now that I was out of the building, I could swear I smelled—

"Mal!" I cried. A familiar figure leaned against my truck, pushing into motion when she saw me coming. My surprised grin withered as I got closer, and her scent hit me. "You stink," I said. At my side, Galen growled softly. I shushed him.

"Hello to you, too." She raised her eyebrows in an annoyingly superior stare.

"Well, you do. You smell like nocturne." My nostrils flared as I caught the scent of blood. "Are you okay?"

"Aside from having a mental hobbit for a sister? I'm great." Her nostrils flared as she took in my scent. "Who's that on you? The outsider?"

"Yeah." I didn't feel like explaining the whole he-was-wearing-my-clothes thing. "What are you doing here?"

"Well, you sounded like you were having so much fun, I thought I'd come play." She glanced at Galen. "Hey, dog."

"I told you, he doesn't like being called that."

"And that, little sis, is why your ass is stuck in a shit-shoveling assignment instead of doing something fun. If you stopped reminding Janus that you can communicate with your furry little friends, he might actually forget why he planted you here." She took a step closer.

Without warning, Galen snarled and lunged at her. I reined in his leash and pulled him back to my side.

"Whoa," Mal said. "Sorry. I won't call you 'dog' anymore, I promise."

I didn't bother looking at her as I responded, focusing my attention on Galen instead. "It's probably just the scent. We've had one too many run-ins with nocturnes lately." I paused. "Why do you smell like nocturne?"

"I was worried about you. I went to your apartment, and a good thing, too. You had a nocturne camped out by your building. I took care of it. You must be getting lazy, letting nocturnes move into your little ghetto."

A nocturne next door? My heart started to pound. We were just there. Did it arrive after we left? Or — and this was more disturbing, because it didn't make any sense — did it let us leave? Galen was still wound way too tight. I could smell his fear, his adrenaline, and I didn't like it. Torn between wanting to protect my dog and wanting to properly greet my long-lost sister, I forced my breath out between pursed lips.

"Are those the documents?" Mal asked.

I risked a glance at her, then down at the papers still clutched in my right hand. "Yeah." I passed them to her and tossed the loaned clothes to the ground. Happy to have both hands free to soothe Galen, I murmured, "That's what all the fuss is about. There should be a drum roll."

"And confetti." The rustle of papers brought a new wave of scent to me, and my nose twitched. As I inhaled, Mal's face filled my mind. Like hers was the face I hadn't wanted to remember, upstairs in Darcy's apartment. But that didn't make any sense. It must just be the way Mal smelled like nocturne that was confusing me. Too much stimuli, too little time.

Never one to miss an opportunity to pass the buck, I turned the problem over to her. "Can you smell anything on them? Besides nocturne, I mean. I was trying to get an ID on the Sankha that gave away the documents, but I ... got distracted."

"Who, you? What happened? Finn took off his shirt?"

"Come on, give me a little credit. Finn's pecs aren't that great."

Mal's laugh played on my eardrums. "Give me a little credit. I was there for the infatuation phase, remember." She raised her voice, thinning it out to a breathiness that was the envy of 900 operators everywhere. "Oh, Finn. He's so pretty. Just look at him. Oh, I wish I could kiss him. Oh!"

I turned to glare at her. "I never said those things. And just because you haven't gotten laid in the last century doesn't mean I'm going to abstain out of solidarity."

"At least I have standards." She sniffed the papers.

I scowled. "I have standards."

She raised her eyes to meet my glare. "Standards? Like what? No garden implements?"

"Or goats. I don't do goats."

Mal laughed again, making me smile. Putting Galen in yet another down-stay, I walked over to her and wrapped my arms around her, burying my nose in her hair. I breathed in so deep, I got light-headed from all the oxygen.

She always felt so frail to me. My natural build was muscular. Hers was feminine, petite, fine-boned. In other words, we didn't look like twins. Her hair was a rich auburn to my black-and-silver, my eyes deep amber while hers were a brown so dark, they were almost black. Her facial features were as delicate as the rest of her, while mine were square and strong. I was taller, she was better endowed. Our ears were almost identical, though. And our senses of humor.

When I pulled away, she waved the papers. "I don't recognize any scents."

With a sigh, I nodded and returned to Galen's side. "I was afraid of that." I hesitated for a moment before asking, "What do you think happens to a person's scent when they turn nocturne?"

Mal froze, her scent growing to occupy more space. She gave me an odd look. "Why do you ask?"

"Well." I told her what I noticed about Janus, and my suspicions.

She swallowed hard. "Hmm. That's an interesting idea. I never really thought about it."

"Tell me you can think of another idea."

Her shoulders lifted as she heaved a sigh. "I don't know, Kell." She looked me square in the face. "But if it is him, we need to eliminate him. Immediately."

That was Mal, always thinking ahead. My stomach turned over. I looked down at Galen, who was staring at Mal as if she were a bomb and he was trying to decide which wire to cut. A thought occurred to me, and I glanced back up at Mal. "Hey, how did you find me here?"

She'd been studying the documents, and looked up in surprise. "I tracked you. Your truck needs its exhaust checked, by the way. It has quite the scent signature."

"Oh. Thanks." I hadn't noticed anything. I'd have to get Trent, our camp mechanic, to check it out. Then a breeze lifted a new scent to us, and both Mal and I looked over at the building.

"Hey, Kelly?" Darcy. "I know you said to wait upstairs, but you're taking forever. Is everything—"

When he rounded the corner of the building and saw Mal, he stopped dead. He and Mal spoke at the same time.

"What's she doing here?"

"You didn't kill him? How stupid are you?"

Confused, I looked from one to the other. Darcy was giving off his strongest fear scent yet, and that was saying something. Mal, on the other hand, smelled like charred dog hair — she was angry. I released Galen from his down-stay and pulled him tight to my side. Feeling my tension, he growled deep in his chest. "What the fuck is going on?" I asked, but I never got an answer.

It happened fast. Mal pulled a knife and threw it at Darcy. Reflexively, I dropped Galen's leash, drew a blade of my own and tossed it to knock Mal's off-course. I was too late. Mal's blade hit Darcy in the stomach, and he fell to his knees with a soft grunt. Even as he fell, Mal moved in to finish the job. Just as she pulled the knife out of Darcy's stomach, I rammed into her with my shoulder. She lost her balance and stumbled backwards, away from Darcy. I could smell his blood, hot and tangy. While Mal was still regaining her balance, I reached into my pocket, grabbed my cell and dropped it behind me, in Darcy's general direction. If he was able, he could call 911. It was the most protection I could offer him.

Of course, he might call 911 and, with his dying breath, give them a description of my truck, complete with the license plate that surely his librarian mind had memorized by now. But I had to take the risk. He still smelled like pack.

Mal shoved my shoulder. I growled back at her.

"What the fuck are you doing?" we yelled in unison.

I caught a scent in the air, of approaching humans. "We gotta go," I said, and grabbed Mal's arm.

"Give me your keys, I'll drive."

"It's my fucking truck, I'll drive. Get in." I whistled for Galen, who was still standing by Darcy. "Hustle up, bud. Let's go." As Galen obediently hopped into the truck, I caught a glimpse of my phone in Darcy's hand. I met his eyes for a moment, then swung up into the truck and roared away.

Chapter 23

When we put some breathing room between us and Darcy's apartment, I pulled over and glared at Mal. "What the hell was that?"

She glared right back. "I was going to ask you the same thing. What are you doing, keeping the outsider alive? Are you going soft? Or is it something else? Maybe you gave the nocturnes those documents. Is this all part of your master plan?"

I couldn't believe what I was hearing. "Jesus, Mal, look at who you're talking to. When have you ever known me to have a master plan about dinner, much less something like this?"

She paused, and I felt anxiety and anger fill the sinkhole that her silence left in me. Then she shook her head, a wry grin shadowing her lips, and all my anxiety drained away. "You're right. Sorry. I just — why was that dumb bastard still vertical? What's going through that head of yours?"

A low growl pulled my attention from her. Galen was staring at Mal, pulling a full-on Cujo at the slightest hint of tension. He must've really been stressed. Guilt tugged on the shirttails of my consciousness, but I pushed it away. I massaged Galen's neck and head, and returned my attention to the conversation.

Except I couldn't remember it. I was so tired, I could barely see straight. Sitting still was a huge mistake.

Mal must have caught something in my scent. "How long's it been since you slept?"

I looked at her, trying to remember. "Well, yesterday, I was unconscious while I healed — Christ, was that really only yesterday? But that doesn't really count as sleep. Before that, I don't know."

"You were unconscious? How — you know what, never mind. You can tell me later." She half-rose, turning so her butt was wedged up against the dashboard. "Come on, scoot over. I'm driving."

"I'm fine," I said.

"Right. I've seen zombies more awake than you. Come on. I'm not going to let you decapitate me because you fell asleep behind the fucking wheel." She tugged my arm, and Galen shifted his weight as if to lunge at her. Only my hand on his collar kept him on the seat. Mal lifted her lip and growled at him. Galen maintained a low growl, but he didn't move again.

In the interest of keeping the peace, I pushed Galen over on the seat and sat in the middle. Mal clambered over me and awkwardly twisted behind the wheel. I felt a flutter of hope. Maybe it would be okay now. Mal was here. Everything would be fine. I leaned my head back against the seat, suddenly overwhelmed with relief.

"Hey, stay with me, kid." Mal's voice pulled me back from the edge of sleep. "We're not done quite yet. I took care of the outsider, so your situation won't get any worse there, but we still have Janus to deal with."

Without raising my head, I angled it so I could see her. "That's why you stabbed him? To protect me?"

"Course," she said, starting up the truck. "If I don't do it, who will? Not you, since you obviously have a death wish."

She was the third person in less than two days to suggest I was suicidal. That seemed significant, somehow. "Coffee," I grunted.

Mal grinned. "You read my mind. How many burgers you want?"

I glanced at the clock on the dash. It was late enough for burgers? That's right, it was noon when Darcy and I went to his apartment. No wonder I was tired. I hadn't eaten for hours. "Three. No, four. Extra—"

"Pickles, I know."

I smiled as she pulled into a drive-thru and placed the order. Mal was the only person I knew, teenage male younglings included, who ate more than I did. She ordered four double cheeseburgers for herself, on top of my four singles. The kid at the drive-thru probably thought we were buying food for our rugby team or something.

I thought I knew the answer, but I asked the question anyway. "Where are we going?"

Mal slanted a glance at me. "To Disney World." Our sense of humor really was identical. "We're going to camp, short-bus. To get you out of the frying pan and clean up this mess."

I nodded and sipped some coffee. Then I choked as I thought of something. "We can't go to camp."

Mal sounded weary. "Why not?"

"Well, for one thing, it's broad daylight. And I was supposed to bring Darcy's body with me." Body. The word echoed inside the hollow of my skull. My voice skipped as a mental image invaded my brain space. An image of Darcy, lying dead in a pool of blood. Darcy's body, growing cold. Darcy's body. Mine. Pack. I swallowed and tried to remember what I was saying. "As proof. That I did the job. I can't go back without it."

Mal looked at me funny, and my stomach lurched. She could probably smell some emotion on me that didn't jibe. "And whose fault is it we don't have him?"

I growled at her because she was my sister and she was supposed to be on my side. And because a little anger felt so much more comfortable than whatever made my stomach churn when I pictured Darcy. "So you've never made any questionable decisions? I guess screwing that werewolf bitch and almost getting mauled to death was a great idea. Or when you decided to break into the kitchens and bake a cake for Nix's birthday? And then forgot about the cake because you started making out with Simone—"

"Okay, okay. You promised you'd never mention that again." She took a sip of coffee. "We're not going back to get him. There's a possibility he isn't dead, and the place could be crawling with cops by now. Going back isn't an option." She looked at me. "Why the hell do you smell hopeful?"

Because now I was picturing Darcy being loaded onto an ambulance, a nice paramedic assuring him he'd be fine while jabbing his arm with an IV like Darcy was a pincushion instead of a sentient being. "Um, I guess I'm glad we're not going back. I just really don't want to go back to Dar— to the outsider's neighborhood. Place creeps me out."

She studied me with a tractor-beam gaze. I held my breath until she spoke. "You wanna wait for dark, before going to camp?"

Relieved that she wasn't pressing the issue of my weird emotions, I considered. I didn't want to get in trouble, but I wanted this whole thing to be over. And I was already exiled. Could my situation get any worse? "No. Let's go."

She thought a little while longer. "I'll vouch for you with the outsider. Say I witnessed everything, you took care of him, we can all live happily ever after. Blah, blah, blah."

If Mal said it would work, it would work. Mal's plans always worked. Except for the cake. And the werewolf. And... I turned to the bag of food.

I really didn't want to think about it anymore.

— «» —

When we reached the forest, Mal and I did a weapons check. "Got everything?" she asked.

"I think so."

"What about the machete?"

"We shouldn't need it, and it's kinda bulky. Besides, they'll probably take our weapons."

"You never know."

With a shrug, I buckled on my homemade sword belt, which consisted of a men's leather belt and heavy-duty shoelaces. Outside of a renaissance fair, you just couldn't find good quality sword accessories anymore. A girl had to get creative.

We took the long way around, since it was still daylight. As we sloshed over familiar ground, I relaxed for the first time in days. The wet terrain distracted Galen somewhat, but he still kept a close eye on Mal. He was bordering on paranoid. I really needed to get life back to normal, for his sake.

When we reached a point where we were far enough away from the businesses to enter the forest, Mal and I stopped and looked at each other. "Ready to dive?" I asked.

She gave me a teeth-baring grin. "Come on in, the water's fine."

We stepped forward into the familiar scents and sounds of the forest. The trees huddled around us, welcoming us home. I took a deep breath, storing the scent-memory for later enjoyment. Then I scowled, because Mal's tainted scent ruined my moment. "How long did it take you to kill that nocturne? You still stink."

"At least I have an excuse. You smell like old gym socks for no good reason."

Her response wasn't really an answer. My face crumpled into a frown, as that scent and her dodge started to pick at my brain. "I showered."

"When, last Wednesday?"

I stuck my tongue out at her, and she reached out and tugged on it. Caught between spitting and laughing, I pulled away, almost tripping over Galen. The worry disappeared.

"Ahem."

Our play ground to a halt. A feeling of déjà vu washed over me as we looked guiltily up at the younglings before us. Mal got us into trouble a lot when we were kids. She was always hatching some scheme to steal food from the kitchens, or nab a couple of horses and go riding in the middle of the night, or sneak into Janus's cabin and leave a dead squirrel in his bed.

"We're here to see Janus." Mal's tone was more severe than Dracula's widow's peak. Dirk jerked to attention, and Cat raised her chin speculatively.

"Yes, Sankha Mal," Cat said, her voice appropriately deferential. Her eyes told a different story, though. They weighed Mal. Cat took her job as patrol leader very seriously, and even a living legend like Mal Faolanni didn't escape scrutiny. "You weren't expected."

Mal's face remained expressionless. "We went the long way around. No one saw. We're here to see Janus."

Cat hesitated a moment longer before telling Dirk, "I'll take them in. Call if anything happens."

He nodded and disappeared into the trees. Then we followed Cat through the forest. They didn't confiscate our weapons, I realized with surprise. Why not? Not that I wasn't grateful. But it was weird. Why last time, and not this time? Maybe Janus had forgiven me. Yeah, right.

The closer we got to camp, the heavier my steps became. What were we walking into? Yes, I trusted Mal, and yes, I knew we were going to see Janus and "clean up this mess." But as much as I trusted her to formulate a plan, I detested not knowing what it was.

Mal grunted. "What the hell's your problem? Something's gonna decide you're prey."

"Nothing. I just don't like following the yellow brick road without knowing what's going to happen when we get to the wizard."

"Sweetheart. That's not the fairy tale we're living. This is the one where the big bad wolf wins in the end."

Cat glanced at her sharply, but didn't speak. Mal's reassurances weren't comforting me for once. "Don't think I'm familiar with that fairy tale."

"Don't worry, I am." Mal's head was high, and her stride was as long as her short legs could manage. "Just trust me, little sister. Would I lead you astray?"

I laughed, and both Cat and Galen looked at me. "Only when you're awake, shrimp."

At Janus's cabin, Cat waited in the outer room with us while Tevin announced our arrival. Even out here, I could smell it. Sour vinegar, Janus's newly acquired scent. Mal looked at me, eyebrows raised. I nodded, my face twisting in distaste. She turned toward the door to the inner room, squaring her shoulders. Galen and I followed her lead, and if my hands spent a little more time fidgeting with the hilt of my machete than necessary, the rest of me looked brave.

And then it all happened so fast, I just didn't see it. I didn't even know when she pulled the blade. While we were walking through the door into Janus's inner sanctum? Or before? In my defense, Mal's scent never changed. No fear, no tension, no trepidation. Nothing even to indicate she was sweating. Even when she raised the blade and threw it, even when it entered Janus's abdomen, her scent was as calm and steady as when she had embraced me less than an hour ago.

It took a second for my brain to catch up to my eyes, and then fear and horror hit with a roar. While Cat tried to tackle Mal, I ran to Janus. I forgot about him being a traitor. Now he was just the man who raised me. I didn't smell bile or feces, which meant his stomach and intestines were intact. He was breathing, which meant his lungs probably were okay, too. The wound shouldn't kill him, at least not right away. I felt relief until I looked in his eyes and saw the sadness there, inhaled his scent and smelled the defeat in it. My mouth fell open. Then a hand crash-landed on my shoulder, shoving me away. I landed on something soft and furry. Galen. I dug my hands into his coat and held onto the one thing in that room that made sense.

Chapter 24

The hand that pushed me away belonged to Finn. With the help of four younglings the size of linebackers, he was able to subdue Mal. A petite shape-shifter could take down two or three muscle-bound hulks. But one against four were odds even Mal couldn't beat, especially when they wrestled her to the ground and two of them sat on her. She was shouting the whole time, that Janus was a traitor and she was only protecting us. Then Ryder shifted his weight so that the air was pushed from her lungs, and she was silent.

Why didn't they just shoot us? I didn't know. Shock, maybe. I didn't care.

I didn't help Mal or try to assist Janus. I was too busy fighting the urge to shift. If I moved, if I spoke, if I so much as took a deep breath, I knew I'd lose control and shift, and the world was enough of a cluster fuck without adding wolves to the mix. And wolves it would be, because if I shifted, Mal wouldn't be able to stop herself. The scent of a pack member freeing herself was too much for any shifter to resist. I clung to Galen and I watched.

Finn carried Janus to the bed. Simone materialized, started to work on him. She said something to Finn, and he told the younglings to take Mal and me to solitary cells. One of the linemen knocked Mal on the head, and two of them carried her limp form from the office. Then Cat and Tevin came over to me. Cat reached down and grabbed my arm, and her rough grip was all it took.

I pulled away with a snarl, rapidly losing all sense of my human half. A young, inexperienced shape-shifter, when she shifts, doesn't retain much humanity. She's just an animal. I hadn't lost myself in a long time, but that day, even before I changed physically, I was less human than Galen.

My wolf half was terrified. The pack was changing. Standings no longer clearly defined. Nothing worse than uncertainty for a low-on-the-totem-pole wolf.

My clothes ripped apart as I shifted. The shouting started up again. Added to my fear. Galen came to my side. They should've just let us run away. But they cornered me and my brother. They tried to grab us. We stood shoulder to shoulder. Growling and snapping anytime a hand came close. Soon we both had bloody muzzles.

One of the males held something that smelled like cold fire. I knew that thing was dangerous. He pointed it at me. I snarled and lunged again. The male jumped back. Dropped his weapon. My nose twitched. I inhaled their fear. They were scared of me, of us. That made me bold. I dove at the smallest one, the female who smelled like sun-warmed leaves.

The little female had teeth. Not in her mouth. In her hand. She bit me in the shoulder. The tooth detached. Stayed in my flesh. Pain. My leg went limp. I stumbled. Frantic barking. My head jerked. I looked at the tall man that smelled like forest floor. He held my brother by the neck. My brother struggled. Tried to wrest free. He needed my help. I tried to take a step toward him. My foreleg collapsed. The female with the teeth shoved me to the ground. She pinned me. Gripped me high on the scruff of the neck. Held tight. Couldn't whip my head around to bite her. Something whooshed toward my head. The world went black.

— «» —

When I woke up, I was still a wolf, but I had my sense back. I stood experimentally. My head pounded, but the stab wound in my shoulder was already healed. My leg held my weight again. After I shook myself, I walked the walls of my cage several times. I sniffed the air coming in from the high windows, searching for some hint of Galen or Mal. Nothing. The scents of stale urine and mold depressed me, so I shifted back to human form. Instantly, I wished I hadn't, because I didn't have a scrap of clothing on. Sitting bare-assed on the dirt floor was extremely uncomfortable. I glanced around the solitary cell, noting from the lack of light at the window that I'd lost the rest of the day.

The air was hot and thick, like an attic on an August afternoon. Standing up and leaning against the relatively cool brick wall, I reviewed my options. I could keep my mouth shut and wait until someone came to interrogate me. Knowing Finn, he'd put that off as long as possible to try and break me down. And he probably wouldn't bring clothes with him, to demoralize me further.

Or I could make a hell of a lot of noise until the youngling that was undoubtedly stationed at my door got sick of me and found a way to get me clothes and maybe even some food. And maybe I could get him to tell me how Janus was doing, and where Mal and Galen were.

"Hey! Hey! How about some clothes in here? Hey, anybody out there? This is inhumane. I'm gonna call Amnesty International on your ass. Come on, mother f—" Well, that was the gist of it, anyway. I didn't get an immediate response, of course. Rapidly, hunger and annoyance sapped my creativity, forcing me to recycle insults. Repetition seemed to work as well as any other tactic, though. Just as I was about to begin my third refrain of comments about mothers in compromising situations with farm animals, the small doggy door set in the wall slid open. The doggy doors had been installed to deliver food and water without risking an escape.

A tray piled with food, two gallon jugs of water — no coffee for prisoners — and a stack of clothes slid through the small opening, accompanied by an angry, "Shut up already." Even though I'd never heard that tone in her voice before, I recognized Cat's voice right away.

"Cat, wait!" The door started to close. "Wait or I'll start up again after I finish my food." The door stopped. I thought fast. Any questions about my sister would only cause the door to slam shut. So I set that worry aside and focused on the others. "Thank you. Look, I just want to know, where's Galen?"

She hesitated, then said, "He's fine. He's stuck in an empty cabin."

Relief. "How's Janus doing?" I held my breath.

"What do you care, wolf?"

I felt her hatred like a hard slap. I liked Cat. She used to respect me. I swallowed my feelings. No time. Getting down on my hands and knees, I put my face as close to the door as I could. "I care, Cat. I didn't know what she was going to do. Please." My voice cracked, and I swallowed to wet my throat. "Just tell me if he's okay."

She made me wait for it, but finally, she answered. "I don't know. Nobody knows." She started to close the door again.

"Wait. They haven't come out to tell everybody he's dead?"

"Didn't I just say that?" Her scent was so hot with anger, I thought it would singe my nose hairs.

Simone fixed him. He was still alive. Why did I care? He was a traitor. But he was also the closest thing to a father I ever knew. "That's really good news. If he was dead, they would let you know."

The only response I got was the doggy door slamming shut in my face.

Well, at least I had some answers. And food. And clothes. The night wasn't out of the crapper, but it was making progress toward the rim of the bowl. I dressed and ate, and then sat down to think.

Mal tried to kill Janus. I never expected her to just up and kill him. Without a trial, or asking a single question. But maybe Mal didn't need to ask. In Janus's office, as I looked into his eyes, I realized what that bitter scent meant.

He no longer carried the confidence of an alpha.

True alpha wolves didn't fight for dominance. They didn't have to. The fighters, the ones who snarled to defend the smallest scrap, those wolves were in the middle to bottom of the pack. Fear of losing even more control over their surroundings made them defensive. Janus never struck me physically before, never, no matter what I did, because he didn't feel he needed to. I might have strayed, but eventually, I would obey. It was simply expected, because he was dominant over me and we both knew it. Somewhere along the way, he had lost that confidence. The sour vinegar smell was weakness.

Mal must've recognized it while waiting in the outer office. And when a member of the pack grew weak enough to endanger the pack itself, especially when that pack member was the alpha male, the pack had no choice but to cut him down. It was just survival, preservation of the strong through elimination of the weak. Trials weren't necessary. Maybe in human terms it was extreme, but in wolf terms, it made perfect sense.

So why did I feel sick when I thought about it? I wanted Janus to explain himself to me. Why do what he did? Why turn to the nocturnes? Could they offer him something we couldn't? Did they tell him they could give him back his strength of will, make him stronger than ever? And how did he get in touch with them in the first place?

My mind careened to Darcy. Did he call 911 in time? Was he alive? If he was alive, what did he tell the authorities? He had been stabbed; people were bound to ask questions. I exhaled my irritation. Why didn't he stay in the damn apartment, like I told him?

And what was it about that whole scene that was bugging me? I felt like something was missing, and I wracked my sore brain, trying to recover it. I wished Tony was here. Mostly because he was smarter than me and would have some ideas about the answers to the questions. But also because his scent might've distracted me from all the questions, and from the smell of urine that, even in human form, I couldn't ignore. Was he getting better? The nocturne ripped him open pretty good. I should've asked Cat about him.

Just as I began to obsess over how very small my cell was, I heard voices outside. Cat arguing with someone, a male. Why did he leave his post, she wanted to know. I couldn't understand the male's response. The deep masculine tones vibrated on a lower frequency, making the words blend together. Fine, Cat said. I thought I caught a rotten scent that made my stomach clench, but in the space of a breath, it was gone. The bolts on my door slid back.

The door swung open, and a hand beckoned me forward. I hesitated. Then I recognized the scent. "Mal?"

"Come on. She'll be back soon."

I hurried forward in a crouch, like no one could see me as long as I was three feet tall. "How? What?"

Mal grabbed my arm and pulled me around the corner of the building, into darker shadows. "Come on. We gotta go."

"Wait." I dug in my heels. "Go where?"

"I don't know. Alaska. I've always wanted to go to Alaska."

"We'll be defectors. They'll hunt us down. And what about Galen?"

She stopped trying to drag me. "We're already defectors. I tried to kill Janus. Remember? And you rode in on the same horse, so as far as they're concerned, you're in on it. It's our word against his. We don't have any proof, and Janus has Finn wrapped around his Oscar Mayer too tight for him to see a damn thing."

I swallowed hard. "I have Finn wrapped around a few body parts of my own."

She snorted. "Wake up, Kell. He's not on your side, he never was."

I closed my eyes as my gut clenched. *Don't make me leave.* "But—"

"So they hunt us down," Mal said, leap-frogging right over my words. "Gimme a break, Kell. Who are they going to send against us? We're Hycene, we're shape-shifters. We were fucking immortal *before* drinking from their bloody Spring. It'll make shooting fish in a barrel look like a sniper competition."

"What about Galen?"

Mal shifted her weight from foot to foot. "He'll be okay. We'll get you another dog. I'm sorry, Kell. But we have to go."

"No. No way. Galen—"

"Kellan. Are you coming or not?"

My stomach had turned to stone. Granite, so hard and so heavy that it pulled my torso forward until my hands were propped on my knees and I struggled to draw air into my lungs. Mal was my entire pack, my fucking archangel come to deliver me. And yet, my "yes" stuck in my throat. Leave? I swore an oath. The Sankhain were all I knew. And even if I could walk away from them, I couldn't walk away from Galen.

Then I remembered Darcy, and a picnic table on a dark night. Survival was always worth it. Mal was right, staying meant certain death. I straightened and looked Mal in the eye. "I'll go with you." She smiled and grabbed my hand, but I stood firm. I was stronger. "But only until we figure out how to clear our names. Only until we find proof, so they'll let us back in. And we're going to find Galen. Now. Non-negotiable."

Mal's nocturne-tinged scent turned soft with sadness. I frowned as I wondered why. "If that's what you want, little sis, then that's what we'll do."

I nodded slowly, not really satisfied. "Cat said Galen's in a vacant cabin." We ran over to the cluster of cabins that housed the Sankhain when they stayed at camp. "Hey. How did you get out of your cell? And how'd you get rid of Cat?"

Mal pointed toward the edge of the forest. "Him."

When I saw the figure standing there, my jaw dropped open. "Dirk?"

I thought I heard her mutter, "Sure." Then she turned back and smiled at me. "Men are so easily persuaded, if you know the right knob to twist."

My head began to pound. Not a headache exactly, more the *thwup thwup* of rushing blood between my ears. I had a memory flitting around in my brain, but my memory-catcher was too tired to grasp it in its net. Then I caught Galen's scent, the sound of his whining, and all thought shut down as the need to see my dog took over.

The door to Galen's cabin wasn't locked. Galen might be talented, but he couldn't turn doorknobs, and so there was no need to lock him in. I opened the door, and he threw himself at me. I melted to my knees, horrified at the idea of leaving without him.

Mal didn't give us time for a reunion. Almost as soon as I buried my face in Galen's fur, she was tugging me to my feet, dragging me toward the forest. Galen lunged at her, and since I didn't have a leash, he caught the back of her right hand. "Hey," Mal hissed. "If you can't control that thing, he's staying here and you can stay with him."

Thing? I bristled, but she didn't wait for a response. Instead, she turned and started to run. I hesitated for just a moment, and then, remembering my fate if I stayed, I took off after her.

Long before we reached the forest, Dirk disappeared into the trees. The scent of rotten trash hanging around Mal grew stronger. I planted my feet again. "Wait. Do you smell that?"

"What?" Mal's voice was downright impatient now.

"Nocturne. It's getting worse."

She waved the observation away like a cloud of fruit flies. "I've probably got some scent still hanging on. Nocturne scent's tough to lose when it gets on you, and it's not like I got to shower. Besides, I'm sweating. We're kind of in danger, because somebody keeps slowing me down."

At her pointed tone, I started moving into the trees. The farther we got from camp, though, the slower my steps got. I was right on the cusp of remembering whatever it was that bothered me. It wasn't until we reached the outer edge of the forest, and stepped into the field beyond, that I realized what it was. Mal hadn't persuaded Dirk to help her, because Dirk's knob didn't twist that way. I stopped moving, grabbed Galen's collar to keep him at my side, and stared at my sister.

My sister, who, right at that moment, looked pissed. "What?"

Please, oh please, let me be wrong. "What did you do with it?"

She stared at me. "Kellan, we have to go. They'll be here any minute."

"The nocturne you killed. At my apartment. What did you do with it?"

"Why the hell are you asking this now?"

"Just answer the damn question." My voice was low, cold, and strong, with just a hint of a growl.

Her tone shifted from angry to cautious. "I shoved it in your dumpster. Can we go now?"

I wanted to howl. I straightened my shoulders and slid my right foot slightly back, flexing my knees and raising my hands in a ready pose. I didn't have a weapon, but neither did she. And of the two of us, I was stronger. "I don't have a dumpster. City-issued trash cans. You never even bothered to stop by my place to check your cover story."

Mal's expression passed from surprised to annoyed faster than a cloud over the moon. "Who knew I'd have to? The Kellan I remember never bothered to ask questions, much less think about the answers."

"Guess you should have come around more often."

"Guess so." She cocked her head to one side, taking in my stance. She smiled at me. A sisterly smile. A familiar smile. Rage flared, and I wanted to smack that smile off her face.

Maybe it wasn't really Mal, I thought wildly. Maybe it was a nocturne who assumed my sister's shape. That was what they did, right? But the scent that the wind brought me shattered that hope. The thing before me had Mal's scent under all that rottenness. A nocturne could look like Mal, talk like Mal. But it could never smell like her. This was no nocturne. It was my twin, my littermate, my other half. My lungs convulsed. I bounced on my feet. Checked my balance and found it solid. "Galen, down. Stay."

"Oh, come on, little sis," Mal said. She closed the remaining distance between us and put her hand on top of my fist, pushing it down. "It doesn't have to be like this. The Sankhain are weakening. You know it's true. Janus hit you, for Christ's sake. Is that the pack you want to align yourself with?"

I closed my eyes so I couldn't see her anymore. Maybe if I wasn't looking into the eyes that I knew better than my own, I would be able to smell the lie on her. Maybe if I couldn't see her face, so much more beautiful than mine, I wouldn't want to believe her quite so badly. "No," I said. "You don't walk away just because things are rough. You stick."

Mal's laugh, which made me so happy before, now made me feel nauseous. My eyes flew open. She smiled at me fondly, and I wanted to punch her. "You and your ideals.

You really bought all those crappy fortune-cookie lines Janus fed you." Her eyes turned hard. "But they were lines, Kell. All of them."

"No." I shook my head.

"Yes." Her voice softened, turned kind, persuasive. "I know, it was hard for me at first, too. But look at us, Kell. He sends me after anemic bloodsuckers. And you? He has you walking dogs. Dogs, for fuck's sake! He turned us into figureheads, a couple of ornaments on a tree to be pulled out and forced to sparkle every once in a while. We're Hycene! We deserve respect!"

Her voice was maniacal, but when maniacal had a ring of truth to it, it sounded exactly like passion. And what could be more persuasive than passion? Had I not longed for a release from my stake-and-tether existence? And here was a friendly face, offering me exactly that.

I shook my head groggily, feeling drugged. Focus, damn it. If it sounded too good to be true, cut out its fucking tongue and stab it through the heart. I dragged in a breath. "It was you, in the hospital," I said. "You and a nocturne. You approached Darcy." Slowly, my brain put two and two together and made eight. "He recognized you, at his apartment. That's why you killed him."

"Oh, yeah, the human," she said. "I almost forgot about him. He was really useful."

My overtaxed thinking cap fell apart. "What do you mean?"

She shook her head. "You really never figured it out, did you? Honestly, Kell, you're good with a blade, but you don't have two brain cells to rub together."

I thought it hurt when I believed Janus was the traitor. That was a stubbed toe compared to the paralyzing ache that pulsed through me now. "Then enlighten me, wise one."

Head cocked to one side, she studied me, eerily resembling one of those raptors in that dinosaur movie. "Fine," she said. "Lesson one: distraction is the key to a successful surprise attack."

"You ... never cared about Darcy? You just wanted to keep us occupied."

She looked genuinely pleased. "Now tell me why."

Even as I hated her condescending tone, part of me preened at her pleasure. "You didn't want Janus and Finn to notice what you were doing."

"And what was I doing?" she prompted.

Grief sapped my energy. My shoulders were too heavy to hold straight anymore. "You were joining forces with the nocturnes. Planning an assault on the forest. Planning to bring your new friends to drink from the Spring."

"Kellan. Come with me," she said again. Her voice rang with evangelical fervor. "Together, we'll be unstoppable. We always have been. We're stronger, faster than all the rest. We'll rule the fucking world, Kell." She looked into my eyes. "I'm your pack, and you're mine. Come with me, and we can build a new pack, one that will never die off."

I squeezed my eyes shut again, tried not to search for the familiar scent I knew was still there. My traitorous nose found it anyway, and I whimpered as I ground my teeth together, to keep from saying yes. "No," I whispered. "Our pack is gone. The Sankhain are all we have left." As I said the words, I knew they were true. I knew where my loyalty resided. Sad but steady, I opened my eyes and looked into hers. "No."

Mal's eyes turned cold. "I'm sorry you feel that way." She lashed out, and I didn't know her fist was coming toward my throat until it hit. I was choking, gasping. She punched my left temple, and followed it up with a jab at my kidney.

I spun, retreating, trying desperately to put distance between us so I could launch an attack of my own. As I took my first deep breath, I caught several new scents approaching. Mal's back-up, the Non-Dirk, stepped out of the trees now that the nocturne was out of the bag. He handed Mal a sword. Bad.

But that wasn't the only scent my nose picked up. Tony ran out of forest. He was pale, and he couldn't seem to stand up straight, but he was there. And he wasn't empty-handed.

With a little finger-wave that almost made me smile, he tossed me my long-lost sword, still sheathed in its shoulder harness. As I pulled the blade free and whirled to face Mal and Non-Dirk, I saw Tony pull a gun from the small of his back and click off the safety. "Good to see you," I called.

"Good to be seen." Then he started firing, focusing on the nocturne that wore Dirk's face. Mal nodded at the nocturne, who switched his direction to advance on Tony.

I told Galen to stay, just before Mal reached me. Our swords met with a bone-ringing clang. Strike, block, strike, block. Adrenaline sang the Hallelujah chorus in my veins, and the rest of the world ceased to exist. It was me and Mal, and the motions we'd gone through more times than memory could hold. This dance was as familiar as the sound of her laugh. I almost forgot that, this time, she actually was trying to kill me.

The scent that grew stronger as we sweated was not only the scent of my pack member and twin. Mal smelled like road-kill, like a dead, half-rotten skunk left out in the sun too long. The understanding of how this came to be her scent distracted me. I stumbled for just a split second. But a split second was all a Hycene needed.

She would've seen the moment I lost focus, probably smelled it coming even before it happened, a slight shift towards anxiety that was such an obvious tell. I missed a block, and she ran her sword through my side. Shocked, I stared at her as she pulled the blade back out. It wasn't real until that moment. Part of me still wanted to believe this was a joke. A prank. A bad dream. But then I felt her blade in me, smelled my blood on her steel, and not even I could deny it.

Suddenly, I understood why Darcy wanted to give up. Did I want to live in a world without Mal?

"Kellan!"

Tony's voice broke my shock-bubble. My sword seemed to rise without the help of my arm, blocking Mal's next strike, this one aimed at my heart. Did I want to live? Yes. Survival was always worth it.

My body wasn't helping all that much. The wound in my side was bleeding badly, taking too long to heal. My movements grew sluggish, my arms heavy. Mal's eyes took on a familiar gleam — she was going to win. Then we'd go to the mess hall, get some ice cream. I'd have to serve her, heat the hot fudge to just the right temperature. It was what we always did after a sparring session.

She drove the hilt of her sword down on my left forearm, and I felt something crack. Pain. My hand lost its grip. My sword clattered to the ground. I fell to my knees. Mal stood over me. "Last chance, little sis. Come with me."

My breath was labored. Harsh. "Go fuck a goat, bitch."

She hesitated. Hope swelled inside me. Nothing was more deadly than hope. "Have it your way," she said, and started to swing the blade for my neck. I watched it come.

But my next breath wasn't my last. I took another, then another. I shook my head, trying to clear my wavering vision. I smelled blood, rottenness mixed with the musk of wolf. Mal's blood? My eyes focused and I saw her before me. She was turned toward the forest, and I saw two arrows sticking out of her back. My blade was on the ground, inches away. *Pick it up*, my mother's voice urged. *Pick it up before she kills you, fool*. I tried to reach for it, but my limbs wouldn't move. *Pick it up!* "Oh, shut up, you old hag," I muttered out loud.

I heard the whoosh of another arrow. This one hit Mal in the shoulder. The impact whirled her around to face me again. Okay, this is it, I thought. Now I die. But another arrow flew and hit her in the butt. I wanted to laugh. Shot in the ass. Her stance began to falter, and I heard her swear. She started to back away from me. "See you soon, little sis," she growled.

She was running away, and I had to let her go, since my head felt like it had floated off my shoulders.

I heard someone call my name, and with an effort that utilized every muscle in my body, I turned my head toward the forest. Tony was moving toward me. He was limping. Dimly, I registered the scent of his blood. In the moonlight, I could see the crumpled form of the nocturne Tony killed. I took a deep breath and called Galen to me. We were safe, for now. Mal would be back, but we were safe for now.

Tony had only taken a few steps before the "dead" nocturne rose. I yelled Tony's name, but I couldn't help. It advanced on Tony with frightening speed. Arrows started flying from the forest again, but the nocturne moved too fast. The arrows missed their mark.

Galen looked from me to Tony. Too dangerous, I thought. I gritted my teeth and prayed. "Galen, sic it!"

When Galen was still two feet away from the nocturne, he leapt into the air, soaring to slam his front paws on the nocturne's chest. He knocked it to the ground and ripped its throat out in one seamless motion.

"Good boy," I said, then plopped gracelessly on my butt. I needed to finish off the nocturne. Head, heart, etc. But first, I needed to figure out how to pick up my sword. My hands felt cold, and my arms felt like they were attached to someone else's body.

"Kell?" Tony was in front of me. Boy, he moved fast. Or, possibly, I'd lost a little time. Bad sign.

I touched his thigh, just below the deep gash that still oozed blood. He inhaled sharply through clenched teeth. I looked up at his face. "You're hurt."

"Uh-huh. Do you think you can walk? I'm not really up to carrying you."

"I'm hurt, too," I said slowly, glancing down at my side.

"Yup, we're a matched set. Like salt-and-pepper shakers." He leaned over and, with a pained grunt, gripped my arm and pulled me to my feet. My vision went all sparkly and I swayed.

"Woo, that was fun. Do that again." Galen trotted up to me, and I reached down to pet him. I couldn't quite coordinate the movement and ended up losing my balance. Tony caught me.

I heard him mutter something under his breath, but I was too distracted to notice what the words were. People were flooding out of the forest, materializing out of nowhere, like some fey creature had animated the trees. At the head of the pack was Finn, brandishing a sword and looking like a Viking conqueror with his blond hair free and wild.

"Oh, good, the cavalry," Tony said. His voice sounded strained.

The sparkles in my eyes were starting to get bigger, blocking out parts of the scene. "Tony?" I said. And then I collapsed to the ground.

Chapter 25

"She's a menace. I'm the only one capable of hunting her down." I stopped pacing and glared at Finn. Then I got sick of looking at him, so I started pacing again. Not that my room in the infirmary left much room for pacing. Take two steps, one-eighty turn, two steps, one-eighty turn. Somewhat lacking in the frustration-relief department. Maybe that was why I was just getting more agitated. Or maybe it had to do with the conversation loop I was stuck in. "I don't understand the problem."

"What's to understand? You're not going anywhere. You're injured, you're losing weight before my eyes, and you have no idea where your sister is. You're not going after her. You're not leaving the infirmary."

"And I'm trying to explain—"

"Enough!" Finn's voice slapped me. I turned to face him and stood still, seething. He looked me in the eye. "This conversation is over. It's not the reason I'm here, and you will not bring it up again. Do you understand?"

I crossed my arms and leaned back on my heels. "I'm not sure, conversation is an awfully big word, lots of syllables. Could you break it down for me?"

Finn's scent began to heat toward anger. "Tell me. How it happened."

"Could you be more specific?"

"Kellan." A warning.

Good. I loved warnings; they usually meant I pushed the right button. I decided to lead by example and be very, very specific. "It's a legitimate request. I've already told you everything about last night, and yesterday when Mal attacked Janus. I don't want to repeat myself, unless, of course, you want me to repeat myself, in which case I'll happily oblige, but if you don't want me to repeat my—"

"I understand the sequence of events," he said. "What I find curious is how, with all of your special abilities, you failed to notice that your sister smelled like nocturne. Or how you failed to notice that she was lying to you. I would also like to know why you failed to follow any of the orders you were given in the last week. Your sister even had to kill the outsider for you."

I bristled. She didn't have to kill Darcy for me. She was just a bigger homicidal maniac than I was, so she murdered him because she wanted to. "Thank you for the specificity." I was trotting out words I hadn't used for fifty years. Finn didn't seem to find it amusing, but I was beyond caring. "In answer to your query, I did notice that my sister smelled like nocturne. But, as previously stated, she fabricated a scenario to justify the foreign scent."

"Kellan."

"Per your second inquiry, with regard to how I failed to notice she was lying. That, I'm afraid, is a matter of personal shame. True, the scent of nocturne masks quite a number of the indicators that would signal a lie. But—"

"Kellan. Stop talking like a lawyer and just answer the question."

"As you wish, my lord. The scent markers for lying are adrenaline-related — cold sweat, mainly, and I think adrenaline itself has a scent I can pick up on. But those markers only show up when the person is afraid of being discovered. I don't think Mal was afraid I'd figure anything out. She knew I wouldn't look for a lie. And I didn't." I missed Galen. He was in the next room, keeping Tony company. He'd started out in my room, but the conversation with Finn got me so agitated that Galen had to be escorted out, for Finn's safety. "And as far as your third question, we've been through that already. I would've followed orders if the orders hadn't been asinine."

Finn stiffened like a snake about to strike. "Kellan—"

"Don't you get mad at me, Finlay. I don't know whose interests you were serving, but you weren't serving mine, or the interests of the world at large, for that matter. You didn't send me Tony because you thought he'd be helpful, you sent him because I pissed you off, and you thought Tony and I hated each other. And ignoring my calls, offering no advice or insight other than 'kill the outsider and clean up the mess?' What choice did I have but to ignore your bloody, and yes, asinine orders, and do my job? Kill the nocturne, secure the documents, find answers. Those should've been the priorities."

He opened his mouth to interrupt, but I was on a roll so big even Charmin wouldn't touch it. "And the outsider? He was a victim, Finlay. A piece on a chess board set up by my sister. And maybe, if I had your help from the beginning, I could've figured out a little sooner what was going on and saved us all a lot of trouble."

We both listened to the silence for a moment. "Are you done?" Finn said.

I started to say yes, but then I thought of something else. "No. How is it that you two chuckleheads never suspected a thing? I mean, Mal had to check in. How did you and Janus not pick up on it, oh master plotter, sir?"

"I — well — our actions are not the ones in question."

I caught an exceptionally unfamiliar scent from him — like mold on the underside of a log. Anxiety. A growl built in the back of my throat. "You did pick up on it. Oh my god. You picked up on it, and you did nothing."

He found his voice. "No. We didn't know anything. We suspected, but we didn't know."

I felt like he smacked me upside the head with a two-by-four. I was actually seeing stars. "Jesus, Finn. She's my sister. How the fuck could you not tell me?"

"Kellan—"

"No!" My heart was beating too fast. My vision was blotchy and out of focus, and my skin felt both hot and cold. Even though I knew I should keep my mouth shut — nothing I said right now would be helpful — I just couldn't stay quiet. "You should've told me. I could've saved her! And even if I couldn't — how could you do that to me? She's my pack!"

"That's exactly why we didn't tell you! You two are so close. You'd go after her, find her, probably get yourself killed in the process. Then she'd disappear, and there would be no one who could hunt her down because you would be dead. And that's if she was up to something, of which we couldn't be certain. We had to be patient, and you are incapable of patience!"

My body bounced from emotion to emotion, so fast I didn't have time to recognize one before I moved on to the next. Finally, out of pity and dizziness, I settled on a familiar face — anger, with a side of sarcasm. "Great plan. Worked out much better this way. I mean, Janus is half-dead, Trini is dead, Tony and Leanna are injured, Dirk is barely alive. But hey, at least you know for sure that Mal is up to something."

It was a mistake, I knew it, mocking the man with the authority to lock me in a cell until I went insane and started talking back to my Rice Krispies. But it was also a mistake to sideline me when my pack was at risk, and by god, I was going to let him know it.

"She wanted me to go with her, you know," I said. "Mal. She wanted me to go. She said we could rule the world, and you know what? She was probably right. But I couldn't do it. I couldn't leave you, and the Sankhain, and the forest. I couldn't walk out on the promises I made." I looked at him, my body feeling weightless and tingly. "But you know, at least Mal was up front about being a lying, deceiving, evil bitch." Eventually.

Finn's eyelids were at half-mast. "Are you saying you regret the choice you made?" His voice wore a careful tone that conveyed danger.

"I don't regret saying no to her." I wished I could achieve that same cool detachment. Instead, my voice shook as I looked at my insignificant other. "But there are plenty of choices I'm regretting right now."

"How unfortunate," he said, and my hands curled into fists. "Luckily, you have ample time to reflect on any future choices you may have to make."

He turned and walked out. The door slammed shut and I was alone.

I wasn't good at alone. Especially not with thoughts and memories like the ones currently in my head. Mal was gone.

Forever. She tried to kill me. The next time we saw each other, one of us would die. And Finn knew, Janus knew, and they kept it from me.

And why the fuck didn't I know? We shared a womb, for Christ's sake. We'd have to be Siamese twins to be more joined at the hip. But I didn't see it, didn't smell it. I was just as dumb as Finn accused me of being.

I broke into a cold sweat. I began pacing again, but all that did was emphasize the lack of breathing room. My heart began to race, and I did the only thing I could think of — I sped up my body to match my heart rate.

After I burned off most of the adrenaline with jumping jacks and squats, I sat down and started doing sit-ups. I didn't want to risk a complete cessation of movement — as it was, the workout couldn't keep thoughts out of my head. How could Finn have kept that information from me? I see-sawed between frenzied rage and freezing shock. Be glad, I told myself. Be glad you found out what a bastard he truly is before you wasted another century on him.

And what about Mal? Could I have saved her, if I knew? At least I could've tried. Now it was too late.

Or was it? I lowered myself to the ground to stare up at the ceiling. Mal still had her own scent, under all that rotten stink. It was that scent that convinced me it was really Mal standing before me. Did that mean she wasn't a full-blown nocturne yet? What if it wasn't a one-way chute? What if there was still time to turn around?

I felt like my chest was going to burst open, there was so much pressure building up behind my ribs. I had to find Mal, bring her back, try to prevent her from turning the rest of the way. If anyone could do it, I could. She was half of me and I was half of her.

I bolted to my feet and started for the door, just as it swung open. A furry body darted through it and rammed itself into me. I fell to my knees, half from joy and half because my muscles were too tired to sustain the impact of Galen's greeting. Because my face was already buried in his fur, it took me a moment to notice his two-legged companions. The scent of fresh-baked bread was easy to place, but the other was less defined. I raised my face to look. Cat and Tony stood above me, Cat looking apprehensive and Tony just looking amused.

"This room smells like a gym locker," Tony commented.

"You don't want to know what it really smells like." My voice was barely a croak. I dug my fingers deep in Galen's fur, finally able to breathe again.

Tony raised an eyebrow, but didn't comment. Instead, he turned to Cat. "I'll distract Simone. But don't take too long. She was already on her way to check on Kellan."

Tony ruffled my hair, handed me a bottle of water, and limped out.

"Wait!" I needed to tell him about Mal. Maybe if I convinced Tony that I needed to get out, he could talk to Finn and… But he was already gone. I turned to Cat. "Cat, listen, I need your help. I need to get Finn back here. Please. He—" I stopped when I saw the look on her face. "Cat. What's wrong?"

"Thank you for seeing me."

"Well, you know, my schedule's pretty full right now, but I figured I could squeeze you in." I sniffed. She smelled like sweat and dried blood, and like… "Tootsie Rolls," I said.

Her eyebrows drew together. "What?"

"You have Tootsie Rolls. You can stay as long as you want, if you share." I gestured at the door. "I'm healing. Simone keeps giving me healthy food. Boiled chicken breasts and broccoli. I think she even tried to feed me kale. I'd do just about anything for some real food."

Cat smiled, the expression looking unsettled on her face, like it hadn't been to visit for a long time. As she pulled a handful of candy out of her pocket, I took a chug from the water bottle. With a mumbled thank you, I popped a Tootsie Roll into my mouth. Then I shoved three more in, to keep that one company.

I chewed contentedly. It took me a while. Four Tootsie Rolls were no easy mouthful. My personal best was a dozen. Mal bet me that I couldn't complete the whole chew, chew, swallow routine, and I almost didn't make it, but… My stomach rolled over and played dead. I swallowed the glob in my mouth and almost choked on it. "Mmm. Thanks."

She made a noncommittal sound. Cat was the one who ran to find Tony, the one who had come to my rescue, the mysterious archer in the trees. Up till that moment, I didn't think she ever shot an arrow with the goal of actually hitting another person. She saved me, and from what Finn told me, she found Dirk half-dead in the forest and held the nocturne at bay so it couldn't finish the job. Hopefully, she could see the value in the violence.

I expected her to ask me about that, violence kind of being my forte. She didn't. "He wanted me," she whispered.

After struggling to understand, I took a guess. "The nocturne? It wanted you how?" Galen rubbed himself against me, reacting to my discomfort.

I could barely hear her. "He — it — said I would be perfect. Perfect for them. For the nocturnes. To be one of them." She took a deep breath, pulled her hands apart and sat on them. "He said I was wound so tight, it wouldn't be hard to turn me. He asked if I ever really felt a single emotion in my life." She looked up at me, her gaze steely. "I don't want to be like them." Her voice cracked, and she cleared her throat. "How do I not be like them?"

Oh, boy. I was woefully out of my depth. "Cat—"

"Don't say you don't know," she said. Her scent, though still afraid, took on a hint of anger. "You know how to feel things."

"Not healthy things," I said. "Jesus, Cat. You wanna talk to someone about feelings, I'm really not your gal."

"I don't want to talk about feelings!" She rocketed into motion, starting to pace. Galen shifted again, this time to keep a closer eye on Cat. "I hate feelings. I don't want to talk about them. I don't want to have them." She gripped her hair in two fistfuls, muscles corded tight. "I don't know how. I just want—" Her breathing ragged, she stopped moving as suddenly as she started.

"Look." My limbs felt twitchy. I glanced at the door. I needed to be out there, searching for Mal, not in here having a talk that required sensitivity and tact. What was the right thing to tell this girl, who survived a childhood of nightmares by not feeling, and now realized her coping mechanism was a different sort of nightmare? How did I keep ending up in situations that were so clearly meant for someone else? "Cat. I really don't think I know the things you think I know." Oh, yeah, that was insightful. "But — look. Right now, you smell angry. And afraid. Both at the same time. If you never feel things, how is that possible?"

She stared at me. For eternity.

I couldn't take it anymore. "Jesus, say something."

"Really?" she said. "You can smell that stuff? On me?"

Praise the lord and pass the ammunition, I actually said something right. "Yes, Cat. I smell that stuff on you."

"Really?"

Impatience struck like the flu. "No, I lied." At her crestfallen look, I backpedaled. "Cat, of course I smell that on you. You smell angry and afraid because you are angry and afraid. You can lie to yourself, but you can't lie to my nose. You feel those things."

"Wow." She looked like I just explained the meaning of life. She actually laughed, and the sound made me feel almost as good as making a certain someone else laugh, once upon a time in a faraway land. My spine sagged under a sudden weight. Cat cocked her head to one side and looked at me. "What did you want to talk to Finn about?"

About saving my sister, of course. You know, the one who brought evil to our doorstep? I couldn't say that to her, not now. "Nothing, I — look, you shouldn't stay too long. Um, could you just send Tony in here for a sec? Maybe you could keep watch outside?"

Promising to return with more chocolate, she left. Tony walked in.

"I need your help," I said.

"Okay. What's up?"

I started to feel twitchy again. With a final scratch between Galen's ears, I stood up and began shifting my weight from foot to foot. "I need you to talk Simone into releasing me. I have to talk to Finn again."

He stared at me. "Why dontcha just ask me to make the sun orbit the earth while I'm at it?"

"Tony, please."

"Kell, nobody can talk Simone into doing anything. If you want to talk to Finn, we'll send a youngling for him. You can talk to him here."

I bounced on the balls of my feet. "I need to get out of here. It's important."

"Why?"

I started tapping my fingers against my leg, fast, syncopated. "I just ... do."

"Kellan—"

"We're wasting time! She might already be—" I took a breath and tried a different track. "Look, maybe you could just distract Simone. Keep her out of the way long enough for me to slip out. I'll come back, I promise. I'm not trying to run away. I just need to..." I couldn't make myself say the words. What I wanted to do was stupid, and if I said it out loud, anyone within earshot would tell me how stupid it was. Hell, I would be forced to tell myself how stupid it was. But I could see Tony wasn't going for the vague non-statements, so I shoved the words out. "I need to find Mal."

The tension drained from Tony's scent as his shoulders slumped a little. "Kell, I get it, but you need to just wait. Finn's got every Sankha in the field on the lookout for her. He'll find her, and then you can go after her."

"No, you don't understand!" My voice was too loud, too high. Galen stood in front of me, looking from me to Tony. I dragged myself back from the Cliffs of Hysteria. "I need to find her, because I think I can keep her from turning nocturne."

"Kellan."

"No, just listen." I started pacing the cell again. I explained to him about Mal's scent, and how, if I could just get face to face with her, I could change her mind.

Galen smelled anxious, but Tony's scent was muted. Sad. Not exactly the energized, jump-into-action response I'd angled for, but that just meant I needed to keep talking. I took a deep breath, to start another monologue, when Tony interrupted me. He stepped in front of me and placed his hands on my shoulders. "Kellan. Listen to me. Mal's gone, okay? Gone fishing, out to lunch, on the dark side of the moon. She's gone. And you can't bring her back."

I shook my head and pulled out of his grasp. "No. No, see—"

He gripped my shoulders again, more forceful this time. "She's gone."

I didn't want to hear it. I refused to hear it, but as long as he stood between me and the door, I had to listen. I struck out with my left fist, hitting him in the chest where the library nocturne slashed him open. He let go of my shoulders and hunched over, his breathing ragged. "Goddammit, Kell."

I winced, remorseful. "If I could just talk to her—" If I could find out why. Because if I knew why, then I could tell her how stupid she was being and convince her to come home.

His scent burned with anger as his long-held temper snapped. "Right, 'cause that worked out so well for you the last time? She tried to kill you, or did you forget that already? I doubt it, 'cause it looks like the little memento she gave you still isn't healed." He gestured at my side. I looked down, seeing for the first time that I had blood on my shirt. The wound had reopened. Damn, when did that happen? Maybe sit-ups weren't such a good idea.

I suddenly felt light-headed and plopped down on my butt. The pain on my side helped me focus. "But—"

"But what, Kellan?" Tony knelt in front of me, the scent of jalapeno focaccia bread strengthening. Like the sight of my weakness made him madder. "She didn't mean to? It was the nocturne talking? Your sister would never really do that, all you have to do is remind her? You're right, it was the nocturne talking, and your sister would never do that. Problem is, your sister isn't there anymore. Just the nocturne that took her place. I don't care what she smelled like. If she was still in control, she wouldn't'a hurt you."

"No." I shook my head, over and over and over again. Shake it hard enough and the events would rearrange themselves, reality would shift and life would make sense again. Or maybe I could knock myself unconscious and I wouldn't have to care for a little while. "No. It's not true. It's just not. I can fix this. Just give me a chance."

Voices outside, then the door to the room banged open. Galen looked up, his hackles rising. Damp earth, along with the scent of newsprint. It looked like I was going to get my chance to talk to Finn.

Chapter 26

"What is going on? Antony? Aren't you supposed to be in bed?"

Tony's anger faded in an instant as he looked over my shoulder at Finn. "Yes, sir. I was just visiting."

"Very well. You're dismissed."

"Yes, sir." Tony started for the door.

"Take Galen with you." My voice didn't sound like mine, or maybe I just couldn't believe I was saying the words. But I needed to talk to Finn without the distraction of Galen's defensiveness.

Tony looked at me, then nodded. "Come on, Galen."

Galen didn't move. He didn't even seem to breathe. My side throbbed. I hadn't felt it during the jumping jacks, the sit-ups, the squats. But now, looking at my dog, so determined to ignore everyone but me, I felt all kinds of pain. I whispered in his ear that it was okay, I'd be with him soon. When I pulled back to look at him, he turned his head and met my eyes. The conviction and certainty there told me he wasn't going anywhere without a fight. My body and spirit throbbed with such a melee of pain, I almost just laid down and surrendered to it. I stood up. "You're gonna have to drag him," I told Tony, my voice flat.

Tony hesitated, then, when he saw the look on Finn's face, wrapped a hand around Galen's collar. "Come on, buddy. Time to go."

Galen resisted. He growled and twisted his head around, trying to snap at Tony and almost nicking Finn's arm instead. Though I wanted to howl and wrap my arms around him, I yelled, "Enough! Galen, out!" Then I turned my back. Before long, the only scent left in the room was Finn's. I turned to face him. "Back already? What'd I do to deserve such a treat?"

Finn's hand swung up, and I almost raised my hands to block a blow. But he wasn't trying to hit me — he was holding up something in front of my face. The newspaper I smelled earlier.

"Explain this," he said.

I didn't want to respond. I was pretty sure that if I opened my mouth, I'd say something that would spur him to violence. Instead, I silently tried to read the paper that was trembling a half-inch from my nose.

LOCAL MAN SURVIVES STABBING. Squinting at the picture, I recognized Darcy's apartment building. "Huh. How 'bout that? He made it." I felt warm and fuzzy inside.

I didn't realize I'd spoken aloud until Finn whipped the newspaper across the room. His scent bubbled over with unheard-of rage. His voice was a low sound that strained at its leash. "That's all you have to say?" I heard the deep breath he took in an attempt to calm himself. "How hard is it to kill one librarian?"

Finn kept his temper on a leash. Mine roamed free. "I don't know," I said. "About as hard as stringing a few words together. Like, 'Kellan, we think something's wrong with your sister.' Which I guess is pretty hard, since a smart guy like yourself can't manage it."

"You will go into town and complete your assignment."

"No."

In the past, when facing blind rage, I abased myself, without fail. Not tonight. I didn't care anymore. Finn was mad? Fine. Great. So was I. I straightened my shoulders and raised my chin, and I waited.

"Perhaps I didn't make myself clear," he said. "That wasn't a request."

"Oh, I understand. And maybe I didn't make myself clear. How about this. Fuck, no. I'm not killing the human. Not now, not ever. I will, however, be happy to leave here and look for my sister."

We stood there, staring at each other, each of us breathing with increasing speed and harshness. "You. Are. Infuriating," he said.

"Right back at you."

When Finn was pissed, he gathered power to him, and it became obvious why Janus chose him as his second in command. Finn was a sorcerer, too, not as strong as Janus, but strong enough. As he drew power from the air around him, the air crackled in response. His skin glowed brighter, his eyes sparked, his lips… He looked like a sun god. He looked like his skin would burn if I touched it. And even though he was a detestable excuse for a human being, part of me really wanted to touch him.

Before I could move, he started talking, and the desire passed. "You used to follow orders. You used to listen. You used to believe in that, in following an alpha. What happened?"

"I don't know, maybe I got sexually frustrated. That can mess with a girl's head, you know."

"Kellan, I'm serious."

"So am I." I sighed. "I don't know, Finn. I think I still believe in those things. I just — I had to go with my gut this time."

His anger evaporated, the crackling power suddenly gone. Suddenly, he was barely there at all. "Janus is—" He stopped. He sounded small. "Something's wrong. I don't know. The wound wasn't that bad, but he just lays there in bed. Could you just — just do this. Just complete this task."

Part of me wanted to say yes, so this sad, shrunken thing would disappear and I could see the familiar, arrogant, self-assured bastard standing before me. But something deep inside held me back. That something made me sad for some reason, but it helped me stand my ground. "No, Finn. I'm sorry."

His scent surged up to fill the room, smelling exactly like it always did. He wasn't depressed. He tried to play me. The plan hadn't worked and now he was trying to come up with a new one.

I wanted to laugh. Or maybe cry. Mal was right. Finn never cared about me. At least now I'd never hear her say I told you so.

I crossed the room and stood before him, jabbing him in the chest with one finger. "You listen to me, Finlay Weaver.

You kept this thing with Mal a secret from me, and now you owe me, and you're going to pay up. First, you're going to stop telling me to kill Darcy Jamison. He's not a problem for us. So take the broken record off the fucking turntable already. Second, you're going to let me go look for Mal. I'm going to find her, and if I think I can bring her back here and turn her back from nocturne to wolf, then that's what I'm going to do. And you're going to let me, because you fucked up and you know it. Get out of my fucking way."

He frowned at me, and his scent was wet, like mud. Confused. "Kellan, you can't bring her back."

"Don't tell me what I can do! I'm going to try. I have to try, so stop fucking telling me what I can do and just get out of the way."

"Kellan, she's—"

"Get out of the way!" I was shouting, screaming. Not the most mature tactic, but I felt hungry and hot and sweaty, and I wanted my dog and I wanted my sister and I wanted the world to make sense again. Cranky shoved Mature out the tenth-story window and watched her splat on the pavement below.

Still Finn hesitated.

This time, I didn't shout, but my voice crackled with effort. "You owe me, Finn."

"It's been twelve hours. She knows we'll send people out looking; she isn't sticking around."

"You don't know that."

"Yes, I do. And you know it too."

I shook my head, trying to dislodge the voice inside that kept agreeing with everything Finn said. "No, I—"

"Kellan, if it were you, what would you do? You wouldn't stay in town. You'd leave, lick your wounds, and come back when you were stronger."

He was right. I wouldn't stick around, waiting to be found. Mal was light-years away by now. I'd never find her, not in time. The fucking bastard was right. And now I couldn't breathe; there wasn't any goddamned oxygen left.

My breath came in sharp, wheezing gasps. "Can't — can't—"

Finn pulled me out the door and dragged me away from the room, out of the infirmary, into the cool shadows outside. "Sit," he said, and I did. He knelt before me. "You followed an order. Was that so hard?"

"Bite me."

His scent relaxed. "Can you breathe now?"

Obviously, I could, but I knew he wanted me to say it. He wanted me to see it and acknowledge it. "Yeah. I'm okay."

A nod. "Good."

As the panic receded, so did my energy. "Are you going to let me go after her?"

"No."

"I might've been able to save her. If you gave me a chance."

"I didn't want to tell you. It's not an easy thing to say to begin with. And I'm not exactly Mal's favorite person." So he knew that, did he? "If you went to her and told her my suspicions, she would've—"

"Said you were lying," I finished.

He smiled darkly. "Yes. And who would you be more inclined to believe, your twin sister and last remaining pack member, who has no history of lying to you, or me, who—"

"Isn't exactly known for openness and honesty."

"Right." He was quiet for a moment. "So when Janus asked what I thought, I told him I didn't think we should tell you. I'm sorry."

The recommendation came from him. Not Janus, but Finn. That shouldn't have shocked me. But it did. And I knew that things had irrevocably changed, not just with Mal, but with Finn, too. "You still owe me."

He leaned back on his heels. "I'll let the outsider go, for now. Provided he doesn't become a problem. But I won't let you go after Mal. You'll get yourself killed, and I can't allow that. We've already lost two of our best warriors. I'm not inclined to lose anymore."

His scent was too warm — it wasn't just about losing another warrior. He didn't want to lose me. I was too tired to tell him that it was too late for that. "If you're going to deprive me of my sister, can I at least get some more coffee?"

He hung his head, but I saw the flash of white teeth that meant he was smiling. "You're going to bring that up every time you want something, aren't you?"

"Absolutely." My voice fell short of its usual attitude, but it came closer. "So...?" Finn rose and held out a hand to help me up. I stood on my own. "Just so you know, I'm still pissed at you."

"Of course you are. And just so you know, you're on restricted duties. You'll be here, scrubbing grout with a toothbrush, for the next few months."

I get to stay. I feigned a sigh. "The nocturnes are looking better all the time."

"No," he said. "That's not for you. You'd never be able to stand the stench. Now let's go retrieve Galen, and get you some coffee."

I never wanted to touch him again. Finn crossed a line by keeping his suspicions from me, and I could never forgive him. But sometimes, it was just really nice to have someone who knew you better than you expected. "Yeah. Okay."

Chapter 27

"Ouch!" At my outburst, Galen pressed himself harder against my leg, and tried to push Simone away with his nose.

Simone gave him a look. "Stop that. I'm trying to help her. And you," she said, looking at me. "Stop being such a wuss. I thought you liked a little pain."

"A little pain, sure. Not—" I sucked in my breath as she poked my wound with her fingers. It had been more than twenty-four hours since Mal stabbed me, and my side was still raw and sore. Worse, it still reopened if I moved too suddenly. Which already happened several times, since I was unaccustomed to treating myself as fragile. I couldn't remember ever taking this long to heal a wound. It was weird, and it made me wonder what I was doing differently this time around, but Simone seemed to take it as a personal affront that she couldn't heal me. "Jeez, Dr. Feelgood, give us some morphine before you do that shit."

"I'm not giving you morphine," she said wryly. "I will, however, give you a lollipop if you stinking sit still for two seconds."

I perked up. My body was craving sugar like it usually clamored for coffee. "Lollipop?"

"I was kidding." She gave my side another probing feel and I jumped. Galen glared at her. She glared at me. "How on earth did you ever manage to get a tattoo?"

I glared right back at her. "With a tattoo artist, you get a fair bit of warning. They actually care about the comfort of their clients."

"Well, then, next time you get a wound that won't heal, go to your tattoo artist." She straightened up and studied me with eyes overshadowed by the dark circles cradling them. "What kind of blade did she use?"

I thought back. "Iron, I think. It smelled like iron. Even before my blood got on it." I shrugged. "I'm fine, really. It's almost completely healed."

"Almost isn't the goal here. And keep the jogging to a minimum, will you?"

"I'll try. But I'd rather ooze blood for the rest of my life than lay around in bed all day. And just to clarify, is a minimum jog two miles or six?"

Simone ignored me. "And you," she said. I turned my head to glance behind me. Finn stood just inside the doorway, looking like he regretted taking the last dozen steps. I never noticed him enter. Galen did — he stood at attention, hackles stiff.

Simone pointed at me. "She needs a steady supply of protein. I know you threatened to throw her back in solitary if she kept stealing food. But you need to either feed her or lock up the smallest younglings, because when she shape-shifts and starts hunting, they'll be the easiest prey."

Finn's eyes widened, like they did the first time I walked into his cabin, pulled off my tunic, and told him to touch my breasts. That memory didn't bring the warmth it usually did. Instead, I felt tired and caged. I wrapped my hand around Galen's collar, for both our sakes. "May we go?" I asked. I wasn't sure whose permission I sought, Simone's or Finn's. They both said, "Yes," then Simone added, "Go to the mess hall and fix yourself some sandwiches. Beef. All right? Gina made pot roast two nights ago, there should be some left."

"Yes, ma'am." Then I skedaddled. When I walked out the door, I almost tripped over Tony. He sat on the bottom step of the infirmary stoop, sunning himself. I swore. "You know, if you wanted to get kicked in the head, all you had to do was ask."

He leaned his head back and grinned up at me. Then he shifted over on the step and I sat down next to him. Barely moving his head, he glanced at me through slitted eyes. "You look like shit."

"Gee, thanks. You're looking centerfold-worthy yourself."

He did look a little pale. But he smelled better. I leaned back and enjoyed the warmth of the mid-morning sun, feeling a slight tug from my side, but not an unpleasant amount of pain. The morning smelled like sun-dried grass, dog, and Tony. If I kept my memory of Mal behind its locked door, I might just be able to enjoy myself.

"I have orders to go eat some sandwiches made from Gina's roast beef. You wanna join me?"

Tony's scent grew stronger and richer. Like a sweet rye bread. "Sure."

The door behind us opened, spilling Finn's scent over the good ones. "Oh. I'm glad you two are here. Antony, Kellan will be restricted to the Academy grounds for the foreseeable future, so you will accompany her to her apartment to collect whatever belongings she requires."

"I don't need a bloody chaperone," I said.

"The last time you were allowed off camp, you came back and tried to kill Janus. I am merely exercising understandable caution."

"You're merely being a dick. Come on, Gigantor. Galen, let's go. Field trip."

When I called Tony Gigantor, Finn's scent flashed from its normal zen calm to something more open, like surprise. Then it turned sour and dry. Like fungus on a downed tree. "I believe Simone ordered you to eat," Finn said.

"I know. I'm not stupid," I said. "Am I packing up the apartment for good?"

"No," Finn said. "We will continue to pay your rent, keep your utilities current, and have someone pick up your mail twice a week. I'm sure that eventually you will be returning."

Two weeks ago, I would've been devastated to hear that my sabbatical at the forest was only temporary. Now, I merely felt empty. And hungry. I was definitely hungry. I looked at Tony. "Ready, Freddy?"

Tony was studying Finn, like he was looking for signs of an incoming hurricane. "Sure. Let's go."

I turned and walked away from Finn, Galen happily following. Tony caught up to me and shortened his stride to match mine. "So I'm your escort?" His tone implied a different meaning for the word.

"Say it like that again and I'll punch you in the junk drawer."

"That'd make it awfully difficult for me to live up to my responsibilities as escort."

Suppressing a smile, I glanced at him. "And I thought you were supposed to be good at improvising."

"Oh, I'm very good."

"Then you oughta know there's more than one way to … escort … a woman."

We arrived at the mess hall, and let ourselves into the locked kitchen. All the Sankhain had a key to the mess, but none of the younglings did. Supposedly that kept food costs down, if younglings couldn't graze as they liked. The plan might've worked, if we didn't teach the older younglings to pick locks.

Tony leaned against one of the islands in the middle of the kitchen while I opened the refrigerator. "So Darcy survived, huh?"

I kept my eyes fixed on the big stainless steel fridge. "Guess so."

"Pretty amazing, how he managed to call 911 and get help there in time. Lucky he had a cell phone. Hey, I tried to call your cell phone yesterday. You didn't answer."

"I lost it."

"Mmm. You should probably cancel the number. What if somebody finds it and calls China a hundred times?"

"What do I care? Finn pays the bill."

Tony chuckled. "While we're in town, you wanna go see Darcy in the hospital? Get your phone back?"

I found the roast beef. "I have no idea what you're talking about."

Chapter 28

I hated hospitals. The disinfectant alone made me feel like someone sprayed kerosene up my nose and lit a match. With the scents of fear, blood, urine, feces, and overall weakness and death, it was an animal's worst nightmare. I broke into a sweat in the parking garage before I even got out of the truck.

Tony, sitting in the passenger seat, glanced over. "You okay?" he said.

"Yeah. Sure." I tried to take a deep breath without taking in any more scents. Pointless, I knew, but my brain needed the oxygen if my human half was going to win this fight. "Just stay here with Galen. I'll be right back." Unless I shape-shifted and started culling out the herd.

"If you aren't up for this, you can wait in the truck with Galen. I'll get your phone."

"I'm fine." If my voice sounded a little harsh, it was only because I was trying to convince myself as much as I was Tony.

"Okey-dokey." He turned back to stare at the windshield, and didn't say anything more.

I should probably apologize. "Look, I—"

"Just go. We gotta get back to the forest before Finn starts wondering if you're planning another coup."

"What do you mean, another coup? I didn't plan the first one!"

He didn't answer, just stared straight ahead like he was watching a movie.

"Fine. Try not to piss off my dog, okay? I'll be right back."

"You said that already."

"Fuck off! Did I say that already?" I got out of the truck and slammed the door so hard, rust fell off the bumper.

A woman at a desk directed me to the sixth floor. I took the elevator — another one of my favorite things, like a solitary cell without the window or the solitude. When the elevator doors finally opened and I stepped onto solid linoleum again, I took a huge breath through my nose. Winding its way through all the other scents came the citrus scent of Bergamot oil. I followed it to Darcy's room.

He was asleep. A woman who smelled like baby vomit and some sort of flower sat in the chair by his bed. When she saw me, she jumped. "Hi," she said, placing a hand on the center of her chest. "You startled me, I must have dozed off." She blinked. "Hey, I remember you. You were at Darcy's apartment that day. The day he was attacked."

Aw, shit. The nosy neighbor with the baby. "Ah, yeah. Sarah, right?"

She studied me a little too closely. Her scent was tinged with a pre-fear almost-sweat. Her body was probably feeling a little too warm, but not quite enough to stimulate the sweat glands. That would happen when she started wondering whether I was responsible for the attack on Darcy.

Suddenly glad that Simone insisted on keeping a bandage over my wound, I raised my shirt. "The guy got me, too. Darcy stepped in and told me to run for it." I looked down at the ground, letting my discomfort turn into a blush that looked like shame. Dropping my voice to a whisper, I added, "I did. I'll never forgive myself."

Baby Vomit reached out and touched my hand. She murmured comforting words. I nodded and arranged my lips in a smile. Then I switched my gaze to Darcy. He looked awful. Hollowed-out, and more pasty than before, which was saying something. I asked Sarah how he was doing.

She straightened Darcy's sheets. As I watched, I wondered if she was just being maternal or if her husband needed to be home more often. "The doctor said he's out of the woods. He had a collapsed lung, and then he had to have surgery to repair internal bleeding. He doesn't have any family, you know. He just lost his sister, so between me and a couple of his friends from the library, we've made sure someone was here with him all the time. It's horrible to be in the hospital alone, don't you think? I didn't realize you two were close. I would have called you."

I shook my head. "I don't know him that well. I, um, I met him sort of by way of his sister." I swallowed hard. "I just lost my sister, too." Saying it out loud made me want to run away. Smelling the pity that dripped off of her made me want to break something big and ceramic over her head.

She told me she was sorry. I thanked her and told her that if she wanted to get a cup of coffee, I'd sit with Darcy for a while. She left, and I lowered myself into the chair beside the bed.

Looking at Darcy lying there like that, I wondered for the eighteen-millionth time why I was there. I told myself that I needed to get my phone back, and I needed to tell Darcy that he wasn't going to be killed anytime soon, at least not by me. But Myself wasn't satisfied with those explanations. She kept asking for the rest of the story.

When Darcy opened his eyes and blinked slowly at me, I smiled with unbidden warmth. He smiled back. "Hey," he said, drawing it out into several syllables and making me laugh.

"Dude, what are you on?"

"Dunno. It's good stuff." His brain worked for a while before he came up with some more words. "What're you doing here?"

The question coaxed out the answer that I didn't want to admit. "I wanted to see that you were okay," I said, then clamped my lips shut. Why did I say that? "And, you know, I need my phone back."

His smile widened. "Yeah. Thanks for that. Sweet of you to lend me your phone."

"Yeah, sweet, that's me. Just call me Pixy Stix."

He laughed, then winced. "Ow."

Guilt flooded me, cold and damp. "Sorry. You okay?"

He closed his eyes and leaned his head back. "Mmmmmmm-hmm, I just forget not to move. Drugs are too good."

"Well, as long as the drugs are good." My voice drifted.

"I think … your phone's in that bag." His eyes slid open and he pointed to a plastic bag that occupied the only other chair in the room. I got up and looked in the bag, which seemed to hold everything that Darcy had on him when he got to the hospital. Sure enough, my cell phone was in there.

I thanked Darcy and settled uneasily back in the chair. "So anyway, you're safe now. I got Finn to agree to let you live. Just don't go around telling people about me, okay? Then I'd really have to kill you."

"Who'm I gonna tell?" he asked. Then his eyes pinched with seriousness. Or maybe pain. The two seemed awfully similar to me. "That woman. She was—"

"The one who approached you. Yeah, I figured." I hesitated, then decided I already had the rice and beans, might as well go for the whole enchilada. "She was my sister. Mal. She's, um … she's a nocturne, now. She used you as a distraction, so my superiors and I wouldn't figure out what she was doing."

"Oh." Darcy's expression was unreadable, but at least he didn't smell angry.

It took me a while to work up to my next words. "I'm sorry. For everything. For her getting you involved. For me not figuring things out sooner, and almost getting you killed. I'm sorry."

"It's all right," he said. "Without your phone, I'd be a … chalk outline on the sidewalk right now."

Logically, I knew what he said was true, but I didn't believe him. How could he not hate me, with how badly I'd failed him? After all, Mal was my sister. If I couldn't trust my instincts about her, how could I trust myself at all?

The room didn't have enough oxygen. What was it with the world lately, always running out of oxygen? "I have to go," I said, and pushed to my feet. I did have to go, before I vomited, passed out, shape-shifted, or D, all of the above.

But Darcy's voice stopped me. "You saved me," he said. "That night, in the field, when you burned that thing. If you didn't say the stuff you said, I never woulda dialed that phone." As I stared at him, he in turn stared at his IV. "Jeez, what are they givin' me? Can't believe I said all that."

I laughed, a short bark of a laugh flavored with sadness and a dash of hysteria. "Next time share the drugs before you share your feelings, okay?"

He looked at me. "Next time? I'm gonna see you again?"

He sounded so hopeful. I felt the hysteria gain momentum. I should've said no. I shouldn't ever have contact with Darcy again. I should've told him to forget he ever met me. "I'll be around."

He nodded, and his eyes drifted closed again. "'Kay."

On impulse, I leaned down and kissed his forehead. "You're a good man, Charlie Brown," I said. "Keep it up, okay?"

A throat cleared behind me, and I straightened guiltily. I turned to see Baby Vomit, holding a cup of — I sniffed. Chai tea. Jeez, they were a match made in tea leaves.

With a last smile at Darcy, I excused myself and left. My hands were shaking and my armpits felt damp. Why did I kiss him? Weirder than weird. I felt like somebody just told me the boys in AC/DC quit the band and became insurance adjusters.

Because I felt so weird, I didn't speak to Tony when I climbed behind the wheel of the truck. I was very, very glad that he didn't have the ability to smell my moods, because I really didn't want to hear about it. As it was, I had to fend off all the questions he lobbed at me. Was I okay, how'd it go, how was Darcy, what was wrong, why had I lost the ability to form polysyllabic words.

Finally, as we reached my apartment, I turned to face him. "I'm fine. Darcy's fine. Everything's fine. And yes, I'm impressed that you used the word polysyllabic in a sentence. I'm sure Alex Trebeck will be calling any day now."

Tony narrowed his eyes. "I'm gonna let that go, since you're wound tighter than a bobcat on a bed of nails. But you better do whatever it's gonna take to unwind, 'cause that was your final free pass today."

He was right. While my list of people who deserved to have their heads bitten off was pretty long, Tony wasn't on it. But he was sitting beside me, and all the people on the list weren't. I sneered at him. "Or what? You'll kick my ass? You couldn't even take down a nocturne with an entire clip of bullets. What are you gonna do to me?"

The look on his face made me want to stick my thumbs in my eyes and press down until my eyeballs popped like overripe tomatoes. I opened and closed my mouth several times, trying to come up with a worthy apology. He spoke before I could. The rims of his ears grew red. "My aim was off," he muttered. He rubbed his chest. "Couldn't handle the recoil."

I knew I should say something encouraging to make him feel better. "Well, at least Galen was there to finish him off for you." Okay, so encouraging wasn't my thing.

As evidenced by the scowl Tony shot at me. "Yeah. Maybe you can loan him to me indefinitely, since I seem to be pretty useless right now."

I dug deeper in search of encouragement. "You're not useless." Better. "And you'll get it back. Muscles heal. They get strong again. You'll get it back." Oddly, his embarrassed scent grew stronger. Maybe I should ditch encouragement and stick to what I did best. I smiled sweetly. "And until then, maybe we can have a couple of the younglings follow you around and make sure you don't bump into any walls or anything."

"You know, it's a wonder Janus didn't dump Finn for you. You're awfully good at this problem-solving crap."

"It's true," I said. "He did ask me to take Finn's place, but I didn't want to hurt Finn's feelings. He's not good at anything else."

"Oh, so you just adopted the stupid act so Finn's ego would remain intact."

My eyes narrowed. "Yes, I did. Purely altruistic. What's your excuse?"

He smiled a twisted, unwilling smile and shoved his door open, jumping out of the truck. He stood next to the open door, his back to me.

I felt something crack inside me. "Tony." He didn't look at me, so I got out and stood in front of him. When he started to move away, I grabbed his shirt and pinned him against the truck. He sullenly met my gaze, but stayed silent.

"Okay, make me work for it. I guess that's fair." I took a deep breath, inhaling his hurt and anger, and that wretched bitch, shame. "Tony, I'm sorry. You didn't deserve that, what I said. And I didn't mean it. Even injured, you're worth a dozen lesser men." Suddenly, the warmth he gave off made me feel a little too comfortable for my comfort level. I took a step back. "Even if you never could manage to kick my ass."

He took a step forward, closing the distance. "Maybe I held back," he said.

I swallowed. I couldn't speak. It was like his heat, his scent, microwaved my brain. Just before my head exploded, Galen hopped out of the truck and woofed impatiently. I took in the spittle clinging to the bright red tongue, the intensity of the panting. Selfishly grateful for Galen's dehydrated discomfort, I said, "Come on. Let's get you some water, big dog."

Upstairs, Galen drank long and deep from his water dish. Tony looked at me. "What do you need to get?"

I thought about it. "I've got clothes at camp already. I can get soap and shit from the supplies there. I guess I just need my blades."

He nodded. "I'll empty out the fridge while you pack 'em up."

Galen started to follow me until he heard the refrigerator door open, then he abandoned me. I emptied the contents of my blade drawer into a duffel bag. Then I looked around the room, feeling heavy and sluggish. I tried to think of other things I might need, and grabbed my two pairs of shorts with the sheathes sewn into the waistbands. Unable to come up with any other distractions, I joined Tony in the kitchen.

I heard the slurp of Galen's tongue as he took advantage of the open refrigerator to lick one of the shelves. I grabbed his collar and dragged him away. Tony pulled his head out of the fridge long enough to look at me. "You realize somebody already discovered penicillin, right?"

I frowned at him, genuinely confused. "What?"

"Well," he said, and stuck his head back into the fridge, "I'm just sayin', you really don't need to grow all this mold. Somebody already—"

"Yeah, yeah." I squashed the urge to shut the door on his head. "Jesus, what's that smell?"

He grunted. "Take your pick. It could be the three-year-old gallon of milk. Or the yogurt that gives new meaning to the term 'live cultures.' Or maybe this thing." He held up a baggie containing an Unidentified Gelatinous Substance. "I think it used to be potatoes. Or possibly pudding." He tossed it back in the fridge and closed the door. "Have you considered just leaving it?"

"To see if it reverts back to a solid?"

He tossed me a grin. "I was thinking more, vacate the building and napalm the sucker. This fridge is just one big biohazard container."

"Suck it up, Gigantor, and toss the food in a trash bag."

"Oh, that's food? Whew. Glad you cleared that up."

I smacked him lightly on the back of the head. "Shut up and work, or I'll make you eat it."

He laughed, but he opened the refrigerator door again. I guessed he didn't want to take the chance I was serious. With a grin creeping across my face, I turned away.

And looked right at my beloved Pollyanna Pickering wolf print. My breath whooshed out of me, my stomach ached and I couldn't stand up straight. Had I ever noticed before, the way that wolf resembled Mal? The eyes were exactly right, down to the concentric circles of brown, shades going from dark to light as they approached the pupils. And the way her ears were cocked, that confident, playful attitude. I could almost feel the heat of her breath as she panted, the way her tail wrapped around me as we slept after a hunt. Memories lanced through me. I forgot to breathe.

I glanced behind me and saw that Galen was several feet away. Safe. I ripped the picture down and smashed it against the wall. The frame splintered and the glass broke, pieces making anticlimactic tinkling sounds as they hit the floor.

"Jesus!" Tony pulled me around to face him so he could grip both my arms. I didn't know why he bothered. It wasn't like I was going to drop to the floor and roll around in the glass shards.

Feeling empty, I stared up at him. "I didn't want to look at it anymore."

I could see the individual muscles of his jaw flex as he took a deep breath. He smelled like sourdough — fear. That seemed odd to me. "Okay," he said. "You don't wanna look at it. So you walk outta the room, or you put it in the closet. You don't trash it."

"Maybe you don't. I did." I tugged experimentally on my arms. He held fast. I could easily break his hold, but it might involve breaking his arms along with it.

"Kellan—"

"What?" I didn't feel empty anymore. Anger filled me up, warmed me. He sounded so patient and rational. I was so sick of patient and rational. "You think you know so much about what I should do? You know what it's like, having your own sister try to kill you? You don't know shit!"

His scent warmed, anger burning away the concern. "Yeah, you're right, I don't know about that. What I know is that I think I remember a time when my mom wasn't high. Maybe I made it up, though, 'cause all my other memories of her, she was getting high or doing something that'd lead to getting high. Like selling herself. Or selling her kid. 'Cause let's face it, a strung-out crack whore isn't worth near as much on the pervert circuit as a six-year-old boy."

I lost hold of my anger. As it slipped away, a trap door opened under me and I was falling through the darkness. I reached out to the only thing I could see. "Tony, I—"

"Don't." He let go of my arms and pushed off of me. His voice was thick with disgust. "I didn't tell you so you'd pity me." He stopped to catch his breath, like he just ran a great distance. "I know more than you think."

My vision went gray around the edges. Too much pain. Too much anger. Too much hate for my body to hold. I backed up until I hit the wall, then I slid down to the floor. My left hand landed in the broken glass, and I felt the skin slide apart. I couldn't help myself — I ground my hand into the glass.

"Fuck, Kell!" Tony crouched in front of me, grabbed my hand and pulled it to him, cradling it in his lap like a baby bird fallen from its nest. At Tony's alarm, Galen came running toward me.

"No! Stop! Down! Stay!" Galen hesitated, then slowly lowered himself to the ground. His ears were back and his eyes showed too much white around the irises. I looked down at my hand, at the blood. Felt the tension drain from me. All the emotional shit of the past thirty-six hours was drowned out by the immediacy of that sweet, sharp pain. Out of the corner of my eye, I saw Galen start to creep toward me. "Galen, stay." I raised my hand, palm facing him. Blood dripped down my wrist to stain my shorts.

Tony muttered under his breath as he carefully picked glass from my slowly-healing palm. It wasn't long, though, before muttering wasn't enough. "Why the hell did you do that?"

I shrugged, a half-assed, spent motion. "It felt good." I wondered idly why my hand was healing so fast when my side was healing so slow.

Tony looked me in the eyes. "I take it back. I don't know that much. You're way more fucked up than I am."

For some reason, that made me smile. "Thanks."

He shook his head and bent over my hand again. "There. I think that's all of it." He returned my hand to me and scooted back a little so he could lean against the fridge. "Please don't do that again."

"I probably will."

His only reply was a grunt.

We sat that way, silent, for what felt like years. I couldn't remember the last time I had been quiet for that long in the presence of someone other than Galen. As my hand healed and my strength waned, I felt the tension rise in me again. The silence that felt soothing a moment ago now grated on my ears like a sixth-grade orchestra rehearsal. "I don't want to go back."

Tony raised his head from its resting place against the fridge. "Huh?"

Galen started creeping toward me again. I got up and moved to the other side of Tony, the glass-free side, and let Galen climb in my lap. "To camp. I don't want to go back."

He squinted at me. "I thought you loved the forest. Loved camp. Exile's the worst punishment in the history of the world."

"Yeah, well. The thought of going back there is making me clench up like a reluctant virgin."

He laughed. "Ah. Um, okay, but we have to go back."

"Yes, thank you, Captain Obvious."

His mouth twisted. "Just because it's not surprising and profound doesn't mean it's not true."

"How would you feel about going back to your mom's? This place that's supposed to be good and safe? Except it's not anymore, and all your memories make you want to scream."

He leaned his head back again and closed his eyes. "My mom's bunghole apartment was never safe or good, but whatever. I get what you're saying. But don't you think it's worth trying to get that good stuff back?" I didn't answer. His scent was blank, plain spongy white bread out of a bag. "So what'd you and Darcy talk about?"

"Nothing much." My skin desperately wanted to peel itself off my body and run off into the sunset to put on a production of *Man of La Mancha*. "I don't know how to do this."

One eye opened a slit. "What? Have a conversation without slicing open your skin?"

"Forget it. I don't know why I even try to talk to you."

"Because nobody else will put up with your crap?"

My shoulders slumped, because it was true. "Mal would've."

"Hmm. Sounds like a cautionary tale for me."

"Fuck you." I pushed Galen off my lap and stood up, but Tony reached out and grabbed my ankle. I considered stopping, letting him hold me back. But my skin was crawling again and the thought of standing still made me want to scream. I kicked him in the shin so he'd let go, and, grabbing the duffel bags I'd dropped a lifetime ago, I headed for the front door.

Galen followed, walking through the glass I'd tried so hard to protect him from. Swearing, I knelt and examined his paws. Nothing. He got lucky. Self-hatred wormed through me, cold and pervasive, as I thought about how my stupidity put him at risk. I had to get out of there. Out of this cage. Outside where there were no walls and I had a limitless supply of fresh air.

A tinkling noise from the kitchen told me Tony was sweeping up the glass. Galen still wore his harness and leash. We could escape. Maybe Tony wouldn't notice, maybe we could have a few minutes alone without anyone talking at us. I reached for the doorknob, and heard only two footfalls before Tony caught up with me. "Kellan, wait."

I stopped moving, but I didn't speak, and I didn't turn to look at him.

"You don't know how to do this without her. I get it, okay?" He paused, his scent souring with anxiety. He blew out a breath that tickled my scalp. "I can't believe I'm going to say this, and don't get all weird on me, okay, but when I saw you on the ground, with her standing over you, and I didn't have any ammo left..."

I was paralyzed, torn between warring desires — to turn around and look at him, or slap my hands over my ears and sing *It's a Small World* at the top of my lungs.

"Not to go all *Beaches* on you or some shit, but the only reason why I made it this far was you, okay?" Tony said.

Curiosity won the war. I turned to face him. "I made your life hell. It was my mission to see your ass so permanently planted in the dirt that some dumb youngling would come along and water you."

He smiled. "Yeah. I noticed. But—" He rubbed a hand over his stubbly hair. "Some kids need kindness. But some of us see a kind hand and wonder what the other hand's gonna do. You were always upfront about being a bitch. I knew what your hands were doing."

My throat closed up. "Tony."

He kept talking, his voice louder as if to ensure he wouldn't have to hear anything I might say. "So anyway, what I'm saying is, there might be people out there who kinda like you. Not that I'm one of 'em or anything. I'm just sayin' they might exist. Somewhere. So, you know, hang in there."

"Thanks for the tip," I said. The awful need to flee passed, leaving me tired but able to stand still. I stuck my hands in my pockets, so I wouldn't do something awful. Like hug him.

"No problem." He went back into the kitchen and finished sweeping up the glass. He added the debris to the bag of perished perishables, before joining me again at the door. "First tip's free. Each subsequent tip is $29.95 plus $3.50 shipping and handling."

I led the way out of the apartment, locking the door behind us.

Chapter 29

Two weeks passed. Galen and I were living in our own little cabin at camp. Galen loved it. I was almost starting to adjust. Tony was healed, with only a few scars to prove anything had happened. Dirk was out of the infirmary and starting physical therapy to regain use of the arm that the nocturne had almost ripped off. Leanna requested a transfer to a place, any place, she'd never been before. No word on Mal's whereabouts. And Janus had yet to emerge from his cabin.

We usually didn't hit ninety degrees until July, but by June tenth, we'd already muddled through two ninety degree days. The heat whittled away my meager patience. One obnoxiously bright Tuesday morning, I marched, with Galen as my vanguard, to Janus's cabin and barged straight into the inner office. As I closed the door in the youngling receptionist's face, I almost gagged on the stench. Not only was the vinegar scent tenfold stronger, but the cabin was also rank with the scent of unwashed human. On the list of most unpleasant scent combinations, this one ranked right up there with bile and lasagna.

I turned to look at Janus. He looked like he'd shrunk. Not just lost weight, but actually become smaller. And he was short to begin with. I consciously closed off my sinus cavity and, breathing through my mouth, resumed my march to his bedside. Galen followed, but at a glacial pace. I think he didn't want to get any closer than necessary to the source of the smell. Couldn't say I blamed him.

I stood over Janus, feet planted and hands on hips, Peter Pan style. And he suddenly stank of cold, rank fear. Great — he was scared of me. Like he wasn't already reeking of Eau de Prey. I gritted my teeth, pretended I didn't know why he was afraid, and focused on my reason for barging into his cabin. "What the hell are you doing?"

He didn't glare at me, get angry, reprimand me for my utterly disrespectful address. He just lay there and stared at the ceiling. And that sent fear shooting through my gut so hard and so fast that I almost doubled over.

I lost Mal. I couldn't lose anyone else. "Hey." I poked him in the shoulder. "I asked you a question."

When several more seconds ticked by, I opened my mouth to talk louder — maybe he just didn't hear me. But then he spoke. "It should not have happened." His eyes slid sideways to look up at my face. When our eyes met, the fear increased tenfold. I would not wonder if our relationship was permanently damaged. If he'd be afraid of me forever, because of what she did. His gaze skittered away. "With Amalea. It should never have happened."

His weakness was so potent, it was almost tangible, a fourth presence in the room. My face twitched as I struggled to keep my disgust from showing. My hands twitched as my lupine half told me to finish him off before he brought a bigger predator down upon the pack. I dug my fingernails into my palms so my voice would be steady.

"No. But it did. Get over it." Right, because I'd adjusted so well to the Mal situation? Hypocrisy, party of one, please. Janus didn't comment; he simply went back to staring at the ceiling. "Oh, for Christ's sake." I started to rip the sheets back, then belatedly wondered if he was fully dressed. Fortunately, he was as proper in his pajamas as he was in everything else.

I discreetly sniffed him up and down. Having seen the wound Mal inflicted, and now knowing from personal experience how thorough Simone was as a healer, I couldn't believe his malady stemmed from that wound. I didn't smell any infection, but I could hear that his heartbeat was slow, uneven. He wasn't sick, I decided. This was something else.

"Get up," I said.

"I am still your leader. You will leave now."

I raised my chin to look down my nose at him. "You're not my leader. My leader is strong. He wouldn't lie down and die, just because something didn't go the way he planned.

It wasn't supposed to be this way. So what?" I pointed at the nearest window. I could see the youngling bunkhouses through it. "You think those kids care about your long-range plan? Your vision of utopia? They care about the fact that the Golden Goddesses of the Sankhain have fallen off their pedestals. They care about the fact that a nocturne and nocturne-to-be breached our borders. They care about having a leader they can look to, so they can feel safe."

"And they shall have that. Finlay—"

"They don't want Finlay. They don't need Finlay. They need you. They need something to remain the same. Something solid to still be there, day in and day out."

"I know you sense it. How ... tired I have become."

He didn't want to say weak. But something told me that if I was going to get him out of that bed, I needed to dump the euphemisms out with the bong water. "You're not tired. You're weak. You've lost something, and you think you can't get it back." I leaned over so that my face filled his line of sight. "Some things you can't get back. A sister. Your thirteenth birthday. A full refund without a receipt. But strength? That you can get back. But you've got to get up off your ass and work for it."

At my crass wording, his eyes finally flashed with something familiar. I felt a surge of power in the room. Janus still smelled like vinegar, but suddenly there was another scent underneath it, something akin to a snake's new skin. I swallowed a smug smile. "Or maybe I'm wrong. Maybe you're just a useless old man and I should finish the job Mal started. Yeah, sure. Let's follow the lead of the evil traitorous bitch. That's a fan-fucking-tastic plan. Yeah, sure, we'll be okay without you. And if we're not, what do you care? You'll be sleeping the deep, restful sleep of a bloody coward."

The fear was gone. Instead, the air crackled with energy. Even Galen felt it — I heard his tags jingle as he rose to his feet and shook himself, to pay proper homage to the display of power. I pulled back, giving Janus space to sit up. Which he did. Slowly and painfully, but he did it. I didn't offer him a helping hand. Instead, I headed for the door. "You'll want to start with a bath. You smell like a homeless person."

"Kellan Alastrina Faolanni."

I stopped, but didn't turn, not wanting him to see the smile on my face or the moisture in my eyes as I listened to his familiar, firm tone. "Yes, master?"

"If ever again you speak to me in such a manner—"

"Yeah, yeah, torture, pain, suffering, blah, blah, blah. I'll be checking on you later. Get cleaned up. And I'll have them send some food in." I paused. "Don't worry. I won't tell anyone that you were... I won't tell."

I barely heard his voice, suddenly flannel-sheets-fresh-out-of-the-dryer soft. "I know."

With a curt nod and a lump in my throat the size of a watermelon, I gathered Galen and left. I waited until we cleared the door before I broke into a run.

Chapter 30

That night, after I finished my evening chores — so demeaning, having chores at my age — I sat in the shadows on the side of Janus's cabin. Galen lay beside me, letting me rub his belly. As I listened to the rise and fall of voices inside the brightly lit cabin, I felt a now-familiar combination of fullness and loss. The feeling crept up on me at the weirdest times. It happened when I sat with Darcy in the hospital, and again in the apartment with Tony. And now here, under Janus's window. Mal and I used to sit here, eavesdrop on Janus, whisper and giggle. We never heard anything interesting, but just the possibility of being caught in the act provided enough excitement for two little wolves, once upon a time.

My phone rang. I glanced at the caller ID, didn't recognize the number, and almost didn't answer. But at the last minute, I picked up.

Mal didn't offer a salutation. "The old man will pick his teeth with your bones, you know."

Her voice stopped my blood in its tracks. Galen twisted to peer up at me as I struggled to keep my voice level. "They're my bones. I can do whatever I want with them."

She never missed a beat. Never had in her life. "Can you? You're a bullet in their gun, Kellan. That's all."

As her blow landed right where she'd aimed, I clenched my fists. My breathing was shallow and fast, my skin suddenly drenched in sweat. "And I suppose the nocturnes are as cute and cuddly as a preschool teacher in an angora sweater?"

She chuckled. I hated her for making me love the sound. But I couldn't make myself hang up the phone. "See you around, little sister," she said. She hung up.

My head spun. I thought I was going to vomit. Why did she call me? To gloat? To mock me, or maybe to try to recruit me? A horrible, insidious emotion crept back into the hollow spot in my gut. Hope. Maybe she'd called because she was still her, still my sister. Maybe she'd called because she regretted hurting me. Maybe she didn't want to let me go.

Those thoughts were dangerous. I'd made my choice that night, and she made hers, and there was no going back for either one of us. I dropped my phone on the ground. Before I could stomp the shit out of it, I caught the scent of fresh bread and heard a sneeze. I looked up as Tony rounded the corner. His allergies had been bad, leaving him miserable and virtually invisible the past few days.

The sight of his broad-shouldered bulk warmed my sweat-chilled skin. "Hey, Sneezy. Where are Dopey and Doc?"

"I dunno, but I just found Grumpy." He plopped down next to me and sneezed again.

"Thanks. I didn't have enough snot on my shoes."

"Shuddup." He picked my phone up and held it out to me. "Almost stepped on that. Yours?"

With a wry twitch of my mouth, I accepted it. "Yeah. Thanks."

Galen managed, without actually getting up from his belly-rub position, to wiggle his body over so that he would be more easily accessible to both of us. Tony accepted his invitation and started scratching Galen's belly, his hand only inches from mine.

"So, Finn came to see me today." His voice was even deeper than usual, thanks to all that congestion. It made my mouth go dry, and I had a hard time concentrating on the words, rather than just listening to the sounds he made with each syllable.

"Hmm?"

"Yup. He's sending me to South Dakota. Some weird livestock deaths out there he wants someone to check out."

I stiffened. Galen sensed it and rolled to his feet to protect me. Because I didn't want Tony to know why Galen was suddenly agitated, I started rubbing behind Galen's left ear. That soothed my dog, and he sank back down into the grass. I searched for a response to Tony's news. "Well. You wanted an assignment out in the big, wide world. This is a good opportunity."

He sneezed. "Yeah, guess so."

"Of course, there's probably a lot of pollen in South Dakota. You sure this is the right time of year to be heading west?"

I felt his shoulder rise in a shrug. "There's a lotta pollen here, too."

"Well, yeah, but..." At a loss, I stopped talking and focused on petting my dog.

The warmth of his skin preceded him as he leaned closer, pressed his arm to my shoulder. "I know you'll miss me, babe. You don't have to say it."

"Call me babe one more time and Little Tony's gonna end up on a bun with ketchup and mustard."

"Oh, not mustard, Little Tony hates mustard."

I laughed, but it didn't last long. I stood up, my balance off-kilter. "Well, have a great trip. Enjoy looking at all the ... plains."

Tony stood. "Here." He grabbed my hand and pressed a piece of cloth into it.

I frowned. The cloth smelled richly of Tony's scents — bread, gun oil, sweat, and a little blood. I read the words printed on it — *Keep talking, I like watching your lips move.* "Your t-shirt."

"I promised I'd give it to you if you gave me a cup of coffee."

"You gave me a bloody, sweaty t-shirt? I know you didn't like my coffee, but jeez."

He reached out and tugged a handful of my hair. Then, so fast, I didn't see it coming, he leaned over and placed his mouth next to my ear. "She wasn't your only pack, Faolanni." His lips brushed the skin under my jaw, and I shivered. "South Dakota's not so far. I hear they even have phones there. Should anyone feel the need to call."

I swallowed hard. "If you sneeze in my hair, I'll punch you in the nose."

He pulled back, his teeth flashing in a smile. "Hey, let's give it a try. Might clear out my sinuses."

"Okay." I pretended to haul back my fist. He laughed and backed away, hands raised in surrender. Then he paused and stared at me a moment, before turning and walking away. I watched him go. "Just a phone call away, right?" I murmured to Galen. "We've got a phone."

Galen wagged his tail at me, and I looked back up at where Tony had been. Instead of Tony, though, I saw Finn. I remembered the jealousy I'd caught in his scent, and felt all my warm fuzzies doused with ice water. Livestock deaths, my ass. He sent Tony away, away from me. I started toward him, but something else grabbed my attention.

The door to Janus's cabin swung open. Power thickened the air like humidity, until it was difficult to breathe. Walking so slowly, looking every one of his one thousand years, Janus emerged from the cabin. He stopped and raised his face to the moon. His expression revealed a younger man, and I forgot about Finn, Tony, and everything in between. Then, as if he knew I was there, Janus turned his face toward me. "Eavesdropping, little wolf?"

Was she right? Would Janus pick his teeth with my bones? Maybe, if it suited him. But Mal had walked away. If anybody needed to worry about their bones, it was her.

"Right, like you ever say anything worth hearing. Sir."

I breathed in Janus's scent, the smell of fresh-cut grass, the smell that meant strength and life and good humor. Then I raised Tony's gift to my face and inhaled. I patted my thigh, and Galen and I walked toward the mess hall. I smelled fresh-brewed coffee.

If you enjoyed this read...

Please leave a review.

It takes less than five minutes, and it really does make a difference.

Reviews should answer at least three basic questions.
(But won't give the story away.):

- *Did you like the book? ("Loved the book! Can't wait for the Next!")*

- *What was your favorite part? (Characters, plot, location, scenes.)*

- *Would you recommend the book?*

Your review will help other readers discover this book. Consider leaving your review on Amazon, Barnes and Noble, Apple iBooks, KOBO, Goodreads, BookBub, Facebook, Instagram and/or your own website.

Brian Hades, publisher

To leave a review on Amazon

~ Even if the book was not purchased on Amazon ~

1. *Go to amazon.com. Sign into your Amazon account. If you do not have an Amazon account, you need to create one and activate it by making a purchase. Amazon will check to see that your account is active before allowing you to leave a review. Amazon has some restrictions, such as not leaving a bias review. For more information on Amazon's policies please read Amazon's Community Guidelines for book reviews:*

   https://www.amazon.com/gp/help/customer/display.
   html?nodeId=GLHXEX85MENUE4XF

2. *Search for and find Pick Your Teeth With My Bones by Carrie Newberry, then click on the book's details page.*

3. *Scroll down to find the Write a Customer Review button. Click it.*

4. *Select your star rating. A rating of 5 is best, 1 is worst.*

5. *If you have a photo or video to share, add it to the upload box.*

6. *Add a headline.*

7. *Write your review.*

8. *Press the SUBMIT button*

To leave a review on Barnes and Noble
~ Even if the book was not purchased on BN.com ~

1. Go to barnesandnoble.com and sign up for an account.
2. Search for and find Pick Your Teeth With My Bones by Carrie Newberry, then click on the book's details page.
3. Scroll down to the review section and click on the Write a Review button.
4. Select your star rating. A rating of 5 is best, 1 is worst.
5. Add a review title.
6. Write your review.
7. Add a photo if you wish.
8. Select if you would recommend this book to a friend.
9. Select appropriate TAGs.
10. Indicate if your review contains spoilers.
11. Select the type of reader that best describes you (optional).
12. Enter your location (optional).
13. Enter your email address.
14. Checkmark that you agree to the terms and conditions.
15. Press the POST REVIEW button.

About the Author

Carrie Newberry studied creative writing at both the University of Wisconsin-Madison and UW-Eau Claire. But when she realized they would no longer let her take writing workshops for credit, she left academia and started working full time at a dog grooming shop. She lives in Madison with two rescued mutts and an enormous collection of books. Pick Your Teeth with my Bones is her first novel, and she is hard at work writing Kellan's next adventure.

Need something new to read?

If you liked Pick Your Teeth With My Bones, you should also consider these other EDGE-Lite titles:

Wolf is a Four-letter Word
(Book Two of the Eternal Spring, Invisible Forest series)

by Carrie Newberry

What do you do when the nightmare is real? That's the question facing Kellan Faolanni.

Following the betrayal of her sister in the previous book, Kellan must set aside her own emotions and thwart an enemy who has the upper hand at every turn.

Kellan, a member of the Sankhain, is a shapeshifter, half-wolf, half- human. Kellan's superiors task her to investigate a man killed by what appears to be a wolf pack.

Meanwhile, Kellan's human friend, Darcy reveals that he's being stalked. Kellan learns that the killer and Darcy's stalker are one and the same: a faery named Aza. But Aza is a high-ranking member of the Shadow Court, and to kill him would start a war with the fey, a war that Kellan's superiors want to avoid at all costs. Kellan must find a way to eliminate the threat and save her friend. Her solution could cost her everything, including a new relationship with another Sankha, Tony, as well as her sanity.

Shadow Stitcher
(An Everland Mystery)

by Misha Handman

Selected as one of the year's most compelling debut novels for Kobo's Emerging Writer Prize, Shadow Stitcher is guaranteed to delight.

This fast paced Noir mystery has a great cast of easily identifiable characters, a plot both easy to follow and intriguing, and an ending that will leave you satisfied.

A former pirate faces mobsters and magic in 1950s Neverland.

Basil Stark isn't the man he once was. A reformed pirate and private detective, he walks the line between criminal and hero, living in the corners of what was once the island of Neverland, its magic slowly fading into the new world of the 1950s. But when a routine missing-persons case turns into a murder investigation, Basil finds himself pulled into a tale of organized crime, murder, unstitched shadows and dangerous espionage. With only a handful of fellow outcasts and a stubborn determination to bring a killer to justice, will he survive the many people who want him dead?

The Rosetta Man
(Book One of the Rosetta Series)

by Claire McCague

Wanted: Translator for first contact. Immediate opening. Danger pay allowance

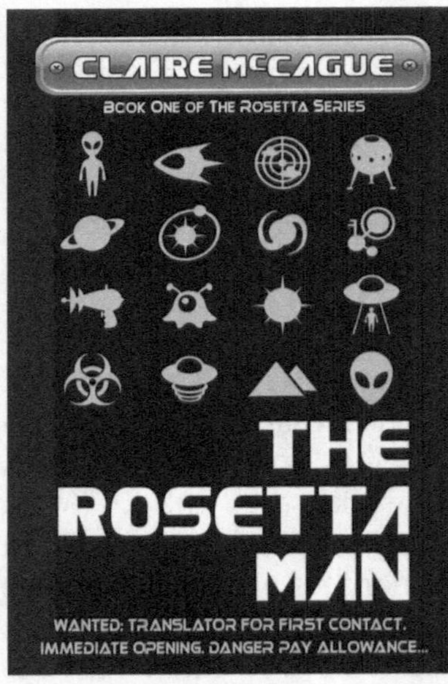

Estlin Hume lives in Twin Butte, Alberta surrounded by a horde of affectionate squirrels. His involuntary squirrel-attracting talent leaves him evicted, expelled, fired and near penniless until two aliens arrive and adopt him as their translator. Yanked around the world at the center of the first contact crisis, Estlin finds his new employers incomprehensible. As he faces the ultimate language barrier, unsympathetic military forces converging in the South Pacific keep threatening to shoot the messenger. The question on everyone's mind is why are the aliens here? But Estlin's starting to think we'll happily blow ourselves up in the process of finding that out.

"What makes The Rosetta Man stand-out? An unusually dense squirrel population for sci-fi. It's light-hearted, accessible sci-fi with exotic present day settings and a pair of aliens who are focused on observing the revealing chaos their visit creates." — Claire McCague

For more EDGE titles and information about upcoming speculative fiction please visit us at:

www.edgewebsite.com

Don't forget to sign-up for our Special Offers

www.ingramcontent.com/pod-product-compliance
Lightning Source LLC
Chambersburg PA
CBHW051608100726
47898CB00001B/280